The
PEACOCK
THRONE

ABOUT THE AUTHOR

Influenced by books like *The Secret Garden* and *The Little Princess* Lisa's early stories were full of boarding schools and creepy houses. These days, even though she's (mostly) grown-up she still loves a healthy dash of adventure in any story she creates, even in real-life. *The Peacock Throne* was the first full novel Lisa ever wrote and has always been particularly special to her, even though it lay unpublished. Now an award-winning published author, she felt it was finally time to dust off and revisit the adventures of Lydia, Anthony, and Marcus, using the skills acquired writing almost a dozen other novels. Lisa is now concentrating on writing their next adventure…

LISA KARON RICHARDSON

The
PEACOCK
THRONE

LION FICTION

For my husband, Joel, whose
support gave me the courage to
chase my dreams. I love you.

Published by Lion Fiction
an imprint of
Lion Hudson plc
Wilkinson House, Jordan Hill Road
Oxford OX2 8DR, England
www.lionhudson.com/fiction

ISBN 978 1 78264 178 0
e-ISBN 978 1 78264 179 7

First edition 2015

Acknowledgments
Cover images: ship © Spectral-Design/istockphoto;
woman © Lee Avison/Trevillion Images.

A catalogue record for this book is available from the British Library

Printed and bound in the UK, September 2015, LH26

ACKNOWLEDGMENTS

Many thanks to all those who acted as beta readers: Jeannie Collins, Lisa Barnette, Allison Barnette, Mom, Dad, and all the others I conned into taking their time to give me feedback. I'd also like to offer sincere thanks to the fantastic editorial team at Lion Hudson: Tony Collins, Jessica Tinker, Kate Kirkpatrick, and Sheila Barnes. Thanks for all you have done to make this story come to life. You're wonderful.

CHAPTER 1

Mayfair, London
Home of the Earl of Danbury
28 March 1802

The tiny snick of the latch sounded. Anthony rubbed at the stubble on his chin and turned a jaundiced eye to the intruder. Pale and dishevelled, his usually unflappable valet came to a halt in the centre of the room.

"What is it?"

"I'm sorry, sir. It's y… your father." The valet paused, seeming at a loss.

Anthony sat up, kicking at the sheets. "Spit it out."

"Jane found him. He is…. He's been murdered, sir."

Anthony clutched the edge of his bed. "What?"

"Your father…" James's voice died away. He waved a hand vaguely towards the hall.

What a ridiculous mistake. Setting his jaw, Anthony jumped to his feet and marched to the door. He would straighten all this out. "Where?" he demanded as he grabbed the knob.

"In his bedchamber."

Servants clustered in the long corridor, their voices an agitated buzz. The frightened gazes following his progress clutched at him. Something was truly wrong. He swallowed hard against the sudden fear. He picked up speed and barrelled through the door to his father's bedroom, driven by the lash of desperate hope.

The old gentleman lay huddled on the bed but there was no mistaking his posture for sleep.

Anthony's eyes shied from the form, staring instead at the blood-soaked bedclothes. Surely, the figure was too small to be his robust father? But he could not force his gaze back to the bed, not just yet. He surveyed the rest of the room. There was no sign of struggle. Nothing appeared out of place, but then, he had rarely entered this *sanctum sanctorum* of his father's experience.

Placing a hand over his mouth and nose to block the odour of slaughter, he steeled himself to approach and examine the body. A curved knife with an engraved ivory handle protruded from his father's chest. His face grew hot; he was trying to absorb the image without allowing its reality to pierce him. Calling on the reserves of his fortitude, he forced his gaze to his father's face.

A grimace obliterated the familiar features. No sign remained of the vigorous, cheerful man Anthony knew so well.

He grasped his father's hand and found it cold and stiff. His thoughts tilted and slid, scattering like dropped coins. His head throbbed in relentless rhythm. He wasn't sure how long he hunched there, but when at last he straightened, his shoulders had grown stiff. With a concerted effort of will he collected himself. Releasing that hand was the most difficult thing he had ever done: it was as if he were giving his father permission to slip away from him. He clenched his trembling hands into fists. Someone would suffer for this.

"James." At least he had found his voice—even if it did sound strained.

"Yes, sir." The young man started to attention, swiping at the tears on his face.

"Send a footman for the magistrate and another to Bow Street for a runner. Then come and help me dress. I'll not receive him in my nightclothes."

James nodded, and ran to do his bidding.

Anthony hesitated. Gritting his teeth, he stepped from the

room. The number of servants in the hall had swelled. Their anxious muttering stopped as he emerged. Stricken faces told of their distress. He needed to reassure them somehow, though his innards swarmed like a nest of wasps.

He had to clear his throat before he could speak. Even then when he addressed them it was in a voice roughened by tightly reined emotion. "His Lordship has… he has passed away."

The silence might have deafened him. They already knew. He cleared his throat and tried again.

"Bow Street is being summoned." A measure of his fury slipped into his tone. "When the runner arrives, I expect you to cooperate with him to the fullest. The murderer will be found and brought to justice. No matter where he lies."

Grief strangled him. He didn't know what else he would have said, but it made no difference. He could not continue. A path opened before him as if he were Moses parting the Red Sea. Anthony made his way through the throng, accepting the murmured condolences with what grace he could muster.

The world had gone mad. There was no other explanation.

James's quiet return interrupted his muddled thoughts. Tamping down the consciousness of his loss in a flurry of activity, Anthony dressed and flung orders about with little consideration for where they landed.

His cravat was in a hopeless tangle. He hurled the thing on the grate. He needed to be doing something. Why was the runner taking so long? His eyes burned and he knew that if he sat down, he would succumb to the pain. He scraped a hand through his hair. He could not sit. The murderer must be caught.

Ever meticulous, James approached with a fresh square of linen, but Anthony waved him off. He would not spend the morning preening while his father's corpse lay down the hall and nothing was being done about it. By the same token he needed to show due respect. He waved his valet back and grudgingly submitted to his ministrations. The instant James stepped away, Anthony stalked from his room and nearly overturned a maid carrying a breakfast tray redolent with ham and fresh bread. He gripped her shoulders to steady her, then shooed her away.

Taking up position in the drawing room, Anthony prowled the edges as if he suspected the killer might yet be lurking beneath one of the couches. His throat remained constricted, his eyes hot. He couldn't sit. He examined the familiar pattern of the red and gold Turkish carpets, then ran a hand along the smooth back of the silk upholstered couch as he passed by. He paused and stared out of the wide front window for a moment but half a dozen gawkers stood on the street, staring and pointing at the house. Londoners seemed to have supernatural ability when it came to sensing tragedy or scandal. Anthony pulled away from the window, retreating to pace about the room again.

It wasn't until a footman ushered in the runner, at last, that Anthony stilled. He had a task now. He needed to get the thief-taker's measure. Large and thick-boned, the bruiser's heavy features were set in what he probably meant to be a reassuring expression. In short, the new arrival looked more likely to commit a murder than to solve one.

He extended a meaty paw towards Anthony, who shook it reluctantly. He was unaccustomed to such familiarity from people he did not know, but the imperative to offer consideration to those of lower rank overrode the etiquette ingrained in him. Perhaps it wouldn't be so very bad to have a formal police force, as other nations did. This man was none too clean. Stubble peppered his pockmarked cheeks and he wore a vest but no jacket. His faded red shirt, a mark of his office, appeared grimy. His hand rested on the cudgel tucked into his belt, as if he anticipated using it at any moment.

"Name's Rodney Perkins. I understand there's been a bit o' mischief."

"My father has been murdered. I believe that qualifies as more than mischief."

Chapter I

"Right you are. No offence intended, I'm sure, Lord Danbury."

Anthony grimaced at the unaccustomed title. "Do not call me that. The title has not been confirmed. It's… it is too soon. I am Viscount Graham."

"As you like, sir. As you like." Perkins rubbed his hands together and looked about. "Where's the body?"

"This way. We left everything as we found it." Anthony led the man up the broad front stair and down the hall to the door of the bedchamber.

"Anythin' missin'?"

Anthony's brow creased. "I don't believe so. His valet may know better than I. The staff reported nothing missing. I'm certain they would have come to me if they had discovered something had been stolen." He was babbling. Taking a deep breath he ushered Perkins into his father's room.

No fire lit the grate, leaving the room chilled despite fine draperies and thick carpets. At the sight of his mother's portrait above the fireplace an irrational urge to throw a blanket over it seized him. She shouldn't have to look down on this atrocity. He hooked his thumbs into the pocket of his waistcoat so the other man would not see that his hands were trembling.

He surveyed the scene again, forcing himself to look at the body with dispassion. He must be alert to anything that might help uncover who had done this.

The runner swaggered about the room as if he were strolling in Hyde Park. He bent over the corpse and plucked out the knife. The slight sucking sound as it exited the body caused Anthony's stomach to heave. For a ghastly moment he feared he would be ill.

Intent on the knife he held to the light, Perkins seemed not to notice Anthony's discomfort. "I'll need t' talk t' the servants, of course."

Anthony nodded to the butler who hovered anxiously behind him in the hall. "See to it, will you, Hemmings?" he said in a choked voice.

"Yes, sir." Hemmings scuttled away.

"When did you find 'im, Lord Da—Graham?"

"I didn't find him. The commotion woke me at about seven. I understand one of the maids took in his breakfast and found him then."

"When did you see 'im last?" Perkins scrutinized Anthony.

"I spoke to him shortly before I left for the Cornwallis's ball last night. Around nine o'clock."

"Did 'is Lordship act scared or upset?"

"Perhaps a little distracted, but certainly not as if he expected to be murdered." Anthony eyed the runner as if he were a particularly loathsome insect. How could anyone believe that he would not have done everything in his power to have prevented the murder if he'd had any inkling that such a potential existed? "If he had been upset, I would have inquired as to the reason."

Perkins met his gaze then nodded, apparently choosing to ignore Anthony's sharpness. "What did you speak of with the ol' gent before you left?"

"I wished him a good night and reminded him I'd be out late. Is that relevant?"

"You didn't see him when you got home?" Perkins knelt beside the bed and looked beneath.

"As I said, I stayed out late. I supposed he had long since been in bed."

The runner paced the room. "Did you see or hear anythin' out o' the way?"

"I wish to God I had. I could have intervened." Anthony couldn't keep the misery from his voice. He'd failed his father at the hour of his most desperate need.

"You recognize the knife?" Perkins held the blade up for Anthony's inspection.

The question gave Anthony a focus, enabling him to force away his guilt for the moment and think logically. He re-examined the knife. Minutely detailed in the pale ivory of the handle, a peacock unfurled its tail in challenge. "No, I don't. It's strange that a murderer would use so fine a weapon, and more so that he would leave it behind. Anyone would recognize it if they had seen it before."

"You might be surprised," Perkins snorted. "Who were your father's enemies?"

Blood rushed to Anthony's face. A hot defence of his father's honour hovered on his lips. He breathed in through his nose. The man was only trying to perform his duties. "He had no enemies. There may have been a few men he quarrelled with over the years, but none with the kind of grudge that would lead to murder. My father was a generous landlord, and upright in his business dealings."

The runner pushed his lips together and out, obviously unconvinced of the earl's virtue. At least he had the sense to keep any arch comments to himself.

"I guess we're done for now then, sir." Scepticism flattened his voice. "Though I may need to speak with you later."

Anthony nodded.

"Good. I need t' see the staff now, starting with 'is valet."

"I'd like to join you for these interviews."

Perkins cleared his throat. "That isn't a good idea, sir. The skivvies won't wanna tell me a thing with you hovering nearby."

Implacable, Anthony stepped forward. "They'll understand I am interested only in finding my father's murderer. I'll make it clear that any minor indiscretions will be overlooked in exchange for their assistance in this matter."

Perkins visibly weighed his options. Anthony smirked. He was the client—the one who would pay the bounty when the murderer was caught. With a heavy sigh, Perkins conceded the point, apparently deciding to save his clout for when it might really be required.

Anthony led the way to the drawing room where he rang for his father's valet. He gestured for the runner to sit and took the seat opposite him on the settee, then stood again. Repose did not suit his humour. He paced near the fireplace, extending his hands to the flames.

Williams appeared swiftly. Spotless and straight-backed, only the dignified old man's face betrayed his grief. His eyes and nose were red and watering, his skin blotchy from recent weeping.

Anthony turned fully back to the room, blinking rapidly to prevent the valet's sorrow from settling on him and drawing him into a display of sentiment before this runner.

"Sir, may I extend my condolences for your loss," Williams said, his voice high and tight.

"Thank you, Williams." The servant's obvious mourning nearly shredded Anthony's thin veneer of control. He cleared his throat. "Please answer this man's questions as well as you are able, so we can find the person who did this."

"I'll do anything to help, sir." The elderly retainer rubbed shaking palms together.

Rodney Perkins adjusted his position in his seat. "What time did Lord Danbury retire last night?"

"About ten o'clock, sir. He felt poorly, and went straight to sleep after he'd changed into his bedclothes."

"Was the old gent angry or upset?"

"He did seem a bit upset, but I couldn't say why."

"Try," Perkins ordered.

The valet wrung his hands and peered about, as if looking for an escape route. His reluctance to discuss private matters filled the room like a fog. Anthony sat forward until he caught the man's gaze. He nodded slightly, and Williams gave in. "Well—it's only an impression, you understand, but I think perhaps he got something by the evening mail that upset him."

"What was it?" The runner perked up like a hound scenting a fox.

"He had several letters. One, though, was..." Williams searched for the word he wanted. "Different—foreign maybe."

"Different?"

"Yes, sir, on fine paper it were and scented with some perfume. I could smell it halfway across the room, I could." As Williams warmed to his story, his native Yorkshire accent broadened. "The seal were odd too. It were a peacock, and the wax itself looked like a peacock." Williams halted. His hands flapped as if motion could convey meaning that words could not.

"What do you mean it looked like a peacock?" Anthony asked.

"Well, sir, the wax were different colours, like—sort of swirled and shiny?" The elderly valet's tone turned the statement into a question.

Anthony nodded gravely, not understanding what the man meant, but impatient to hear what else he had to say. "Go on."

"The handwriting looked different too. I knew it were foreign as soon as I spied it. His Lordship turned quite red when he read the letter. I thought he meant to tear it up, but he didn't. He got up—didn't even finish reading the others—he went straight to his desk and began writing."

"What was he writing?"

"I don't know, sir."

"What'd you do with the letter?" Perkins asked.

"I never touched it. I imagine it's still on his desk. The maids know not to touch anythin' on his Lordship's desk."

"Lead on then." Perkins planted his hands on the arms of his chair and levered himself upright. "Where is this desk?"

Anthony took charge of the short procession across the hall to the study. He gestured to the desk standing at the far end of the room. Close on his heels, Perkins nearly trod on him in his eagerness to inspect the desk where a partially open letter lay in plain view.

Of good quality stationery, the paper looked as described. From where Anthony stood, he could already smell the perfume permeating the missive. The distinctive scent made him think of warmer climates. Ornate script flowed and looped across the page in a manner no Englishman would countenance. Anthony picked up the letter and removed the covering page to better observe the seal. He had never seen sealing wax like it before: a brilliant swirl of iridescent blue, purple, and green flecked with gold. It did indeed resemble a peacock's feather. The imprint of a peacock, tiny and intricate in the wax, looked like the engraving on the knife used to slay his father.

While Anthony examined the seal, Perkins read the letter. With a nod they traded objects of interest. The letter's odd script and ceremonial tenor made Anthony's mouth go dry.

Dear Sir,

I am writing as the representative of his most Royal and Gracious Highness Shah Zahir-ud-din Akbar of the Great Mughal Empire, etc. In the year 1758, you and the crew of your ship, the Centaur, *were involved in the nefarious theft of the Peacock Throne from our kingdom. Sir, you may have imagined you had escaped vengeance, but your day of reckoning has come. Our emissary will visit you. The time has come for you to assuage your conscience or suffer the consequences dictated by perfidy.*

Jahan Pasha

CHAPTER 2

"I've come about a murder." Lydia Garrett wedged her pattened foot in the kitchen door before the scowling footman could shove it closed.

His green and gold livery seemed to expand as the fellow swelled with indignation. His gaze scoured her person, no doubt taking in her worn dress and pelisse. "Be off."

Lydia jammed an elbow into the narrowing gap. Perhaps she had miscalculated, but she had no one to send as a proxy. "I need to see his Lordship. It's important."

The footman shoved her arm out of the door. "He's not home to the likes of you."

"I have information." Lydia braced for the impact of the door against her inadequately protected toes.

It halted, mid slam. Grudgingly the footman sized her up again. "He isn't home. You'll have to come back."

That was unexpected. Lydia straightened, but didn't remove her foot from the door, just in case it was some sort of trick. "When will he be back?"

A great sighing and rolling of eyes met this query. "His Lordship don't consult me before leaving the house."

She sighed. What kind of person wasn't at home at this hour? It was probably for the best, however. It had taken her longer to find Danbury's town home than she had expected. Morning light was beginning to burnish the eastern sky even through the smoke of the morning cook fires. If she didn't get home soon, she'd be caught and there would be more than the piper to pay. "If he wants my information he can find me at the Green Peacock coffee house on Brant Street. But please ask him to be discreet."

Without waiting for a reply she withdrew her abused foot and hurried towards home. She'd done all she could for the day. With any luck she was one step closer to catching a killer.

* * *

It had been an exceptionally long day. Groaning, Lydia settled in her favourite nook, tucked up close beside the kitchen chimney where she could soak in the stored heat of the bricks even though the fire had been banked for the night. She'd been run off her feet, and every time someone had opened the front door, she'd been sure it would be Lord Danbury. Why didn't he come? Surely even a lordship would be interested enough to pursue discussion about a murder.

She'd been so sure.

Lydia let her cheek rest against the rough bricks and removed her shoes. Normally at this hour of the day she'd have been sitting with Cousin Wolfe in his cramped office, surrounded by the smell of books and joint salve and having a lively discussion. But one week ago "normal" had been robbed of meaning. She would never sit and debate with the old man again. Never hear his crow of delight when she scored a mental point. Never again feel the warmth of familial affection. They were all gone now.

Lydia squeezed her eyes shut.

The bell in the main room plinked dispiritedly. She tiptoed the two steps to the kitchen door and pulled it open the inch and a half it would allow before its hinges emitted a shattering screech of protest.

Through the crack she could just make out the figure of a man shutting the front door. He raised a finger to his mouth, shushing himself as he did so. Fenn. As usual he was so drunk he was nearly pickled. She eased the door closed and leaned against it. With any luck he'd head straight up to bed.

Instead a weight slammed into the door, sending her staggering forward.

"Evening, Fenn."

He closed in, yawning. "Help me t' me bed." At twenty-two he considered himself a debonair man of the world, or so he'd given Lydia to understand over the years. She looked with distaste at his overlarge, raw-boned features. His complexion was the dull red of the dissolute. Hair sprouted from his head in spiky thatches, the hue and texture of dirty straw.

"I don't think so." Lydia turned her head to avoid his gin-laced breath.

Fenn grabbed her arm, grinning mawkishly at her. "Come on then, me fancy li'l cousin. Keep me company."

"Let go, Fenn." Lydia struggled in his grasp.

"Don't put on airs." He was growing surly. "Mum wanted to toss you out on yer ear. You owe me for saving you from the street."

"You know your father disapproved of this behaviour." It was a feeble attempt to put him off, but it was all she could manage when most of her attention was focused on getting hold of something with which to drive him off.

"He weren't no father of mine. Wolfe was a weak old man. Mum never shoulda married 'im."

Fenn had hold of her neck now, forcing her head down for a drunken kiss.

The fingers of her flailing hand brushed the water pitcher sitting on the table. She snatched it and hit him a hard blow on the head. His eyes rolled back and his body sagged towards her, carrying her to the ground beneath him.

Kicking and shoving, she wriggled away then scrambled to her feet.

For a moment she stood perfectly still, looking at the heavy pitcher in her grip. That was good quality stoneware.

Stertorous snoring assured her that she hadn't killed him. She set the jug back on the table and returned to her tiny alcove. Her traitorous knees grew suddenly wobbly and she dropped onto the perch. Had she really just struck Fenn? The reality of her daring made her feel as if she was choking. A bubble of hysterical laughter caught against the fear that constricted her throat.

She could not stay at the coffee house any longer. In the week since Mr Wolfe's death, Fenn's advances had become increasingly difficult to ward off.

She pulled on her shoes.

But how could she leave now? Her heart ached at the thought of the gentle old man who had sheltered her for so long. If she weren't around to prod the magistrate into action, the murderer would never be caught.

And besides, where was she to go?

The bell in the front room clattered grimly. Lydia froze. Trust Fenn not to latch the door behind him. She quelled the urge to kick him where he lay. Hands pressed flat against her abdomen, she debated. Who could it be at this hour?

"Hello?" The voice was definitely male, but no burglar would announce himself.

Lydia pushed through the door into the dining room. She stopped short upon sight of the customer. A fine young gentleman stood just inside the door examining the coffee house. Tall, well built, and well dressed—with gleaming Hessians and a cravat so white it seemed to glow—he most certainly was not the calibre of customer usually attracted to the dowdy establishment. His hair was cut short in the Brutus style, with rather severe sideburns, and his dark blue eyes were intent as they studied the shabby coffee house.

The last thing she needed was a pampered dandy to wait upon. "We're closed."

"Your door was unlocked." A charming smile lit his features.

Head whirring with quick mental calculations, Lydia decided it would be quicker, and less noisy, to wait on the fellow than it would be to argue. She sighed. "I'm afraid the kitchen is closed but I can get you a pot of coffee and some toast."

He opened his mouth, but Lydia was in no mood to listen to complaints. She spun on her heel and hurried back into the kitchen. She snatched up one of the De Belloy pots and scooped in some ground coffee then put a kettle of water on to boil.

She edged around Fenn's prostrate form and hurried up the stairs to her garret room. In a trice she had piled her worldly possessions into a haversack. She hurried back downstairs and dumped the bag on the table. She whisked the kettle off the fire and poured water into the pot to steep while she toasted a couple of slices of bread.

Mere moments after she'd left her customer gaping, she backed through the door into the dining room carrying a tray. With any luck he had wandered off to annoy someone else, and she could retrieve one last thing before fleeing this house for good.

But for the second time in as many minutes luck had left her to fend for herself. The gentleman sat patiently at a booth. She set the tray down with an ill-tempered rattle.

"I've come to speak with a young woman."

Lydia plopped her hands on her hips. "We're not that kind of establishment. Be off."

He flushed. "Not in that way. Listen, she didn't leave a name. I'm the Vi—the Earl of Danbury."

"*You're* the Earl of Danbury? I thought—oh, I don't think you can help me at all." Lydia rubbed her temples. This man must be the son or grandson of the man her uncle served under.

His Lordship set aside his coffee cup. "I came because I want *you* to help *me*. What do you know of my father's murder?"

CHAPTER 3

Marcus Harting lounged in a comfortable armchair. A fire warmed the room nicely, and when he downed the drink at his elbow, it was replenished almost immediately. Masculine conversation swirled about him, though he took no part, preferring for the moment to observe. He had long favoured this particular room of his club. The familiar atmosphere acted as a balm.

A footman in immaculate livery approached, bearing a note on a silver salver. Marcus accepted the missive with a languid hand, noting with pleasure as he did so the way the snowy cuff of his sleeve fell just so as he moved.

He read the note and arched an eyebrow. "Where is the gentleman?"

"In the Greek study, sir."

"Thank you, Peter." Marcus flipped the servant a coin and rose. The speed of his progress was belied by his carefully maintained insouciance as he sauntered through the club. Men stood in clusters talking or lounged in comfortable armchairs. He nodded at one or two acquaintances as he passed, but did not linger to converse. The heavily carpeted stairs took him up to a green, silk-hung hall lined with the portraits of past club presidents. The door to the Greek study stood ajar. He slipped in and closed it firmly behind him.

William Pitt stood and welcomed him with an extended hand. "Harting, you're looking well. Thank you for coming to see me."

A dapper man, the former prime minister had a narrow aristocratic face and gracious manners. He dressed well, but a mere glance at his incisive eyes quieted any impulse to classify him a dandy.

"How may I be of service?"

"Pray have a seat. Would you care for something?" Pitt motioned to the decanter near his chair.

Marcus accepted and waited. Pitt poured, then pushed his fingers together into a steeple, and sat for a moment in brooding silence. Marcus sipped from his glass. He did not prod. He had worked with Pitt before on certain sensitive matters, he even liked the man, but Pitt would speak when he was ready and not before.

"I hope your recovery progresses well." Pitt nodded towards Marcus's right leg.

"I am fully myself again. Thank you." He smoothed the fine buckskin of his breeches, the mere reference to his prior injury causing a twinge of remembered pain.

"We appreciated your assistance in that matter."

"Think nothing of it." Marcus gave an airy wave of his hand. He would never let on how much his last mission had cost him. Just as he would never be seen about London in anything less than a perfectly tailored coat. Standards had to be maintained.

Mr Pitt sat silently for a long moment, while Marcus fought the temptation to fill the gap with a rush of words.

"There has been a great deal of political upheaval recently. A vote of no confidence is expected in a matter of months, and when Prime Minister Addington's government fails, I shall be called upon to replace him. There are some serious matters, however, which must be dealt with immediately. Mr Addington does not have the political resources at hand to deal with all of them, so I have been asked to handle some of the more delicate issues."

Marcus nodded, understanding.

Pitt continued. "May I ask if you know of Lord Danbury's murder?"

"The newssheets have been filled with little else."

"We have received some garbled intelligence from an agent in France mentioning the Earl of Danbury in connection with one Jahan Pasha. I have reason to be concerned from reading the report that Bonaparte has hatched some scheme in India."

"Trying to reach Tippoo Sultan in Mysore again? Would he repeat his invasion of Egypt?"

"Bonaparte wouldn't repeat such a futile undertaking. He lost his best chance to get to India through Egypt when he abandoned his men there in '99."

"Then he has resorted to underhanded methods to get what he wants."

A wry grin creased Pitt's face. "And for a moment I thought you had underestimated our adversary. I ought to have known better."

Marcus raised his glass in salute and Pitt continued.

"The information we have is incomplete. Indeed, it is all speculation. I would like you to look into the matter of Lord Danbury's death. See what you can uncover. I wish I had something more solid to give you." Pitt set his glass aside and leaned forward, his elbows on his knees. "I believe Le Faucon is involved."

The blood thrummed in Marcus's ears. "The Hawk again."

"It is vitally important that we discover what the French are plotting. I fear England has taken the Peace of Amiens too much to heart. People are flocking to the continent like schoolboys fleeing Eton at the end of term. It cannot last. There are reports of an invasion force gathering along the French coast. When war comes again, we must be prepared to face the onslaught."

Marcus wanted to refuse the commission—he had scarcely recovered from his last jaunt—but he could not bring himself to do so. He had vowed to bring down Le Faucon and his puppetmaster, Fouche, even if it cost him everything he owned. This was too good an opportunity to pass up.

* * *

The serving girl inhaled sharply. Her regard, which had not been precisely friendly, now bordered on hostile. "It was my cousin, my guardian, who was murdered."

CHAPTER 3

Anthony felt as if he'd stepped into some strange pantomime where a familiar story had been set on its head. "Your cousin?"

"Yes, he was murdered."

Anthony shook his head. "My father, the Earl of Danbury, was murdered one week ago today."

As if she were a guest rather than a maid the girl thunked onto the bench opposite him. Eyes wide and face pale she shook her head as if she weren't seeing him any longer. "Then they were murdered the same day. There must be some significance."

Anthony leaned across the table towards her. "Who was your cousin and why would you think there is some connec—"

"He owned this coffee house. He—" She held up a hand. "Please excuse me. My cousin left a… well, there's something you should see."

Nodding acceptance he sat back and sipped at what was a surprisingly good cup of coffee. He reached into the pocket of his waistcoat and touched the letter notifying him that his title had been confirmed. He pulled it out. He was officially the Earl of Danbury. He had always known that the day would come when he would accede to his father's rights and responsibilities, but he still didn't feel prepared. His fingers caressed the parchment, folding and unfolding it. How many men had spent their lives striving for such honours? He would trade the title in a minute if it would restore his father to him.

He shoved the letter back into his pocket.

If her cousin's murder occurred the same night as his father's it was just conceivable that they were related. But the connection eluded him. Most likely it was nothing. Some phantom delusion; but at this point he had no other clues to investigate. It couldn't hurt to humour the girl and find out why she would think there could possibly be a link.

He gazed about the coffee house, wondering about its former owner. The Green Peacock defined shabbiness. Care had been lavished on spotless tables and grates, but the furnishings had been mended several times, by the look of them.

The entire street had seen better days. The shops and taverns—once prosperous—now stank of the Thames and decay. Most of the respectable inhabitants had long since fled westward to be replaced by seedy people with murky pasts.

Come to think of it, the serving girl seemed out of place. What was it? He considered.

Of course! With a triumphant slap of his hand against the scarred table, he had it. Her accent had no part in this rundown area of London. She sounded as if she would be more at home in Mayfair than this scruffy coffee house. How had she come to be in such a place?

Raised voices wafted from the other room, and Anthony frowned. An instant later the serving girl reappeared carrying a small haversack. Anthony studied her. He often didn't really see servants—one of the pitfalls of his class and upbringing, he supposed. They were little more than part of the décor in any establishment. Now he regarded her intently. The girl certainly bore closer inspection well. Classically sculpted features were saved from coldness by their animation. Auburn hair curled becomingly about her face and temples. Large, deep brown eyes put him in mind of the chocolates at Gunter's. An enigma. The girl's speech and bearing were those of a lady, while her employment at this coffee house precluded that assumption.

"I'm sorry, sir, it will have to wait—"

A man burst through the door hard on the girl's heels. He caught up with her in a couple of large bounds and grabbed her shoulder, swinging the girl around to face him.

"Did you think you'd get away with that?" He shoved her, sending her staggering. As she sprawled, her heel caught the brute's calf, tripping him. The man let out a bellow as he nearly fell. He grabbed the girl's hair, yanking her head back.

Anthony's toast clattered to the table.

"Fenn, please. Look…" Her words were cut off by a sharp kick to the ribs. The girl sucked in air, a painful gulping noise.

"Always thought you were better," the bully spat. He raised his hand to strike her as she jerked free and scrabbled away from him on all fours.

Anthony's arm shot out, seizing Fenn's and twisting it up behind his back with a quick, sharp movement. Almost without realizing it, he'd come up behind the lout and taken him by surprise.

"What do you think you're about?" Anthony framed his question politely, but allowed his tone to remain threatening.

"Wha' d'ye care?" The ruffian struggled to free his wrist.

Anthony repeated his question, tightening his grip. Fenn howled, his eyes shifted. "The trollop's been stealing. I caught her. See the bag?"

Twisting in Anthony's grip, but still unable to free himself, Fenn turned his vindictive attention back to the girl. "It's the beak for you. Ready to dangle, my fine lady?"

"Unless you want to visit the magistrate you will cease this moment." Anthony enunciated as distinctly as possible. He released the young man to toss a few coins on the table to pay for his coffee. Then turned to the girl. "What's in the bag?"

Shakily the girl clambered to her feet and retrieved it from where it had fallen to the floor and emptied the contents onto the closest table. A pitiful pair of worn dresses and a few undergarments toppled out.

"Did you steal anything from this establishment?"

"No." Her voice sounded ragged. She hugged her ribs protectively.

"Lyin' little rat." Fenn rushed forward, striking a violent blow that sent her tumbling. Her head cracked resoundingly against the hearthstone and she lay deathly still.

Anthony collared the lout. He had itched to punch something for a week. Now he allowed himself the sublime pleasure of knocking the bully senseless. The hours spent sparring in Gentleman Jack's fashionable ring had at last been profitably put to use.

He flexed his fingers and stepped over the brute's prone figure.

It was a certainty that he'd get no information from this Fenn character. He sighed. Someday he must learn to curb his impulsiveness.

There was nothing for it. He needed the girl. He wasn't convinced there was a link between the murders, but even if it was a remote possibility he wanted to know precisely what she knew. But they could hardly remain here to chat. Fenn might rouse at any moment and he'd be as mad as a badger. Anthony picked up the maid's unconscious form and carried her out to his carriage.

CHAPTER 4

A rough bump jolted Lydia back to unpleasant reality. An involuntary gasp of pain escaped her lips, and she struggled to sit up. Groaning, she leaned forward, holding her head.

"You're in my carriage." A gentle male voice from the shadowy corner answered her unasked question.

"Who are you?" A spike of fear skewered her to the seat.

"Careful," he said, sitting forward so that she could see his face more clearly.

"The Earl?"

"Yes."

He dabbed with a clean linen handkerchief at the blood trickling from her lip. She flinched away from the touch and he sat back.

Lydia sucked in a lungful of air. She refused to succumb to the darkness again. She needed her wits about her to discover what this gentleman wanted. In no condition to fight, she sat back, rallying her strength and biding her time in case she needed to bolt.

* * *

Anthony suppressed a sigh as he stared at the girl. She looked as timid as a caged sparrow. Her glance darted about as if searching for a means of escape. He needed to gain her trust before she tried to fly the coop. The girl leaned back against the seat and closed her eyes. He needed whatever information she might have. The runner's investigation was going nowhere.

He would take her home with him. There he could find out what she had to tell him away from prying eyes. Her wounds would need to be tended, and perhaps he could find a friend in need of a maid—then she wouldn't have to return to the Green Peacock at all. A neat solution all around. He rapped on the carriage roof.

"Home, Martin." Settling back comfortably into his seat, he tried to think of some topic of conversation. He had never been in such an odd situation. "Might I know your name?" Perhaps not the most ingenious of openings, but at least it was practical.

The girl widened her eyes as if he had pulled her from a deep reverie. "Lydia Garrett." Her dark eyes held his in a steady gaze. "Why did you take me from the Peacock?"

"I couldn't leave you there. If convicted of thievery you might have faced the gallows."

"He wouldn't send me to the gallows. There would be no one left to do the work."

"No?" Anthony cocked an eyebrow. He'd always been rather proud of that particular ability. He felt it gave him a rakish air.

For some reason the girl flushed. "No," she said. Her tone cut the topic off at the legs. "Why did you really take me away?"

"I don't know why you should refuse to accept altruism as my motivation." He flashed her a smile. They were almost home. He needed to gain her trust before she tried to flee. Perhaps it would be best to state the facts openly. He held his palms up. "I admit it. I do have need of you—preferably conscious—to tell me more about your cousin's death. It's possible you may be right and his murder is related to my father's, though I can't see why that might be the case."

Lydia narrowed her eyes. She opened her mouth, probably to deliver a cutting remark, but a particularly rough bump caused her to gasp. She swayed in her seat. For a moment, Anthony feared she would faint again.

"We'll have a physician in."

She shook her head and grimaced, what little colour she had draining from her face. "No, sir." Her voice was so fragile he could scarcely hear her over the rattle of carriage wheels and hawkers' cries.

"I intend no offence, my girl, but you don't look well."

Lydia dabbed gingerly at her bleeding lip. "Some hot water to wash with will put me to rights."

"I insist." Anthony held up a hand. "I need you in proper working order."

She almost smiled, but the slight upward twitch at the corners of her mouth was turned back by a fierce scowl. She stared at him for a long moment. "I will tell you why I believe the murders are connected on two conditions."

Anthony angled his chin and one eyebrow up a fraction, waiting to hear her terms.

"First, if I tell you what I know, you will not go hire some Bow Street runner, and leave me in the dark. My cousin was my last… I owe him a great deal. I need to know who did this. I need justice." Tears pooled in her eyes and Anthony pressed his handkerchief into her hand.

"Is there a second condition?"

Her lips tightened and she breathed in deeply. He could see her shepherding her emotions together. She did not speak until she was once more composed. "As you pointed out, I can't return to the Green Peacock." She paused pointedly. "Fenn will be even angrier now. You must promise to write a letter of reference for me, and assist me in finding a suitable position elsewhere."

Anthony couldn't blame her. A woman alone needed a mercenary edge to survive. What would he have done if their positions were reversed? The silence stretched between them. He narrowed his eyes and studied her, but she met his gaze, refusing to flinch or fidget.

"I'm willing to agree to your terms." He saw the girl exhale and realized she had been holding her breath awaiting his response.

The horses rattled to a halt and Anthony stole a glance out of the window. "Ah, we're here."

* * *

Lydia welcomed the cessation of movement. She had managed not to disgrace herself by fainting again, but the continuous jostling put her tenacity to the test.

A footman hurried to open the door of the carriage and the young gentleman led the way. Lydia followed more slowly, her legs threatening to fail her. She clutched her ribs and tried to breathe shallowly. She must keep her wits about her.

The grand houses on the fashionable cul-de-sac stood solid and graceful, guarding their quiet street from incursion by the unwashed masses. Even the air here behaved more genteelly than it did on Brant Street. The wind fluttered past like a fine lady in trailing lace, rather than darting and snagging at one like a ragamuffin.

The gazes of several servants pierced her, and she imagined she could hear their disapproving thoughts. Using the handkerchief the gentleman had given her, she dabbed again at her face, trying to wipe away any signs of squalor.

She kept her movements deliberate for fear she might break one of the treasures that graced the front hall. None of the fine houses she had visited as a child could compare to the elegance of this London mansion.

The gentleman led the way to a spacious study. He motioned for her to sit, and seated himself behind the desk. Obeying gingerly, she tucked her skirts close. She didn't want to sully the fine leather or beautiful carpets. She peeked at the soles of her shoes, hoping she hadn't tracked anything disgraceful in with her.

"Can you read, Lydia?" At her nod, he handed her a letter.

She read the short missive and then, brow creased in confusion, looked up. "I don't understand. Who is Jahan Pasha?"

"I haven't been able to determine that, but his letter arrived for my father on the day of his death."

Lydia glanced again at the letter, fingering the distinctive seal as if she could discern the answer to a puzzle from the ridges of wax.

"I'm beginning to see. That morning—after they took his body away—I found a patch of wax on the hearthstone while cleaning away the mess. I thought it odd because we don't generally have dealings with the type of people who can afford sealing wax this fine, nor is Mrs Wolfe one to pay for fancy wax candles when tallow will do. I didn't assign any particular significance to it at the time." She glanced back up at him.

He half stood, palms flat on his desk. "Did you say Wolfe?"

"Yes." Involuntarily she reared away from his intensity, wincing as she did so. "My guardian." Deliberately she sat forward again. She would not be intimidated by this man. Or, at least, she would not show that he intimidated her.

He sat back down. "Mr Wolfe served as boatswain on the *Centaur*."

"Yes. How did you know that?"

He tried to hide a quick smile behind his hand. Lydia almost smiled herself. He had brought her to his home in order to interrogate her, not the other way around. He made no comment, however, but rifled through a sheaf of papers on the desk.

"The first I heard of Mr Wolfe was in a letter my father wrote to me on the day he was murdered. My valet found it stuffed into one of my boots. Here." He pulled a couple of pages from the pile and handed them to her. Once again he sat quietly while Lydia read.

My Dearest Son,

It is with a heavy heart and much misgiving that I write to you. If, as I hope, the cause of this narrative is merely the delusion of an old man, then please forgive the fancies of age. I received by the evening post a letter which disturbed me a great deal.

The Centaur *was my first command. When I took it, I was younger than you are now, though I thought myself very experienced. I have made a great many mistakes in my life, son, but none I regret more than the one I made on that journey. I acted outside the scope of my orders and my crew and I paid dearly.*

I have no defence for my actions. I can say only that I was in the grip of a terrible conceit.

Worse than my faulty judgment is that I involved my crew in the matter, and in doing so cost several of them their lives. I have tried by the rest of my life to atone for my actions of so long ago.

Son, I do not have the time to recount all the details, but I beg you to find my old boatswain, Rudolph Wolfe. Give him my best compliments and pray him to tell you the tale.

Of all the things I have done right in my life, you and your mother were the best and brightest. I have ever been proud of you and I know you will carry out this last wish. Thank you, son. Do not grieve over much; we will see one another again.

Father

Lydia glanced from the letter to his Lordship and back again, trying to wrap her mind around the information. He had been forthright. It was time to offer him some of what she knew. "I found Mr Wolfe in the kitchen." Lydia could almost see and smell his corpse again. She forced herself to speak, though an acrid taste fouled her tongue. "I'm always the first to get up in the mornings, to stoke the fires and begin the morning chores. He had been stabbed."

She raised her eyes to meet Lord Danbury's and the force of his gaze made the words shrivel and stick to the roof of her mouth. She swallowed hard and tried again. "The oddest thing I noticed was that the murderer left behind a fine knife with a carved ivory handle. It was more valuable than anything a thief could have possibly hoped to cart away from the coffee house. The magistrate confiscated it as evidence, of course."

"What was the carving?"

"A peacock."

CHAPTER 4

Her interrogator leaned closer, his attention fixed on her as if she were the only person in the world. "Was he stabbed from the front or the back?"

"The back. There were two wounds." Poor, poor Mr Wolfe. They had stood together so long against the petty cruelties of Mrs Wolfe and the misbegotten Fenn. She shut her eyes against the tide of sorrow. The Earl must think her an utter ninny. She had done little but weep and snivel since she had met him. If only she could think clearly.

"So he either turned his back on his attacker, or did not know he was there. Did you notice anything else out of place?"

Lydia fought back the distress that threatened to choke her. Her head ached, her throat burned with the effort of stifling her nausea. "The door was off the latch. The magistrate declared that someone must have neglected to secure it. He thought thieves happened on the unlocked door and came in to rob us—a simple crime of opportunity."

"And the murder?"

"When Mr Wolfe caught them, they killed him, then fled in horror at what they had done." She rubbed at her temples. "No one had the slightest interest in listening to my protestations."

Lydia's head swam. Thumping, throbbing pain coursed throughout her frame, making it difficult to hear above her own pulse. She dabbed at the blood oozing from her split lip, determined not to mar the elegantly upholstered chair in which she sat.

The gentleman seemed to notice the fatigue plucking at her composure like an importunate beggar. "I'll have no more argument from you. Someone must take a look at those injuries." He raised an imperious hand to stifle her protests and rang for a footman.

"Mrs Malloy, please."

The liveried young man bowed shortly, glanced covertly at Lydia and departed on his quest. A small, stout woman with an ample bosom and sparkling eyes appeared a moment later.

"Your Lordship?" The question was aimed at the Earl, but her gaze lingered on Lydia.

"Mrs Malloy, our guest is in need of medical attention. I shall leave it to you to decide whether your stillroom ministrations will suffice, or whether the doctor ought to be called in."

As if she had received permission, Mrs Malloy tsk-tsked over Lydia's condition. "Come along, child." She extended her arm towards Lydia like a hen guiding its chick with outspread wings. Over her shoulder, Mrs Malloy addressed his Lordship. "I'll put her in the spare maid's room, shall I?"

"As you see fit." His Lordship's attention had already reverted to the papers on his desk.

The woman patted her hand. "Don't worry, child. I won't hurt you. I want to help you feel better."

Lydia had been dismissed, but it was only right to tell him the rest of what she'd seen. "Your Lordship, there is something more you must know." Obediently she stood and backed around the chair before Mrs Malloy's motherly onslaught.

His Lordship looked up from his papers, the gleam of a hunter in his eye.

The drumming in Lydia's head picked up tempo. The fine room whirled. Lightheaded, she gripped the chair back. She opened her mouth to speak, but could make nothing emerge. Mrs Malloy placed a hand on Lydia's arm, steadying her.

Darkness encroached on the edges of her vision. His Lordship stood up, sending his chair toppling backwards. There should have been a crash as the chair landed. Why was there no crash? Confused thoughts scurried like mice as Lydia struggled to remain coherent despite the thrumming in her ears. Then—nothing.

CHAPTER 5

M arcus hated the foul odour of these low taverns. It was a pity so many of his commitments required that he frequent them. His valet would have a devil of a time beating the stench from his clothes—a shame, since he particularly liked this new jacket. Barely concealing his disgust at the thick miasma of smoke and close-packed, reeking humanity, he pushed his way through the throng to the place where his contact sat drinking.

There was the slightest whisper of movement in the crush at his side and Marcus whirled. Gripping the would-be pickpocket by the wrist he administered a sharp rap on the young man's hand with the heavy knob of his cane.

"That sort of lark will land you in Newgate."

The lad jerked free, raising his bruised fingers to his lips. Without a backward glance he melted into the crowd as if he'd never been there.

"Young people these days." Rodney Perkins shook his head.

Marcus settled himself beside the runner. "What can you tell me about the Earl of Danbury's murder?"

"Not a bloomin' thing—if you'll pardon my language—aside from what's been reported in the rags."

"Come now, Mr Perkins. You must earn your keep. What have you been doing all this time?"

"I ain't turned up a speck of evidence. This one's no easy bit o' work."

"What of the threatening letter that was found?" Marcus gritted his teeth, fingers drumming against the head of his cane. If Pitt was right—and he was rarely wrong—time was of the essence. Perhaps it would be better to take matters into his own hands.

"I ain't turned up a single whiff of any Jahan Pasha." Perkins' contempt for a foreigner—be he real or imagined—edged his words and turned his lips up in a sneer.

"Oh?" Marcus allowed a hint of superciliousness into his tone.

The runner raised a hand. "Look now, I done everythin' any man with sense could be expected to do. There ain't been no one in London by that name so far's I can tell. None of the ports have record of 'im and neither does anybody else. I wouldn't 'ave said it at the time—he seemed right grieved—but you ask me, I think the son done for the ol' gent to get at the money and title."

Marcus sat back and crossed his arms. It was possible. Murder had been committed for less. But then what could all this have to do with Bonaparte's scheming? Could the son be the traitor he had been looking for? He was highly placed in society and could have access to much of the information that had been passed along. Perhaps the murder had been committed, not out of greed, but out of fear of being named to the authorities. Or, perhaps, the old man had been the traitor and the son had killed him rather than allow the family honour to be besmirched.

Tossing a crown on the table, Marcus stood. "Contact me if you learn anything more."

Perkins tugged on his forelock and scooped the coin into his shirt with a deft motion. "Right you are, sir. Right you are."

* * *

Was it morning or evening? Lydia lay unmoving, considering the dim grey light that filtered through the thin curtains. She turned her gaze to the figure in the chair next to the bed, but could not summon the will to move any other bit of herself.

CHAPTER 5

Mrs Malloy hummed gently, her rocking chair creaking rhythmically as she attended to some mending.

So she was still at his Lordship's house.

Mrs Malloy seemed to sense she had awakened. "You gave us a fright, my girl."

Lydia's jaw and right cheek felt stiff and swollen, making her words clumsy and slow. "I'm sorry for the imposition. I assure you it was not my intention." Stiffly, she began to move aside the bedclothes.

"Don't stir a muscle from that bed. Get back under there." The housekeeper's words were sharp, but the tone gentle. Too tired and sore to argue, Lydia eased the coverlet back in place.

"Lord Danbury will want to know you are awake." Mrs Malloy set aside her sewing and stood. "I expect you to stay put."

Lydia hadn't the slightest desire to ever move again. "Yes, ma'am."

Mrs Malloy left the room in a swish of bombazine and lavender scent.

With gritted teeth, Lydia gently probed her ribs with one hand. Sweat beaded her forehead and a hiss of pain whistled through her teeth. Every movement, every breath would be labourious for several days, but she was fairly certain they were not broken, merely bruised. Nor was her skull cracked, though it gave a fair imitation of being split open.

The room darkened as night chased the sun away: now she knew what time of day it was. Her eyes grew heavy, she began to drift off. A squeak from the door roused her and she blinked groggily.

Lord Danbury peeked into the room, though he did not enter. "How are you?"

"Better. Thank you. I am sorry for the imposition." Her cheeks burned and she pulled the coverlet higher.

Lord Danbury waved away her apology. "I am sorry. I should have intervened sooner." He opened the door an inch or so wider. "How did you come to be at the Green Peacock?"

"My father was a vicar, but he and my mother were killed in a carriage accident when I was fourteen. After some confusion, I was sent to live with Mr Wolfe, my father's cousin. He was the only family with which the solicitor was able to establish contact."

"And he owned the Green Peacock? Is that how you came to be working there?"

She nodded.

Lord Danbury gazed at her for a long moment. Lydia caught at her lip with her teeth, but offered no other details.

At last he pushed away from the doorframe on which he had been leaning. "As promised, I will see what I can do about employment for you. I'm sure some acquaintance or other is in need of a maid."

Lydia nodded gingerly.

He must have taken her slowness for reluctance. "Do you have any accomplishments?" He looked dubious.

"Arithmetic, Latin, French, and Geography. I could manage music, dance and deportment."

He nodded, more to himself it seemed. "Perhaps a governess then?"

It was a higher post than she had dared hope for. "I should like it very much."

He turned to go.

"Lord Danbury, I would be qualified. I was well educated."

He nodded and offered her a slight smile before closing the door. He may even have believed her.

Sinking deeply into the pillows, Lydia stared after him. How often would her life be so resoundingly upended? Sighing, she considered making an escape. She would rather leap from the top of St Paul's golden dome, but perhaps returning to the Green Peacock was possible. At least it was a life she knew—the only home she'd had since her parents' deaths. She had been able to manage Fenn for years. Surely she would be able to manage him a while longer? But no. She was deluding herself. There was no going back.

She worried a stray thread on the coverlet as she evaluated the situation.

Her mother's family owned a home in London, but Lydia

wouldn't have the courage to approach them. Besides, if they refused to acknowledge her, then she was content to act as though they didn't exist either. It might be cold company, but she had her pride.

It seemed she would have to trust Lord Danbury a bit longer. She had nowhere else to go.

CHAPTER 6

Anthony slammed into the library in search of something to distract his mind. Another day wasted. Every trail he pursued seemed fraught with difficulties. It had been three days since he had discovered who Mr Wolfe was, and the information had led precisely nowhere. He stuck a finger down his collar and tugged to loosen his cravat. Why James thought he could only achieve the perfect mathematical knot by strangling him, he'd never know.

The presence of a slight figure sitting quietly in his favourite chair brought him up short. The young woman grimaced as she rose. "Good evening, sir. I apologize if I've intruded. I was told I might wait for you in here."

With a start, Anthony realized that the young woman before him, dressed in a maid's uniform, was Wolfe's cousin. He smoothed the furrows from his brow and summoned a smile to cover the sudden racing of his pulse.

"Mrs Malloy is allowing you out of the sick room now, or have you escaped?"

"She said I might get up, but ordered me not to over-exert myself." The girl smoothed the front of her borrowed dress. "If you have a moment, it is important that I speak with you."

Perhaps the day was not an entire loss after all. He settled into a chair, prepared to offer his whole-hearted attention. "Certainly."

"I must thank you for your kindness."

"No need, no need." Anthony found himself bobbing his head like a demented cockatoo. "Lydia, wasn't it? Think nothing of it. You

42

are the first and only person so far to give me any real information. I have been keeping you here for my own reasons." Belatedly realizing how that might be construed, he rushed to assure her. "Nothing dishonourable, I assure you." His cheeks burned. Good heavens, he must sound a regular flat.

He thought he saw a smile but she tucked her chin down and looked at her hands, folded primly around the book in her lap. "Yes, my Lord, that's why I'm here."

Anthony leaned forward.

"I always woke first to prepare the kitchen for the morning trade. But on the evening before Mr Wolfe was killed…" She paused. "You must promise not to use the information I divulge for any purpose other than bringing the murderer to justice."

Anthony inhaled deeply, trying to maintain a pleasant demeanour. He leaned forward a bit more. And then another bit. If he could reach down her throat and rip the tale from her he would. "I have no interest in Mr Wolfe's affairs except where they cross my father's."

Her eyes searched his face and then she nodded once. "I found him in the kitchen stuffing some papers behind a couple of loose bricks in the mantle. He was as anxious as a cutpurse hiding his ill-gotten gain so I made him some tea to settle his nerves." A wistful smile lit her features.

Anthony jerked upright. Another fraction of an inch and he would have toppled into the chit's lap. The information might indeed be valuable, but what was it about this girl that had him so out of kilter?

A pink flush crept up her neck and into her cheeks. Once more she bent her head. Had his attention embarrassed her in some way? "As he drank it he told me the papers were reminiscences of his days at sea, but he didn't want Mrs Wolfe or Fenn to know about them. He feared they would mock his efforts."

"He made me promise not to tell anyone where they were hidden. I agreed, of course, but he remained distracted all evening. The next morning I found him murdered."

She looked up then, and met his gaze again. The restrained sorrow in her eyes made his breath take up lodgings in his throat. Perhaps her embarrassment was at her own failure to prevent her cousin's death. He well knew the weight of that particular guilt. He opened his mouth but she continued.

"I wouldn't be telling you about it now but for the fact that those papers might have something to do with his death. Based on the letter your father wrote, this all began decades ago."

Anthony settled back into his chair. "I suppose it's time."

"Pardon me?"

"Bow Street is investigating the murder. I suppose it is time I introduce you to Perkins. I have been considering whether you ought to speak to him, and now I believe it would be for the best. What you've told me could be important indeed. You don't mind speaking to a runner, do you?"

She blinked at the sudden turn of the conversation. "Not if you think it important."

Anthony dispatched a footman to summon Rodney Perkins, and then returned to the discussion.

"The question we now face is how to retrieve those papers. Would Mrs Wolfe sell them?"

Lydia hesitated. "Mrs Wolfe will not give them up if she knows someone else wants them. It's her way."

"I could make it well worth her while."

"But you would have to explain how you knew, not only of their existence, but of their hiding place."

"I would…"

She shook her head. "Once you admitted that I told you of the papers you would have to pry them from her with a crowbar." She gave a small shrug. "We never got along well."

"What would you suggest?"

"I should go back. Then I could retrieve the documents and slip them to you after dark." Her quiet words sounded as sombre as the tolling of a church bell at a funeral.

"I cannot allow it." Anthony stood and began to pace. "Surely you know as well as I what the consequences could be. That brute Fenn would enjoy making you pay for the humiliation he suffered at my hands."

"What did you do to Fenn?"

Anthony paused in mid-stride. He had forgotten she did not witness the decisive action. "I knocked him senseless." Satisfaction added relish to his tone.

A wide grin spread across her face. "Impossible, I'm afraid."

His eyes widened. Did she question his veracity? He whirled to address her.

"He was already entirely senseless." An impish light sparked in her eyes, and he found himself chuckling at her small jest.

He must not allow himself to be sidetracked by a pretty, witty maid. "He may again accuse you of theft. You could be tried and hanged."

"I've considered the possibility, believe me, but the more I think on it, the less I believe he would do it. Which is not to say he will be pleasant. But trade has been slow of late at the Green Peacock. Mrs Wolfe didn't have the funds to hire someone to do the work. Fenn has probably had to take over most of my duties. He should be glad enough to have me back, for a short time at least." The rush of words made him think she was trying to convince herself as well as him.

He cocked his head to the side. There was something going on here. It was plain as parchment that she did not want to return to the coffee house. Dreaded it, in fact. "Why this insistence on placing yourself at risk?"

Her gaze clashed against his, flint and stone sparking one against the other. "The last person in this entire world who cared one farthing about me has been slaughtered. I will see justice done, and if that meant facing a hundred Fenns I would do so without a moment's hesitation."

He held out his hands in a placating gesture. "I only meant there must be another way. Your Fenn would be as likely to burn the papers in front of me as give them to me. But I still think it would be placing you in too much danger to send you back there unescorted."

They pondered the problem silently for a while, the only sounds in the room the crackle and hiss of the fire in the grate and the steady tick of the clock on the mantle. The evening shadows deepened and spread.

Anthony stood and set to pacing. "Would I be able to sneak into the coffee house and extract the papers with no one the wiser?"

It was a daft, wild, ridiculous notion, and the girl opened her mouth as if to tell him so, but then she narrowed her eyes. Her fingers stroked the fine-grained leather of the book in her lap. "I think it would be possible. We would want to wait until Fenn takes himself off for the night. Then it should be fairly easy. He often forgets and leaves the door off the latch. If that won't work, the window to my old room in the garret doesn't close properly. I could get in that way."

She held up a hand to forestall his protests.

"It's small but *I* can squeeze through. You would be far too large. If you must be involved, I could go down and let you in through the kitchen door. It shouldn't take more than a moment to get the papers." Lydia paused, then engaged his gaze. "I am willing to do nearly anything if it will mean catching Mr Wolfe's murderer, but if he meant to provide for his family with what he stashed away, some money, or the deed to some property or something, I won't allow them to be removed. I will not be the thief Fenn accused me of being."

Having stated her conditions she pulled back her shoulders, but turned her eyes downward as if bracing for a tirade. What an interesting young lady she was proving to be. "I'll agree to those terms. They do you credit."

Her gaze again found his as she smiled. "Thank you, sir."

"Now we have some planning to do." He led the way to the study, where he took the seat behind the desk and motioned for her to take the seat before it. Only compunction for her safety had made him hesitate, but he had to concede the point. She must be involved in the escapade. She alone knew the location of the hiding place. And she alone could offer a plausible tale if caught inside the coffee house in the middle of the night. As long as he was near, she should come to no harm.

Looking across the desk as she noted down their plans in small neat script, Anthony congratulated himself for having taken her away from that miserable den. He must think harder—try harder to find her a suitable position. He would find some means of repaying her for her service. Reclining into the comfortable chair, he tilted his head as Lydia proposed another idea—though he hadn't heard what she said.

A footman announced Perkins.

"Say nothing of Wolfe's papers or our plans," he muttered as he stood to receive the runner.

She nodded minutely while he greeted Perkins. He'd all but forgotten that he'd summoned the man. And now he regretted it, but he would have to tell him something. The runner had to be devilish curious at the sudden summons, though he hid the emotion with practised skill. His attention had obviously fixed on the girl seated before the desk. His small, round eyes examined her as if regarding a fish to be filleted for supper.

"Mr Perkins, it is good of you to come. This young lady has information which may be useful to us."

"How is it you didn't come forward before?"

"Excuse me?" Her brow cleared and she shook her head. "Oh, no, I'm not a maid here. These clothes are borrowed. Perhaps…" She looked to Anthony for assistance.

In brief outline he explained how he had discovered the letter from his father and managed to find Rudolph Wolfe's residence, only to learn that he too had been murdered. He gave Perkins the letter to peruse. The runner turned an apoplectic shade of crimson, and seared him with a reproachful glare, but held his tongue.

When Lydia had completed her recitation of the facts around

her discovery of Wolfe's body, Perkins sat back and tapped his lip thoughtfully.

"You think as these men were killed for summat to do with this voyage they took, what was it, some forty odd years ago?"

Anthony and Lydia voiced their agreement.

"And why would that be, exactly?"

"We don't know," said Anthony.

Perkins addressed Lydia. "Did Mr Wolfe ever speak to you of these things?"

"No, sir. I knew nothing of the matter until his Lordship allowed me to read the same letter you've just seen."

"I hate to admit it, but we're at somethin' of a dead end. I ain't been able to find no one called Jahan Pasha, or this Shah Akbar."

Frowning, Anthony leaned forward. "You've found no trace at all? I confess my inquiries have been unsuccessful, but I had hoped with your greater resources…"

Perkins cut in. "I'll wager no one by those names 'as come into the country anytime recent, at least not legal like. There's no record of 'em in London or anywheres nearby. You sure you told me everythin', Miss?"

"I told you everything I can recall about how I found Mr Wolfe's body. I did not hear anything in the night, or see anything suspicious out of my window, if that is what you mean. Do you think mention of those men might be a blind?"

Perkins eyed her as if she were particularly obtuse. "If you think of anything you forgot, send for me."

"Certainly."

"And if I have questions for you, where will you be?"

She opened her mouth but closed it again. Anthony stepped in smoothly. "You may call for Lydia here."

Looking back at the girl he frowned. Her complexion had turned ashen and dark circles settled beneath her eyes. He berated himself for a fool. Her exhaustion showed plainly. She needed rest if she were to recover from her injuries.

CHAPTER 6

"I fear Mrs Malloy will have my head on a platter for keeping you from your sickbed. Please retire; you need to gather your strength."

She looked from one man to the other. "If you are certain I am no longer needed, I believe I will."

With their reassurances she bade them goodnight.

"Do you think she's tellin' us the entire story?" Perkins was watching him closely.

"I'm sure she hasn't lied about what she found. She came up with the details about the knife, and so on, independently. She hadn't any description of my father's death when she told me her tale."

The runner narrowed his eyes, perhaps noticing that he had not answered the question. "Unless it were from the newssheets." Despite his obvious scepticism, Perkins said no more about it, but admonished Anthony to bring anything else he might find to his attention immediately. "After all, sir, whoever did this has already killed twice. We wouldn't want to put a third to his conscience."

* * *

Marcus watched as the door to the fine house closed firmly behind Perkins, and the runner crossed the street. Stepping from the shadows of the mews, from which he had been keeping a discreet eye on the household, Marcus grasped the runner's shoulder.

"What did he have for you?"

"Oi!" Perkins clutched his chest dramatically. "You gave me a fright."

Marcus did not find him amusing. He cocked an eyebrow.

"All right, guv'nor, all right. Seems his Lordship in there 'as been doin' some investigatin' of 'is own. 'E showed me a letter from his dad, what he writ the same night as he was murdered. He admitted to something unsavoury in the letter, but he weren't specific. He wanted the son to find an old mate. Man by the name of Rudolph Wolfe, what owned a coffee house. This here Wolfe happened to

49

get hisself killed the same day as old Danbury, if you can credit it, and he's got a girl in there what worked for him."

Both Marcus's eyebrows went up now. "Does he, now?"

"What's more, I think they're still hidin' somethin'. I don't know what they kept back, but I'd wager my next reward packet. They were careful not to say *somethin'*."

"Good work, Perkins; good work. Do let me know if you turn up anything else." Marcus slipped the man a handful of coins.

Perkins glanced at the money in his palm. "Yes, sir. You know me, sir. Always pleased to help if I can." The runner tipped his cap and slouched away, jingling the money in his hand as if it were a musical instrument.

Marcus scowled. Danbury would not get away with withholding any further evidence. This puzzle would be solved, despite the lack of information and an arrogant, interfering heir who thought he knew more about investigation than the professionals.

He settled in to watch the house. Twilight slid off the edge of the abyss into full darkness but he remained at his post long past the time when the candles had been damped and the door secured. The night watch made his rounds twice before Marcus abandoned his post with a disgruntled sigh. He'd be back. If the man was up to something, Marcus would find him out.

CHAPTER 7

Lydia convinced Lord Danbury to wait until Saturday night to enter the coffee house, because the shop stayed closed on Sunday. Fenn would almost certainly go out in search of diversion and Mrs Wolfe had a habit of ensuring a good night's sleep by taking a substantial dose of laudanum. Lydia had no doubt that the woman would be abed early, leaving them a clear field.

The days slumped past, as halting as recalcitrant children. But as plodding as they were, they at least served the useful function of giving her body time to heal. When she finally shed her borrowed dress and donned her own shabby garments on Saturday evening, however, her heartbeat rang oddly loud in her ears. She stared at her image in the glass the maids shared. What if the evening's adventure landed her back at the Green Peacock for good? Her hands grew clammy, and her throat dry. Sucking in a deep breath she forced herself up the stairs.

Hands clasped behind his back, Lord Danbury paced in the study. An almost wild light gleamed in his eye. "You're ready, then?"

"Yes, sir."

He halted. "Are you well?"

"Quite well."

"I could find another way in. You needn't be involved."

"And let you have all the fun?" Even as she said it her tongue felt thick.

He nodded as if she had passed some sort of test and strode from the room, leaving her to follow. Despite the bravado of her words, it took all her courage to follow Lord Danbury out to the carriage.

* * *

Marcus stood half dozing as he kept an eye on the house from the darkened mews. His hireling should be here in half an hour or so. Rubbing his gloved hands together he thought longingly of his club—his warm, comfortable, well-provisioned club.

Drat Pitt and all politicians anyway.

A carriage rattled up in front of the house and Marcus started to attention. Finally something unorthodox was happening. Awash for a moment in the light from the open door, Lord Danbury and a girl glanced about furtively as they bustled out to the carriage. The hour had grown too late for any legitimate business. And that girl was dressed like a scullery maid. She was neither a fine lady nor a demirep ready to spend the night in frivolity.

Marcus nearly crowed in exhilaration. He had known they were up to something. They didn't even have a footman in attendance. The coachman sat alone on the box. It could only mean they wanted as few as possible to be aware of their activities.

Taking advantage of the lack of attendants, Marcus darted to the side of the carriage and eased onto the backboard, being careful to keep his head low so they would not spot him. Unwitting of the stowaway, the carriage clattered off into the night.

* * *

Emerging from the coach, Lydia took the lead, guiding Lord Danbury through a warren of alleys and side streets. Neither Lydia nor his Lordship had spoken during their journey. The murky darkness hindered their progress and they moved cautiously, having no desire to meet anyone on this particular errand.

Music and hazy light spilled along the street as the door of a nearby bawdy house opened and an obviously inebriated young man teetered out. He waved a cheery good-bye, which was answered by a chorus of ribald humour and raucous laughter before the door shut firmly behind him. Making an attempt at dignity, the fellow tried to straighten his cravat. Having hopelessly disarranged it he set off, his course wobbling and unsure, presumably towards home.

Lydia and Danbury stayed silent and still in the shadows until he had disappeared around a corner.

"The fool is going to get himself killed," whispered Lord Danbury ferociously.

Something in his tone made Lydia turn and look at him. "You know him, then?"

"The idiot recently inherited a large fortune. He seems bent on spending it all as quickly and uselessly as possible."

Lydia understood his frustration. The dolt would undoubtedly wake on the street somewhere to find himself the possessor of a pounding headache and a bruise the size of a goose egg, while at the same time missing his expensive coat, cravat, shoes, hat and walking stick, as well as his purse—if indeed there were anything in it left to take.

The desire to follow and see the poor fellow home tugged at her. A single glance at Lord Danbury's impatient figure silenced the notion. Perhaps it would do the man good to learn such a lesson, painful though it might be.

Pushing the young man's folly from her mind, she led the way through the gloom until they reached the rear of the coffee house. They had scarcely taken up position across the street in an alcove when the door opened and Fenn appeared. She stiffened at the sight of him and held her breath. He was so close. How could he fail to spot them hovering in the shadows? But he hummed a gin-house tune and seemed to be looking forward to his carousing.

Gradually she let out her breath as Fenn made his way down the street with a jaunty stride.

"I think it would be safe to go in now. He doesn't generally leave until Mrs Wolfe is in bed," Lydia whispered, before darting across the street to try the back entrance. No matter how she jostled the handle it would not budge. She grimaced in annoyance. Fenn *would* remember to lock the door on the one night she wanted to get in. She motioned for Anthony to follow her to the edge of the coffee house. About nine feet above them a narrow eave nestled in the crook of the house.

"My window is there." Lydia pointed out the tiny opening above them.

"It looks rather small," Lord Danbury said dubiously.

"I'll fit." She wanted to be done and gone. Her heart pounded in her throat, and her lips were growing chapped from being worried by her teeth, but she had to know what lay behind Mr Wolfe's death. She wiped her palms on her skirt. "Help me?"

Sucking in a deep lungful of air, Lydia stepped up into the basket Lord Danbury made of his hands. Then she stepped to his shoulders. From that vantage, she was able to get enough of a grip on the edge of the overhang to haul herself up the rest of the way. Perched precariously on the narrow ledge, she paused to catch her breath. Her ribs ached from the effort of the climb and she held them protectively. Sweat sprang to her brow. Palms flat on the window she jiggled it gently from side to side. The bolt slipped down into its chamber with a satisfying snick.

Again she rubbed damp palms on her skirt as she paused for a moment to see if the sound of the latch had roused any sign of life from Mrs Wolfe. Ever so carefully she raised the window, mindful of each squeak and groan of the wood. It seemed to take ages, but eventually she had it opened all the way.

Thrusting one arm through, she pushed through the window at an angle until she had enough leverage to redistribute her weight and pull in the other arm. Hands planted on the garret floor, she pulled her lower body through. Her bodice caught at the waist on a protruding nail. The unwelcome sound of tearing cloth caused her to wince—to her over-sensitive ears it sounded as loud as a night watchman's rattle. She reached up with one hand and freed the torn fabric, then proceeded to worm her way through the window. Until—

For a heart-stopping moment she feared her hips had stuck fast. She wriggled madly and lost a bit of skin, but at last she found herself fully inside the familiar old room.

Lydia scrambled to her feet and, taking care to make no noise, leaned out of the window and signalled Lord Danbury. He retreated to even deeper shadow and she lowered the sash back into place.

Congratulating herself on her foresight, she pulled a tiny vial of oil from her apron pocket and liberally doused the hinges of her door. She eased the door open, breathing a sigh of relief when no hideous screech sounded.

She knew the house so well she did not need a light in order to reach the stairs and make her way down them, which was just as well since no light was to be had in the dreary interior.

Breathless from nerves she slunk into the kitchen, unlatched the door and peered outside, motioning Danbury to enter. He darted in from the darkness and stepped aside, making way for her to close the door behind him.

"Where is it?" he hissed.

"Over there." She motioned towards the big fireplace at the end of the kitchen.

The fire had been banked for the night and provided no illumination. Lydia felt the wall near the fireplace, her fingers sensitive to each variation in the rough brick surface. It took but a moment to find the two loose bricks and pry them out. Danbury took them from her almost reverently.

Lydia reached inside the gaping hole. Her groping was rewarded by the smoother texture of a paper-wrapped parcel. The package slid out easily.

Grinning like an imbecile, she handed the thin package to Lord Danbury and hastily replaced the bricks. They turned to go, but then froze. Someone rattled the latch. Lord Danbury leapt for the cellar door. He yanked it open and held it for her.

Too late.

The back door opened and Fenn's figure filled the doorframe.

"Oi! Who's there?" Menace charged Fenn's voice.

Adopting a frantic manner was fairly effortless under the circumstances.

"Fenn," Lydia cried, running to him.

"You!" His tone held a mixture of surprise and suspicion.

"Oh, Fenn, it was awful." She began to cry, her turbulent emotions easy to convey.

"Quit yer blubberin'." He came in and lit the lamp. "Where've you been all this time, runt? Come back to rob the place for real?"

"The man, the one who was here, he took me away." Her voice faltered and she allowed another small sob to escape. "It was horrible."

"Why'd he want t' do that for?"

She lowered her voice to a dramatic whisper, though the quake of fear it held was real enough. "He's a swell. His friends—well, they're depraved."

Flabbergasted, Fenn did not respond for a long moment. "That gent stole you away? I knew he weren't no good the minute I clapped eyes on him."

"I escaped and came here straight away."

"How'd you get in?" The edge of suspicion crept back into his voice.

"Fenn, you know you often forget to lock the door." Lydia bit her lip. He might easily remember locking it when he left.

She needn't have feared. He grimaced and she could practically see the wheels of his mind grind into sluggish movement as he prepared to justify his lapse. She forestalled him by her next comment. "I don't think they've figured out I'm gone yet. You needn't worry that anyone followed me here."

Fenn blinked, the grim pronouncement obviously striking him with aspects of the case that had heretofore escaped his notice. The blood drained from his face. She could almost feel sorry for him. Almost.

"You'll have the whole blinkin' lot swarming about the place.

What were you thinking to come back here, you little fool?" He cuffed her on the side of the head.

"Fenn, you're not going to throw me out in the street, are you? Please, you don't know what they'll do to me if they find me." She clasped her hands together in front of her in supplication, and took another small side step. She had slowly repositioned them so Fenn had his back to the cellar door.

Fenn seemed intrigued by her remark. He scratched his head and a gleam of malicious interest flared deep in his eyes. "What'll they do if they find you?"

She covered her face with her hands and began to sniffle. "It's too dreadful." Through her fingers she saw Lord Danbury peek around the corner of the cellar door. With a furtive wave of her hand she motioned for him to sneak out the back. Pulling Fenn down, she whispered the rest in his ear, as if it were too terrible to speak out loud.

Danbury had scarcely squeezed through the back door when Fenn, his eyes wide, felt behind him for a chair and sat down heavily.

He seemed unable to do any more.

"Don't worry, Fenn. I'm sure they couldn't do anything to you. Even if they do come here, you're a tough one."

If possible, Fenn turned even paler. Grabbing her by the arm he hustled her out of the door. "I don't know what you were thinking, but you ain't stayin' 'ere."

"Fenn, you can't do this. Please, I need your help."

Her pitiful cries had no effect.

"Don't want none of your kinda' trouble, you hear? We don't want nothin' to do with none of those swells." He shook her. "If I catches you hangin' about, I'll skin you and take you back to the devils meself."

He gave her a shove, sending her staggering into the street. A shadow detached itself from the deeper gloom of the alley and move towards her. Fenn slammed the door shut, latching it and ramming the bolt home with a clatter indicative of shaking hands.

Danbury rushed forward to catch her. "Did anyone ever tell you that you should be treading the boards? You could do marvels with Shakespeare."

Lydia gave a snort of laughter, but did not otherwise dignify Lord Danbury's remark with a response. "Come on." She tugged on his sleeve wanting to be away as quickly as possible. The relief bubbling through her felt tenuous, as if her escape might be snatched away at any second.

CHAPTER 8

Marcus observed the nefarious doings of the two housebreakers from a safe distance. What could the wealthy lord want from a rundown coffee house? Whatever it might be, it ought to prove highly interesting. And he now had the leverage he needed.

As if playing some demented parlour game he crept close behind the earl and his companion. He tightened the grip on his cane, holding it just below the heavy knob that could break bones if necessary.

"Lord Danbury, what brings you out at such a late hour?" He kept his voice light, but the sound of it brought the pair to a dead halt.

Danbury turned only his head. "Ah, Harting, how are you?"

"I am decidedly well. Miss, I do not believe I have had the pleasure."

"May I present Miss Lydia Garrett. Lydia, the Honourable Marcus Harting," Danbury said woodenly. "He is the fifth—"

"Fourth," Marcus corrected lazily.

"Fourth," amended Danbury, "son of the Viscount of Wiltshire."

"I am charmed." Marcus took the girl's hand and raised it to his lips before turning his attention back to Danbury. "We should chat."

"Yes, well. We…"

"Come now, Danbury. I saw everything. I'm sure there is a perfectly reasonable explanation for your actions. I would enjoy hearing it." When his quarry said nothing, Marcus adopted his blandest smile. "It would pain me to have to call the watch and see you taken up for theft."

With a disgruntled sigh, Danbury gave in to the inevitable. "Perhaps you could come with us? I'll explain on the way home."

Humming a merry tune, Marcus followed the downcast pair back to the waiting carriage and climbed in behind them. Despite the lighthearted melody, Marcus scrutinized his quarry. He was taking no chances with these two. The most dangerous traitor England had suffered in centuries was still at large and he needed answers.

* * *

If it had not been for the flash of decisive intelligence Anthony had seen gleaming in Harting's eyes and the fact that he obviously meant to try his hand at blackmail, he'd have thought him a bit simple. His monotonous humming could drive a person to distraction.

The man was about the same age, perhaps twenty-six or twenty-seven, his form as lean and tall as a whip, and dressed as nattily as Beau Brummell. But his usual air of languid vapidity was absent. His family had money and influence aplenty, and on the few occasions they had met heretofore, he had struck Anthony as inoffensive enough. What was he up to?

The continued drone of Harting's humming peeled away at Anthony's good breeding as if it were an orange. Indignation rose in his chest. Why was he prying into Anthony's personal affairs in such an ungentlemanly fashion?

He smothered a growl as it tried to escape. Harting's usual indolence belied the idea that he should interest himself in anything beyond his own person—just Anthony's luck that he should spark the fop's curiosity.

"Sir, as enchanting as your melody is, I pray you to cease." At the sound of Lydia's voice, Harting broke off in mid-note.

"Please accept my humblest apologies, Miss Garrett." He

lowered his head in formal salute. "From what part of the country do you hail? Perhaps I know your people."

"That is highly unlikely, sir." Her tone might have cut glass. "In fact, Lord Danbury and I were just coming from my cousin's home when you met us."

"Ah, indeed? I suppose that explains such a late night visit."

"Of course it does." Anthony pounced on the explanation. "Her aunt is very ill. Lydia was good enough to rush to her family in their hour of need."

"I suppose that also explains why Miss Garrett had to climb in through a window—her aunt was simply too ill to come down and open the door?" Harting narrowed his eyes and leaned forward, meeting Anthony's hot gaze. The dandy had disappeared, to be replaced by a man who was no fool. "Listen, Danbury, this is not a game. I want to know why you would crack a rundown coffee house, and I mean every detail."

The blood drained from Anthony's face and hands, already chilly in the crisp air. "What is this about?"

"That needn't concern you. What should concern you is the fact that I will call for the beak unless you cooperate."

Seething, Anthony clamped his mouth shut.

Lydia glanced at him and then back at Harting. "What possible interest could you have? Perhaps—"

Harting smiled in a most unpleasant fashion. "Miss Garrett, I should be the one asking questions, not the reverse."

Lydia pursed her lips and regarded the inquisitor with a molten gaze. Quietly she sat back against her seat and folded her hands in her lap.

Confronted with the brick wall of their silence, Harting changed tack. "Come now, I understand your feelings, and I give you my word of honour that I have no intention of trying to blackmail you with the information. I simply must know what all this means. Ennui is my greatest enemy and this promises to staunch its relentless tide for at least a few hours."

The patronizing demeanour was more than Anthony could bear. He half stood in the jostling carriage. "I have no desire to provide your entertainment for the evening." Blood pulsed in his ears and he snorted like a bull. If someone were to wave something red at him he would likely have charged.

He felt a tug on his arm. Lydia stood next to him, swaying to keep her balance.

"We are trying to discover who murdered Lord Danbury's father and my cousin. Please search for amusement elsewhere. Our work is in deadly earnest."

Harting remained seated, but his eyes flicked to Lydia, obviously reevaluating her. "Perhaps I could assist you." His tone had turned suddenly mild; all its mocking condescension evaporated as if it had never been.

The carriage jolted hard, dumping Miss Garrett unceremoniously into her seat. Anthony tottered, but Harting placed a steadying grip on his elbow. Anthony wrenched his arm free, preferring to fall rather than allow himself to be assisted by the fop.

"Believe me, Danbury, nothing would give me greater pleasure than to see your father's murderer brought to justice."

Anthony heard the ring of sincerity in his tone. What did Harting want? After a long moment he resumed his seat. They had little choice. And what would it hurt to tell the fellow what he wanted to know? In the meantime, Anthony would have the chance to find out why he wished to know. Perhaps Harting knew more of the murder than he let on.

* * *

Lydia remained silent and all but forgotten in the dark corner of the carriage as Lord Danbury provided a terse explanation. How had she gotten mixed up in all this? The tension between the two men was so patent it might have been a fourth presence in the landau.

The horses slowed to a stop before Lord Danbury's house and

the two gentlemen stepped out. No one turned to assist Lydia from the landau, and she was more than happy to leave it that way for the moment.

Lord Danbury led the way to his study and ushered his guests inside. "Let's see what this night's work has netted." He pulled the paper-wrapped parcel from beneath his coat and tried to loose the knotted string holding it closed. After a moment's frustration, in which his agitated fumbling made the knots worse, he uttered a low oath. Dropping the package on his desk he rummaged about for a knife to cut the string.

Lydia picked up the package and worried the knot. Of all his sailor's skills, Mr Wolfe had always been proud of his knots.

With a triumphant grunt, Lord Danbury held aloft a penknife just as Lydia extended the opened parcel.

He had the grace to laugh. "I suppose I'm a bit anxious to see what is in this." Accepting the proffered package he folded back the wrapping paper.

Inside lay a leather-bound book of foolscap and a handful of loose papers. Danbury's hands trembled slightly as he picked up the book and examined it. Lydia glanced at Mr Harting, who reclined negligently in his chair. His posture declared him uninterested, but his presence in this house forbore that conclusion. Disquiet roiled her belly, but she turned resolutely away from him. She was far more interested in finding what her cousin had so carefully hidden away.

"He kept a log of the journey." Lord Danbury's cheeks flushed crimson, and his eyes glittered in excitement. He leafed through the pages. "No, it is more a diary than a log."

Unable to restrain herself any longer, Lydia reached for the loose sheets. She glanced at the top page and then read it again, more thoroughly. "Lord Danbury, I believe this must have been written by your father."

She read aloud.

"This document is a complete explanation of the circumstances surrounding the disappearance of the great Peacock Throne of the Mughals in 1758. My name is Captain Richard Douglas; I am the youngest son of the Viscount Graham."

"He must have written this long ago," Lord Danbury murmured.

"In 1757 I was fortunate enough to be appointed post-captain and given charge of the Centaur, *a 28-gun frigate. We were sent out to India on a mission to protect English trade in the region.*

We had good cruising and were doing well for ourselves in the matter of prize money when we turned in to Bombay for a complete refitting. The process in those parts takes even longer than it does at an English dockyard. I had plenty of opportunity to become acquainted with the East India Company officials and, through them, some of the members of the Mughal's family.

I cannot adequately describe the atmosphere of those days. The Mughal Empire had long since been crumbling into ruin; armies had invaded from the north. Yet at the court, frivolity reigned. Gold and jewels flowed about the royals like water, while the people starved. Decadence was the order of the day. The richness of the palace hid the rotting corpse of the empire, but poorly.

While we were taking on a load of fresh water and fruit for the crew in preparation for sailing, a young lady approached me from the shadows with a request. I knew her to be a member of the Mughal's family and gave her every consideration.

This lady begged me on behalf of her cousin to take the jewelled Peacock Throne to a place of safety. It had been placed in hiding after an Indian holy man had prophesied that if the throne were captured, the light of the Mughals would be extinguished forever. But if the throne escaped the Shah's clutches, a new Mughal empire would arise from the ashes of the old.

CHAPTER 8

They had come up with a scheme to spirit the throne out of the country in a manner no one would suspect. That was when my services were requested.

At first I would have nothing to do with their plan. Would to God I had listened to my own reservations, but I did not. I allowed myself to be persuaded when an official from the East India Company also approached me.

I followed him to a dilapidated old warehouse lying empty and unused in the seediest part of that sordid port. Wishing mightily that I had not agreed to this folly, I yet allowed him to show me a huge crate tucked in a shadowy corner and half covered with dirty canvas. I gripped my sword and made ready to fend off any attackers that might rush from the darkness. The man lit a nearby lantern, and then taking up a crowbar he proceeded to open the front of the crate. Pulling out the old straw that padded the interior he worked with feverish intensity. When he stepped away, the feeble light of the lantern revealed the polished glint of gold.

All thought of thieves fled. I stepped forward to get a better look at the treasure ensconced in the crate. It was a throne, though not what an English mind might picture. This was a platform on four curved legs with a waist-high railing and a seat at the back. The entire thing was fashioned of gold and encrusted with priceless gems. Even the feeble light of the dingy lantern caused the throne to glitter. Rubies, emeralds, pearls and diamonds vied within their golden setting to see which could most dazzle the beholder.

Large enough to seat at least two reclining people, the throne even had a small golden canopy suspended above the seat. It too was covered in jewels. On each of the columns that supported this canopy, the delicate image of two peacocks separated by a tree had been formed by the intricate placement of jewels. Awestruck, I gaped at the thing for several moments.

My guide finally brought me back to my senses by tugging on my sleeve.

In pure bedevilled curiosity I asked how much the Mughal would pay for my assistance. The answer stunned me. One hundred thousand pounds.

My mind worked furiously. God help me, but I decided then and there. Greed was like a fire in my blood. I would put it before my officers because I could not pull off the scheme alone. We would treat the Mughal's bribe as prize money, but with the added benefit that the Admiralty need claim no share. All that would be required of us was a detour away from our appointed duty, and that would be easy enough to justify to the Admiralty. We had only to say that we spotted a ship and gave chase, or that we were caught in a blow.

I raced back to the Centaur. *On the ship I held a meeting of all the officers and put forth my proposal. The men were unanimously in favour of my proposition.*

Under cover of night we manoeuvred the throne into the hold of the ship, and then went about the rest of our business as usual. We left port with the next tide and made our way with all haste to an island chain in the Indian Ocean. We found an island with a natural harbour. Ships often put in to take on fresh supplies of water and fruit, but at the time there was no permanent settlement. It is not large, but a mountain rises straight from its centre and undoubtedly much of the island has never been truly explored. It had the reputation of being a hiding spot for pirates, and if pirates could use it for nefarious purposes why could we not put it to more profitable use?

We made our landing in the harbour. Scouts were dispatched to find the best hiding place for the throne. Eventually my first lieutenant returned with news of a cave located strategically up the side of the mountain. It was dry and spacious and, most importantly, well concealed from cursory examination. A little artifice masked the place completely. It was no easy task to transport the throne. It took days, and three of my men were crushed when the crate toppled from its cart. In the end, though, we managed to get that monstrosity up to the cave and hidden.

We never returned to Bombay. As we neared the port we received orders to join Vice-Admiral Pocock's squadron with all haste. I dispatched a letter to my contact in the Mughal's family, advising of the throne's safety, but I had no notion of whether it was ever received. As we worked our way around the southernmost tip of India we were attacked.

A French ship of the line and two frigates, undoubtedly on their way to join their own squadron, came upon us and gave chase. The Centaur *and her men gave a good showing, but we were no match for three ships. We would have been taken at that moment but for a squall that hid us long enough for us to limp away. We found shelter on the lee side of a small island. The French ships scoured the sea for their prize, but we dismasted* Centaur *and remained hidden in our little cove.*

When we at last felt that the French must have moved on, we performed what repairs we could. Short-handed as we were, every hand took shifts at the pumps, myself included. We sailed from our haven on 20 August 1759.

Just two days later we spotted another sail on the horizon. Chinese pirates had come upon us. Our pitiful condition was patent or they would never have had the temerity to attack a king's ship.

The fighting was the most brutal I have ever witnessed. The pirates fought as if possessed. My crew was the bravest set of men I've had the privilege of sailing with but we were outnumbered and overpowered.

When all had been lost those few of us left alive jumped overboard. Less than a handful survived. The pirates finished looting the Centaur, *and then set fire to her. In disbelief we watched as the ship became a floating pyre for our comrades, many of whom were not yet dead, but injured. In my nightmares I can still taste the smoke and ashes of that inferno.*

We lashed together wreckage from the Centaur *and made a raft. To shorten a story that has already been made too long, suffice it to say that we made it to safety and eventually found our way back to England.*

Knowing that the Peacock Throne may remain where we left it, possibly lost forever to history, is a powerful temptation to greed. We have undertaken to write out this confession as a safeguard against our own natures. None of us have the means to return for the throne alone, but if we ever do, each will be aware that the others will hold him accountable. That throne has been hallowed by the blood of our comrades. We will leave it buried."

Scrawled at the bottom of the page were the signatures of three men.

CHAPTER 9

The room remained utterly silent for a moment. Enthralled by the tale, Anthony had been transported to a time and place long ago. He blinked, slowly bringing the comfortable, well-furnished study back into focus. It seemed anticlimactic somehow, to find himself safe and secure in the midst of London, rather than in the heart of the Indian subcontinent.

Harting broke the silence. "It's hard to believe no one ever went back to retrieve the throne."

"Shortly after the Seven Years War my grandfather and then father's elder brother died. Father resigned his commission to come home and assume the title. I don't know that he would have had the opportunity."

"I doubt the others would have had means to do so." Lydia rifled through the pages once more and then extended the document to Anthony.

He took it and gazed at his father's hand, not reading the words so much as tracing the form of each familiarly shaped letter. His throat burned. If he could not find the murderer, perhaps there was a way to encourage the murderer to reveal himself. "I've had a thought."

Harting and Lydia waited politely.

"I'm going to mount an expedition to retrieve this cursed throne." He tapped the confession with his finger. "And thereby solve the murders."

"May I point out that you have no business trying to solve anything? That's what runners and magistrates are for." Derision coated Harting's tone, thick and heavy.

Anthony regarded him coldly. The man knew nothing about the situation, yet he felt compelled to stick his oar in. "You may not, sir. I know I'm sadly lacking in experience. But I will not stand idly by while my father's murderer walks about freely. It is obvious to me that whoever murdered my father and Mr Wolfe was intent on finding information about the throne. Why else should they seek out my father and Mr Wolfe? To exact revenge at this late date? No, it's more likely they demanded the location of the throne before they murdered them. He will either follow me or lie in wait for my return. And then I'll have him."

"Perhaps he meant to ensure he would not be pursued or wanted to ensure their silence about the whole affair, or perhaps…" Harting shifted to stare at him with curious intensity. "Maybe the man was known to your father and he could not risk being identified to the authorities."

Anthony narrowed his eyes. "If—"

"If they have this information and are looking for the throne then time is of the essence," Lydia said.

Harting straightened his cuffs. "Such an expedition will be enormously expensive."

"I will go to any length in order to find those responsible for my father's death." Anthony glanced at the mantel clock. "It's far too late this evening, but I shall begin making arrangements first thing in the morning." Anthony began searching through one of the stacks of paper on the desk. He had been trying to sort through all the financial affairs and had seen something about a ship….

"There is one more problem." Lydia was perched on the edge of her chair. "The confession does not specify the location of the throne. By design I would suppose."

Anthony dropped the document he was pursuing. She was right.

Harting was smothering a grin.

"The diary. Perhaps there is a mention in there." Anthony grabbed for the volume and began leafing through it. He stared at first one page and then another. The lines of ink were faded and stained in places, but the real problem was the penmanship. He couldn't make anything of the script. "I can't read this."

"Penmanship was not one of Mr Wolfe's strengths. But I am usually able to decipher it." Lydia extended a hand for the diary. "I would be pleased to assist you."

Anthony glanced at her and for the first time noticed a tear near the waistline of her dress. "It looks as if you are a trifle worse for wear." He motioned towards the torn fabric. Harting, too, turned an intent gaze upon her. Anthony cringed inwardly. Drawing attention to the tear had been an ungentlemanly thing to do.

Lydia grabbed at the cloth and clutched it together. "Lucky these are not my good clothes."

It was, in fact, the only garment she could call her own. In spite of his acute embarrassment, Anthony smiled. She was stout-hearted to offer jokes at her own expense after everything. He really must see to getting her settled in some suitable position before he left.

He glanced at the clock on the mantelpiece. "We can get an early start in the morning." He rose and stepped away from the desk.

Harting and Lydia took the hint. Both stood to take their leave.

Harting tapped the head of his cane with a long finger. "Just don't attempt any more nefarious activities. You'll get caught."

The man certainly had an abundance of highhanded gall. Anthony regretted being so forthcoming and showed him the door with little ceremony. He would be asking some questions about Mr Harting, that was for certain.

Despite his indication to the others that he meant to seek his bed, he paused only long enough to remove his jacket, then returned to perusing the diary. He must wrest from it the secrets of that long-ago journey.

* * *

Anthony cracked open a single eye and groaned. He'd lain his head down only for a moment, to rest his eyes, but now sun spilled through the gaps in the drapery and his face rested in a puddle of spittle. Wiping his mouth, he sat up and surveyed his desk. He had made almost no progress on the dratted diary.

A footman entered and announced the arrival of Mr Harting. Anthony groaned, but nodded permission for the man to be shown in. "But bring in tea."

The footman nodded.

A moment later, Anthony rose to greet his guest with outstretched hand. "Harting, I did not expect to see you so early this morning." Had not expected to see him again at all, in fact.

"It's nearly noon."

The quirk of Harting's mouth confirmed Anthony's suspicion that he was being made sport of—again. "Precisely. I thought active members of the ton such as yourself made it a habit not to rise before three."

The quirk grew into a full-fledged smile. Harting held up a hand. "I deserved that." His tone grew sober. "What do you know of Miss Garrett?"

Anthony hesitated. What *did* he know of her? "You know as much of her character and background as I do based on what I told you last evening."

"Then it would seem at this stage that I know a great deal more about her than you do."

The urge to snarl came over him. What was it about Harting that got his hackles up? "What should I know about the chit then?"

Evidently enjoying the moment, Harting sat back. "Her father was a clergyman from respectable, though not affluent, stock."

The cad was enjoying spinning out the tale. Anthony declined to give him the satisfaction of begging him to continue.

"Her mother, however, was born Callandra Westham."

The name sparked vague recognition, but Anthony could not place it.

Harting continued. "Miss Westham married Mr Andrew Garrett without her parents' permission. Enraged that his daughter would disobey him, her father cut her off entirely. To my knowledge they never saw one another again."

"What was the objection, if Garrett was respectable?"

"Ah, then you didn't recognize the name. I had thought you might."

Anthony gritted his teeth.

Oblivious to his danger, Harting went on. "Perhaps I should have styled her Lady Callandra. She was the eldest daughter of Charles Westham, the Earl of Glenford. He had great hopes for her. By all accounts she was one of the great beauties of her generation. He aimed at nothing less than a Duke for his girl."

Dismay settled over Anthony like a cloak. Surely he ought to have discerned nobility in Miss Garrett at once. Even knowing her demeanour and speech were different, he had treated her as a servant rather than a lady, even calling her by her Christian name— the granddaughter of Old Glenford, no less. Why hadn't she said something? "What happened to her parents?" he managed to croak.

"Seems they were both killed some six or seven years ago in a carriage accident."

"Glenford refused to acknowledge his granddaughter even then?"

"That is a bit vague. He was ill at the time. The doctors never expected he would pull through. My contact believed that Mrs Garrett had heard of his illness, and hoped to reconcile with him before he died. It was as they were travelling to her family's estate that their carriage overturned and the Garretts were killed. Though the old man obviously pulled through."

"Irony is an ugly master."

"I would assume that Miss Garrett's family solicitor tried to contact the Westhams, but whether they did not respond because of a disinclination to be burdened by the girl, or because of the turmoil surrounding the Earl's illness at the time, I cannot say."

Anthony rubbed his face with both hands. He did not need this complication. "So the solicitor dug up some far-flung relative on her father's side and palmed the girl off to them."

Harting nodded. "Her small inheritance was gone within a matter of months."

"How do you know all this?"

The fellow positively smirked. "Cultivating the gossips does occasionally reap benefits."

Anthony ignored the look. If he allowed himself to be distracted by such mannerisms he'd throttle the fop and then he'd never solve the murders. "No. No, I don't think so." He sat back in his chair. "Your information is too precise. How did you come by it?"

While it did not wipe the smile from his face, the skin around his eyes tightened as Harting gave him a shrewd appraisal.

He waited, hoping that Harting would squirm.

He didn't.

"I occasionally assist the Home Office." His tone was so bland he might have been announcing that the sun had indeed risen that morning. "I did not come upon you by accident last night."

Somehow, Anthony had thought not. "You're a spy." It was at last his own turn to smirk.

Harting frowned. "I am not a spy."

"As you wish." The man was absolutely a spy. A sneaking, creeping spy.

CHAPTER 10

"Mrs Malloy?"

The elderly housekeeper clutched at her chest and dropped the quill she had been holding. "Lord, child! You gave me a fright."

"My apologies." Lydia backed away, biting her lip. The poor woman had turned as white as a maid's mobcap. "I did not mean to startle you."

She waved a hand. "I'm all right, girl. I'm all right."

Mrs Malloy settled back in her seat. She pulled a handkerchief from her sleeve then dabbed at her brow. "'Tisn't your fault, my dear girl. I'm all at sixes and sevens when I am doing the household accounts." She rifled the pages of the ledger in front of her.

"Perhaps I could be of assistance? I came to see if there was aught I could do to help repay Lord Danbury's kindness. My father taught me mathematics."

"I can manage well enough. I've muddled through 'em for some fifteen years now."

"Yes, ma'am. I meant no disrespect."

The older woman's features softened some and she smiled. "I expect you didn't, at that." Mrs Malloy looked down at the ledger and piles of paper on her desk. She flushed pink and pursed her lips. "Perhaps, just this once, you might assist me with the accounts." Her expression gentled even further and she waved a hand over the mess. "I would like to get to Sunday service if I can. If Lord Danbury has no need for you, mayhap you could join me."

How long had it been since she had been in a Sunday service? "I would greatly enjoy that. I haven't been to church in an age."

For a time, Mrs Malloy hovered nearby, double-checking Lydia's calculations, but soon she drifted away to other tasks in her cluttered pantry.

"You seem to have a real head for figures."

"I handled the accounts for my cousin's coffee house for some three years." Lydia kept her gaze trained on the neat columns of numbers. She had long ago learned to downplay any achievement in order to avoid rebuke or ridicule.

"It is no wonder then you were so quick on picking up what was required." Unlike the odious Fenn, Mrs Malloy did not seem the least bit intimidated by Lydia's education.

The rustle of a house alive with people continued in the background, but Lydia settled into the undemanding task, and an easy hush descended as they worked companionably side by side.

"Oh my, time has gotten away from me. I must be getting ready if I'm to make it to service." Mrs Malloy pushed aside the menu she had been preparing and stood. "You do wish to come with me?"

Lydia glanced up from the accounts. "I had forgotten that I have nothing appropriate to wear, and I couldn't bear being a discredit to you."

"Betsy, our tweeny, is about your size and has a good frock she might lend you for the day. I'll speak to her about it."

The door opened and one of the housemaids bobbed a curtsy. "His Lordship is asking for you in the study, ma'am."

"Yes, of course." She turned back to Lydia. "I will see you in the mews in twenty minutes." Mrs Malloy nodded civilly and sailed away in a flurry of rustling skirts.

* * *

"Miss Garrett?"

Lydia glanced up from careful consideration of a mews cobblestone she had been scuffing with the toe of her worn slipper.

Mr Harting stood before her, looking especially debonair in a dark blue jacket and buff breeches. His complicated cravat stood out in regal splendour, and his hat and cane gleamed in the afternoon light. He truly was a dashing figure, especially in contrast to the groomsmen mucking out the stalls nearby. Offering a quick curtsy, Lydia licked lips that had suddenly gone dry.

"Good day, sir."

"May I have a moment of your time?"

"How may I be of assistance?" She glanced up at him warily from under her lashes.

He drew her aside and lowered his voice. "I understand that you have some illustrious forebears."

"Illus…" As the implication of his words dawned on her, she drew away, the breath growing tight in her chest. "What concern are my family connections to you?" There. She had kept her voice well modulated. He could not possibly know the turmoil he was causing.

"Your family has served the crown with great success over the years."

"My mother's family." She scrutinized his face for any hint as to where he was leading this conversation.

"Your family. I had hoped to find you similarly patriotic."

"Speak plainly. What do you want from me?"

"I must request your aid with a matter of grave importance." He glanced about, and pitched his voice even lower. "I assist the Home Office. My… colleagues believe there is a highly placed traitor in London. He goes by the name Le Faucon, the Hawk. We believe that it is not someone employed in the ministry but rather someone with access to those who are. The cost extracted by this person—both in men and material—has been very great indeed."

Lydia stared at Mr Harting as if he were speaking Dutch. What could he mean by sharing such information with her? Was he making sport of her?

He bent his head even closer to hers. "I tell you this so you will understand the importance of what I must ask you to do."

With narrowed eyes, Lydia nodded slowly.

"Lord Danbury is in a position to have come by much of the information we suspect this traitor to have passed on. He knows the right people. In addition, he had the opportunity and the means to have done away with his father. He inherits everything including the title and lands. I am told that his holdings amount to an income of some 40,000 pounds a year."

Lydia gaped. She couldn't help it. That was a colossal amount of money. Still she shook her head in disbelief. This had to be some feeble jest. "I cannot vouch for all Lord Danbury's loyalties, but I'm certain that he had nothing to do with his father's death. And I'd be grateful—"

"You scarcely know the man."

Lips pursed as indignation warred with the consciousness of her station. Lydia struggled to convey her perceptions. "I… he is so sincere. It's obvious that his father's murder has wounded him deeply. He…" Her words tumbled over one another in her haste to defend the man who seemed to share her own sense of loss. Taking a deep breath she began again. "If he had killed his father, why would he so diligently seek the murderer?"

"As a means of diverting suspicion from himself. Or maybe he has not been after the murderer at all. Perhaps he has been after the location of the throne all along."

A horse pawed the ground nearby and tossed its mane. Gratefully she took the opportunity to break Harting's gaze. She wanted to show her displeasure as clearly as the horse but settled for shaking her head, denying the possibility that Lord Danbury could be so treacherous. A worm of doubt wriggled into her heart. "I simply cannot believe it. You are making sport of me—"

Mr Harting interrupted her with his palms outstretched, as if fending off an attack. "Not at all, Miss Garrett. I would never make light of such a matter. All I ask is that you stay close to him and if you find anything suspicious, pass it along to me."

Again Lydia shook her head and opened her mouth to speak.

CHAPTER 10

"Miss Garrett, you must know that I was thorough in my investigation of your situation. I understand the loss of your parents and your many struggles."

How dare he? A scalding flush swept up Lydia's neck until it burned her cheeks. She clenched her jaw to hold back the torrent of abuse she wished to heap on his head.

He placed a finger under her chin and raised it until her gaze met his. He stared hard into her eyes as if trying to read something in their depths. "I only mention it because this type of service to the country is rewarded handsomely."

No doubt this sort of offer had worked well for him in the past, but he had miscalculated with her. She desperately needed some sort of income, but she hadn't fallen so low as to spy on a friend for it. Jerking her chin free, Lydia controlled her voice with difficulty. "His Lordship has been nothing but kind to me. I will not betray his trust."

This time Harting took her hands. She tried to pull free, but though it seemed effortless he retained his grip until she looked him in the face. Earnestness emanated from him like a cloud of cologne. "There is no betrayal. If he is not guilty you will be doing him a good turn by eliminating him from my consideration. If he is guilty then he has already betrayed you. He's betrayed us all. You will be the hand of justice."

Conflicting loyalties tugged at Lydia. Lord Danbury had fought for her and provided for her, asking little in return. He had treated her with kindness. The faces of the women she knew from Brant Street floated in her mind's eye: mothers, wives, and sweethearts— so many had lost men to the incessant fighting on the continent. Didn't she owe Le Faucon's victims some consideration? What if she could prevent further losses? If Harting was correct, the traitor had been responsible for many deaths, including Mr Wolfe's. And she had vowed to bring her cousin's murderer to justice. A vow that gave no consideration to the possibility that she might not like the answer. Now that the issue had been raised, she could not ignore the potential that Lord Danbury had some involvement in the murders.

Lydia scowled at Harting, loathing him for putting her in this position. She pulled her hands free and lowered her eyes. She did not want him to see the tears welling in them. "I will do as you ask…" Defiance flared again. "But only to prove you wrong."

"Agreed." Harting again took one of her hands, this time raising it to his lips. She could almost see the force of his personality fade as he assumed a mantle of foppishness. "Until we meet again."

* * *

Anthony paused as he caught sight of Harting and Miss Garrett engaged in conversation down in the mews. Spurred by curiosity his eyes remained fixed to the scene. Resting an arm against the wall, he leaned close to the window, straining to hear.

What could Harting want with her? Perhaps he wished to discuss his investigations into her past? Anthony drew aside the drapery a bit. She blushed and looked flustered, angry even. Blood pounded in his ears. Was Harting propositioning the girl? He wanted to fly down the stairs and flatten the cad. He could yell down to the stable hands to seize the louse and hold him until he reached them.

Restraint, he cautioned himself. Restraint. Miss Garrett could handle the advances of a would-be roué like Harting. Though if the bounder tried anything more, Anthony promised himself, he would have the pleasure of teaching Harting a lesson.

If only he was close enough to hear what they were saying. Anthony flexed his fingers.

Harting raised the girl's chin and Anthony ground his teeth. When he took her hands in his, Anthony started down the stairs. One simply did not manhandle a young lady in such a way.

Would he have thought it so grossly improper if he had not known of her heritage? He pushed the thought away. She was under the protection of his household and she obviously needed someone to help her handle the scoundrel.

Barrelling through the door, he almost collided with one of the maids carrying a coal scuttle.

"Pardon me, yer Lordship." The girl bent her knees in an imitation curtsy and promptly stepped to the side, smack in his way again. They both stepped to the other side. They performed the uncomfortable dance until Anthony stopped, gripped her arms and shifted her out of his way.

He was breathless when he threw the door open and entered the courtyard. Harting was gone. Miss Garrett turned in surprise at his abrupt arrival. Her eyes were red-rimmed and slightly damp.

"Are you all right?"

"Yes, my Lord." Her brow furrowed and she gazed at him as if perplexed.

Anthony ran a hand through his hair, no doubt disarranging it further. "Ah, well. Harting is gone then?" Babbling like an idiot was becoming a positive habit.

"Did you need something? I can fetch one of the footmen to go after him. He passed by not long ago."

She did not mention their conversation. Of course, such an experience must have been trying, and recounting it would be distressing. Anthony sought a way to retreat.

"No, that won't be necessary. I'll send a note around to him later. Are—"

Mrs Malloy bustled up in her Sunday finery. "Do you need anything, sir?"

"Not at all, Mrs Malloy; not at all. Going to church? I hope you enjoy the holy offices. Perhaps, Miss Garrett, you would stop by my study when you return? There is something I wish to discuss." Anthony backed towards the door as if trying to escape a pack of wolves, rather than two mildly confused women.

"Of course, Lord Danbury. I can stay and begin going through the diary. I was not aware that you had awakened."

"No. Uh, no. That can wait. We will get to it when you return. I do appreciate the offer. I was unable to make much sense of it myself." He clasped his hands behind his back and managed a smile. "Ah, thanks then. I will see you…thanks." Darting inside, he shut the door firmly.

* * *

Lydia returned from Mrs Malloy's church with more than enough food for thought. The ritual and reflection of the service had calmed the worst of the turbulence in her emotions.

"Lord Danbury is waiting for you in his study," one of the footmen said as Lydia handed her borrowed wrap to its owner.

She nodded her thanks, and turned as if facing a firing squad. All that Mr Harting had said that morning rushed back. What would Lord Danbury say? Should she confess that she had been press ganged into becoming a spy against him?

The idea that Lord Danbury was some sort of agent for the French could not be borne. The whole notion was simply ridiculous. She would write a note and, with regret, decline Mr Harting's request after all.

Mind made up, Lydia hesitated at the door to the study. A servant would just go in. Should she act as a servant, or a guest, or…? Lydia exhaled hard through pursed lips, causing the hair that framed her face to flutter in the sudden breeze. Finally she rapped the door sharply with her knuckles, and entered before any response was forthcoming.

Lord Danbury looked up at her arrival and flushed.

"You asked for me?"

"Yes, Miss Garrett." He rummaged amongst the papers on his desk for a moment, before retrieving a small package.

"This was delivered for you."

Lydia accepted the proffered package.

"It's from Mr Harting?" A note of inquiry shaded his statement.

Lydia's gaze snapped up in surprise to meet his. Her brow furrowed. Harting was making more than a nuisance of himself. What could he possibly want now? Her fingers itched to rip into the parcel.

"Are you ready for me to begin on the diary, my Lord?"

"Please, be seated and open your package. I can wait a few moments."

"Certainly." Lydia took a chair and tore into the wrapping paper. A gasp escaped her lips as a stack of pristine Bank of England notes was revealed. Her hands trembled as she plucked out the letter that accompanied them.

Dear Miss Garrett,

Please find the enclosed per our discussion of this morning. Excuse my presumption but I have arranged for an appointment with Madame D'Arcy for you tomorrow afternoon. I shall come for you after luncheon. You must be properly outfitted.

May I suggest that you inform Lord Danbury that I have uncovered some holdings of your father's and have advanced you these funds based on the strength of your expectations. I will of course corroborate this statement.

Your humble servant,
Harting

Lydia could feel the blood draining from her face. Had he been there, she would have flung the letter and money at him. Which was, no doubt, why he had not personally delivered the package.

"I trust it is not distressing news?"

Dragging her gaze from the missive, Lydia tried to meet Lord Danbury's eyes. His glance strayed from her face to the pound notes protruding from the wrapping.

"He… I…" Drat the man. He had offered the only plausible explanation for the funds. How she would have liked to come up with something brilliant, or to spill the whole story out to Lord Danbury. "Mr Harting learned of some investments of my father's whilst investigating my background," she said. "Knowing I am at low water he was kind enough to advance me funds on the strength of my expectations."

"It looks as if you will be well provided for, for quite some time." He sounded as if his cravat were too tight.

Lydia could not prevent the blush that heated her cheeks. She had never been good at telling tales. At least now she had acknowledged her background, if in a round about way. She braced for more questions but none were forthcoming.

When she gathered the courage to look up, Lord Danbury had returned his attention to the papers before him.

He had requested her presence, and now he acted as if she did not exist. Her cheeks burned and she cleared her throat. "I hope that you will still abide by our agreement. This… inheritance improves my situation, but it will not provide for my needs forever. I must still find employment."

His Lordship looked up with a scowl. "I'm known as a man who keeps his bargains."

"I'm sure that those who know you well hold many favourable opinions, but I know you very little and I simply wish to know that the change in my circumstances has not affected our agreement."

"You have my word, Miss Garrett." He turned his attention to the papers on his desk, dismissing her as if she were a servant.

"Thank you." Her tone was as tart as he deserved. "Well, I do not wish to trouble you any more than necessary. I will certainly find other lodgings so that I am no longer trespassing on your kindness. Of course, I will still decipher the diary. And you did request my presence. Did you have need of something else?"

"It had to do with the preparations for the journey. You may not wish to pursue such things now, however, since you have come into this unexpected inheritance."

Lydia could not maintain her hauteur. Not when she had committed to spy on this man who had done her no wrong. She gripped the package so hard her fingers ached. "My Lord, I beg you not to shut me out. I am as committed to catching my cousin's murderer now as I was before. No amount of money would ever change that."

He regarded her as if trying to see into her soul. Lydia swallowed hard and blinked rapidly. Even if he tossed her out on her ear, she would find a way to catch Mr Wolfe's murderer. And she was keeping the money too. That would serve Harting right.

Relenting at last, Lord Danbury sat back in his chair. "No, of course not, Miss Garrett. I know you cared for your cousin a great deal. Please forgive me."

"There is no need."

Lord Danbury waved a hand as if pushing their ill-tempered words into the past. "With murderers and spies abroad I would sleep better if you would continue to stay under the protection of my roof."

Guilt dug into Lydia's heart like the talons of an angry bird. "You have been more than kind, but I cannot continue to impose upon your hospitality."

He flung down his papers, and pushed away from the desk, turning his back to her. "You misunderstand. It would be a kindness to me if you would stay. I… with all that…" He rubbed at his temple. "It is possible there is danger. Our investigation is bearing fruit, and I—I cannot change the fact that I was not there for my father when he needed me. I would appreciate it if you would stay." He turned back to face her. "Besides, it would be more convenient. I am in great need of your assistance in this matter. Oh, and I've asked Mrs Malloy to move your things into the guest room at the top of the stairs."

Shocked, Lydia protested. "My Lord, such a move is not necessary. I was more than comfortable." In fact, the cosy little nook she occupied was the pleasantest place she had lived in for many years.

"If Lord Glenford ever discovered that I housed his granddaughter in the maids' quarters, he would suffer apoplexy."

Another kind of ache tore at Lydia's heart. "The chances of that are slim indeed." She rested a hand on the desk. With any luck he would hand her the papers he had been poring over and change the topic of conversation.

"How did you end up as a servant at the Green Peacock?"

This was not the change she had been hoping for. "I was not a servant... precisely. I simply was sensible of what I owed Mr Wolfe for providing me with a home. I truly did not mind the work. It helped him to keep the coffee house going. Mrs Wolfe and Fenn were never much use in that regard." Lydia looked away. Discomfiture made her fingers itch to be busy with something.

"And Fenn kept you sensible of your position of dependence." Lord Danbury's grip cracked the nib of the pen he held. He thrust it into the pen stand and wiped his hand on his handkerchief.

"Mr Wolfe kept Fenn's behaviour in check. It was only after his death that the situation became intolerable."

Danbury reached an ink-stained hand across the desk to cover hers. Their gazes met with an intensity that made her chest compress as if her stays had been pulled too tight. It was impressed upon her again how handsome he was. How his midnight dark eyes could nevertheless seem bright and shining.

"I know you are still convalescing, but Mrs Malloy tells me you have a gift for organizing things, handling accounts and so on. I'll need a great deal of assistance as I arrange this expedition, if I'm to leave as soon as possible."

That was better. Relieved, Lydia set aside the packet of notes. "Tell me what you require. I will help in any way I can."

* * *

Throughout the afternoon and into the evening, Anthony worked steadily. But his concentration was unsteady. His gaze kept drifting from his documents to the composed form of Lydia Garrett across the desk from him. She was painstakingly copying the incomprehensible scrawl into legible script. He suspected that she represented a mystery as deep as the one they now pursued.

He could not rid himself of the image of her opening Harting's parcel. The shock had been writ plain on her face. Had she been surprised to receive money? Or simply by the amount? The way she shied from his questions like a nervous foal was certainly curious. Had Harting found an inheritance for her as she claimed, or was he paying for some other service he wished her to render?

Tension throbbed behind his eyes. He rested his head against his forefingers and thrust his thumbs against his temples. It was best if he did not think along those lines. He forced his attention back to the letter he was composing. Captain Campbell would be surprised to hear from him so urgently.

Some hours later, Anthony glanced up from the victualling list he perused to catch her rubbing her eyes. Drat it all. He was working the poor girl like a galley slave. "We'd best put these aside for the time being."

Miss Garrett shook her head. "That's not necessary. I only needed to rest my eyes for a moment. Mr Wolfe's penmanship was dreadful, wasn't it?"

"My eyes are all but crossing from my own handwriting. I cannot bear to think what they might be doing had I spent the afternoon staring at his wretched scrawlings. We'll come back to these this evening, and perhaps the words won't blur and jump about."

Miss Garrett set aside the papers, though perhaps a touch reluctantly. In truth, he was loathe to put them aside as well. Every moment's delay meant that their enemies were that much further ahead of them.

CHAPTER 11

Lydia was waiting when Mr Harting arrived for her shortly after luncheon the next day. She had loitered in front of the house for some fifteen minutes in the hopes of making as little a scene as possible. True, she had no reputation to think of—but even so she hated to draw more adverse comment to herself than necessary. She was already a nine-day wonder in the servants' hall. They didn't know what to make of her, and in truth, she no longer knew what to make of herself.

"Miss Garrett, you are looking well this afternoon."

He was probably relieved she wasn't wearing the borrowed maid's uniform. Her own clothes were worse quality, but at least they didn't scream servant quite so loudly. Poor, perhaps, but not servant.

He presented his arm and after an instant Lydia accepted. She gritted her teeth. She didn't want to think well of him. He was a manipulative rogue. But apparently he did not mind being seen squiring a lady of no consequence such as herself about Mayfair.

His smile hinted that he had the power to read her mind. "I'm glad you received my package. I half feared you would send it back."

"I was going to, but Lord Danbury was present when I opened it and I had no explanation for the contents other than the one you so *thoughtfully* penned." Lydia did not bother to keep the acerbity from her tone.

Harting chuckled. "I could not have planned it better had I tried."

From under her lashes, Lydia sent him a glance that could pierce armour. She forbore from commenting. Anything else would undoubtedly only add to his enjoyment of her predicament.

"Why is it so important to you that I have a new wardrobe?"

He raised an eyebrow and glanced at her down his long nose. "You should be properly outfitted as befits your station – not as if you are some scullion from the East End. Besides, I expect any woman on my arm to look her best, and the people you will be interacting with will respond better to a lady than a street urchin."

"I'm to play a role then?"

"You are to be your charming and educated self, while you never ever forget that you have an assignment which you must not lose sight of." His expression sobered. "Miss Garrett, I have not asked you to do this lightly. The stakes are..." He shook his head. "I find no pleasure in placing you in an awkward situation. I simply wish to find the traitor, and if that means putting a good man under close scrutiny in order to eliminate him as a suspect, so be it. I would put a hundred good men under such surveillance in order to find the one guilty fellow." His colour had risen, but his step never strayed from its desultory pace.

How had she suddenly been placed in the wrong? Lydia cast her gaze down at her feet. She bit her lip to keep from responding, but after a moment the words spilled past the safeguard of her common sense. "So in your mind the end justifies the means."

"It's not as simple as that."

"Oh?"

For the first time in her experience he looked almost flustered.

"One must think of the greater good. Is it better that good men die, or that innocent men be investigated for something they did not do?"

"Perhaps I am simple, but it seems that a great many good English men have died to maintain our traditional English liberties. This current war against the French is a prime example. We don't abhor French domination simply because they are French, but because their system of government, even under the banner of Liberty, Equality, and Fraternity, offers none of those things. As a nation we have offered up our life's blood in order to protect from the French the very liberties which may come under attack from our own leaders were your philosophy to take hold among them."

Harting contemplated her for a long moment, his probing gaze at odds with his languid motions. "I believe I have chosen wisely indeed, in this case."

"How can you say such a thing? Even if I do find something to assist your cause I cannot testify against his Lordship. I have no legal standing with the courts."

"That is why you must bring any proof you find to me."

His lips quirked up again, and an almost uncontrollable urge to throttle him with his own cravat welled within her bosom.

"Ah, here we are. Madame D'Arcy's." He turned aside at a well-kept shop.

He had successfully diverted her wrath.

For the moment.

"Who is Madame D'Arcy?"

Harting eyed her again; he seemed perpetually to be revising his opinion of her. "She is the smartest mantua maker in Mayfair. She is in great demand with the highest ladies of the land."

"Then why are we here? I have no need for such expensive frippery."

"That is what you think." Mr Harting held the door open for her with a gentlemanly flourish. "Besides, she owes me a favour."

A tall, exquisitely dressed woman held her hands out to Mr Harting in greeting. "My dear, it has been an age. Where have you been hiding yourself?" If this was the proprietress her title was clearly an affectation.

As inconspicuous as a kitten among lions, Lydia lingered near the door. In spite of herself, she drank in the sights and scents of the shop. A flowing summer frock in dainty cotton clothed a dress form, its lace as ephemeral as frost. She leaned forward to examine the detail. Nearby, a few bolts of luxurious material lounged against the wall. Unable to resist, Lydia caressed a piece of sky blue silk.

She started up guiltily when Mr Harting called her. Judging from his tone, it must have been the second or third time.

At his side, Madame D'Arcy also regarded her oddly and Lydia blushed. "I apologize. I was not attending."

"This is what you have to work with?" Madame D'Arcy said in a whisper, which Lydia could hear perfectly well. "Ah, well, it could be worse." With barely a rustle she turned and headed for the far door.

"Madame D'Arcy has her book of sketches for you to go through. You must look and decide what you want."

Despite the modiste's dismissive behaviour, excitement bubbled within Lydia as though she were a child about to try ice cream for the first time. She had not bought clothes for herself since well before her parents were killed. The three dresses she had owned were all made from Mrs Wolfe's old gowns. The idea of purchasing something new thrilled her to her toes. She could not seem to wipe the imbecilic grin from her face. Lydia caught Lord Harting once or twice concealing a small smile of his own. Surrounded by such lovely things, Lydia couldn't even find it within herself to be angry with him for his condescension.

Several large books were presented to her for inspection. Overwhelmed by the sheer number of charming options, Lydia hesitated. The styles were disarmingly different from the round gowns she was familiar with. These dresses featured slim silhouettes and dainty puffed sleeves. They looked modern and daring, and yet classical at the same time.

With a shrewd look, Madame D'Arcy assessed her. "I assure you, these are in the latest styles from the continent. With your slender figure, you will look well in these gowns."

"They are lovely." Lydia caressed one of the drawings with gentle fingers. "I simply do not know where to begin."

Madame took matters in hand. Lydia's head whirled—dress patterns, fabric swatches and trims tumbling over one another in her mind. Two dresses were to be delivered that afternoon, the rest within the week. After leaving Madame D'Arcy's, Mr Harting directed her to another shop to purchase hats. A third store provided hosiery and slippers, underclothing, handkerchiefs, gloves and all the final, innumerable elements needed to complete her toilet. Mr Harting did at least allow her to handle these purchases on her own, while he waited outside with a gaggle of husbands, fathers, and brothers.

Deeply concerned about the amount of money being spent, she paused at the door to the emporium and shot him a searching look. He leaned towards her and whispered in her ear as if he had the power to read her mind. "Give no thought to the cost. The ministry has agreed to outfit you in the appropriate manner for this case."

"Why should the ministry care one whit—"

He did not answer, merely nudged her shoulder and urged her inside the shop.

* * *

Lydia quickly put away the few packages they had elected to carry back with them. The altered dresses had already been delivered and she pulled one from the wardrobe, simply to look at it again. It was, by far, the loveliest gown she had ever owned. She sighed. When would she ever have the courage to wear it? His Lordship would probably think she was pasting peacock feathers to a chicken. She returned the gown to the wardrobe, and closed the door with a touch too much force.

She hurried down the stairs to Lord Danbury's study. She had been longer than she intended and he was no doubt awaiting her return.

The deep furrows of his brow lightened considerably at her entrance. "You are back. I shall be heartily glad to leave the duties of a landlord behind for a time."

Her heart plummeted. How could she betray this man who had

been naught but kind to her? She wanted to seize him and shake him, and tell him to toss her out on her ear while he still had the chance. But she did none of those things. Instead she greeted him politely and resumed her place on the opposite side of the desk.

She must not lose sight of the chance to find Mr Wolfe's murderer.

They worked steadily through the evening in quiet companionship. Lydia continued copying the diary, while Lord Danbury wrote letter after letter, and constructed list after list. Lost in their separate tasks the hours slid by unheeded.

Monotony weighed upon her. She could scarce keep her eyes open. Page after page she transcribed, until her hand had moved far past pain into numbness.

Lydia read a sentence and had almost completed copying it, when it dawned on her what she had read. The blood drained from her face and her fingertips went cold. She dropped her pen, splattering her fingers and the blotting paper with droplets of ink. She read it again.

"My Lord, I've found it." The words shouted so loudly through her being, that it was difficult to realize she had done naught but whisper.

Danbury regarded her quizzically as if unsure whether he had heard her speak.

Shoving away from the desk, she snatched up the diary. "I have found it."

Lord Danbury dropped the papers he was perusing to accept the diary as she thrust it into his hands.

She pointed to the passage in question.

"Here. They took the throne to Abundance Island." They had done it. Now that they knew which island to search, Lord Danbury's plan had ceased to be a hare-brained scheme and become a looming reality. They might just manage it.

Lord Danbury stared at the open diary as if he were looking into the Book of Life. He could not seem to tear his eyes away from the words it contained.

All at once he jumped up and rushed to a table where he had spread out a large map of the Indian Ocean.

"Well done, Miss Garrett." He spared her a glance and a flashing smile that made a warm glow flit through her belly.

His trembling finger slid over the map as he sought the island. His motion slowed, and he turned a disconcerted gaze to hers. "It's not here."

CHAPTER 12

Lydia drew nearer, cradling the diary. "I would stake my life on it that it says Abundance Island."

Lord Danbury's shoulders slumped slightly. He stared at the map as Lydia took up position by his side. His eyes continued to scour every inch for the island.

She read and reread the diary entry and then turned the page. "Here! He included coordinates on the next page." Lydia read off the numbers. Their heads nearly touched as they bent to find the location.

Triumph flared in Lord Danbury's eyes. "Here it is. It was renamed Mahe at some point." He whooped and swept her into a rollicking country dance. Breathless and laughing, they whirled and cavorted. Hands clasped and facing one another, they bounded to one end of the room and back.

A footman's voice at the door announced Mr Harting.

Abruptly conscious of the picture of lunacy they must be painting, Lydia broke free of Lord Danbury's hold and spun to face the meddlesome agent.

Harting's single raised eyebrow spoke more elegantly than any words.

Lord Danbury straightened his waistcoat and cleared his throat. "Good evening, Harting. I believe we've found the vital bit of information we've been searching for."

Lydia continued to edge away. This was the sort of mortification that impetuosity purchased. She must school her emotions better in future. Propriety and a plan. Those were to be her bywords.

Lord Danbury turned to her before she could make her escape. "Miss Garrett, I was hoping you would also join us for dinner."

Lydia swallowed. Her position in the household was becoming more confused by the moment. She had never dreamed of being asked to dine with his Lordship. Wrapping composure about herself like a shroud, she inclined her head. "As you wish, my Lord. And since you have been so kind as to honour me, would you then please excuse me? I must dress for dinner." She did not wait for a reply, only nodding at Mr Harting as she all but fled from the room.

Safely ensconced in the new guest room to which she had been moved, Lydia found that several packages had been delivered. She donned the dress of fine green muslin she had so admired earlier, then sat in a comfortable armchair, holding a new pair of silk stockings and garters in her hand.

She sighed as she slid on the hose and stepped into a pair of kidskin slippers. This was the pinnacle of luxury.

Moving to the glass she took earnest stock of her appearance. Gone was the shabby serving wench and even the pale maidservant. In their place stood a young lady of grace and consequence. An imposter. Lydia turned from the glass and made her way blindly downstairs, joy swallowed in doubt.

Mr Harting had been cooling his heels in the drawing room. He stood swiftly upon her entrance, offering a half bow. And then he drew back his head, cocking it minutely to the side as if he had just recognized her. Determined to do justice to her mother's tutelage, Lydia made her curtsy and chose a seat, sitting down gingerly in her finery.

Harting played the gallant. "Miss Garrett, you look radiant."

"You are very kind, Mr Harting." She could not prevent the flush that crept up her neck and into her cheeks. It was infuriating to respond so when she knew very well that his admiration was not sincere.

Harting leaned nearer and lowered his voice.

CHAPTER 12

"I have decided to take your Lord Danbury into my confidence—at least to an extent. If, as you hope, he is not guilty then I want him on my side. If he is guilty, then I want him to labour under the illusion that I have swallowed his tale whole-heartedly. You must play along."

* * *

Anthony paused at the entrance to the drawing room. Harting sat with his head bent close to Miss Garrett, speaking to her softly. They might as well have been sharing the same couch. At least she didn't appear too happy about it. Should he say something? Rebuke Harting for forwardness? After all, he was her guardian in some way, wasn't he?

Clearing his throat pointedly, he entered the drawing room. "I believe our meal is ready," he said too heartily.

Harting and Miss Garrett both stood at his entrance. His gait checked slightly when he saw Lydia fully. "Miss Garrett, you have a new gown."

Idiotic. It was the only word that fit. He was idiotic.

The pale green made her look especially fresh and winsome—a sylph from some forest glade where spring was born. But he had never been good at saying the right thing.

A faint pink flush coloured her cheeks. "Yes, sir."

Anthony held out his arm to lead her into the dining room. At least he could seat her beside himself, rather than that rogue Harting. "Shall we go in?"

* * *

Once Marcus set aside professional indignation at an amateur's interference, Danbury's idea to roust the murderers had grown on him the more he mulled it over. In light of British interests it might not be a bad plan.

They had no way of knowing who might have learned that the Peacock Throne had come into the hands of the *Centaur's* crew. Although the old Earl and Rudolph Wolfe apparently kept their vow of silence, the other surviving seaman may not have been so reliable. Even the Mughal's representative could have spread the information. Particularly if he had come under duress. Half a century after the event it would be well nigh impossible to determine who might know of the affair.

Danbury's plan to provoke action on the part of the murderer was brilliant in that it challenged the murderer, and with luck would lead the culprit pell-mell into their hands. Assuming that, after telling him where the throne had been hidden, the two men were murdered to prevent them from divulging information about the throne and its location to anyone else, it seemed a reasonable hypothesis that the murderer had plans to retrieve the throne. They just had to beat him to the island, or at least catch up with him while he was about his task.

There were, of course, drawbacks to Danbury's plan. They might miss the murderer altogether. Worse yet they might actually find the throne and have to decide what to do with it. The logistics would be nightmarish. Moreover, there was the danger—not for himself, but the others.

Marcus had no desire to go to any godforsaken island in the Indian Ocean, but he could not allow Danbury to go on his own. Aside from the possibility that he was a traitor, if the young imbecile encountered trouble and got wounded or killed, the blame would be laid at Marcus's door—even if by no one but himself. Perhaps he would get lucky and determine that the whole tale of thrones and jewels had all been a hoax. He kneaded his knee, fingers sensitive to the ridge of scar tissue discernible through the fabric of his breeches. Alas, that wasn't his kind of luck. It was highly likely that this little adventure wasn't going to end well.

He sighed and approached the necessary conversation in a roundabout way. "Have you uncovered any new information from the diary?"

CHAPTER 12

Danbury grinned like an idiot. In fact he had been grinning like an idiot since Marcus had come in. This could not possibly bode well.

"Yes, we did. Mr Wolfe revealed the location of the throne. His coordinates match those of an island named Mahe, part of the Seychelles chain."

Marcus summoned a smile. It probably looked more sickly than celebratory, but he could muster no enthusiasm. "How are the preparations coming along for your expedition?"

"The details are coming together more quickly than I dared hope. The peace will make things much simpler. I plan to set sail in April or May. It is impossible that the murderer could be any quicker. Even if he could afford to mount his own expedition, what are the odds he would have access to a ship of his own that could make the journey at a moment's notice?"

His stomach gurgled and Marcus set down his soup spoon. "That is a question for the gentlemen of Tattersalls. Still, I think you are correct." It was his prerogative to collect information, to horde it for himself, not to share it with all and sundry. It felt wrong. He had already revealed more information than was his wont. But now he needed to share even more. Just enough so Danbury could make a noose for himself with it if he were so inclined. After all, if he was the traitor, then Marcus wouldn't be sharing anything Danbury didn't already know. "Danbury, there are some things you must know. The danger you face is greater than you may have realized."

The happy glow drained away, leaving Danbury's face taut and hard. "What are you hiding?"

"There are greater matters at stake than solving these murders."

Danbury jumped to his feet, nearly upsetting the crystal. He glowered at Marcus. "What are you hiding?"

Lydia glared at him, icy disdain making her features all planes and angles.

Marcus measured his response. "If I divulge this information, you must keep it in the strictest confidence."

Danbury continued to glower.

Marcus held up his hands in a placating gesture. "I know I can trust you, and when you hear what I have to say, I think you will acknowledge that you would have done the same."

Miss Garrett's cool voice slipped between their heated ones. "Let's sit and talk. Lord Danbury, please heed him. There's no sense wasting effort on misplaced anger." She placed a hand on Danbury's arm, guiding him back into his seat and handing him a drink. Marcus swallowed a smile. Without a doubt he had chosen a capable confederate.

"We all know Henry Addington's government is not going to last long, and when he is gone, Pitt will be Prime Minister again. He has been out of the public eye but has remained actively involved with what is occurring in government. I have worked with him on several occasions when there were… sensitive matters to be handled."

Danbury shook his head and opened his mouth to speak but Marcus forestalled him with an upraised hand. "I am well aware that I have the reputation of a fop and a layabout. I have cultivated that perception. Please hear me out."

Danbury nodded, though a tic in the muscle of his cheek seemed to shout that he had not relinquished a dearly held plan to throw Marcus bodily from the room.

"One of our spies in France heard rumours of a new plot. He did not have many details—only that it involved India, and your father's name was mentioned." He nodded towards Danbury.

"That's absurd." Danbury's hands flexed rhythmically into fists.

"We had to find out. In my opinion he was murdered through the machinations of the plotters. As you have already surmised, I believe they are after the throne," Marcus said.

Danbury subsided once more into his seat.

"Pitt asked me to discover what I could. When I first learned about the throne, and that you had been concealing information from the runner, I was livid. My first thought was that you could be part of the plot." He waved away the objections. "Upon consideration, I know you would have had nothing to do with your father's death. I believe your motives are as you have stated, or I would not be telling you this even now."

Lydia caught his eye. "I assume you told Mr Pitt about the throne when you learned of it."

"I went to him directly, and he was grateful for the information."

Danbury ran a hand through his already tousled hair. "What does any of this have to do with the French and their plots?"

"I explained what you found to Pitt, and over the past few days, the bits of rumour have been pieced together. Napoleon is amassing an invasion force near the coast, but the blockade has been so effective that he doesn't have the means to get his men across the channel.

"Meanwhile, the Peacock Throne is a powerful symbol of the old Mughal Empire in India. It was used each time a new Mughal was crowned, and the people came to attribute almost mystical powers to the throne. We believe the French are searching for the throne in order to return it to India. There they will use the throne as a rallying point. A symbol, to inflame a rebellion against the British by backing a claimant to the Mughal Empire—the Peacock Throne will be their badge of authority. A metaphor for the independence they have lost. Conflict in India would require the Admiralty to divert a large portion of our fleet, not to mention our troops, to the Indian subcontinent, leaving the channel vulnerable."

"Opening the door for France to invade England," Lydia finished for him, her face paling.

"Precisely," said Marcus, with a grim smile. "There are many among the various Rajahs, Sultans, and so forth, who would welcome a unified banner that they could join without losing face or the possibility of ceding part of their territory or authority to a local rival. The Marathas are among the most vocal and difficult of the local chieftains who have expressed dissatisfaction with English influence in their land, and unfortunately, we have not handled

Indian affairs as well as we might. Technically, of course, it is the East India Company, not the British government, involved in India, but that is changing.

"Pitt is well aware of the threat of violence in the area. The India Act he authored and pushed through Parliament to re-organize the East India Company was only one of his efforts to reform the corrupt elements of the system; elements which cause such resentment. War in India could be devastating, not only in opening England up to invasion, but also economically, since India is such an important trading partner. Either way, Bonaparte's hand is strengthened, and England is in trouble."

"What can we do to help?" Danbury asked.

Marcus blinked. He had not expected such easy acquiescence. "What do you mean?"

"There must be a way to stop old Boney or you wouldn't be here."

"Ah. Well, I believe you are correct. We must find the throne. It's vital to keep it out of French hands. And I want to accompany you on this expedition."

* * *

Lydia might have saved Danbury the effort of trying to dissuade Mr Harting from his intention of joining the expedition. She had already experienced how unreasonable the man could be when he wanted something. Unsurprisingly he remained adamant in his conviction that he must participate in the venture.

But perhaps it wouldn't be a bad idea to have Harting along. If nothing else, he could do his own prying. Since he'd taken Lord Danbury into his confidence, did that mean she was released from any obligation to ferret about for proof of disloyalty?

"Other than the captain, no one will know of our plan to put in at Mahe except you and me," Danbury explained to Harting.

Lydia blinked and straightened in her seat. "And me. I'm going too."

CHAPTER 12

Lord Danbury pulled his head back. "This journey will be far too dangerous for a young lady."

"Young ladies frequently make the journey out to India, and this voyage to Mahe should be shorter than that," Lydia said.

"Those ladies do not have murderers following them," Lord Danbury pointed out. He wore the longsuffering expression of a parent dealing with a recalcitrant child.

Heart in her throat, Lydia nevertheless persisted. "I would be pleased to pay you for my passage."

"This has nothing to do with the expense. It would be too…"

Lydia cut him off. "I appreciate your concern. But I was under the impression that you are a man of your word. Indeed I was assured so very recently. We agreed that I would pursue my cousin's murderer along with you."

"I'm sure you would be a great asset, but I would be constantly fearful for your safety."

"Lord Danbury, I have lost as much—even more than you. I am not only bereft of a beloved relative, but a home as well. In direct proportion I am determined to see someone brought to justice. I am responsible for my own safety, and I promise to be careful. Please, I beg you. I must be part of this."

He sighed and set aside his glass.

She flung out her last argument. "And if I remain here alone, who is to protect me from the French? What if they should make me tell them of your plans?" She forced a tear. "What if they murder me as they did my dear cousin?" Her cheeks and lips burned as with fever, but she did not retract the argument. Lord forgive her, but she would see justice done, not just for his Lordship, but also for poor Mr Wolfe. Who would care for him and his case if not her?

Her last words seemed to have struck a chord within Danbury. She held her breath.

He sighed again. Lydia scented victory but had the sense to keep quiet. Harting's head swivelled between the two of them as if at a tennis match, but he also waited in silence.

"All right," Lord Danbury said at last. "But you must be cautious."

"I will be very careful," Lydia tried to reassure him.

"If that is settled?" Harting waited for acknowledgment. "Danbury, I suggest you also be exceedingly careful of the crew you take on. Loyal and honest men can be hard to come by. It would be an unpleasant irony to be murdered for the throne by your own crew. You wouldn't want to harbour a viper in your bosom."

Lydia flushed and looked down at her plate. Even her ears burned with embarrassment, knowing that she was her own breed of viper.

* * *

A midnight hush blanketed the house. Lydia eased open her door and poked her head into the hall. Satisfied that no one was about she slipped from her room. The delicate lawn of her new nightdress brushed her legs, while the heavy brocade of her dressing gown weighed down her shoulders. She had never owned such fine things in all her life. Sighing, Lydia headed for the stairs. Time to pay the piper.

The door to Lord Danbury's study stood ajar. It creaked loudly as she crept through. Her heart lodged in her throat. Of late it seemed to have taken up permanent residence in that unsuitable location.

She dropped a small vial of headache powder beneath a chair. It was not much of a ruse, but if anyone discovered her here, she needed some sort of story, and it was the best she had been able to manufacture.

Taking her seat at his Lordship's desk, Lydia stared at the piles of papers. Whether Danbury would be formally accused of treachery had yet to be proved, but no one would ever accuse him of being overly neat.

She reached for the nearest pile. For a moment she could not read the documents. Tears of shame and frustration blurred her vision. She blinked them away. This was a necessary evil. Lord

Chapter 12

Danbury would be angry with her if she was discovered going through his papers in search of any evidence that might tie him to France, Fouche, or Le Faucon, but really she was helping him. Not only would she prove him innocent, she would get Harting refocused on searching for the real traitor. If he knew her motives, Danbury would thank her.

CHAPTER 13

Lydia stood in the courtyard watching the loading of an immense amount of baggage—so much that both of the Danbury landaus had been pressed into service for the trip. A flurry of activity had galvanized the household in recent days. From footmen to maids, it seemed everyone had an errand to run.

Legacy awaited them in Portsmouth. Was it really possible that she was about to set sail for an exotic island in the Indian Ocean? She shook her head at the vagaries of her existence.

Mrs Malloy tapped her on the shoulder. "This is for you." She extended a small paper-covered parcel.

"Dear Mrs Malloy, you have been so good to me." Lydia embraced the older woman. They had grown close over the weeks of Lydia's sojourn in the house. Mrs Malloy had taken her under her wing and Lydia had learned much about the running of a large household, offering in exchange her own expertise in managing the household expenses. Now when they returned to London, she might have another possible avenue of employment. And perhaps even a letter of reference from Mrs Malloy, which would be worth far more than its weight in gold. Beyond all that, Lydia would miss her. She had been an oasis of calm practicality.

"Take care. And come back soon. I need your help with the accounts." Mrs Malloy smiled despite the tears pooling in her grey eyes.

"I shall miss you, Mrs Malloy. Thank you for all your kindness." Lydia sniffed and held her eyes open wide.

"I'll be praying for you, girl. But remember, justice is one thing and vengeance is another." With one last squeeze of her hand, Mrs Malloy stepped back.

Lord Danbury and Mr Harting awaited her. She turned and climbed into the carriage, blinking rapidly. She would not cry. Lord Danbury would have her out of the carriage in a trice if he suspected the slightest weakness. She needed something to distract her mind.

Lydia leaned forward and watched as London rattled past in all its stateliness and shabbiness, splendour and grime. Would she ever see it again?

It was not until they left the city behind them, and the gentlemen were involved in desultory conversation about mutual acquaintances, that Lydia opened Mrs Malloy's package. Inside she found a small Bible. Used, but still an expensive gift on a housekeeper's salary. Lydia bit her lip. She had taken her father's Bible with her to the Green Peacock after his death, but it had disappeared like all her other meagre treasures. She cracked open the spine and turned to the first whisper-thin page.

My Dear Lydia,

I hope this book will come to mean as much to you as it does to me. I hesitated to mention it before for fear of raising melancholy memories, but I knew your mother. She was a fine lady and I always admired her. You can be proud of your lineage. I believe she'd be proud of you.

Yr obt. svt.
Martha Malloy

Lydia blinked furiously. Tears could wait. They had to wait.

The carriages kept up a steady pace throughout the long morning, stopping only to change horses and allow the passengers to eat at noon. Despite the landaus' excellent springs, the road was in terrible repair, and the passengers were jostled until Lydia thought her teeth might rattle loose from her head.

Conversation had long since languished. Lydia could not read any longer and it even grew difficult to think. Every thought was jarred out of place as soon as it formed.

A dismal rain began to fall. The roads degenerated into lengthy tracks of mud. As they entered the small hamlet of Lower Ditton, the lead carriage sank almost to its axels in thick country mire.

Passengers, footmen and coachmen piled out into the cold drizzle to take stock of the situation. Fixing his hat lower on his head, Lord Danbury sent Lydia ahead to the inn to fetch assistance and, she suspected, to get out of the rain. He and Harting stayed to direct the servants in extricating their vehicle.

Lydia slogged through the mud. Her pattens helped some, but she held her skirts high anyway. She was not going to allow a new gown to be ruined so soon.

The inn looked grumpy and dilapidated, with sagging eaves like an old man's lowering eyebrows. As if the rain had washed away any veneer of good manners, the innkeeper sniffed in apparent disapproval of her bedraggled appearance. Not that he was a fashion plate himself: his boots were down at the heels, shirt cuffs frayed, apron a constellation of spatters and stains. Lydia peered back out through the deluge; it was the only inn visible. One would have thought that on such a well-travelled route there would be more accommodations to hand.

Lydia shoved sodden tendrils of hair away from her face, and pasted on a cheery smile. "Good evening, sir. Our coach has had a mishap, and we are in need of assistance and lodging."

In a few moments, Lydia dispatched the post boy with a team of horses to help drag the landau from the mire, and arranged for rooms and a hot meal. The cook put kettles of water on the fire so the gentlemen could wash when they came in.

Taking possession of the most comfortable nook in the threadbare private sitting room, Lydia reserved the seats nearest the fire for the gentlemen. They would be as cold as Fenn's heart after their set-to with rain and mud.

Some twenty minutes passed before a flurry of activity announced the arrival of the sopping and disgruntled gentlemen. Lydia poured two steaming cups of tea and added healthy doses of sugar to help ward off a chill.

"I'm sure you are near frozen. This ought…" She glanced up and broke off in mid-sentence.

They looked as if they had been in a wrestling match with the earth. From head to foot they were smeared with gelatinous muck. Lydia opened her mouth but Lord Danbury preempted her with an admonitory hand.

"Don't ask." A glob of mud dropped from his raised arm and landed with a loud plop on the wooden slats of the parlour floor.

Lydia bit her lip—hard. A sense of the absurd tickled the back of her throat. She couldn't help it. A chuckle slipped out, and then another. More laughter burbled up, clamouring to escape.

Lord Danbury held his glower for a moment, but then she caught his glance sliding over to Harting. The grim line of his mouth tremored. For an instant he seemed to struggle with his composure. He lost the battle; an explosive guffaw escaped. In an instant they were all laughing.

Standing half bent, Danbury clutched his side. "Harting," he wheezed, after a long moment, "you look ridiculous."

* * *

Lydia bustled about, showing the footmen where they could get warm and clean, and directing the inn's sleepy-eyed maid to take the hot water up to their chambers. Lord Danbury reappeared, freshly bathed, and attired in a clean suit of warm wool. He sank, sighing, into the chair Lydia had reserved for him and propped his feet on the grate.

Harting appeared a few moments later, shooting his cuffs and sniffing the air in appreciation as the meal was brought in. Piping hot beef stew, and crusty bread along with warm apple cider filled the platters presented by the innkeeper and his wife. The simple, hearty fare proved warm and filling.

"This establishment isn't exactly prepossessing, but you have managed to goad the staff into a credible showing." Lord Danbury pushed his bowl away, sighing in contentment.

Lydia nodded in acknowledgment of the compliment. "I trust you are recovered from your… exertions?"

"Almost. You mustn't rush a man's recovery. It is highly dangerous to all concerned." He stretched his feet towards the fire again, warming them lazily against the grate. He looked like a self-satisfied cat, sunning itself in a window.

"What damage was done to the landau?"

Lord Danbury grimaced, his indolent satisfaction disappearing. "We were quite lucky. There was no real damage to the carriage. We cannot proceed, however, until this abysmal weather clears up." He shrugged in almost Gallic fashion. "The post boy is apparently a bit of a sage regarding the weather. He advises me that the rain will stop within the hour. Then we simply wait for things to dry out a bit. As it is, we wouldn't make a mile before becoming stuck again."

Glum silence descended, as drenching as the rain. Lydia picked at a loose thread from her wrap. She crossed her ankles in ladylike fashion; but one heel bobbed up and down in incessant rhythm. Each time she realized what she was doing, she stopped and shifted positions. In a few minutes she would catch herself at it again. The minutes hobbled by.

The murderer seemed to be slipping right through her fingers. She'd been so busy with the preparations that she hadn't thought about the possibility that the killer wouldn't be lured by their grand plan. But what if he learned of the expedition and simply decided to wait for them to bring the throne back to England and then steal it? If that were the case, she supposed, they would have an opportunity to catch him when they returned. At some point he must make a move for the treasure he murdered to obtain. It was a good plan. It had to work.

Once more she stilled the nervous movement of her foot. She couldn't help it. Her body knew they had no business sitting here when a murderer roamed loose. But what could they do? They were trapped.

* * *

Unable to bear the dour restiveness that pervaded their parlour, Anthony took refuge in his room, but he carried the atmosphere within him like a disease. He'd no sooner entered than he set to pacing. There must be a way to get to Portsmouth more quickly. If the roads weren't dry in the morning he'd take one of the horses and ride south on his own. The others could follow later.

He stopped. Was that a sob coming from the next room? Ears aquiver he waited in tense expectation. Small though it was, he detected the sound again. His frown deepened and he ran his fingers through his hair.

Heaven knew Miss Garrett had had things to cry about in their short acquaintance, but she had never uttered a word of complaint. What could have happened to provoke her to it now? Abstracted, he lay down on the lumpy bed.

Perhaps she was unequal to storming about the world trying to track down a murderer. The more he thought about it, the more he could not believe how reckless he had been to bring her with him. He couldn't imagine now why he had allowed it—though he rather enjoyed having her nearby. She was certainly different from the society misses of his acquaintance. Not hardened or unladylike, but certainly more experienced in the ways of the world and consequently more independent. And to his mind, more vital.

A vision of her glowing face and shining eyes as she showed him the island's name in the diary flashed before his mind's eye. At times her loveliness caught him entirely off guard, and made the breath catch in his throat.

Still, expecting a young lady to face the danger inherent in their investigations, and the rigours of travel, was a bit much. Ladies had delicate constitutions; such stresses could cause collapse in the best of them. He would speak to her before his departure in the morning. She would see that it was best for her to return to London.

* * *

Marcus lay awake, though fatigue bludgeoned him like a battering ram. Sleep no longer heeded his summons. He lay supine, and tried to convince his conscious mind to retreat. If only rest were a dog to be lured with sweetmeats.

The more he came to know Danbury, the more he doubted his involvement in the plot. Drat the girl, but Miss Garrett was most likely right on that score. Still, he had learned to never rely on appearances. The traitor who had gulled the ministry for the last five years was a cunning adversary. He would not give himself away easily.

His mind drifted to Miss Garrett. She presented a conundrum. He had never met a young lady like her. He turned on his side, attempting to punch the meagre down of his pillow into some sort of shape. He gave up. He ought not, but nevertheless he conjured up the girl's image. The spirited gleam in her eye, the graceful arch of her neck, the way she cocked her head when she was reading. Most of all the smile that kissed her lips when she was delighted. At least she knew him as more than a fop.

Would it make any difference?

For the first time since he had assumed the role of a dandy he truly regretted the necessity of the masquerade.

* * *

Lydia tossed upon her feather ticking. The delay had them all at sixes and sevens. And she was the worst of the lot. What was she to do once they had discovered the murderer? Where was she to find employment, much less shelter and sustenance? Once his Lordship no longer had common cause with her, he would move on to other more important matters. She had no idea whether he would follow through on his promises. For that matter, she had no guarantee that he would indeed take her on board the *Legacy*. He could change his mind at any time and there was little she could do about it.

If only she could be enfolded in her parents' embrace once more. She missed them. Oh, how she missed them. The hurt of their loss had been rekindled fresh and new with Mr Wolfe's passing. She curled up on her side and covered her mouth to stifle the sob that tore at her throat.

The hours marched on in the steady rhythms of a country night. The moon rose and peered in through the web of barren tree limbs at her window. The wind rattled the branches, shaking away the rain. From deep in the inn someone set to snoring, a deep, gusty sound like the workings of a great bellows, soothing in its own way.

Lydia's eyes flew open. Heart pounding, she sat up in breathless anticipation. The rasp of covert movement in the hall stood out in stark contrast to the sleepy sounds of the country. Climbing from her bed she grabbed her wrapper and crept to the door. Slipping the latch, she opened it warily and poked her head outside. In the darkness of the hall, she could just make out the bulk of a dark figure surreptitiously slipping into Lord Danbury's room.

Abandoning caution, Lydia flew after the creature, yelling with all her might. The figure hesitated for a vital instant at the sound of her voice. A jumble of impressions assaulted her. Lord Danbury sitting up, features frozen in a scowl. A knife, gleaming in the cold light of the moon. The flash as metal sliced air, cloth and flesh in a wicked arc.

She leapt at the invader, latching on, her forearm tightly clamped around his throat. The attacker shook himself like a wet dog trying to dislodge her, but she stuck like a burr.

Now on his feet, Lord Danbury hovered nearby, dodging and weaving. He hugged his left arm tight against his chest, but his right hand was curled in a fist. He delivered a rigid jab to the intruder's nose. Lydia heard the crunch of bone and the man's head snapped back, hitting her ear with a blow that set it ringing. It wasn't the first time her ears had been boxed. He could be the killer. She clung to him with all the strength she could muster.

The attacker, having failed to extricate himself from Lydia's furious grasp, backed violently into the wall, slamming her between it and the force of his own weight. On the third blow, Lydia's grip failed. She collapsed to the ground gasping for air and trying to shake the stars from her vision. From his pallet on the floor, a blinking and bewildered James managed to fight his way from the tangle of his blankets and jumped to her side.

Lord Danbury charged at the man, but the intruder was like a cornered fox bent on escape. He fled stumblingly from Danbury's onslaught, placing only one blow—but that landed on Danbury's wounded shoulder.

Harting stepped from his room as the man emerged. The assailant shoved Harting hard, sending him backwards a few steps, but not knocking him off his feet.

The attacker did not pause to look back as he fled down the stairs, bowling into the innkeeper who had come to investigate the chaos. Picking himself up, the man fled out of the door and a moment later the sound of a horse taking off at a gallop reached them. Harting, having given chase, was trapped by the bulk of the clumsy innkeeper trying to right himself in the narrow stairwell.

Panting, Lord Danbury slumped against the wall of the corridor, holding his injured arm to slow the bleeding. The innkeeper could not seem to decide whether to hurl indignant exclamations after the fleeing intruder, or offer a solicitous hand to Lord Danbury. Ignoring him, Danbury turned back to his room.

Dazed and breathless, Lydia rose on wobbly legs.

CHAPTER 13

"Are you injured, Miss Garrett?" Danbury held out his good hand to steady her.

"I'm quite all right." She was far more concerned about Lord Danbury's injuries than her own.

Shaking her head gently to clear it, she dispatched the fussing and fluttering innkeeper to the kitchen for bandages and warm water. The innkeeper's wife relit the candles, and shooed away the small crowd that had assembled. Harting returned to report that the man had ridden southeast.

"It would appear, my friend, that someone is dead set against your making this journey," Harting said.

Lord Danbury glowered at the agent. He might have argued, but at Lydia's insistence he sat down, a tacit acknowledgment that he was in no shape to take off on horseback after the fellow.

Lydia eased the fabric of his nightshirt away from the wound, peering intently at the edges. A clean cut. "It will hurt, but the wound needs to be probed for any stray bits of cloth. If left in place they could fester and cause an infection."

He nodded, his head bobbing almost drunkenly.

James was turning a delicate shade of apple green. She nodded at him with her chin. "Brandy for his Lordship."

The valet swallowed hard and, looking relieved, made his escape from the room without protest.

"You seem to know what you're about." Harting stood at her elbow watching her work. "How is that?"

Lydia carefully cut away Danbury's sleeve. "I have a little training in physic." She rinsed the gash with the scalding water provided by the innkeeper. Despite her gentleness, Lord Danbury grew pale and taut as she assessed the damage and pulled out a few fine threads.

Harting continued to stare and she turned to him. "Do you wish to take over?"

"Heavens no. I am congratulating myself again on having the good sense to ensure that you were brought along."

"Congratulate yourself over there. I need the light." As the

115

lamp was brought nearer, Lydia stooped until she was on eye level with her charge. "Your Lordship, the knife sliced through the upper part of the arm, but it seems that the attacker caught only muscle. No tendons or ligaments that might have left a permanent impairment."

He nodded once in acknowledgment, too dazed or in too much pain to argue that she should not be the one providing ministrations. And really, he was generally a sensible man—there was no one else to do it.

Lydia sopped up the blood and then held the wound open so that the depths could be examined. She removed two tiny scraps of cloth with tweezers provided by Harting's valet, making a mental note to question why Harting had tweezers at a later date. Danbury's breathing turned shallow. No doubt he kept from crying out by sheer stubbornness. Sweat stood out on his brow even in the nighttime chill. The clenching and unclenching of his jaw and the odd grimaces were enough to tell Lydia of the pain he endured. She motioned with a slight movement of her chin and Harting positioned himself nearer so he could catch Danbury if he fainted. At last she was able to clean and bandage the wound. Finally she fashioned a sling to protect it from further injury.

The innkeeper produced a vial of laudanum and she dosed his Lordship, which eased his pain and soon had him nodding off. Three of the footmen were brought in from where they had been sleeping in the stables. Pallets were prepared on the floor in front of the guest room doors. Armed with stout cudgels, the footmen were charged with keeping out intruders.

"Are you satisfied now that he is not a part of this plot?" Lydia hissed to Harting as she checked the sleeping Danbury's wound one more time before leaving the chamber.

"This event would seem to preclude that assumption, although he did escape nearly unscathed."

A most unladylike growl emerged from the back of her throat as she fought the impulse to strike him. She pushed past him without another word. She could not get the better of him in a verbal joust tonight.

Sleep came slowly. Infection posed a serious danger with such a wound. Questions about their attacker chased one another through the corners of her mind. How had the man found them? Someone must have been following them. She drifted into a fragile doze only after getting up and straightening the twisted bedclothes for the third time.

Morning dawned sombre and windy. Rather than lie in bed brooding, Lydia washed and dressed, relieved to be able to rise at last. Having forgotten the footman sleeping on her threshold, she tripped over him. After soothing the startled man, Lydia hurried downstairs to order breakfast and determine whether there was a real physician nearby who would be able to look in on his Lordship.

Instead she found Danbury already seated at one of the long public tables, trying to eat without moving his left arm. He looked up at the sound of her approach.

"I couldn't sleep," he said by way of explanation, and waved his fork vaguely at the many platters of food spread out before him.

Lydia took the seat across from him, and placed a napkin in her lap. "How are you feeling?"

"As well as might be expected." Lord Danbury grimaced around a bite of eggs.

"Perhaps we should postpone leaving, so a surgeon can examine your wound."

"I'll be fine. This attack proves the murderers are still interested in what we're doing. We cannot delay a moment."

Lydia didn't argue. He did seem in remarkably good spirits. And she knew him well enough by now to know he would not be dissuaded from a purpose once his mind was set. He and Harting were much alike in that way. She must simply see to it that his strength would not be taxed.

They ate in contemplative silence. Moments later, a grinning

Harting appeared. In no frame of mind for such a display of cheerfulness, Lydia glowered at him.

Harting sat down and helped himself to eggs. "I had already grabbed for the intruder when he shoved me last night."

Lord Danbury grunted at the seemingly pointless announcement and continued eating. Despite an almost obsessive desire to snub him, Lydia set aside her fork and gazed at Harting with narrowed eyes. He never said anything to no purpose; indeed usually there were at least two purposes being served.

"I thought I felt something pull away from his coat, but with only the light of the candles, I couldn't find anything after the fracas last night."

Now even Lord Danbury had perked up and turned an expectant gaze upon him.

"Morning light is a vastly different thing, however." Harting reached into his pocket and pulled out a small object. "I found this."

CHAPTER 14

Danbury and Lydia leaned forward to examine the large ebony button that nestled in Harting's palm. Engraved on the front was a tall, square-rigged merchant ship, sails billowing.

"This must have come from an expensive garment." Lord Danbury took the button and revolved it thoughtfully between his fingers.

"There is certainly a naval air about it," Lydia said.

"I don't believe it's from a uniform. Perhaps we should look for a merchant seaman."

Harting reclaimed the button and turned it over to expose a tiny amount of cloth and thread still affixed to the shank. "It appears to have come from a dark blue coat."

"Now all we have to do is find a mariner who owns a blue coat with a missing button. How many of those can there be?" Lord Danbury jested feebly.

Harting pocketed the button and suggested they continue the search in the hope that the attacker left some other clue behind. They searched the inn and courtyard minutely. Despite painstaking effort they found only a length of grubby twine, half a hook-and-eye closure, and a wealth of crumbs and dust. Calling an end to the fruitless endeavour, they repaired to the private sitting room Lord Danbury had hired.

Danbury summoned his perpetually disgruntled coachman to report on whether the roads were dry enough for travel. The man arrived, hat in hand, looking only marginally gloomy. In response to the question, he narrowly avoided smiling.

"Well, your Lordship, tain't rainin' but the sun ain't shinin' neither. The wind's picked up and if it keeps dry, the roads should be fit fer driving real soon. Mebbe a couple of hours."

"See you're ready to go at the first opportunity, Burke. We must not delay any more than necessary."

"Yes, sir. I'll be ready." The coachman tugged his forelock and hurried back out to the stables.

"If we cannot take the carriages, I'll hire a horse and ride on ahead. There are too many things yet to do in Portsmouth for me to remain here. If that happens, Miss Garrett, you will come later with the carriages." Lord Danbury tapped the map lying open before him.

"Riding such a distance would almost certainly prove damaging to your shoulder. It would be foolhardy to cause further delay by injuring yourself anew," said Lydia.

"I can ride ahead and make sure that the arrangements are properly completed." Harting propped his boots on the grate.

Lord Danbury's jaw grew tight and Lydia thought she heard the grinding of teeth. He acknowledged the sense of the suggestion but it was clear to see he did not agree to it.

"Listen, friend, it occurs to me that the attacker made straight for your room. How did he know which room you were staying in and how did he get into the inn?" asked Harting.

Lydia opened her mouth and then closed it again. She had not thought to ask such questions.

Harting summoned the innkeeper, who appeared with apologies on his lips. The poor man was abject in his distress. Lydia could nearly read his thoughts. They were writ plain enough on his face. It was obvious from his restlessness that he didn't need someone from the upper classes making trouble for his inn.

When Harting asked to speak to each of the live-in staff, the man all but tripped over himself in his haste to comply. One by one, the post boy, cook, and upstairs maid paraded in, looking nervous. They were each dismissed after a couple of questions, leaving only the scullery maid.

A tiny scratching at the door announced the presence of the lowest member of the household. The scrawny young woman entered timidly, twisting her apron in red, chapped hands. Her eyes were red-rimmed as if she had been weeping.

"May I ask your name?" Harting spoke soothingly as if addressing a wild animal.

"Sarah Emsley, yer Honour," she whispered.

"Thank you, Sarah. We have a few questions for you."

The girl's nod was barely perceptible. She seemed to be holding her breath. This must all be overwhelming—well beyond her experience. No doubt she feared being blamed for something. Lydia tried to offer an encouraging smile, but the girl had eyes for no one except Mr Harting, sitting with all the awful solemnity of a magistrate in the seat of honour.

"How long have you worked at this establishment, Sarah?"

"Three years, sir." Her voice remained a mere breath of sound.

"Do you like the work?"

"It's all right."

"Do you know many of your customers?"

"Most of 'em."

"Would you remember someone if they weren't a regular?"

"Mayhap I would."

"Did anyone approach you to ask about our party yesterday?"

The girl crumpled as if she were a bit of blotting paper balled up for the rubbish bin. Bending over, she sobbed loudly into her apron. Lydia hurried to the girl's side, and put a comforting arm around her shoulder.

"It's all right," she soothed. "Come now. Don't carry on so. There's no need for this. We aren't interested in getting you into trouble. We simply need to know about this person. Hush now." It took a few moments but the girl managed to collect herself. She clutched Lydia's hand as if she might offer absolution.

"I'm sure I didn't mean to do wrong. I never thought fer a second the gentleman were a wrong 'un. He were ever so nice and polite to me."

"Why don't you just tell us how it happened?" Lydia gentled the girl onto a couch.

"Lizzie Dalton took sick yesterday so I got stuck waitin' tables in the common room. This right gent come in lookin' for a good supper. I poured him a draught and he were quite pleasant. Said as how he were travellin' through on his way to the coast. He thought as how he'd seen his friend's carriage in the yard, and asked if Lord Danbury were stayin' here. I said as how you were. Then the gent said as how he hadn't seen you in an age and wanted to know which room you were in so he could pay his compliments. I told him a'course, and then said as how I thought you were in the private sitting room." Tears again welled in her eyes and the girl's words choked off.

"You're doing well." Lydia offered an encouraging smile. "Did this gentleman have anything else to say?"

The girl nodded. "He were ever so nice. Told me as I was pretty and how I shouldn't have to work so hard fer my livin'." Sarah's ears turned scarlet. "He talked about settin' me up in a cottage near London. I…I left the latch off the door so as he could come t' see me last night. But he never come." With a whimper, the girl again buried her face. Lydia patted her back. It hurt to realize one had been played for a fool.

Lydia looked to Harting.

Harting spoke quietly, taking care not to frighten the maid. "Can you describe the man for us?"

Sarah mopped at her face with a handkerchief Lydia handed her. "He were a gentleman. His manners were so nice and he spoke well too. He were taller than most. He wore a good wig, well powdered. Kind of old fashioned, I s'pose."

"What of his clothing?"

The girl closed her eyes and screwed up her face in a caricature of someone thinking hard. "He had a fine, dark blue jacket of broadcloth. I'm sure it cost a good deal." She turned again to Lord Danbury. "I'm sorry, yer Lordship, I never thought fer a second he meant anyone harm."

CHAPTER 14

"Think no more about it, my dear," Lord Danbury said. "We'll not mention any of this to your employer, but do be careful in future. You deserve a good deal more than that fellow promised."

Sniffling, the girl nodded again. She could add nothing to what she had already told them, and Lord Harting dismissed her after a few more minutes.

"It's a pity she could not be more specific in her description," Harting said when the maid had gone.

Lydia frowned. "She did her best."

"No doubt, but her description could fit half the male population of England." Harting stood. "If you will excuse me, I must send a message to Pitt."

* * *

Anthony paced and grumbled. He hated delay at any time, but this situation magnified his impatience a thousand-fold. Surely the roads were passable by now? If he were forced to spend another night in the dreary inn, he would be a candidate for Bedlam. Bored with his own grousing, Anthony brought his attention back to his surroundings. The peeling paint and dusty, mostly empty, bookshelves held no interest. He needed a distraction.

Miss Garrett still sat quietly in an armchair, plying needle and thread with quick, neat dexterity. Had she been there the whole time? Of course she had. He wondered if her experiences at the Green Peacock had taught her how to fade into the background. Anthony coloured and sat down. He was an ill-mannered boor to keep a young lady company in such a manner.

"I cannot say why I am so unsettled. A sense of urgency hangs over me that I cannot escape."

She set aside her needlework. "I feel it too. I think we all do." Her luminous eyes met his with such a depth of understanding that he held his breath for an instant.

"Tell me, how did you learn physic?" Anthony asked.

"My mother," said Lydia. "When she married, she wanted to be the finest vicar's wife in England—to make Father proud. She made all the usual rounds to visit the ailing, though she hated to see their suffering, and felt helpless to alleviate their pain. When she could stand no more she began to borrow books about medicine. She read everything she could get on the subject." A far-away smile touched the girl's lips. "Then she developed a friendship with the stillroom maid at the great house, and learned about herbs, and plants, what things made good physics, and so on. She even took to assisting the local surgeon. All so that when she visited the sick, she could offer more than pity. When I grew old enough to accompany her, she began to teach me what she knew."

"You must be very like her."

Lydia flashed him a brilliant smile. "That is one of the kindest things anyone has ever said to me." She took her sewing up once more. "Tell me about your mother."

"I never really knew her. She died when I was very young."

"I'm sorry." Her smile faded like a wilting rose, and a flush crept up her cheeks. Anthony rushed to reassure her.

"Don't be. I used to listen to my father tell stories about her. I believe she was the reforming influence in his life. He always said he wanted to be the man she thought he was."

"It sounds as if they were very happy."

"They were. I have very little memory of her. Only impressions really—a gentle voice, soft cool hands, dark hair and eyes. As a boy I used to stare at her portrait for hours, trying to will animation into the features."

"Sometimes I'm afraid I will forget my parents' faces. When someone is there, you think such a thing would be impossible, but when they're gone, memory fades and one is left only with the essence of who they were." A distant look crossed her features.

"I'm fortunate to have portraits of my parents."

"I think my mother sat for a portrait about the time she came out but, of course, her family would have it. I did have a miniature of the two of them. They paid an itinerant artist to make it, and it was fairly good. It was misplaced somehow shortly after I arrived at the Wolfes'."

A shuffling in the hallway announced the approach of one of the footmen. Anthony sat up, every nerve a tingle.

"Pardon me, sir. The groom says as how the road is looking fine and the landau is waiting your convenience."

"Excellent." Anthony bounded to his feet, beaming. "At last, some good news. Now where is James? I want to leave immediately."

CHAPTER 15

The short caravan reached Portsmouth as twilight claimed the city. Lydia welcomed the bustle of Portsmouth after the isolation of the road. They found a good inn and ate a hearty supper before retiring early to their rooms. Though the inn's proprietor grumbled over the arrangement, footmen were again placed on guard duty in the hall.

Lydia woke early. With the assistance of one of the footmen, whom Lord Danbury insisted accompany her at all times, she headed out to the apothecary's for a few supplies, including bandages and a healing salve for Lord Danbury's shoulder. She had changed the dressing the night before and it appeared to be mending well. Still, she refused to allow gangrene an opportunity to take root.

The briny scent of the air communicated clearly that they were near the sea. She inhaled deeply, a sense of excitement beginning to press out against her chest. The salt-scoured shops, with their peeling paint and exotic mix of clientele, held an unaccountable charm. Even the overflow of rowdy, landlocked sailors lounging in the streets due to the peace did little to quash her spirits. Still, despite her sense of expectation, she remained on guard. Everywhere she looked there were dark blue pea jackets and it seemed that an unaccountably high number were missing buttons.

She scarcely saw Danbury and Harting. They were off and away, each on business of his own. It would be a relief to climb aboard the ship. They all needed a reprieve from the fear of attack.

And then the time was upon her, with the last-moment breathlessness that always seemed to accompany highly anticipated moments. As eager as schoolboys on an outing, they piled into the carriage and drove down to the quay.

Lydia accepted the help of a stout oarsman as she climbed gingerly down into a teetery skiff. Waves slapped against the side of the small boat pushing it up against the dock and then sucking it back. Her stomach lurched. Why hadn't she ever paused to consider that travelling by ship meant being surrounded by water? And why, oh why, hadn't she ever learned to swim?

Lord Danbury skipped down into the boat as nimbly as if he were a mountain goat, and with as much subtlety. Lydia clutched the side as the boat bobbed and weaved drunkenly. They were going to capsize, and she was going to drown right there in the harbour.

Only slightly slower, Harting joined them. Lydia closed her eyes and swallowed hard. In a moment, the oarsmen were pulling with sure, swift strokes for the ship.

A spray of evil-smelling water splashed into Lydia's face. She released one white-knuckled hand from the seat to dash it away. These were not the sea waters physicians encouraged patients to bathe in. The harbour of Portsmouth was befouled by the waste of the city's inhabitants and the many ships at anchor. Every sort of effluvia floated on the insalubrious liquid. Unable to keep her nose from wrinkling, Lydia peeked into the rippling brown waves. It was worse than the Thames.

With an expert hand, the coxswain guided the skiff right up to the ship. The gentlemen latched onto the net and began their ascent with fluid dexterity. Even Danbury's injured arm didn't seem to give him pause, while Lydia looked on in consternation. She could make the climb, but not with the sailors leering up from below. And first she'd have to release her hold on the plank that served as her seat. She bit her lip.

One of the sailors took pity on her. "It's all right, Miss. They're lowerin' a boatswain's chair for you."

Lydia looked up to find an odd contraption descending towards the skiff like an angel from on high. The men helped her into it as if it were a swing and she a playful shepherdess posing for a portrait. The seamen let go as their friends from above hauled her up with a sickening lurch. Lydia's stomach contracted. The ship rolled, and she slammed into the hull with a resounding thud. A chorus of apologies rained from above. If she ever made it aboard alive, she would spend the rest of her days there. Anything to avoid this torturous process again.

At last the sailors restored her to her feet, and she stood on *Legacy*'s deck, gazing in awe at the cobweb of ropes and cables, the rush of coordinated activity, and the gleaming brass. She had already entered foreign territory.

"Miss Garrett, are you quite all right?"

"Hmm?" Bemused, she turned to Lord Danbury. "Oh, yes. Thank you, I'm perfectly fine."

Harting clapped Danbury on the back. "How did you manage to hire such a fine craft on such short notice?"

"She's a beautiful little frigate, isn't she?" He was positively smug. "Fact is, I didn't hire her. My father bought her after she had been retired from naval service and began to fit her out as a private man o' war, complete with a letter of marque."

"You own a privateer?" Lydia shook her head.

Danbury grinned. "She was scheduled for completion in a month, but the dockyard was able to move up the date, with the persuasion of a bonus for quick work."

Captain Campbell hurried to meet them. A short, stout man with a barrel-chest and a fringe of red hair encircling a bald pate, he led them to the quarterdeck with the air of a bridegroom introducing his bride.

"My *Legacy* here is a beautiful ship. That she is. Well built, sound, and weatherly, you couldn't ask for better, my Lord."

"She will do well, then?" Danbury asked. His tone conveyed confidence that the answer would be in the affirmative.

"Better than well." He ran a rough hand over the smooth wood of the rail, caressing the ship with a lover's ardour. "Your father, God rest him, spent a great deal on her refitting, but it was money put to good use."

Lydia turned her eyes upward, examining the complex web of ropes and sails. Some were drawn in close to the yardarms. Some were full and billowing, and filling the air with an audible sense of the wind's movement. The cloth flapped and the rigging creaked in pace with the lapping waves. She looked to the nearest ship in the harbour, an East Indiaman, for comparison. By her account, *Legacy* was smaller and sleeker, though she still had vast yardage in her sails.

Campbell caught the direction of Lydia's gaze. "*Legacy*'s more heavily armed than an Indiaman, and has an advantage in her speed. She can lead any merchant ship she comes upon in a merry dance." He rubbed his hands together in contained glee. "Lord Danbury's father ensured she should."

When she looked at Danbury, she noticed that he, too, had a kind of barely controlled excitement. If time and tide had been right he would have ordered them to sea immediately.

Captain Campbell waved a hand at the hive of activity around them. "I've manned her with experienced seamen. Most of them are old navy hands what got landlocked when the peace was declared. If we ever have a need, I guarantee that *Legacy* will make a fine showing for herself."

A young man in a neat, dark navy coat climbed onto the quarterdeck and approached the captain. The buttons matched the one Harting had found at the inn, and one of his buttons seemed to have been replaced. The thread used to sew it in place was a lighter blue that showed up against the ebony of the button. But that was hardly conclusive. During her foray through Portsmouth's shops she'd found more than one establishment that seemed to be doing a roaring trade in buttons of the same design.

She stepped closer to the young man. A head taller than his captain, he held himself with stiff formality that made him appear older. She tried to imagine him in a powdered wig and he easily fit the scullery maid's description.

"The buttons on your coat are quite unique."

He looked down at his chest as if surprised to find any buttons there at all. "Not at all. Every port in England carries them, or similar. Shopkeepers seem to think all sailors wish to emblazon their profession across their wardrobe."

"True enough. Even I have buttons like that." Captain Campbell patted his ample belly. "Your Lordship, Mr Harting, Miss Garrett." He nodded to each in turn. "Allow me to introduce Dan Cabot, my first mate. If I were still in the service he would be my first lieutenant, and a fine one at that."

Lydia watched the fellow closely. "Were you in the navy then, Mr Cabot?"

"Briefly." He did not elaborate.

Captain Campbell rushed to fill the social void. "Let me give you a tour of the ship. She's just as beautiful within as without, I can tell you that much."

Lord Danbury had been all over *Legacy* the day before, but he joined them on their rounds, pointing out with all the pride of ownership what he felt to be the most interesting features of the ship. Lydia's mind whirled with capstans, and mizzen masts and fore jeer bitts abaft. It was an alien world, full of strange objects and foreign notions. Even the floor beneath her feet moved. She would take a step only to find the deck meeting her too soon or too late. More than once she staggered. Perhaps it was this phenomenon that gave sailors their legendary reputation for being drunkards?

Captain Campbell assured her that she would grow accustomed to the sway of the deck and learn to move with the ship. He was a kind man and she smiled her thanks.

Lydia could not have said what she had expected, but she was pleasantly surprised at the accommodations below decks. Mr Wolfe's tales of life at sea had prepared her for far worse.

"This here's the greater cabin." Captain Campbell made an

expansive gesture. Every bit of the space had been put to economical use. And there was no doubt that *Legacy* was a fighting ship. Two cannon punctuated the outer wall on either side, their bulk taking up most of what might otherwise have been large, sunny windows. A dining table and chairs occupied the centre of the space, and a great sideboard rested against the bulkhead.

"This will serve as a fine command post." Lord Danbury nodded his approval.

"Aye, sir. On an Indiaman, I think they calls it a saloon," Captain Campbell said.

Danbury clapped him on the back. "None of that civilian twaddle for us. This is by rights the greater cabin, and that's what we'll call it."

The captain beamed his approval and continued the tour.

Beyond lay a simple private space with a hammock and washstand, writing desk and stool, as well as one of the seemingly ubiquitous cannon. The room's best feature was easily the stern gallery windows, which let in a good deal of light and could be opened to air the cabin. Adjacent to this was the quarter gallery and a private seat of ease. Lydia had been hanging back, but a glimpse of her bags piled beneath the hammock made her start forward.

She approached Mr Cabot. "Have I been given the captain's quarters?"

His manner was as rigidly correct as if they were aboard a ship of the line. "Yes, Miss."

"That wasn't necessary. I would happily accept something else."

"As owner, Lord Danbury had the right to claim these quarters, but he insisted that you should have them. And if I may say so," Mr Cabot rubbed his nose delicately and looked away, "the quarters below are quite *close*."

"Oh, I see."

"I suggest that you accept the arrangement graciously."

Accepting the censure, Lydia subsided and allowed him to proceed with the tour.

On the deck below, cabins for the gentlemen and ship's officers lined either side of the long wardroom. Seeing the accommodations, Lydia conceded that Lord Danbury had likely made the proper decision, but a bit of her still felt unworthy of the consideration.

The sun rose with the change in tide, bringing with it a clean salty breeze. With a barked command, Captain Campbell had the crew hopping to their duty. The sails captured the breeze and flapped to life, sounding as if the ship were clapping her hands in her excitement to be underway.

Lydia closed her eyes and raised her face to the breeze. Exhilaration swept through her. They were on their way. It seemed scarcely credible.

Legacy picked up speed until she fairly skimmed along the waves, putting crew and passengers alike in high spirits.

Captain Campbell left the quarterdeck to Mr Cabot's command and took his passengers down to the greater cabin. He unfurled a large map and showed them the charted course. With wide eyes and a racing pulse, Lydia leaned close. The captain's strong, knotty hands described their ports of call as he ran a long finger along the route. As he pronounced the exotic names, a thrill shot through her. She put a hand to her stomach to calm its roiling. This adventure was no carefree lark. They hoped to capture a murderer.

* * *

Captain Campbell and the other gentlemen stood as Lydia entered the dining room. "Miss Garrett, you've met Mr Cabot. May I also present Dr Marshall?" He extended a hand towards the gentleman who offered a small bow in her direction. "Dr Marshall isn't some wheedling surgeon, as most ships have. He is a real Harley Street physician, a credit to the ship. He has lords aplenty among his patients."

The doctor was a thin man, almost to the point of gauntness, the skin stretched tight over his cheekbones. His middling brown hair was pulled back in a neat queue. Everything about him spoke of meticulous care, right down to his clean and trimmed fingernails.

"I'm delighted to make your acquaintance, sir."

"And I yours, Miss Garrett. You are a beauty amongst beasts, I see." He regarded her with clear grey eyes.

"You are too kind by far." She forced herself not to fidget under the scrutiny of the assembled gentlemen.

He nodded formally, his eyes twinkling, and resumed his seat.

"What has induced you to abandon your patients for a cruise to the Indian Ocean?" asked Harting.

"I suffered a round of illness recently myself, and find that I must take an extended holiday from my practice. When I heard of this voyage, it seemed the perfect opportunity to indulge both my health and my interest in the natural sciences."

"We are certainly pleased to have you aboard, Dr Marshall. I have very little knowledge of botany, but I am ever eager to learn." Lord Danbury smiled broadly at the doctor.

"Be careful what you wish for. I love having an audience at which I can direct my brilliance." A wry smile curved his lips. "Although Miss Garrett, I understand that my presence may be entirely superfluous. That was quite a neat job you did of patching up his Lordship. Where did you learn the art of physic?"

Lydia explained briefly as steaming platters, bowls and tureens were produced until they covered the table in wild profusion. She had made out the victualling orders herself, so the quantity and quality of the fare should not have startled her, and yet somehow she had half expected to subsist on ship's biscuit and grog for the entire journey. Her tale did not take long to tell. "To be honest, I greatly enjoyed learning how to care for those in distress. It provided a sense of fulfilment I've found in little else."

She bit her lip and looked down at her plate, concerned that she had revealed too much of herself, but the good doctor merely nodded gravely. "I've already seen that you have a measure of skill. If you still have an interest in such things you would be welcome to join me in the surgery. An extra pair of hands is always welcome."

He made no comment on her sex, nor did he question her faculties.

She beamed at him in response. "I would be grateful for the experience and I promise to try not to weary you with all my questions."

Convivial conversation abounded as freely as the food. Only the slosh of water against the hull of the ship and creak of the rigging reminded her they were at sea, rather than dining in the heart of London.

Talk soon turned to politics.

"The peace will never last." Captain Campbell spoke with a good deal of ardour. "Old Boney is ambitious, and ambitious people aren't satisfied with peace. He's the sort that wants action, always action."

"The newssheets say Bonaparte is preparing an invasion force," said Danbury.

"The French will have to get past our naval blockade first." Harting shot Danbury a cutting glance, though his tone and manner remained trifling. "They've little hope of that at the moment. France suffers from an unfortunate shortage of competent naval commanders since they beheaded most of their experienced men a few years back."

"Don't underestimate Boney. He's a creative genius. What he can't gain by force he'll take by some other means." Mr Cabot had remained largely silent, eating with almost mechanical precision, but now his words underscored the captain's point.

Campbell turned his attention to Lydia as if to reassure her and raised his glass. "Don't you worry, Miss Garrett. Mr Harting is correct. The Frenchies are well contained. The blockade was right effective in keeping them cooped up in their ports. Besides which, we have our guns if we were to need 'em. That's four eighteen pounders, twelve eight-pound long guns and six twelve-pound carronades, not to mention our chasers. *Legacy* is the neatest little frigate you could imagine. She's quick and makes as little leeway as anyone could wish. We can outrun anything they could send after us without turning a hair."

CHAPTER 16

Anthony was finally discovering what had shaped his father into the man he knew. The discipline Captain Campbell maintained, the camaraderie among the crew, the sacrosanct daily routines that constituted the rhythm of life aboard ship: it all captivated him. He had been given a window into what had shaped his father's soul.

As the owner, Anthony had free rein of the ship, and he made a nuisance of himself as he followed the men about with unending questions. As his shoulder healed, he even took a hand in the work to be done, which, when he wasn't in their way, seemed to endear him to the crew.

He spent a portion of each morning teaching Miss Garrett to defend herself. He began by giving her a little dagger and showing her how to use it. Then he taught her to shoot a pistol. God willing she wouldn't need to use any of these masculine skills, but if she did, then they were worth the effort of acquisition.

In point of fact, the effort expended in helping Miss Garrett to acquire the skills to protect herself was far from onerous. Watching her lithe movement as she obeyed his instruction stirred something within him, quickening his pulse.

The afternoon breeze had a bite to it as it skittered across the deck. Perspiring, Anthony welcomed the playful wind as he hefted his sword. The weight felt good in his hands—right somehow. He'd always loved swordplay, the brisk action, the clear bell-like clang of blade on blade, and the strategy. Especially the strategy. Pitting his wits against an opponent's. Finding the one perfect instant to strike the decisive blow. The makings of a pleasant afternoon.

He toyed with the idea of teaching Miss Garrett to use a sword. He pursed his lips and squinted against the glare of the sun. She sat on an upturned crate with the wind whipping tendrils of hair about her face. Yet with her head bowed over a small black volume, she managed to look as serene as if she idled in a London drawing room.

Perhaps it would not be a good idea. It took a great deal of strength to handle a sword for any length of time, and it required years of training to master. Knowing Miss Garrett, she could probably manage it, but they didn't have the time.

A throat cleared behind him. "Care for a match?"

A grin creased Anthony's face, and he turned to find Harting holding a sword of his own.

"Delighted."

"Then *en garde!*" Flashing a grin of his own, Harting attacked.

Steel clashed against steel. Exhilarated, Anthony parried. They feinted and lunged their way across the deck until they were both laughing and winded.

Now this was living.

They collapsed onto a crate in the waist of the ship.

"Well handled, my friend." Harting clapped him on the back.

"You are more daring than I'd have credited."

"And you are more skilled."

Anthony snorted. "I'm as dry as the desert. Would you care for a drink?"

"By all means."

Together they made their way down to the wardroom. Anthony pulled the stopper from the decanter and poured them each a dram.

Harting claimed the most comfortable chair and put his feet up with the air of a man settling in for the duration. "That is better."

Anthony took the seat across from him. "I hadn't any notion you were a swordsman."

CHAPTER 16

"Not a dandified pursuit?"

"It does provide opportunity for one's hair to be disarranged."

Harting put on a show of mock distress and patted his short locks, trimmed to resemble some ancient Roman emperor. "Horrors. Send for Charles and my wig."

Anthony could not help but laugh. He leaned back in his chair and closed his eyes. A pleasant hush blanketed the room, broken only by the ambient sea. He had nearly dozed off when Harting's voice fractured the peace.

"What do you mean to do with Miss Garrett when this is all over?"

He stiffened. "I'm not sure I take your meaning. I don't intend to do anything with her."

"Come now, man, you must realize that this little jaunt is doing her no favours."

Anthony sighed. "Everything was a great deal simpler before I knew of her relation to Glenford."

"No doubt. But the fact remains that you allowed her to accompany you."

"I understand that you have found an inheritance for her. Will there be nothing more from that source?" Anthony let some of the suspicion he had harboured since seeing the packet of money she had received surface.

Harting simply blinked once like a particularly slow milch cow. "Her father's investments may provide for some of her needs, but the principal ought to remain untouched in order to provide for her old age."

The man must be a devil at the gaming tables. Anthony was still convinced there was more to the story. She had been entirely too flustered when she had opened that package.

"I have made some inquiries. She won't be a suitable governess, of course, after an unchaperoned jaunt such as this, but she would make a fine housekeeper or perhaps a companion for an elderly lady."

Harting settled back into his seat and closed his eyes. "Just so long as you are considering her future. It would disturb me greatly to believe that someone thought he could impose upon a young lady in such dependent circumstances." His tone was as tough as dried salt pork.

Anthony shot him a glance. For the first time in their acquaintance he truly believed in Harting's abilities as an agent.

* * *

Lydia fell into the habit of spending her mornings with Dr Marshall. He was an excellent teacher. Able to find something new to say or explain about even the most mundane of sprained ankles. Far from tiring of her questions, he encouraged her curiosity. A novel experience indeed.

In contrast she spent much of each afternoon in company with Mr Harting, playing games of whist or casino, devising puzzles, or reading on the deck. Lord Danbury's preoccupation with all things naval often kept him otherwise engaged, and yet spending time with Harting was not the punishing task she'd feared.

He was witty, and as their acquaintance grew he set aside his foppish mask entirely. Beneath it she found him thoughtful and unexpectedly modest. Slowly she came to suspect it was not so much a mask as a suit of armour.

Her resentment dissipated. His manipulations were employed only in the pursuit of what he thought right. She could scarcely fault him for that, and began to look forward to their time together. What drove him? He had no need of money, so why had he offered his services in an occupation that most believed thoroughly discreditable?

For the first several weeks of the voyage, the weather remained almost constantly fair, with a westerly breeze that made *Legacy* fly atop the waves.

Lord Danbury gleefully marked the halfway point on a map.

CHAPTER 16

"Captain Campbell says we may make the journey in just about four months." The gentlemen hurried up on deck to stare at the horizon, as if land was already in sight.

Grinning, Lydia turned her attention to her cousin's diary. She had read it, and reread it, trying to parse meaning from the tiniest of clues. She was hoping to anticipate what they might encounter on the island of Mahe. From what she could tell it had claimed the lives of at least two of *Centaur*'s crewmen. The island itself might be an opponent as deadly as the murderer.

* * *

Lydia Garrett was an anomaly. Marcus regarded her as she spoke animatedly with Dr Marshall at the dinner table. She could hold her own in any of the drawing rooms of London, but unlike the dressed up dolls of the ton, she had experienced the underbelly of society. Her independent turn of thought intrigued him even when it irritated.

Danbury also watched her. Covertly, Marcus inspected the Earl. He looked disgustingly hale and hearty. Life at sea agreed with him. He probably enjoyed the country too. Marcus flicked a weevil off his plate.

At his insistence Miss Garrett had managed to procure some of Danbury's correspondence. But she still seemed to resent the task, and cooperated only to the letter of their agreement. Perhaps she had allowed the Earl certain liberties… No. Marcus quashed a jealous impulse. They couldn't have hidden such a liaison aboard ship. Every man-jack in the vessel would know the instant any sort of attachment was formed. Besides, such thoughts dishonoured Miss Garrett. She had never given the slightest indication that she held her virtue cheaply.

* * *

The good weather could not hold out indefinitely. The following afternoon the wind picked up and changed direction. A heavy bank of storm clouds lowered in the northeast. The seamen went about the business of preparing the ship for a storm as calmly as they went through any of their routines. Lydia glanced up from her needlework as Captain Campbell approached.

"Good afternoon, Captain. Would you care to have a seat?" She motioned to a nearby barrel.

"No, thank you, Miss. I just wanted to assure you that there is no cause to fret. *Legacy* is a fine, tight ship. She don't hardly even notice a storm."

"It's kind of you to reassure me. I know what a capable seaman you are, and if you say it, then I'm certain there is no cause for alarm."

Captain Campbell blushed and nodded. "Well now, that is kind of you, Miss. You might want to go down to the greater cabin. The bluster is going to arrive any minute."

Harting joined Lydia as she stood. "What did you do to that man?"

Lydia glanced up at him. "I? I did nothing."

"Oh no?" Harting was getting entirely too much enjoyment from the situation. "You made that crusty old seadog blush. I believe you have every man aboard charmed and ready to do your bidding."

Lydia could not feign ignorance. It was certainly a flattering boost to one's confidence to be the only woman aboard a ship. Still, it was scarcely her fault; it was simply the nature of things. Mentally she prepared her defence as they strolled to the nearest ladderway.

Harting forestalled her with a shake of his head. "I'm not saying you've done anything devious, but it is true nonetheless."

"I have been nothing but courteous."

"And how many ladies of quality do you think have been courteous to these tars? Most of the gentry show these fellows nothing more than the heel of their boot."

"Well, there you have it. I've found the flaw in your logic."

Lydia's sense of humour returned, and she smiled in self-mockery. "I'm not even one of the shabby gentility. Merely a vicar's daughter, turned maid of all work, turned spy. It's been a decided downward spiral."

"You are much more, my girl. Don't allow anyone to tell you differently. My man Charles is a bigger snob than any of the peers I know, and he thinks you are a fine lady." Harting paused at the top of the ladderway. "So do I."

Lydia blushed furiously. She could not meet his eyes. "Perhaps it is easy to act as a lady, since all of you have treated me as if I were one."

Harting cleared his throat. "I think I will take another turn or two around the deck. Would you care to join me?"

Relieved that the intensity in his manner had been replaced by more customary nonchalance, Lydia shook her head. "Thank you, but I think I will read for a while."

* * *

The sharp bite of a stiffening wind drew some of the heat from Marcus's cheeks. He was an utter fool for putting Miss Garrett on the spot in such a way. How could he have possibly expected her to respond to such a statement? With a grunt, he kicked at a coil of rope on the deck.

"Everything all right, old man?" Danbury, coming along the deck, cocked an eyebrow.

"Fine." Marcus stalked away towards his cabin.

* * *

Lydia sat with the diary in hand, but she wasn't reading. She gazed into the middle distance, seeing nothing.

Lord Danbury entered the greater cabin. "Do you know what's wrong with Harting? He nearly took my head off just now."

"Oh?" With an effort she turned her attention to his Lordship.

"I suppose life aboard ship is hard for some." He extended a sheaf of smudged notepapers. "I'm writing up a record of our adventures. I thought that I might forget something that might prove later to be of importance, so I wanted to capture it all while things are fresh."

Lydia accepted the offering. Smiling, she shook her head. "Your penmanship is disgraceful, you know. Nearly as bad as my cousin's."

"I received the worst wallopings of my life over penmanship," he sighed.

"Would you like me to transcribe these into something more legible?"

"Would you?"

Over the weeks they had developed a sort of partnership. Her knack for organization, and lack of occupation, had prompted her to offer Lord Danbury clerical assistance. He had accepted her help with an air of relief.

"Certainly." More fodder for Harting. She suppressed the sigh that threatened to overwhelm her. She had never come up with anything remotely incriminating, but he always demanded more.

"It looks like the weather is changing. We might be in for a rough patch." Lord Danbury sank into a nearby chair and crossed his long legs in front of him.

"Captain Campbell warned me that a storm was brewing."

"That must have been why Harting was in such a foul temper," Lord Danbury mused. "Did you know these are the very waters where Sir Francis Drake had many of his triumphs?"

"Oh yes?"

"He made a name for himself here before heading off to the West Indies."

Lydia made a sound expressing suitable interest.

Lord Danbury continued. "Some of the seamen are almost entirely uneducated, but they have an amazing knowledge of maritime lore."

CHAPTER 16

"They're good storytellers too." Lydia stripped all wryness from her tone.

Lord Danbury caught her inflection anyway and chuckled. "That they are, though you have to watch out for what is true and what is story. I'm afraid there is a great deal more of the latter in most of their tales."

Lydia fetched the portable writing desk, and set about the task of deciphering Danbury's chicken scratches into English. He, meanwhile, continued his pleasant, inconsequential talk. They passed the afternoon in comfortable companionship, while the menacing cloudbank gained on *Legacy* as if she stood still.

CHAPTER 17

Harting rejoined them during the supper hour. Lydia tried to catch his eye, but he avoided looking in her direction. Captain Campbell appeared only briefly at the meal. Something must have changed his opinion of the coming storm. Despite his efforts at equanimity, tension communicated itself in the hunched line of his back as he bent over his plate and ate without even seeming to chew the food. He excused himself as soon as he had finished his meal.

Lydia put down her soup spoon. She stared into the bowl. Its contents sloshed about with the rhythm of the ship. The movement was pronouncedly more violent than she'd ever noticed before. The soup would spill at any minute. She glanced up to find Lord Danbury's gaze upon her. Neither he nor Harting made any move to eat more. Somehow, up until this moment, she had convinced herself that she wasn't adrift on the sea—merely on a very tiny island.

Her stomach seemed suddenly to be filled with lead, as if she had taken on ballast. Saliva filled her mouth as if she were going to be ill. She swallowed it back. She could not—would not—give way to fear before these gentlemen.

Harting stood. "Perhaps we ought to get a breath of fresh air while we still can. If it's a large storm, we might be stuck indoors for several days."

Relieved, she stood and allowed herself to be led from the table.

Lydia could scarcely believe how quickly the wind had picked up. The fierce clouds were nearly upon them now. *Legacy* ploughed her way through the sea, flinging up spray, which was snatched by the gale and spit back at them in gusts. The waves were building, and the deck beneath their feet heaved with strain.

The crew had double reefed the topsails. Several men remained in the tops, their glasses trained on the cloud bank that bristled with lightning and thunder. Their actions held an element of haste that had not been there earlier in the day. A few paused in their work to cast anxious glances at the lowering green-black clouds. Jolly banter had been replaced by an eerie hush, punctuated only occasionally by an order or a curse.

A large wave seemed almost to pick up the ship and drop it. A heavy weight crashed into the small of Lydia's back. She staggered forward, her head colliding with Harting's solid form, bowling him over as if he were a cricket stump. The planks of the deck bit her palms.

"I'm so sorry. Are you all right? Lost my balance." Lord Danbury bent to help Lydia to her feet. He had to yell to be heard.

"Perhaps we ought to admit defeat." Harting clutched at his hat as it attempted to take flight.

The rain hit in full force, drenching the ship within seconds. They scrambled for shelter in the greater cabin, nearly tumbling down the ladderway as they made their way below decks. Due to the risk of fire, the lanterns had been doused, leaving the passengers in almost total darkness. The violence of the ship's pitch and roll increased. Lydia was soon disorientated. She groped for a chair and collapsed into it on the roll.

Along with the howl of the wind, she could hear objects sliding about. Dread trickled in with the rain and sea, turning Lydia's feet and hands icy.

Something slammed into her leg, wrenching a squeak of pain from her. Another piece of debris collided with her chair. With the gloom so complete, she could not see to avoid the blows. She drew her legs up onto her seat, flinching as other unidentifiable objects skittered by.

The storm grew more vicious. A particularly violent wave seemed to drop the ship off a cliff. Lydia's chair toppled over with her still in it. She let out a yelp. Scrambling for purchase, she tried to stand, but couldn't find her feet on the plunging deck. Lord Danbury and Mr Harting both called to her. She could hear them fumbling in the dark, and then, beneath the howling of the wind, two thuds in quick succession.

"Oof." One of them sounded as if the breath had been knocked from him.

The other swore.

The furniture continued to skate and tumble about them. It was too absurd—the sort of comedy London's burlettas turned prodigious profit from each year. If she hadn't been so terrified she would have laughed.

Legacy slid down into the trough of another enormous wave and Lydia's breath seemed to hover in her throat, unsure whether it was coming or going. She hiccoughed. How could the ship possibly survive such a beating? Sudden tears forged hot trails down her cheeks. *Not drowning. Please God. I couldn't face drowning.*

Grateful that darkness masked her features, Lydia abandoned, for the moment, her attempt to stand upright.

"We should go to our cabins," Lord Danbury yelled, abandoning decorum to be heard above the crash of sea and sky and ship.

She righted herself against the bulkhead. Stumbling and staggering, she made her way to the aft cabin. Not bothering to search out a nightdress, Lydia wrapped herself in a cocoon of blankets and all but fell into the hammock. It was a long time before her teeth stopped chattering and she could feel her fingers.

She lay listening to the ocean and the wind fighting to claim the ship. Her heart thudded in an uneven staccato. Her stomach surged and plunged with the heaving of the ship and the swaying of the hammock. Any moment she would be ill.

A lump lodged firmly in her chest and clammy perspiration coated her body.

CHAPTER 17

If only she could have a little light. It would make all the difference. It was so disorientating in the darkness that she didn't know which way was up. It could hardly be described as a fixed point. She retched; dizziness swamped her senses.

What had she been thinking to believe that she could do this? The first challenge and she was a whimpering, snivelling mess. Teeth clenched, she sucked in a breath. She refused to be a mewling coward.

She began to fight her way from the hammock, making it swing even more erratically. She could not afford to be ruled by fear.

At last she managed to extricate herself from the hammock's embrace. Even if they died during this storm, at least she would know that she had pursued what she thought was right. There were worse ways to die.

Grimly, Lydia groped for the hatch and made her way out into the storm to be sick.

* * *

By morning, the storm had mostly blown itself out. Wind and rain still lashed petulantly at the ship, but the maniacal power had waned.

Eyes gritted with sleep, Lydia crawled from her hammock. Her legs felt as wobbly as a newborn lamb's. But despite this, she was almost jubilant. They had survived. Shivering, she pulled on a dry gown and pinned up her hair.

The greater cabin looked like a doll's house upended by a naughty child. Every stick of furniture was overturned—even the large sideboard. Lydia picked her way through the soggy mess. Standing in the middle, hands on her hips, she shook her head at the destruction. Then she reached for the nearest chair and righted it. She might at least make herself useful in some small way. Her appearance on the deck the evening before had prompted consternation and she had been sent back to her cabin with a bucket. Unable to face the hammock, she had wedged herself into the seat below the window, hugging that wretched bucket as she stared out of the windows. The roiling, ever changing wall of water at times hurried the ship along, and at other times seemed to try to snatch them back. All the time she'd had the sense that the waves were designed to draw them into some giant maw—that they were a quick snack before the sea found heartier fare elsewhere.

The gusting rain slowed to a sullen drizzle before Lord Danbury and Mr Harting appeared. Lydia had restored most of the furniture to its proper place, sorting out what could not be salvaged from what merely needed repair. She had mopped up the water and picked up the odds and ends scattered about. When they arrived, Captain Campbell hard on their heels, she was busily sorting out the sideboard.

"Why, Miss," the captain said in astonishment, "you didn't do all this yourself, did you? I was going to send in a couple of the lads."

"It's no trouble. Your men have quite enough on their hands with the rest of the ship to look after."

"Well, it don't seem right somehow, but I'm grateful for the hand and no mistake." He turned his attention to the gentlemen. "I don't think we were blown too much off course. Won't be able to tell for certain until the clouds clear a bit more and we can get a proper reading."

Lord Danbury had been lamenting the delay this storm would cause. At the news, his dour expression lightened and he straightened. "If that's true, it's a credit to your skill. I'm obliged to you, sir, for coming to tell me."

Campbell nodded. "Best be getting back to the quarterdeck. These seas are still a mite rougher than I'd like, and I don't want to be away too long."

"It's amazing we've survived—a downright miracle if we have not been blown weeks off course," Danbury said.

"A miracle?" Harting countered with an ironic smile. "You are attributing our survival to the work of a deity, Danbury?"

"Perhaps I am."

Harting raised his eyebrows.

Lydia looked up from her task. "Do you believe in God, then, Lord Danbury? A God who works miracles?"

Lord Danbury opened another cabinet. "My father did."

"Perhaps, then, if God's gracing us with the miraculous," Harting tossed a waterlogged book at Danbury and grinned wickedly, "we should be asking the Almighty for another miracle—that we might find the murderer."

Lydia glanced at him, but she wasn't sure from his even tone whether he was speaking in jest. Thoughtful, she resumed her work.

* * *

Lord Danbury steadied Lydia as they emerged from the greater cabin and made their way up on deck for a breath of air. Sails hung in limp, disheartened shreds and the rigging had been snarled into hopeless confusion. Most of the crew was aloft, attempting repairs. Everything on deck and much of the below decks was a sodden, splintered mess. As she viewed the chaos, Lydia decided that his Lordship was correct. It was a miracle they had survived. She said nothing until they had completed the circuit. "Surely God spared us." Awe thinned her voice.

"Nonsense, my dear." Dr Marshall's hearty hail as he joined them made Lydia start. "What saved us last night was solid heart of oak, masterful engineering, and judicious seamanship. God sent the storm, not the salvation."

Danbury took advantage of his grip on her arm to steer her down the ladderway and into the greater cabin. He most certainly did not wish her to challenge the doctor.

The scent of a warm meal nearly tempted her into silence, but she refused to be put off so easily. As the doctor settled in across from her she spoke. "You have an unusual view of God, sir."

"A more realistic view I am afraid, my dear."

"Reminiscent of the ancient Romans whose gods toyed with

mankind and were motivated by greed and spite." Lydia forced a smile as she placed a napkin in her lap and changed the subject. "I'm pleased to see you are well, Doctor."

"Yes, perfectly, thank you."

The conversation drifted to the effects of the storm on the ship as the captain claimed his seat.

Just twelve hours before, she had been convinced of her imminent demise, and now she was chatting about the events over a pleasant meal. Although, perhaps not everyone on the ship had been so lucky? She set aside her fork.

"Did the storm cause any casualties, Doctor?"

"A handful—the bruises and broken limbs usual in such an event."

"I should have thought sooner, and come to assist you. Perhaps I can help after lunch?"

"I will count on it. Your assistance will be most welcome. My loblolly boy was one of those injured. A trifling matter of a broken arm and wrenched shoulder, but it does make him abominably slow."

"I didn't realize you had much experience at sea," Lord Danbury said.

"I was pressed as a surgeon's mate many years ago when I was quite young. My mother paid the price for my release, so it did not last long."

"Then you are well acquainted with seafaring life."

"Well enough. It at least provides opportunities for an enterprising botanist. There are always exotic locales to be explored." The doctor accepted another portion of plum duff from the captain.

After dinner the doctor accordingly offered his elbow and Lydia took it. "Excuse us, gentlemen." She nodded to the others at the table.

The dank orlop deck was fetid and dark. Below the water line, the only light came from smoky lanterns. As ever when she came to this part of the ship, Lydia breathed shallowly, forcing herself not to cover her mouth and nose with a handkerchief. If mere night air was dangerous, how did any patient survive this atmosphere?

His medical equipment encompassed a handful of hammocks, an apothecary chest and a mixing table. The surgeon's cockpit was to the fore. She had glanced at the tools it held only once and had no desire to do so again.

"Where ought I to start?"

"A drop, please?" A young seaman held up a horny palm.

Marshall moved forward. "Normally a job for my loblolly boy." He gestured at a figure in the last hammock. "He came to us the day before the storm. One of the most typical wounds you'll see on board ship. An arm broken when it was caught in a block and tackle."

Lydia reached out a staying hand. "I can do it."

She worked throughout the afternoon wiping brows, dispensing gruel into hungry mouths, and offering reassurances.

For the hundredth time a voice croaked for her attention, requesting water. Lydia lowered the dipper into the hogshead and, careful not to spill, approached the sailor. His lips were cracked. Perspiration stood out on a brow that looked pallid beneath a heavy tan. With obvious effort he raised himself on one elbow. His other arm had been broken and was bound tightly to his chest.

Lydia lifted the dipper to his mouth and he drank deeply.

"Thank you kindly." He fell back with a grunt of pain.

"Certainly." He looked younger than she. Unable to resist the impulse, Lydia smoothed the damp hair back from his forehead. She yanked her hand back. He was burning up with fever.

Biting her lip, she carefully unwrapped his bandages to reveal his injured arm. A foul odour soured the air and made Lydia gasp. The wound was livid, and swollen to bursting with infection.

"Doctor."

"Yes, Miss Garrett?" He did not look up from the powder he was mixing.

"I believe this young man needs your assistance." Lydia fought to keep the welling panic from her voice. He was seriously ill, or she was Josephine Bonaparte. "Right now."

At that, the doctor did raise his head. "What can I do for you, Larsen?"

"I'm all right, sir. No need for a fuss."

Marshall raised his glance to Lydia's. She nodded minutely.

"He feels quite warm to me. Perhaps you could re-evaluate his arm?"

Dr Marshall placed a hand on the man's brow. Frowning, he pulled his watch from his waistcoat pocket, and grasped the man's wrist. Then he lifted the dressing and scowled. "Ah, I see. A preparation of febrifuge would answer, to begin with." His voice was low, a conversation with himself rather than his breathless audience. Marshall drifted away. Lydia glanced from the retreating form to the sailor and pulled a stool closer to the sailor's hammock.

A thin white line ringed the sailor's mouth where he had compressed his lips tightly together. "Am I going to die, Miss?"

Lydia swallowed. Her eyes and throat stung. False reassurance hovered on her lips, but she could not bring herself to utter the platitudes. "I don't know."

He blinked rapidly and turned his face from her.

"I do know that my father—he was a vicar—didn't fear death. To him it was the beginning of another adventure. But Dr Marshall and I will do everything in our power to ensure that you don't go on that adventure just yet."

CHAPTER 18

Through the open portholes, Marcus caught the sound of a shout ringing from the tops, immediately followed by the pounding of feet. He set aside his book, anticipation rising in his belly. The talk around the table stilled. A moment later a young man swung into the greater cabin. He whipped off his hat and bobbed his head in greeting. "Mr Cabot's compliments, sir, and land has been sighted. Two points to larboard."

Danbury was first out of the door, flinging his napkin to the table and standing so precipitately that his chair toppled back with a thud. The rest followed in close succession.

On deck, an obliging sailor pointed him in the right direction, and Marcus raised his glass. Far in the distance, he made out a tiny green speck dotting the horizon.

Lydia turned to Lord Danbury. "That's Mahe?"

"Yes, I think so." Danbury's eyes were bright. "Now we will see." He rubbed his hands together and laughed, a hearty sound that drew others to join him.

Marcus raised his glass again and eyed the island. He had never seen a more welcome sight. And yet he couldn't shake the sense that danger awaited them on Mahe. He well knew the ruthlessness of murderers. Once someone had killed to obtain a goal, it became easier to do so again. The people they were dealing with had killed at least twice.

Danbury and Miss Garrett were too naive. During their voyage, Marcus had come to admire Danbury's tenacity, intelligence, and enthusiasm, but the earl didn't truly appreciate the risks they ran. How could he? He'd never come face to face with men such as they now sought to trap. He was apt to be rash and it would take a great deal of effort to compel him to caution.

They stayed on deck watching the green speck transform itself into a jewel of an island as they drew closer. All the time he was considering what challenges might await.

* * *

Legacy drew into Mahe's natural harbour as the sun set. The place had attracted sailors for hundreds of years. Anthony drank in the view as if it were an intoxicating vintage. Beautiful beaches gave way to a series of verdant mountains. Huge granite boulders jutted from the hills, providing rugged contrast to the lush greenness that predominated. The shallower water became a hue Anthony had never seen before in nature, though he had heard it described—a brilliant, luminous Prussian green. A mixture, it seemed, of the vibrant blue of the sky and the green of the island itself. Every hue and shade seemed more vivid than the colours of England.

A small village had grown beside the harbour since *Centaur*'s crew had put in so long ago. It wasn't much to look at. A handful of ramshackle shanties clustered along the shore. They looked as if they provided little in the way of shade, much less shelter. The inhabitants apparently excelled at scavenging; the shacks looked as though they had been formed mainly from bits of shipwrecked vessels. Scant effort had been made to tame the natural vegetation, resulting in a riotous profusion of greenery that almost overran some of the structures.

Captain Campbell approached and Anthony turned to meet him. "Captain, you've done splendidly. I can practically feel the sand underfoot already."

"Aye, my Lord. I've no doubt you're champing at the bit to set ashore. But I counsel you to wait until morning. The moon's waning and it'll be nigh impossible to accomplish anything before dawn."

He'd waited long enough. Anthony opened his mouth to say so, but Mr Cabot appeared at his shoulder. "There's less than an hour's worth of daylight. By the time we lowered the boats and rowed ashore you'd be compelled to return to the ship."

Harting shrugged as eloquently as a Frenchman.

Anthony sighed, but his better sense prevailed. "We will leave at first light, no matter who is or is not prepared to depart." He shot a withering glance across Harting's bow.

Thus, in the pearly grey prelude to dawn he rose and dressed. Miss Garrett found him pacing the foredeck and annoying the watch.

"Good morning, my Lord."

"Good morning. I trust you slept well."

"I'm afraid that I did not."

Anthony ripped his gaze from the beckoning shore to look at her more closely. "Oh?"

"Too unsettled." She waved a hand towards the island. "I suspect I wasn't the only one who tossed and turned during the night."

Anthony managed to stop pacing, and smiled. "My dear young lady, you are too perceptive by half."

"Perhaps breakfast would make the wait more bearable?"

Anthony raised an eyebrow. At the moment he had less desire to eat than to clap a bucket on his head. What he wanted was to get on that island. He was giddy with the nearness of their goal. Perhaps he could swim for it? He leaned over the rail slightly. The water was so clear he could see straight to the bottom. It might not be a bad idea at all.

"My Lord?" Miss Garrett placed a hand on his sleeve. "You'll need your strength if we are to be climbing all over Mahé in search of the throne." She offered a sweet smile.

The pleasure of her company, without Harting's eternal presence, might be worth the delay. She was looking particularly well. The warmth of the day and the flush of excitement had brought pink to her cheeks and a sparkle to her eyes. Yes, a few more minutes wouldn't really be a delay at all.

CHAPTER 19

D aybreak found Lydia watching a launch being lowered into the water. Lord Danbury and Lord Harting climbed down the rope ladder while the seamen rigged the boatswain's seat to lower Lydia to the gig. Capable hands held the sling, but repetition had not robbed the procedure of its power to terrorize her.

If only she could climb the ladder like the men. At least the ladder was in no danger of plummeting into the sea. She did not breathe deeply until she landed safely in the gig, and the sling had been hauled back up to the deck.

The oarsmen bent their backs with a good will, and it took only a few moments to reach shore. Up close, Lydia found the island even more charming. Lively little birds darted amongst the foliage and trilled to one another. Small, creamy-white flowers with buttery centres adorned many of the trees, and their sweet smell wafted on the air.

Lord Danbury hopped from the gig as the bottom ground up against sand. With a gentlemanly gesture he turned and reached to swing Lydia down from the boat, his hands warm and strong on her waist.

A little thrill swirled through her—probably the effect of the sudden motion. Or perhaps the delight of being on solid ground once more. She could not afford for the cause to lie in any other quarter. Not given their respective positions. Nor could she afford to believe that his hands had lingered longer than strictly necessary.

Holding her skirts clear of the water she waded the last few steps to firmer sand. Beside her, Lord Danbury staggered.

"This ground is very unsteady."

Harting too swayed almost drunkenly. Nor was Lydia unaffected. The earth to which they had been returned seemed very different from that which they had left.

"Never fear. It is simply the effect of having been so long at sea. You shall regain your land legs as quickly as you gained your sea legs." Dr Marshall seemed to note Lydia's gaze on the flowers. He plucked a particularly beautiful specimen. "They're called frangipani."

"They're lovely." Lydia accepted the blossom he extended to her, and held it to her nose, inhaling deeply.

Lord Danbury spread his arms to take in the view. "Everything seems brighter somehow." He turned to Lydia, his jaw set, a gleam in his eye. "We will capture the murderer, and we will obtain redress." His tone turned savage at this last, a strange counterpoint to the beauty of the island.

"Oh?" said Harting. "I pray you, my friend, do not forget that larger things are at stake than your desire for revenge."

Lord Danbury seemed to tuck his feelings back in as swiftly as if they were a handkerchief in his pocket. "No, of course not."

"I'm glad to hear you say it," said Harting.

Danbury smiled grimly, turning back to the business at hand. "Let's see what the inhabitants of this handsome spot can tell us."

Suddenly cold, as if she'd been tossed in an icehouse, Lydia accepted the arm he extended to her. Rage lurked beneath Lord Danbury's affability. Perhaps he meant to do more than return the killer to London for a trial. More than prevent Bonaparte's wicked schemes.

A white man with a grizzled beard sat outside the front door of the nearest shack. Tilted back in a chair with his feet off the ground, he watched their approach between lazy puffs on his pipe.

"*Bonjour, monsieur,*" Lord Danbury hailed him.

"Mornin'," the man said with a gruff nod.

Danbury blinked twice. "You're English."

"So are you."

"I believed Mahe to be inhabited by French plantation owners."

"So it is, so it is. But we've a few stout Englishmen among these frog eaters."

"I am glad to hear it. It's always good to come upon an Englishman abroad," Danbury said.

"Aye, it's good to hear an English voice. What brings you fine folks to Établissement?"

"Établissement?"

"That's the fancy name for this here village." The old man waved a hand at the handful of houses.

"Ah, well. Can you tell me if any ships have put in recently?"

"No, sir. We haven't had any visitors for nigh on three months." He plucked the pipe from his mouth and scratched a grizzled chin. "There a reason you're asking?"

"We're on a mission, my friend, and we need help from someone who is familiar with this island."

The man returned the front legs of his chair to the earth with a thump, and stood, extending his hand. "Name's Jeremiah Long. I've lived here for twelve years. I guess I know the place 'bout as good as anyone."

"Pleased to meet you. I am the Earl of Danbury; this is the Honourable Marcus Harting, and Miss Garrett." Lydia nodded politely, but both she and Harting remained silent, allowing Lord Danbury to maintain the lead in the conversation. "I believe we should like to discuss matters with you, Mr Long."

"There's no sense in letting everyone in town know your business." He motioned them into the shade of what turned out to be a shop.

The tiny mercantile was nearly barren. A handful of assorted tins, boxes and bags looked as if they had been spread out to maximize their effect on potential customers. Instead the display ended up looking even more meagre.

Long gave an apologetic wave at the contents of his shelves. "Haven't had any ships to trade with recently."

"Are there many caves on this island?" Lord Danbury asked when they had shuffled into the cramped space.

"There's a goodly number."

"Is there plenty of fresh water, even in the mountains?"

Long's brow furrowed. He was obviously becoming curious, but he answered readily enough. "Oh, aye, plenty of good water to be had if you knows where to look."

"Is the terrain difficult to negotiate?"

"Well, some of it's pretty steep going. There's a few trails— mostly to the spice plantations. The rainy season is nigh upon us, and sometimes the mountains are hid by clouds for days at a time. It can be dangerous going."

"I see." Lord Danbury nodded thoughtfully. After a moment's silence he nodded once more, decisively. "Mr Long, I'd like to hire you to be our guide. We're looking for a fairly large cave somewhere on this island. We'll require help to find food and water and someone to make sure we don't become lost or walk off the edge of the mountain."

"What's this all about? There's legends of pirate treasure being hidden on this island. Is that what you're after?"

"No. My father and his crew visited Mahe years ago. They weren't pirates, but when he died, I learned he left something here which must needs be retrieved." Lord Danbury's answer, though vague, was enticing.

Lydia shot a sideways glance at Lord Danbury. They had discussed the plan and Danbury hoped that if their enemies appeared, they would hear gossip of the search, and it would provoke them to make a move. But was it wise to bring someone they didn't know into their confidence so quickly? What if—Lydia choked the thought off before it could go any further. She had to stop worrying about events as if they were knots she could untie. But what if the spy did come?

CHAPTER 19

* * *

Miss Garrett and Harting stepped back into the sun, leaving Anthony to haggle with Mr Long. He snorted indelicately at the price Long demanded. "Highway robbery, and you well know it."

"A man has to live," Long shrugged.

Anthony offered him a third of his original price, and Long pretended to be shocked. In the end they agreed upon half his first demand. As the bargaining concluded, Long stuck his head through the hole in the wall which served as a window.

"Danielle."

A young woman turned from where she had been hanging laundry to dry on bushes behind the store. She was quite lovely, with golden hair that gleamed in the sun and a lithe figure.

Long gestured at the young woman with his chin. "My wife. French, but she speaks fair English."

Danielle presented herself at the window. She looked from her husband to Anthony and back again. Closer up, her eyes were a match for the sea surrounding Mahe.

"Get in here and help me, girl. I'm taking these folks up into the mountains and we're going to need supplies."

"*Qu'est-ce que c'est?*"

Long cut her off. "Get on in here." He turned to Anthony. "You want her to come? She was raised here, and knows Mahe like nobody."

"We can use all the expertise we can get."

"Expertise!" Long snorted a laugh that made it clear he considered that too high-flown a term to describe his wife. "That's a good one, milord." Anthony had the distinct impression that had he been anything less than an earl, Long would have slapped him on the back.

Leaving the couple to begin their preparations, Anthony stepped outside to join Harting and Miss Garrett. The bright tropical sunlight blinded him, and it took a moment to spy them. They stood conversing with a pair of men at the far end of the dirt path that constituted the sum total of the main street. Anthony walked towards them, feeling conspicuous as he ran the gauntlet of stares from the few individuals he passed. The gazes were not hostile, but neither were they friendly.

"Ah," Harting said as he approached. It was his turn to perform introductions. "Danbury, this is Monsieur Paul Laurent and Monsieur Pierre-Louis Poiret."

Anthony guessed they were French noblemen dispossessed by the revolution. Monsieur Laurent—a tall, spare man with a balding pate and skin turned nut-brown by the sun—looked at the world down a long, narrow nose. Although slightly shabby now, his clothes had once been of the highest quality.

A good deal younger, Monsieur Poiret appeared to Anthony to be eighteen or nineteen. While not especially good-looking, he held himself erect and managed to convey friendly interest by the tilt of his head and a welcoming smile.

"I am very pleased to meet you." Monsieur Poiret extended a hand to shake in the English manner.

"A pleasure."

"We've been telling these gentlemen about your father's legacy. They were suggesting some areas we ought to search," Miss Garrett said.

"Oh, yes?" A great, boiling bellow welled up in Anthony's chest. He wanted to issue his challenge in a shout, to dare the murderers to come for him. When he had them in his grasp…

"Yes, your—" Monsieur Laurent looked between Anthony and Miss Garrett and paused, patently unsure what relationship existed between them. He backtracked. "Miss Garrett 'as been telling us a fascinating story. I did not know there were caves 'ere, but I 'ave not lived 'ere for too long."

"Do you not recall the runaway slave? Did they not catch him in a cave? I am sure I heard something," Poiret said.

"Ah, *oui*, that is true," Monsieur Laurent adjusted his cuffs awkwardly.

"You have much work in front of you if you do not know where this cave might be. How long do you think it will take you to complete this task you have set yourself?" Pierre-Louis asked.

"It doesn't matter. I will stay as long as necessary and do whatever it takes to find it."

"I admire your persistence, monsieur. Family is most important. The memory of one's parents ought to be honoured." A shadow passed over Poiret's features and drowned out the merry light of his eyes. Monsieur Laurent gripped the young man's arm. "It 'as been a great pleasure to meet you, but we must be getting back to the plantation. I am sure you will understand." With a nod of farewell he whisked his friend away.

* * *

Lord Danbury led the way back to the beach. The crew had been ferrying supplies ashore. Everything from tarpaulins and rope to cookware and a medicine chest was piled on the sand. Looking at the mountain of boxes and crates, Lydia could not imagine they were missing so much as a thimble.

Together she and the gentlemen took an inventory of the supplies, then ate a cold luncheon brought over from the ship. The sun climbed ever higher in the sky, making the beach a hazy inferno.

Lydia dipped her handkerchief in the surf and dabbed at her face. The gentlemen looked even more miserable than she in their coats, waistcoats, cravats and shirts. At least there was a slight breeze coming off the water.

Dr Marshall trooped past in shirtsleeves, weighted down by a number of baskets, clay jars, even a hatchet and a large musket.

Harting turned to address him. "Are you going collecting, Doctor?"

He halted and returned to their party, though his eyes seemed fixed on the lush greenery of the forest. "Yes, there are some amazing specimens on this island. This place must be unknown to natural philosophers. I've already found a species of coconut that I believe is distinct." He paused and looked at his audience. "Gentlemen, the heat will drive you mad if you remain in that get-up. For heaven's sake, take off those heavy things. You're dressed for England, not the tropics."

"Yes, Doctor. You're right." Lord Danbury gave way without even a token protest.

"If my cronies could see me now." Harting grinned blissfully as he tore off his jacket.

Lydia turned away discreetly to see their valets looking stricken as they raced across the sand to collect the discarded outer garments.

"They'd be shocked at your bad form, I'm sure." Danbury rolled up his shirtsleeves and mopped his brow.

With a farewell nod, Dr Marshall headed into the jungle.

"Shocked? They would probably never speak to me again. In fact, they would make a pact to cut me off if I presumed to approach them." Harting didn't sound especially distressed at the notion.

"Why do you maintain friendships with people of such little depth?" Lydia asked.

"They're not so bad as all that, and we do have a shared history," Harting shrugged.

"Yet there is more to you than they could ever appreciate." Lydia again wetted her handkerchief and dabbed at her face.

Danbury followed her example. "Precisely my feeling. For instance, how did you come to be an intelligence agent?"

"That is a long story—one I am not at liberty to share." Harting seemed to constrict, shrinking in on himself ever so slightly as if consolidating his power should he need to spring.

Lydia looked away towards the ship. She hadn't even asked the question and yet felt as if she had been snubbed. How like Harting to demand unwavering faith and yet mistrust everyone so completely.

"I must admit that when you first revealed yourself I didn't—" Danbury trailed off as if regretting that he'd spoken.

Harting waved away the offence. "You'd be amazed at how effective it is to dress as a dandy. People underestimate me. They say things they shouldn't. I've cultivated the image since becoming an agent."

"Now we're getting to it," Danbury guffawed. "You're hiding behind that silly exterior in the hope that I will let something incriminating slip."

"I would deny it, but you've caught me out." Harting held his hands up in mock surrender.

Lydia summoned a feeble smile, but again turned her gaze towards the ship. Danbury was far closer to the truth than he realized. From the corner of her eye she saw him glance her way and hoped that he'd attribute her red face to the bite of the sun.

"Enough about me." Harting motioned down the shore. "Why don't we explore? There's no great rush to get back to the ship."

Turning the conversation to inconsequential matters, Lydia and Danbury joined him. The sun glared at them, hot and vivid; only the cooling ocean breeze saved the beach from feeling entirely like a furnace. Lydia gaped at giant boulders strewn along the beach, and enormous palm trees. So different from England; God must surely have an infinite well of creativity to have devised all this.

Her hair kept slipping free of its bonds, as wilful and desirous of a game as a child. Baking in the sun, she grimaced. She was sure to return home with spots not only on her reputation, but also on her skin. They walked and walked, each new vantage point providing some new wonder to be examined and collected. When at last they turned back, Lydia considered removing her half-boots to let the water lap at her feet. But she discarded the notion. She might have no reputation, but that didn't mean she had to act like it. Her own sense of modesty dictated against such a display among gentlemen.

The sun bid its adieu in fiery streaks of brilliance. Danbury posted guards to protect the supplies, and the adventurers returned to *Legacy* for one more night aboard ship.

Lydia eyed Lord Danbury. He seemed to be bearing up well, though obviously restless to make a start. He was a good man, an honourable man. But had his father's murder changed him?

What had he been like before he had been seized by this single-minded determination to track the murderer? A tiny sigh escaped her. It made no difference. After this affair, her usefulness and his obligation would be at an end. She would return to her own world. She obviously had no part or parcel with the world of the *haute ton* that the gentlemen inhabited.

She smoothed her skirts. Until that time, Mr Wolfe deserved justice as surely as the former Lord Danbury. She would see that he received his due.

* * *

Morning light found the party headed north along a narrow dirt path that circled the island. In addition to the Longs and the gentlemen's valets, a complement of three sailors and Mr Cabot, the first officer, joined the excursion.

The heat and humidity grew oppressive when they left the beach for the forest. Although sheltered from the sun by the dense foliage, the greenery also served to extinguish any hint of a breeze. Danbury and Harting had abandoned sartorial elegance in favour of practicality. They wore lightweight cotton shirts, buckskin breeches, and sturdy riding boots reaching to the knee.

Lydia was dressed in a simple muslin gown with short sleeves and a single petticoat. Comfortable leather half-boots protected her feet. She tied her hair back, but damp tendrils kept escaping into her eyes. Danielle Long wrapped a scarf about her hair in cunning fashion, keeping it neatly bound up and off her neck. But at Lydia's inquiry into how it was done, she made a face as if she did not understand the request and turned her back.

The trail became increasingly steep and narrow until they came to a cotton plantation. Here the trail petered out altogether.

Mr Long hailed the house, and asked the owner for permission to cross his land. The formality might have been overlooked, but Lord Danbury felt it wisest to foster whatever goodwill was available. The owner granted his permission willingly enough, but eyed the group speculatively as they passed. His slaves also paused to watch them as they trooped along. Lydia adjusted the knapsack on her shoulder and kept her gaze trained on the path. In single file, they must have looked as if they were on parade. Or perhaps a line of convicts headed for the prison hulks.

The way grew increasingly steep, slowing their pace. Lydia found a stout branch to use as a walking stick to make the climbing easier. She divided her attention between keeping an eye on the thick undergrowth that snatched and plucked at her feet, and looking for a cave. It didn't work very well: she tripped several times.

She wasn't the only one. Rest stops came with increasing frequency as the press of the humidity sought to suffocate them. She sat gasping and gaping, mouth as wide as a frog's as she tried to find some oxygen in the soup that masqueraded as air. An almost desperate yearning to return to *Legacy*'s breezy deck plucked at her resolve, fraying it one thread at a time.

All she had to do was turn around. As long as she went downhill she would eventually reach the beach and she would just follow that around until she came to the ship. Instead, sticky with sweat and slightly dizzy, she leaned into her walking stick and climbed.

They fanned out to cover the terrain as thoroughly as possible. Danielle Long took the position in the middle, leading the little donkeys, which were tied together in a line like the camels of a caravan. Her husband brought up the rear to make sure no one strayed or came to grief on the rougher terrain.

Here in the middle of the thick jungle, Mahe seemed to have grown. All at once their task had ballooned out of all proportion. Buoyant confidence evaporated with the realization of how difficult their job might prove. They had sailed thousands of miles to get here, but this island, only thirteen miles by seven, might defeat them.

CHAPTER 20

Luncheon provided an excuse to stop for a time. In spite of the effort hiking required, Anthony could not summon an appetite. Worry clogged his throat, making eating difficult. Might he have simply led the French to the prize they sought? He could not bring himself to consider what he would do if they beat him to the throne and escaped.

He hadn't precisely believed the task would be easy, but now, in the middle of the thick green maze of a forest, the challenge seemed not simply difficult, but impossible.

Energy only slightly renewed by the meal, he stood. It was time to move on. They climbed ever higher up the side of the mountain. Huge granite boulders littered their path, and they had to detour frequently.

Spirits at low ebb, Anthony broke from the forest cover into a clearing. Below him the island spread her green skirts and the sea lapped at her toes. With the exception of the Longs, the group stopped as one, staring in awe at the beauty of the scene. In the open space the breeze reached them again. Anthony raised his face to it gratefully. The sun hung suspended near the horizon. He watched as it settled into the sea, erupting in a blazing glory of gold and ginger and crimson.

"We'll camp here tonight," Anthony called to Long, who had turned to wait on them. "Twilight's coming on and we ought to set up camp."

Shrugging, Long dropped his knapsack. A general bustle ensued as the donkeys were unloaded, and they set about pitching the tents.

Long disappeared, returning some time later with a bunch of yellow fruit shaped like crescent moons. He showed them how to peel back the thick rind and expose a pale, firm flesh inside. He glanced at Harting, who cocked his head, and then at Miss Garrett, but she already had a bite in her mouth.

When she smiled Anthony took a tentative bite. The smooth, sweet fruit took him by surprise. "What are these called?"

"I learned of 'em in Guinea when I was a boatswain's mate. They called fruit like this *bannann*, so that's what I call 'em."

"It's delicious." Anthony devoured his and accepted another.

"Thought you folks might like 'em." Long ducked his head and turned away to other business. A smile tugged up the corners of his mouth, though he seemed to be trying to push it back down. The old fellow seemed pleased that they had liked his offering.

"Miss Garrett, would you be willing to assist me with some notes?"

Agreeable as always, she pulled out a quarto volume and a stub of pencil. They sat a little apart, overlooking the sea while supper was prepared. He dictated his observations of the day's hike, and she dutifully captured the comments. They needed to keep careful track of the ground they had covered to avoid backtracking.

Anthony paused to watch as the sun embraced the sea at the edge of the horizon. Something tight and hard constricted his heart and throat at the same time. He turned his back on the view. He must concentrate on the task at hand. Once he had set matters right, then he could return to his normal life. He would find a young woman to court and settle down to the responsibilities of a landlord.

Firelight framed Miss Garrett's hair in radiance. Bent over her notebook she looked like a Da Vinci Madonna complete with golden glow. A questioning smile bowed her lips as she glanced up at him expectantly.

He scrabbled for something to say. "It was good of you to offer your services in this way. I don't believe I've thanked you properly."

"Think no more on it. I'm pleased to help in any way I can."

"I should find some means of thanking you."

"My Lord, the only thanks I desire is the satisfaction of seeing my cousin's murderer brought to justice."

"Do you still believe we might succeed?"

She met his scrutiny with a limpid gaze that seemed to pierce through the shadow of his own doubt. "I'm convinced of it."

"I'm rather glad that you accompanied the expedition. I wondered if it was wise, but you have been a most pleasing travelling companion. Never complaining." It sounded cold and flat, an accolade to be awarded a servant. But then he could hardly say that she had made him forget all about his vow to find a proper young lady to court.

"Thank you, my Lord."

"Let us leave this for now. Supper should be ready any moment."

She grinned at him and the Madonna vanished to be replaced by a pixie. "I'm glad you suggested it. I am near to perishing from hunger."

Anthony's natural sanguinity resurfaced. He would put it all right. One thing at a time. All it required was effort and perseverance.

* * *

It had been a long while since Marcus had exerted so much physical effort. He lolled against a rock, utterly spent.

His valet, Charles, sniffed. "Would you like a shave, my Lord?"

Marcus acquiesced immediately. He might be willing to forgo the formality of jacket and waistcoat for the rigours of the climate, but he had no intention of becoming a complete barbarian.

Charles nudged him awake when the meal was announced. Marcus rubbed his cheeks and yawned. *God grant that they find the dashed throne soon.*

He joined the party around the campfire, but conversation lagged, dwindling into nothing once the food had been consumed.

One by one the group drifted to their tents. Mahe's tropical heat had proved a cruel master, draining the energy from the party as if they had been forced through an enormous sieve.

The successive days blurred into a haze of effort and exhaustion. They spent their time in endless trudging up and down, their progress dismally slow. The heat surrounded Marcus like wet woollen blankets, smotheringly thick. To add to the misery, biting insects plagued the party.

A number of small caves were found, each causing a thrill, each causing a delay. The entire group clustered expectantly around these holes in the ground. Most had entrances too small to have allowed the throne passage inside. Even so, in every instance Danbury insisted on a torch, and explored the dank recess as completely as possible. Sometimes this required only a cursory glance. Other times the process took much longer. Each time, Marcus wanted to throttle him.

With each disappointment, Danbury would slump, then breathe deeply and square his shoulders. He ate little and grew hollow-eyed and fractious. Marcus could hardly say any more whether he wanted to hear the cry of discovery or not. Perhaps it had all been a mare's nest and the traitor remained in London sowing the seeds of further treachery.

* * *

On the fourth day of searching, Lydia woke and crawled reluctantly from her tent to discover the campsite shrouded in a heavy fog. She could see no more than five or six feet in front of her. The damp chill felt almost shocking after the sweltering heat they had been enduring. A welcome change.

Amidst much waving of arms and stalking about, Lord Danbury conferred with Long, but finally conceded that it would be too dangerous to continue the search with the blanketing haze in place. Mid morning the fog birthed a steady downpour that saturated everything in sight. The rain wasn't especially cold, but made it impossible to keep a fire going, and with the sun banished by the clouds, the atmosphere grew distinctly cool.

Lydia would never have expected to wish for a return of the glare of the sun, but as she ate a cold lunch of dried fish and fruit, she did. Although at least the rain had driven off the cursed mosquitoes. She scratched discreetly at one of the numerous red welts on her skin.

"Are you regretting that you came?" Lord Danbury settled beside her.

"Yes." She mock scowled. "But I won't be when we find the throne and catch the murderer."

"I am in perfect agreement." He grinned. Rivulets of water streamed from his hat. "Who would have thought such a beautiful place could be so utterly miserable?" He hunched his shoulders inside his coat—to little effect, Lydia guessed, since the coat was soaked through like everything else.

"At least someone looks more miserable than you or I." Danbury motioned with his chin towards the two valets who crouched beneath a stand of *bannann* leaves. The poor men looked like waterlogged rats. Lydia raised a hand to hide a grin.

"Poor James." She looked from Danbury to the valet and back again, smiling impishly. "Actually there is little to choose between you."

Cocking an eyebrow, Danbury put on a show of hauteur. "Madam, I will have you know that the drowned monkey look is the height of fashion this season."

"Then it is a pity there are no marriageable young misses about to see you in such sartorial splendour."

"I'm certain they would fight over me given the chance." Danbury struck a heroic pose, then howled as the movement dumped water from his hat brim down his collar.

Lydia laughed in earnest and Danbury joined her.

Evening descended before the rain wore itself out and moved on. Clothing, blankets, and other sodden supplies were spread out on nearby shrubbery and tree branches to dry. With all the firewood soaked, they could not get a fire lit to dry things and warm themselves. Lydia resigned herself to spending a restless night in damp clothing.

She rose early, waiting on the sun to return and warm her—resolving not to grumble about the heat ever again. When dawn finally broke, she lifted her face to the light, luxuriating in the warmth. With a grimace, she noted how dark her skin had grown in the previous days.

An image of her mother flitted through her mind. The daughter of an earl—reared in a home where such things as complexion were of paramount interest.

In spite of everything, Lydia hoped—believed—that her mother would not have reviled her choices. She might not appear much of a lady, but she had pursued the course she felt most honourable. If Lydia could retain the regard of only one person in the world, it ought to be her own. At least that was the lesson her parents had taught her. It had kept her in good stead thus far. Pray God she would not regret the decision.

Lydia whirled at the sound of a greeting. Focused on fond memories of her mother, Danielle Long's approach had gone unheeded. Lydia put a hand to her heart as if to slow it. She barely avoided narrowing her eyes. What did the woman want? She had gone out of her way, more than once, to snub Lydia. "I'm sorry, Danielle—you startled me."

"*Je suis déso*—I apologize, Miss Garrett," Danielle said. Her hesitant English had a stiff formality about it, making her sound older.

Lydia waited a moment for the woman to continue, but she stood mute. "Is there something I can do for you?"

"We approach *Le Jardin du Roi*. It is the plantation of Pierre-Louis Poiret. He is a most pleasant man."

"We met Monsieur Poiret in the village," said Lydia. "He did seem quite pleasant."

"There is a stream with a…" Danielle hesitated, making a downward motion with her hands. "A water drop?"

"A waterfall?"

"*Oui*, a waterfall. I think perhaps Monsieur Poiret would not mind if we wash there. You will to speak to Lord Danbury of this?"

"I shall be delighted. I would love a good wash."

"*Oui*, it is a good place. I go there as a child before Monsieur Poiret came."

Lydia mentioned the matter to Lord Danbury as they ate breakfast. Having lost the previous day to rain, he balked. But when his valet, James, added a rather acerbic opinion on the subject of clean linen, the decision all but made itself.

Mr Long carried a note to the plantation from Lord Danbury, while Danielle stayed behind to lead the group. Shortly after midday they came to a stream. Danielle followed the skipping water for a way until it plunged abruptly into a ravine some thirty feet below.

Lydia helped Danielle hand out lunch. *Bannann* in hand, Lydia peered over the edge of the ravine into the swirling pool below and shivered in anticipation. Despite her resolution of the night, the wilting power of the sun had renewed her longing for anything cool. The prospect of a wash in the crisp, clear water set her skin tingling with the promise of relief.

Jeremiah rejoined the party and handed Lord Danbury a note. Every conversation around the small camp trailed off, and an expectant silence hung in the air.

"He is delighted that we should desire to use his waterfall, and begs we visit his home and stay with him for the night," Danbury said. He passed the note to Lydia. She hid a smile at the florid language of the missive.

The gentlemen gallantly insisted that Lydia and Danielle should avail themselves of the waterfall's delights first. Toting knapsacks full of washing, they made their way down the hillside to the ravine floor. The steepness of the climb prevented Lydia from truly taking in the view until she reached the relatively level ground at the base. Pausing to wipe the perspiration from her face, she gazed about in awe. The beauty of the place made her heart skip as if it were doing a country dance.

Truly, God's creation was wondrous. Sunlight danced among the spray creating a multitude of brilliant rainbows. Sweetly scented flowers proliferated, perfuming the air. Danielle pointed out frangipani, ylang-ylang, jasmine, and even vanilla orchids.

Stripping down to her shift, Lydia entered the water. She scrubbed her laundry against a large rock with a piece of lye soap. She scraped her fingers against the stone until her knuckles were raw. It didn't matter. The prospect of soft, clean cotton against her skin, rather than material turned stiff and scratchy by filth and perspiration, outweighed other concerns.

The sun stared down as if taking an interest in their work and it would have been unbearably hot if she were not crouched in the water at the edge the pool. She beat the garments against the rocks and rinsed them, then spread them on the nearby bushes to dry.

Returning to the water, she waded in. A delightful shiver ran up her spine as the cool water embraced her, caressing and cosseting, washing away all signs of exertion. She sighed and allowed herself to be drawn deeper.

Her foot slipped on a slick rock and she went under. Flailing and splashing, she rose to the surface. One precious gasp of air but her feet could find no purchase. She sank again. Panic edged in on her. She sucked in water. A vision of the slick, mossy walls of the vicarage well spiraled from her memory and seared itself against her closed eyelids. She might have been six again.

A hand gripped hers and hauled her up. Her thrashing feet found the bottom and the darkness receded. Her head broke the surface and she coughed and sputtered.

"You are all right?" Danielle released her hand.

Lydia could not speak, but she nodded as she floundered into shallower water. With trembling fingers she pushed her sodden hair away from her face. Her heartbeat slowed from a gallop to a trot and she summoned a weak smile.

"Thank you."

The Frenchwoman shrugged as if her aid had been of no consequence.

Lydia retrieved a precious cake of sweet lavender soap from the shore and extended it to Danielle. "I would be most happy if you would use some." *Not too much*.

The young woman held it to her nose, and inhaled deeply, sighing prettily. "I have not such a thing since my marriage." A wistful gleam came into the girl's eyes.

Lydia's better nature warred with her desire. "I would be delighted if you accepted it as a gift."

Danielle smiled and immediately slid under the water, rising to lather her hair with the French-milled soap.

Lydia covered her discomfort with a smile, and waded back into the pool. She moved hesitantly. Her throat constricted, making it nearly as difficult to breathe as if she had been under the water again. She must learn to swim, or the unreasoning fear might cripple her.

Of course, Danielle took to the water like a mermaid. Her pretty features were more content than Lydia had ever seen them.

"You really love this place, don't you?"

"*Oui*, I do. *C'est très belle*. As a girl, I am 'ere much. I swim or make houses with the palm leaves."

"I can see why. It is magical—as if no other human has ever touched it."

"*Vous comprenez*. Like it waits for me."

"Has it been a long time since you have been here?"

"Since my marriage to Jeremiah, before Monsieur Poiret owned this land."

"You must have missed it."

"*Oui*." Danielle raised her chin, inhaling the perfumed air with closed eyes.

CHAPTER 20

Determined to best her fear, Lydia dipped her head under the water as Danielle had. Gasping, she emerged and wiped the water from her eyes. It could have been worse. She would try again later, or perhaps another time.

She cast about for a way to spur further conversation with the reticent young Frenchwoman. "How long have you been married?"

"Four years." A scowl flashed across Danielle's features.

"But you cannot be any older than I. How old were you when you married?"

"Fifteen. My father, he thinks it is a good match. Jeremiah did not ask a large dowry."

"You are so much younger," Lydia said. Such alliances were quite common; still, compassion welled up in her for the bewildered young girl Danielle must have been.

"Jeremiah can be hard but 'e is not a bad husband. And I am a woman married *honorablement*."

The asperity in Danielle's tone might have been a torch as it touched Lydia. Her cheeks flamed and her mouth dropped open. The Longs must believe she was mistress to one of the gentlemen.

"Oh, but no—no, it isn't like that."

Danielle's responding smile was as thin and cruel as a paper cut. "Of course not."

Lydia blinked rapidly. She would not cry in front of this woman. Which one did they think she was bedding? She swallowed back the hot defence that sprang to her tongue. *Madame* Long would not understand the relationships, or even care. She had attributed the woman's distance to her difficulty with English, when in truth she must disapprove of Lydia as a fallen woman.

Danielle looked away, but offered no apology. Instead she offered the soap back to Lydia.

"Thank you for the use, but I could not keep it. It is too fine."

Swallowing the lump in her throat, Lydia accepted the sweet-smelling little lump and waded towards the shore. "The clothes must be dry now, and I'm sure the gentlemen are ready for their turn."

She wrapped the creamy bar in a cloth, and placed it back in her knapsack. Then she dressed as quickly as she could. Humiliation left an acid taste in her mouth.

They hiked out of the ravine in silence. Lydia didn't know what to say. In any case she could not manage small talk at the moment. For her part, Danielle had reverted to her usual taciturnity and made no attempt to start a conversation.

At the top, Lydia pasted on a smile and described to the gentlemen the beauty of the waterfall, encouraging them to take their time and enjoy the reprieve from tedious trudging.

Mr Long led the way—Danbury and Harting hard on his heels. They looked as though they were practically salivating at the thought of a good wash. Right behind them the valets toted the laundry, and bringing up the rear were the sailors and Mr Cabot, who—although voicing indifference to the possibility of a thorough wash—were delighted at the prospect of a romp.

There was no decorous wading for the men, as when Danielle and Lydia had bathed. Raucous whoops of laughter and the sound of splashing reached the women, even above the noise of the falling water. Despite the turbulence of her emotions, Lydia could not help but smile. It seemed men never did outgrow their tendency to act like little boys, particularly if presented with the opportunity of shoving someone into a body of water.

Lydia combed out her long hair. It had even more of a tendency to curl when wet. If she did not tend it now, it would become hopelessly tangled. The steady motion of the brush soothed her flayed emotions.

Loneliness threatened to swamp her. To whom could she confide her hurt? People were ever willing to leap to the wickedest conclusion. She couldn't imagine approaching either of the gentlemen on such a subject. They could do little in any event. No one could successfully order someone to change an opinion. She braided her hair quickly and returned it to its knot at the nape of her neck.

She was used to loneliness. It would pass.

CHAPTER 21

Anthony eventually rousted the other men away from the delights of the water. Damp but refreshed, they climbed from the ravine, ready to complete the journey to Pierre-Louis Poiret's plantation.

"*Le Jardin du Roi*—Garden of the King?" Anthony asked Jeremiah.

"Aye."

"They must be royalists." Anthony raised his chin to allow James to tie his cravat.

Jeremiah snorted, but offered no other comment.

The cultivated plantation grounds were not far distant. As with the other plantations on the island, the main house was located near the centre of the spice gardens. Anthony regarded the scene with pleasure.

The cheery house was white with dark blue shutters and trim. Wide windows stood open to catch every stray breeze, and a large, shady veranda edged the residence. A dirt path led up to the house. Rutted though it was, it felt positively luxurious to be walking on a path again.

Pierre-Louis Poiret had evidently been informed of their approach. He awaited them on the veranda.

"Welcome, welcome, my friends. I am delighted to see you again."

A manservant appeared behind him carrying a tray of glasses.

"Please come and be seated." He gestured to a nearby grouping of chairs on the shady porch. "You must be very hot and weary with all your walking."

Another servant appeared behind the first, and escorted the others to the servants' quarters where refreshments had been prepared for them. Only Mr Cabot—with the status of a ship's officer—remained with them.

"This is nice," Pierre-Louis said, once his guests were seated and served. "Very nice indeed. I must confess I have a great affinity for the English. Some of your countrymen were once very kind to me. They were even so gracious as to teach me your language while I was yet a boy. "

"It was kind of you to invite us to stay with you," Harting said.

"Not at all. Not at all. You are most welcome. It can be lonely on this island and up here on the mountain we are isolated in so many respects. It will be good to have such pleasant company for a change."

Monsieur Laurent came hurrying around the corner of the house. At the sight of guests, his steps slowed.

"Good afternoon." He inclined his head formally to the assembled party.

"There you are, Laurent," cried Pierre-Louis. "Isn't it delightful? Our friends have come to stay with us."

Laurent's smile was bland. "'Ow nice."

"Yes, it is," said Pierre-Louis firmly. "I have been unable to find your lovely wife. I wanted her to meet our guests."

"I shall look for 'er." Laurent directed a stiff bow towards the group. "If you will excuse me." He departed, returning the way he had come.

"Laurent," Pierre-Louis said with a sad shake of his head. "He is a good fellow—invaluable in so many ways." He offered a charming smile. "We should talk of more interesting things. Dinner will be in one hour. We are not normally formal, but it is a special occasion to have guests so you will find suitable clothing in your rooms."

"Now that will be a nice change of pace. I am weary of these grubby old togs." Harting's gesture was eloquent of disdain.

"Servants will attend you at once." Pierre-Louis motioned to one of the waiting slaves with a flick of his wrist. The man scurried away. In a few moments he returned, followed by several others.

"Ah, here they are," Pierre-Louis said in satisfaction as he stood. "They will show you to your rooms. I will see you all again at dinner."

* * *

Lydia had a bedchamber of her own. The slave woman opened the door with a flourish. The charming room captivated her instantly. Fresh white linens contrasted with mahogany dark wood. Stark white walls had no need of artifice. Wide shutters had been pushed back, and the windows flung open to reveal sloping spice fields on the hillside below, and beyond, the jungle all the way to the glittering sea. The room felt cool and inviting with its simple comfort and lack of pretension. Lydia sighed with delight and inhaled deeply as the breeze carried with it the scent of the nutmeg grove and the vanilla orchids. She could hardly keep from flinging herself down on the bed.

The slave took charge of her knapsack, and began to unpack her few things.

"You don't have to do this." Lydia reached to take the bag back.

"I been told t' tend you." The girl clutched the bag as if Lydia wanted to steal it.

"No, really. You needn't wait on me. In England I am little more than a servant myself."

"Yes, I must." The look in the girl's eyes flickered like a candle from bewilderment to fear.

Lydia gave up the argument. "At least tell me your name."

"I'm Sophie," she replied with a quick duck of her head. Her dark skin was the same colour as the nutmeg grown on the plantation, and just as smooth and glossy. Her tight-ringleted hair

was caught up and bound at the base of her neck and she moved with grace.

"I'm Lydia Garrett. You speak English well. Where are you from?" Lydia gave in to temptation, and perched on the bed.

"I'm just a slave, Miss. My fam'ly came from Africa. I don' remember it. My English is why I'm away from de kitchen." As if anxious to turn the conversation, the young woman abandoned Lydia's knapsack, and went to the wardrobe. She drew out a gown, holding it up for Lydia's inspection.

Made of fine cotton, the dress looked light and airy. The creamy yellow colour reminded Lydia of freshly churned butter. In modern fashion it had a high waist and narrow skirt. Embroidered randomly over the skirt and bodice were dark green palm fronds—the needlework so delicate the leaves looked almost real. Fitted sleeves reached the elbow. A narrow ribbon of dark green velvet delineated the skirt from the bodice, tying at the back and trailing gracefully.

"This is absolutely lovely." Lydia reached an admiring hand to stroke the fabric.

The girl bobbed her head. "Thank you, Miss."

At the proprietary tone, Lydia looked up. "Did you make this gown?"

"Yes, Miss."

"You have a wonderful talent. The ladies of London would be climbing over one another to get such a beautiful gown."

"Do you think so, Miss?" The girl looked at her eagerly.

"I do. Why does Monsieur Poiret have such clothing? I did not understand him to be married."

"No, Miss, he's not married. Master has me make all de newest fashions for his sister. He's hopin' for her t' come live wit' him."

"I didn't know he had a sister."

"Dey haven't seen one anot'er in many years. She lives in France and he has a hard time reachin' her."

"The aristocrats in France have had to be discreet if they do not wish to face the guillotine."

"Yes, Miss." Sophie replaced the gown lovingly in the wardrobe, and produced a pair of ivory coloured slippers for Lydia's inspection.

"These are lovely as well," Lydia said, examining them. "Were they also made here?"

"Yes, we do many things for ourselves here. Ships come, but not so much, and it costs much to order things from France or England."

"And yet it seems you lack for nothing."

"Yes, Miss. You would like me to put up your hair?"

"That would be very kind."

Sophie brought a basin of warm water, and Lydia washed.

"Do you know of any large caves in the area?"

Bent over the dressing table sorting various pins and baubles, Sophie froze in mid-motion. "Caves?"

Lydia turned to her. "Yes. We're here to search for something Lord Danbury's father left many years ago. We understand that it was stored in a cave."

Sophie shook her head in quick, hard jerks. Turning her back, she hurried to the wardrobe and again removed the beautiful gown. "I don' know 'bout no caves."

Lydia opened her mouth to press the point, but the girl met her gaze. Rounded eyes, swimming with unshed tears, spoke of deep-seated dread.

The girl must know something. But whether it was about the throne was unclear and now was not the time to torment the poor thing with questions. Lydia patted Sophie's arm. "Don't fret now."

The girl visibly swallowed and then nodded. She raised the gown and Lydia stooped so she could lower it over her head. Sophie carefully did up the long row of tiny buttons down the back. She sat Lydia down in front of the vanity, and swept her hair up and away from her face, securing it with a couple of gold pins. When they were finished Lydia stood up to see the results in the glass.

"You look beautiful, Miss."

The gown was a trifle too long and the slippers too large, but overall she did look nice. The cream and green was becoming with her auburn hair. Lifting her skirt and poking her slipper-shod foot out, she gave it a shake.

"These feel light as air after wearing boots for so long."

"I'll show you de drawin' room," Sophie said.

Conversation stopped and the gentlemen stood as Lydia entered the room.

"*Mademoiselle*, you are lovely," Pierre-Louis said.

Lord Danbury and Mr Harting added their voices to the compliment.

"Thank you," replied Lydia. Both the gentlemen had taken full advantage of the hour to shave and have their hair trimmed, as well as being rigged out in formal dinner attire. "I imagine your valets were relieved to make you appear as gentlemen again."

"I don't know about my valet, but *I'm* glad to look like a gentleman again," Mr Harting said.

"Well, you are all dashing."

Poiret went about his duties as host. "You have met my friend Paul Laurent, but may I present his lovely wife, Madame Laurent."

A stout woman of middle age, Madame Laurent wore a gown in a style popular a decade earlier, with a tightly corseted waist and wide, panniered skirt. Heavy ornamentation weighed it down. She had even powdered her hair and piled it in a high pompadour.

Lydia curtsied to the older woman. The woman did not smile. She sized up the party, Lydia in particular, with a critical eye even as the appropriate pleasantries were exchanged. It seemed unlikely that they passed muster. Danielle's innuendo of the afternoon set her cheeks alight once more. This old harpy probably thought the same.

Glancing around for an escape route of some sort, Lydia fidgeted with her fan. What was she doing here? She had no idea how to behave at a formal dinner party. If she could just draw one of the gentlemen aside she could tell them of the maid's strange reaction and then she could plead illness.

"We are waiting for Mr Cabot, then we will go in," Pierre-Louis said.

As he spoke the man entered. He looked extremely uncomfortable out of his uniform. The jacket appeared too small, the pants too loose, and he had retained his own battered boots, but he smiled in response to their greeting.

"Shall we go in?" Pierre-Louis asked.

He took Lydia's arm to lead the parade into the dining room.

The dining table was of the same dark wood as the other furniture in the house, but ornately carved with vines and flowers. The walls provided relief for the eye with their stark white simplicity, and again the view was so breathtaking that artwork would have been redundant.

The heady aroma of nutmeg, pepper, cinnamon and any number of other delights swirled around the table. Lydia grew almost dizzy with the scent, and sat gratefully when a servant pulled a chair out for her. Her stomach gurgled in anticipation and she clasped her hands discreetly over her middle to muffle any further comment from that quarter.

It felt novel to sit at a table and dine on something that had not been prepared over a campfire. She restrained herself from devouring the hot, crusty French bread like a maddened goat. The closest they had come to bread in weeks was the ship's biscuit they had brought with them.

The conversation did no more than limp along initially, but Pierre-Louis Poiret was skilled at oiling the gears of social mechanism and soon had everyone interacting with one another— if not comfortably, at least cordially.

After the meal Madame Laurent led Lydia away to the veranda to catch a bit more of the breeze while the men enjoyed their port.

The Frenchwoman's stays creaked as she seated herself in the breeziest corner. Lydia took a nearby chair. Long, awkward silences were punctuated by brief bursts of pointless conversation.

Sophie appeared and bobbed a curtsy. "For you, Miss." She

extended a small slip of paper to Lydia then turned on her heel and scurried away.

Ignoring Madame Laurent's disapproving sniff Lydia opened the folded note.

If you want to know more about caves come to the nutmeg grove.

CHAPTER 22

"Please excuse me." Setting aside her tea, Lydia stood and hurried after Sophie. It was strange, but something urged her to trust the girl. Madame Laurent's huff of disdain followed her as she hastened into the gardens. No doubt she thought Lydia was on her way to a tryst with her lover, whoever she assumed that to be.

It didn't matter. What mattered was locating the throne. She stumbled over an upturned root and slowed. She had not the faintest notion where the nutmeg trees grew. Hoping Sophie was nearby she called out, "Hello?" Her voice sounded tentative even to her own ears.

She opened her mouth to try again when a hand gripped her arm. She gasped and opened her mouth to scream before she recognized Sophie in the moonglow.

"This way, Miss." Sophie tugged on her arm.

A sharp rebuke died on Lydia's lips. They halted beneath a stand of trees and Sophie held her finger to her mouth. Lydia nodded and rubbed her arms. Mist pooled and puddled around them, gathering in the hollows and snagging on the tree limbs.

A voice hissed behind them and Lydia whirled round.

"*C'est elle?*"

Sophie nodded and gave Lydia a little push forward, and then replied in French. "She's a good lady. Kind. I think we can trust her."

A large African man loomed away from the shadow of the trees and Lydia wanted to hide behind Sophie. Instead she stood as straight as she could and met the searching, dark-eyed gaze.

"You're looking for the caves?"

"*Oui*." Her tongue cleaved to the roof of her mouth. She rummaged through the baggage of her mind for her disused French.

"This will cause trouble."

"I'm sorry for any inconvenience. I would not press, but it's most important."

"We do not want you to keep looking."

Lydia's stomach churned and she feared she would lose her dinner. Still she straightened and raised her chin. "Who is 'we'?"

Sophie intervened, impatience colouring her voice. "We don't have to fight. We can help each other."

She drew them to a cluster of wide stumps and warily Lydia sat.

Lydia sent up a silent prayer for guidance.

Sophie reverted to English, perhaps because she could tell Lydia would be more comfortable in her own language. "This my brother Emmanuel. He and two others run away from his master near a month ago. That man is wicked cruel. He… Never mind, you don' care 'bout that. They been hidin' in the caves and I think I know what you after." She planted her hands on her hips. "You help these men escape the island on your ship, I'll tell you where it is."

"How could you possibly—?"

Sophie shook her head impatiently. "It's a great seat covered in jewels."

Lydia's mouth fell open and she closed it with a snap. "If you know where it is why not just take it for yourselves?"

Sophie looked at her as if she were a bit simple. "How a slave explain where they get jewels? We can't eat 'em. A throne is no use to us—not unless we crown a king of slaves."

"Of course." Lydia held up a hand.

Sophie still eyed her as if reassessing her capability. "Hire a cart and oxen from Monsieur Poiret to carry your supplies. The throne is too big for donkeys. Tell him you have not found what you sought and you are goin' home. I will meet you when you are away from the house and take you to the cave. But you mus' take my brother and the others with you. No more slaves." She turned to her brother and spoke rapidly in a language that Lydia couldn't even guess at.

When Sophie had completed her speech, Lydia licked her lips and spoke in French. "I cannot promise. It's not my decision to make alone."

Emmanuel shifted restlessly and she hurried on. "I will tell the gentlemen what you've said. I think they will be amenable. Whatever they decide, I vow to keep your confidence. No one else will know of our meeting or what you have told me."

Sophie and Emmanuel looked at one another for a long moment. Finally Sophie turned to Lydia. "Give me your answer tonight."

Lydia returned to the veranda just as the men emerged from the house. She wandered over to the edge of the porch hoping to draw one of her comrades near and confide her news.

Far below in the natural cove overlooked by the plantation, a ship lay at anchor. A sickly lump settled in the pit of her stomach.

"That is not *Legacy*, is it?" Lydia gestured towards the ship.

"No, it can't be *Legacy*. It's too large." Danbury joined her, squinting through the darkness. "It looks more like…" His face paled as a breeze caught the flag at her mainmast and snapped it to life. "It is a French ship of the line."

CHAPTER 23

Marcus surged towards the railing. He stared hard through the gloom. Confound it, they were right. He struck the rail with his open palm and swallowed a curse. What were the Frogs doing? Were they unloading men to begin a search? He needed a spyglass.

Miss Garrett edged closer. "I must—"

"Is something amiss, my friends?" Their host hovered at his shoulder.

Marcus plastered on a smile full of bonhomie. He nudged Anthony in the ribs. "Nothing to fear. We're at peace with ol' Boney." He turned to his host. "Our nations have been at war so long it's difficult to remember peace has been declared."

"Do warships often put into this harbour?" asked Danbury.

Poiret peered down the mountain. "Usually they put in at Établissement."

He took Miss Garrett's hand and raised it to his lips. "You have no cause for fear here, *ma chère*. Even if the war has recommenced I bear Bonaparte and his ilk no friendship. That rabble dispossessed me of my rightful lands and title. I will not allow them to take you."

Miss Garrett made her curtsy and thanked Poiret sweetly, even as he continued to hold her hand.

Marcus clapped him on the back, perhaps with a tad too much force since the other man staggered forward a step. "I'd be most grateful for a touch more of that claret."

"Of course." Poiret released Miss Garrett and led the way to a pleasant seating area.

The Laurents and Mr Cabot excused themselves, pleading weariness. *Now to be rid of their host.*

Marcus rather liked Poiret, but he needed to discuss developments with his companions, and he couldn't do that in the presence of a Frenchman, no matter how disaffected.

The hour grew later and later still. Finally, Marcus could stand no more.

"Another glass with you, sir."

When Poiret made to stand, Marcus waved him back.

"Allow me to pour."

At the table he pulled a tiny vial from his waistcoat pocket. A few drops in the Frenchman's glass would be all that was required. Marcus handed the drugged drink to Poiret with silent apologies. Their host would suffer an aching head in the morning, but no worse.

In but a few moments, Poiret's words began to slur and he looked a trifle dazed. Another moment and his head slumped forward and he began to snore. Marcus called for one of the servants and had him taken off to bed.

Danbury spoke as soon as the slave had manoeuvred the staggering Frenchman into the house. "Who would have conceived that they would have access to a ship of the line?"

Miss Garrett sat forward in her seat. "My Lord—"

Marcus leaned towards Danbury. He had no desire for any of the household to hear this conversation. "We must consider our course of action. There could be as many as six hundred men on that ship and we have not a third that number. Is it feasible to continue the search or should we flee?"

Miss Garrett held up her hand. "My—"

"I hate to abandon the search, but we can't hold out against such odds. Perhaps we should leave tonight? They won't know where we are so soon, but do we wish to tempt fate?"

Miss Garrett rose and planted herself between the two. "Listen to me."

* * *

Anthony scrubbed his fingers through his hair. He needed to do something to stimulate thought. "You're certain she knows what we seek?"

Seated primly again, Miss Garrett inclined her head. "I refuse to believe there is more than one jewelled throne hidden on this island. Perhaps she came across it when searching out a place for the men to hide from their master."

He shook his head. "All she wants in return is that we take these men off the island with us?"

"We must pledge that they will never be returned to slavery."

Anthony snorted. "I can agree to those terms readily. If it means getting the throne I'll buy them an Admiral's commission."

"That would be a feat." Harting sighed and rubbed the bridge of his nose. "But we must consider. If we aid these slaves we will in essence be stealing."

Miss Garrett paled and then two blotches of colour smeared her cheeks. "As one who was considered no more than chattel by certain of my relations—"

Harting put up a hand. "I'm not defending the institution of slavery. I am a friend to Mr Wilberforce. But we must consider the implications. If we agree to this, we will be unable to seek aid from any of the landholders in the area. With the French here in such numbers we must evaluate the hazard. Perhaps we ought to abandon the notion of removing the throne from the island."

Anthony vaulted to his feet. "And leave the throne to these murderers?"

"Lower your voice, sir." Harting's nostrils flared. "What are we to do with the blasted thing once we've got hold of it? Lead them on a merry chase back to England?"

Anthony's lips curled back in a snarl. He'd had enough of Harting's supercilious presumption. "Why not? I don't give a curse for the throne other than as bait."

"*Legacy* is no match for a ship of the line. And the great ships don't travel alone. She's not here by chance, and I would wager she has her wolf pack nearby. We cannot play act that we are the hunters any longer."

Blood pulsing in his ears, Anthony moved towards Harting.

Miss Garrett's hand on his arm pulled him up short. "We have difficulties enough without being at odds with one another." She looked directly into Anthony's eyes and he sighed.

She focused upon Harting. "You once told us the French intended to spark rebellion by returning the throne to India and setting up a puppet."

He nodded.

"What if we pull the fuse from their plot by returning the throne ourselves? We could call it a goodwill gesture from the British nation or some such. You'll know how to characterize the matter."

Anthony opened his mouth to protest, but before he could utter a word she had turned back to him. Her hand still rested on his arm and the grip tightened. "My Lord, you know that I desire the murderer's capture above all. But we cannot complete that task if we are slaughtered on this island. We must escape if we can and try for him another time."

Chapter 24

No amount of pleading could induce the sun to speed its course, but morning eventually dawned. Fog shrouded the island as if a blanket had been pulled over her while she slept. No matter how hard she stared, Lydia could not discern whether the French ship still lay at anchor in the cove.

It had taken the better part of an anxiety-plagued hour for her to convince Mr Harting that the chance to retrieve the throne was worth the risk of capture. She doubted she'd have succeeded had it not been for Lord Danbury's shrewd support. His determination to catch the murderer rivalled her own. She smiled at the memory of his passionate arguments. He was such a contrast to Harting's cold containment. Fire had carried the day, however.

Following the scheme outlined by Sophie, Harting negotiated with Poiret for the use of an ox cart and a pair of the beasts, leaving behind the donkeys they had brought and stating that they were heading back to Établissement. Danbury sent the Longs back to Établissement with instructions to Captain Campbell to bring *Legacy* around to a cove on the other side of the island. Rather than returning to the village and parading the throne along the main street, the ship would come to them. With God's help they would be well away before the French realized they were gone.

They must avoid any action. Hearty though the men of *Legacy* were, seeking a battle with a ship of the line would amount to inviting a massacre.

CHAPTER 24

* * *

With a confident stride, Danbury took the lead, followed closely by Harting. Just beyond sight of the plantation house, Sophie joined them.

She shot a glance behind her and then squared her shoulders. "This way."

They followed her in silence, the trek leading them slightly south, and a little lower on the mountain. They had not even become winded when, half an hour later, Sophie slowed and motioned the rest of the group forward.

"There is the entrance," she said, pointing.

Following her motion, Lydia noted a grouping of the granite boulders that peppered the mountainside. Even knowing a cave must be there, Lydia could detect no opening.

As one body, the party moved closer, circling the outcropping. Scarcely discernible amongst the undergrowth and a thick draping of vines lay the mouth of the cave. Impatiently, Lord Danbury thrust aside the foliage. The sailors lit several torches. Sophie again took the lead, guiding the group into the close darkness of the cave.

Some six feet inside, the cave widened into a larger chamber. Boards and rocks were piled together, partially blocking the entrance so that only one person at a time could enter. The sun quickly lost its power to pierce the gloom as they travelled further into the belly of the mountain.

Flickering torches cast eerie shadows and caused the darkness to huddle in the corners. Lydia shivered. Atmospheric. The perfect place for the heroine from one of Mrs Radcliffe's horrid novels. Lydia was determined that she would neither scream nor faint.

From behind a pile of rocks three figures emerged. Their tattered clothing and dark skin made it clear they were the escaped slaves. Making no attempt to play the dandy, Harting stepped forward and extended his hand.

The runaways eyed it for a moment, then Sophie's brother stepped forward and grasped it. "I am Emmanuel; this is Louis and Jean."

"Marcus Harting."

"The treasure you seek is this way," Sophie gestured stiffly.

* * *

Holding his torch aloft, Anthony took the lead. Anticipation made him salivate and he swallowed. A centipede skittered across the floor before the light and his lips twisted in revulsion. At the back of the chamber the cave narrowed to form a tapering hall. This passage extended some thirty feet before the cave abruptly widened again.

There, tucked back against the rock wall so that it did not become visible until he cleared the passage, sat an enormous crate. Several of the boards had been pried away, revealing the throne. After all the time they had spent searching, the suddenness of its appearance left him speechless.

Wonderment swept through him as the first beam of torchlight illuminated the gold of the throne. Years of grit coated the gold and enamel now, but it still glowed in the firelight. A singly inlaid peacock was visible. Detailed with infinite delicacy and haughty with the assurance of the beautiful, it looked almost real in the wavering light.

He stepped forward and caressed one of the columns. "I can understand how they were all seduced by this. It is beautiful."

"And deadly," said Miss Garrett tartly.

"Hmm?" Anthony shook himself as if from a dream. "Yes, you're right. This thing has caused the death of too many men."

Anthony turned to Sophie. "I cannot express how much you have helped us. We might never have found the throne without your help."

The girl nodded gravely. "I must go back before I'm missed."

Miss Garrett clasped the girl's hand and whispered something in her ear. When she stepped away tears stood out on the girl's cheeks. She turned to her brother and embraced him.

"Be safe." The words were little more than a whisper, but the cave had grown silent with all eyes on the emotional parting.

Emmanuel bent his head until it rested on top of his sister's. Tears streamed down his cheeks and he did naught to check them. He smoothed her hair and then cupped her face in his hands as if trying to imprint her features on his memory. "I will find a way to come back for you." His voice cracked.

The girl squeezed his hands in hers, then turned and fled.

Anthony turned away. It seemed shameful to gawk at the man's anguish as if it were no more than a Punch and Judy pantomime. As he turned he caught sight of Harting. For an instant it appeared that tears sheened his eyes. Anthony blinked and stepped closer, but the agent turned away as if studying the crate encasing the throne. A moment later Harting turned back. No hint of sensibility lingered on his features. Instead he wore a nonchalant—even bored—expression, as if impatient to be on the move.

Anthony shook his head. This was not the time to worry about Harting and his foibles. He put the men to work repairing the crate, and cutting and smoothing good-sized branches from nearby trees.

It took more than three hours before they could attempt to move the throne. There wasn't room to negotiate the ox cart into the cave and get the throne atop it, so they looped ropes around the crate, and formed two teams of men to haul it.

The cut and trimmed branches were laid before the throne to make a rolling path. Miss Garrett ran back and forth, collecting the branches already traversed and repositioning them in front of the throne so it could continue its slow progress. Anthony and the other men bent their backs to hauling the throne.

The thing must have weighed more than a ton. Anthony strained with all his might. When finally they wrested the crate from the maw of the mountain, he collapsed on the ground, grimy, exhausted and panting.

The other men followed suit. Miss Garrett passed among them with a skin full of water. Anthony drank deeply, the lukewarm liquid wondrously welcome to his parched throat.

* * *

As the men prepared to raise the throne to the cart, Lydia was shunted to the fringes of the group, her offers of assistance brushed away.

With great care they lowered the throne to its side. The ropes were repositioned, and Lord Danbury handed the ends of the rope to a sailor, who scaled an overhanging tree like a monkey. The man looped the line over the sturdiest branch and fed the rest through a complicated series of block and tackle that his Lordship had included in their stores. Lydia had considered its weight many times, and wondered at its purpose. Now it was more than proving its worth.

In teams, the men hauled on the ropes until the throne began to rise from the ground. One of the oxen shied and Lydia rushed to help Harting gentle the beasts backward, until the cart was in place.

She held her breath as the men lowered the throne.

An ominous creaking issued from the ox cart.

Her mouth felt as if it had been stuffed with cotton wool.

Lord Danbury grimaced.

The cart held.

A whoop of satisfaction hailed the completion of the manoeuvre. Danbury turned to her and clasped her hands in his. He raised them to his lips but then blinked and dropped them as if she'd burnt him.

Unsure of how to respond, she rubbed her palms on her skirt.

Now they only had to get the throne off the mountain and onto the ship. Even to Lydia the thought held more mockery than good cheer. The effort required would be tremendous—almost overwhelming. How had the *Centaur*'s crew managed to get the throne all the way up to the cave in the first place?

"We will show you a path. It is not far." Emmanuel's deep-throated French silenced everyone near. A reminder that the enemy could be all too close.

The seamen lashed the throne to the cart to make it as steady as possible. Emmanuel walked before the cart, scouting out the easiest path by which to take the throne. Several sailors armed with long knives followed, hacking at the branches and overhanging vines to clear a way for the cart. Lydia and Lord Danbury walked on either side of the ox cart guiding the animals. Finally, Harting, armed with a pistol and musket, brought up the rear of the procession, keeping an eye out for attack.

The day took on a gruesome monotony. In the roughest areas they stopped altogether. Everyone in the party helped to flatten the undergrowth, move rocks, and uproot bushes. The three-mile trek loomed large.

By noon they had gone less than three quarters of a mile. Lord Danbury halted the grinding progress so they could eat and rest for a few minutes.

Lydia sat gratefully, far more interested in the water she clutched than the bread and cheese. She gestured up the hill at the swathe of trampled ground they had left behind them. "At least we're subtle."

The gentlemen's eyes followed her gesture.

"We'll have to hope they don't stumble on our path," Danbury shrugged.

"Or if they do, that they won't understand its significance," Harting added.

"'Course they gon' find that trail and they gon' follow it straight to us. 'Cause they not worryin' with this great... monster." Emmanuel aimed a kick at the wheel of the cart.

"Careful, my friend. You wouldn't want it to land on your foot," Danbury said.

A faint crack sounded. Every eye turned towards the mountain.

"What was that?" asked Lord Danbury.

"It sounded like gunfire," said Harting.

"Nah, it was this cart, about to give up the ghost," chimed in one of the sailors.

"Let's go," said Danbury. Uneasiness showed in his eyes and in his quick, jerky movements as he shouldered his gear.

Lydia sprang up and shouldered her knapsack.

Emmanuel pointed downhill to the northeast. "We should come to a path soon. We'll be able to go faster. But it's steep in places. We gon' have to help the oxen by pulling back on the cart, or they be overtaken and crushed."

It took nearly an hour to reach the promised path.

Lydia surveyed the rutted track. At least the greenery did not press so closely. She swiped away trickling perspiration with her handkerchief. The ox she walked next to flicked its tail, smacking her in the back of the head. With her walking stick she tapped the ox's haunch.

Birds chattered about them, screeching at the interlopers for disturbing their midday nap. Even next to the noisome ox, she occasionally caught the scent of an exotic blossom. A slip of a waterfall trickled down the side of the mountain, tempting her beyond bearing. Again Lydia lagged behind a little. What harm could it do to get a cool drink and wash her face?

"'Allo!"

Lydia jumped back from the splashing water. Stumbling over her own feet, she sat down hard on the dirt path. The men raised their weapons, each swinging about to face the sound.

CHAPTER 25

Lydia offered up a sigh of relief as Danielle Long came into view, hurrying down the trail.

"Wait for me," the Frenchwoman called, waving at them. Having captured their attention, Danielle's progress slowed.

Lydia tapped her foot. After a long moment, she turned back to the water. At least she could take advantage of the delay to wash her face and neck. It would be heaven to remove her boots and let the cool water splash over her feet. She settled for cupping her hands and gathering a refreshing draught.

Breathless, Danielle rushed up to Lord Danbury's side, clasping his hands in hers. Lydia narrowed her eyes. She really did not care for that woman.

"You 'ave made good progress," Danielle said when she could speak. "Better than I would 'ave thought." A flood of words washed away her habitual sullen silence. "Is that the throne? It must be *très grand*. The crate is huge. It is heavy, no? What will you do if it rains?"

Danielle directed the hail of questions at Lord Danbury. While he was trying to decide which of her ridiculous questions to answer, Lydia interjected a query of her own. "Where is Mr Long?"

Danielle glanced at Lydia and sniffed. "He shows the captain how to get around the island. He sends me back to help and tell you that your ship is coming."

"But how did you find us?"

"Will they be able to rendezvous tomorrow morning?" Danbury asked at the same moment.

The Frenchwoman ignored Lydia in favour of his Lordship. "*Oui*. Yes. I think so—Mahe is a small island."

The young woman's colour was high. Her eyes shone bright with some emotion, and she fluttered her hands as she spoke. Lydia shot a glance at the gentlemen. Neither seemed to have marked the change in her manner. Perhaps it was due to Jeremiah's absence. No doubt she felt freer without his presence. Whatever the reason, she was chattering like a magpie.

Danbury gave a nod to the crew and the trek resumed.

The hours ground away tediously. It seemed they were making no progress at all. Surely, Lydia had been staring at the same clump of ferns for nearly an hour.

Danielle had affixed herself to Lord Danbury's side. She trotted along merrily, as if there were no threat hanging over them and it weren't hotter than Hades. Lydia heartily wished Danielle would revert to her tight-lipped demeanour.

Danielle shrieked. Lost in reverie, Lydia jumped as if she had been scalded. Danbury pitched forward, thudding against the side of the ox he guided. His head struck the side of the cart and he slid to the ground beneath the oncoming wheels of the vehicle. Lydia yelped. She grabbed her ox's ear, tugging hard. Startled by the commotion, the oxen stopped in confusion.

Danbury had just enough time to roll away from the advancing wheels. Heart thudding in her chest, Lydia rushed around the animals to make sure he was not harmed. She found him sitting up and rubbing his head. She dropped to his side. Danielle stood apart, wringing her hands.

"Monsieur, I am so sorry. You are all right? You might 'ave been crushed. Please, you 'ave not hurt?" Agitation thickened her French accent and shortened her grasp on English syntax. "*Mon Dieu, mon Dieu*," she moaned pitifully.

The others clustered near, all exclamations and questions.

"I am fine, Mrs Long. No harm done." Lord Danbury stood and held out his arms to demonstrate his unscathed condition.

"*Dieu merci.*" Danielle sat on the ground with a thump. "I... I trip, I fall." She gestured helplessly.

"Mrs Long stumbled and fell into me. Unfortunately it was just as I was stepping over that boulder, and I was off balance," Lord Danbury said. "As I said, no harm's been done—" He bent down at Danielle's side. "Are you quite well, Mrs Long?"

Danielle lowered her eyes. "It is nothing—only my ankle. It will be fine. I will be more careful." She made as if to stand, but collapsed back to the ground with a squeak.

Lydia knelt to examine the injured ankle. Danielle groaned as she probed the area gently. Lydia bit the inside of her lip, but forbore to roll her eyes. Kindness, she reminded herself. Her father had always taught that—longsuffering, gentleness, love.

"It's not broken. Nor is there any swelling I can discern. Perhaps it's sprained." Lydia retrieved some rolled bandages from the medicine chest and bound the ankle tightly.

"Now we'll see if you can walk on it." She took Danielle's hand to help her to her feet.

Mr Harting supported her other arm. She tentatively put weight on her injured limb. When she did not swoon, someone produced a sturdy branch for her to use as a cane, and with its aid Danielle hobbled a few steps.

The excitement over, everyone fell back in line and they resumed the journey. The pace lagged even slower to accommodate the injured woman. Danielle did not resume her place by Danbury. Instead she straggled behind, until coming abreast of Harting. Judging from the woman's breathless flutter of exclamations at the tragic thing that had nearly happened, she seemed to have overcome any consternation she may have felt. It proved the opening salvo in another bombardment of words.

Lydia looked back to see Harting politely inclined towards the young woman. Her hand rested on his arm as he assisted her along the path. Despite his apparent attendance to her chatter, Lydia saw the quick movements of his eyes and the frequent turning of his head. He remained vigilant for any sign of threat from the French. Sighing, Lydia returned her attention to her own footing. The last thing they needed was further delay.

Lord Danbury didn't call an end to the day's exertions until darkness had edged in close enough to touch. They had reached the base of the mountain. The worst of the terrain lay behind them. Emmanuel reckoned they had another half a mile to go.

From their impatient movements and short tempers Lydia guessed that Danbury and Harting would have liked to press on. But common sense prevailed. The cloak of night made further travel with the throne madness. An unseen hole or rock could send the cart over, and the throne with it. The danger was too great to chance, so the men hurried about the routine of setting up camp for one last night.

Rather than erecting a separate tent for Danielle, Lydia offered to share hers. They prepared for bed in silence, a marked contrast to Danielle's talkativeness throughout the day.

The heat and humidity were oppressive. No stray breeze penetrated the jungle at the base of the mountain. Restless and perspiring, Lydia woke in the middle of the night. She tried to go back to sleep, but the thick, motionless air defeated her. In silence she picked up her boots, settling down outside the tent to put them on. This done, she straightened and sought out the guards so they would not be startled into shooting her later if they came upon her unexpectedly.

She had spoken to two of the guard and was looking for the third, Anthony's valet, James, when she heard a rustling nearby. Instantly alert, she stopped and called out softly to the darkness. "James?" She waited in vain for a response. Cautiously she crept towards the noise. "James, is that you?"

Again she heard no response. Heart in her throat, Lydia stole towards the rustling. Stooping to pick up a heavy branch, she continued to advance. A low moan caught her ear, sending a shiver up her spine. The darkness hung as thick and heavy as a curtain, hiding the source of the sound from her view. Mustering her courage, Lydia called again in the sternest voice she could manage.

"Who is it? Show yourself!"

The underbrush rustled again, and she caught sight of a figure on the ground. Another moan came from the dark mound, and then a raspy whisper.

"Miss… help me."

Lydia dropped her club and ran to the speaker. "Sophie? Sophie, what's wrong?" She knelt in the brush beside the slave girl.

The girl rasped something unintelligible. A slight nod of her head directed Lydia's attention to her side, which she clutched tightly.

Lydia gasped at the dark, sticky smear down the girl's dress. Blood, and quite a lot of it. Sophie's head lolled back. Lydia pulled her up.

"Let's get you to some light so I can look at this wound."

She half carried Sophie to the campfire. In obvious agony, the girl moved haltingly. Lydia tried to be gentle, but Sophie was insensible when they collapsed together near the fire. Fetching a cup of water, Lydia lifted it to Sophie's dry lips. Somewhat revived, the girl spoke feebly.

"Miss, de French is comin'. I saw dem talkin'." Her words trailed off in a wince as Lydia gently probed her wound.

Lydia glanced up from her examination. "Who did you see?"

"Madame Long and a Frenchman. They don' know I'm close by. Miss, I think she kill Mister Jeremiah."

CHAPTER 26

Lydia rocked back on her heels. Her lungs felt like a broken bellows, unable to inflate properly.

Gasping and grimacing, Sophie continued. "I's taking laundry to the waterfall. An' I hear. She tell him 'bout the plan to move the ship."

She groaned as Lydia swabbed the wound and applied a padding of folded handkerchiefs. It was rough, but it would have to do for the moment. All the while her mind worked furiously.

"I start to run 'way. The man heard me an' shot, but I—" Sophie's breathing grew reedy with the effort of speech and she gasped to a stop.

Danielle must have been trying to delay them in a bid to allow the French ship time to catch *Legacy* and cut off their escape.

Lydia stroked the girl's brow and her eyes fluttered open. Bending low, Lydia hissed into her ear. "Sophie, be very quiet and still. Danielle rejoined us. I think she may have even tried to kill Lord Danbury."

Sophie's eyes turned fearful at the news.

"She is in my tent. We will try to take her unaware. Stay here where you will be out of danger." She placed the girl's hand over the padding on her wound. "Hold this in place. You've bled a great deal, and you must try to staunch the flow. I cannot imagine how you managed to come so far."

Not waiting for a response, Lydia jumped to her feet. She had to find Danielle before that traitor suspected her plot was uncovered.

Lydia considered going to Harting and Danbury, but they would have to be roused, booted, and armed. Instead she located the guards and briefly explained.

Stealthily they approached the tent. Lydia lifted the flap, and ducked in. A glance revealed that Danielle no longer lay curled on her blanket. Lydia left one of the guards to watch the tent and capture Danielle should she return. She sent the other guard to scout in one direction—she took the opposite.

She was still reluctant to rouse the camp. It would put the Frenchwoman on guard and she might escape or try something desperate.

The stifling darkness limited her vision. Frustration flared. This was wrong, all wrong. She couldn't waste time wandering aimlessly. Haste was of the utmost importance. Every sense strained to pierce the gloom, to catch a hint of where the woman could be. What was she doing? What would cause them the greatest delay?

With a flash of insight she realized where Danielle would go. The throne. Abandoning her cautious circling of the camp, Lydia hastened silently to where the cart and its precious burden had been secured.

A figure crouched at the side of the cart. Lydia threw herself forward. Danielle turned as Lydia wrenched her away from the cart. The Frenchwoman clutched a knife in her hand.

Lydia gasped. The woman was diabolical. Heedless of those who might have been hurt, Danielle had been fraying the ropes securing the throne to the cart. At some point in the morning it would have tumbled to the ground.

The knife glinted wickedly as Danielle lunged at her. Lydia grabbed the arcing hand before the blade could bury itself in her flesh. But Danielle's rush toppled them both over. Rolling on the ground they grappled for the weapon. Struggling beneath the other woman's weight, Lydia held Danielle's arm with all her might. The sharp metal dipped again and again, like a snake seeking to destroy her.

With a desperate shove, Lydia was free of her attacker for an instant. Now she was on top and had the upper hand. She pushed hard at

Danielle, trying to force the knife from the woman's grasp. She almost had it— almost. The Frenchwoman bucked violently. With a twist of her wrist the knife jabbed at Lydia again. She cried out. A scarlet thread blossomed and spread across her bicep, turning into a stream that washed down her arm and onto the face of the woman beneath her.

From somewhere seemingly far away, Lydia heard a shout. She could pay it no heed. Danielle's whitened fingers were talons gripping the knife. They were on their sides in the dirt again, wrestling for their lives. It took every bit of strength Lydia possessed to keep the knife from striking again.

Men poured from their tents forming a jagged circle around the combatants. Cries pierced the night. Someone produced a torch. The light reached Danielle. She blinked and dropped the knife, which tumbled to the ground. She went limp in Lydia's grasp. Strong arms reached in to separate them.

Harting assisted Lydia to her feet. He took her arm in gentle hands and examined the wound. She panted, unable for the moment to catch her breath. She locked her knees to keep from collapsing. Her teeth began to chatter. With her free hand she swiped at hair that hung in her face, shoving it behind her ear. Numb fingers could not seem to stop trembling.

"Sophie… hurt. By the fire…needs help," Lydia gasped.

Emmanuel whirled towards the fire. The other men surrounded Danielle. She cursed them all roundly in French.

Brow crumpled, Lord Danbury looked from Lydia to the other woman and back again. "What is all this?"

Chest heaving, Lydia tried to catch her breath and relate Sophie's story at the same time. It seemed to take a long time, though it could only have been a few minutes by the clock. "I believe she meant to fray the ropes, hoping they would break sometime in the morning. She wanted to delay us long enough for the French to cut off our retreat." Lydia's injured arm burned. Her palm was sticky with her own blood. She wiped it against the already filthy skirt of her dress. There would be no salvaging this gown.

"Someone might have been killed." Danbury's hands tightened into fists.

"Sophie thinks Danielle may have killed Jeremiah," Lydia said.

"The accident yesterday…" Shock lit Danbury's face. "Madame Long has much to answer for."

Two sailors had taken Danielle's arms. She stood silent and petulant when Lord Danbury turned to her.

"What have you to say?"

"It is all lies." She thrust up her chin in a contemptuous nod at Lydia. "Your trollop doesn't like me because I am prettier, and you were friendly to me. She attacked me and then made up these terrible tales."

Harting cocked his head and smiled. "Come now, Madame. We all know that is untrue. Miss Garrett is much lovelier than you. That's why you had to settle for an old man like Mr Long."

Rage flared in Danielle's eyes and she showed her teeth. "There were many men who desired me. Only Long bid on me like a slave. *Bien*, he regrets it now, doesn't he?"

Harting pounced. "So you did kill him."

Caught by her own boastful pride, Danielle tried to bluster, but with no success. She crumbled in an outburst of vindictiveness. "*Oui*, I killed the old pig." She turned to Lord Danbury. "And I tried to kill you. Monsieur Bonaparte restores the glory of France. We will defeat your pitiful island, and I shall dance with Le Faucon in Paris."

Danbury turned ashen, his lips a slash in the granite of his face.

Danielle extended a hand to him, apparently deciding she ought to change tack. "I 'ad to, Monsieur. You do not know what it was like with Jeremiah. So tedious. I met Le Faucon in the village while Jeremiah delivered your message to the ship. All he desire is information. And for this, he swear to take me to France. I did not decide right away." She said this as if it indicated her virtue. "I try to make Jeremiah to stay in the village, but he would not. I tell him I would make sure you knew the message had been delivered. But he never listened to me. I did not want to kill the old fool, but he never listened."

"You killed him because he would not go away?" Harting asked.

"*Oui*. You understand. I did not want to, but he would not stay in the village. Such a stupid old man." She glanced at the faces surrounding her.

"It sounds as if you had already made up your mind to assist Le Faucon." Lydia eyed the traitor. She bit her lip to keep from screaming at the woman. Even as she trembled from the effort of their scuffle, she longed to lunge at her and resume the battle. She flexed the fingers of her good hand. She would rip out the woman's hair at the roots.

Danielle slumped. It was obvious she would find no sympathetic ear among this audience. Lydia smirked, but then her heart clenched. Scheming and wicked Danielle might be, but she was also a pitiful dupe.

"*Oui*, I told Monsieur Le Faucon what you search for and also where your ship was being moved. He will stop you."

Danielle stopped as she caught sight of Emmanuel standing at the edge of the circle of light. Her eyes grew round. The look of disgust on his face seemed to touch her as nothing else.

"You!" She turned to Harting. "This man is dangerous, an escaped slave."

"And your paramour shot his sister."

"He wouldn't have had to shoot her if she weren't sly. The stupid girl crept up on us." An injured note crept into her voice at being so ill-used by Sophie. "*Monsieur*, I beg you, do not let him harm me."

"*Madame*." Hauteur oozed from Harting. "He would not descend to your level."

Danbury nodded and gestured towards Danielle. "Bind her hands and keep a guard on her. We need to hurry. Take only the essentials. Leave the tents and everything not absolutely necessary."

CHAPTER 27

Danbury set a couple of men to re-securing the throne to the cart and finally turned to Lydia, his manner gentling considerably. "How is your arm?"

"Fine. The cut isn't deep." Lydia held the arm up for his inspection.

"She might have killed you. What were you thinking, going after her without help?"

"I did have assistance. The guards helped me search for her. I simply happened to find her first."

"You ought to have wakened me."

"There wasn't time."

He narrowed his eyes and sighed heavily. "I could have helped with the search as well. You were injured fighting with her."

"We had to be as quiet as possible so as not to alert her, and anyone who came upon her might have been hurt—she had a knife. Not that I knew that when I started out."

"Precisely. It was dangerous, and you should—"

"How is Sophie?"

"Sophie?" He ran a hand through his hair and looked towards the campfire. "I don't know."

Harting reappeared at Lydia's elbow. "The bullet passed through her side. No vital organs seem to have been hit. She lost a lot of blood, but as long as no infection sets in…"

A bit of the tension eased from her shoulders. "I am glad. I don't know how she made it such a long way with that wound."

The sky lightened by smudgy degrees as they set off. Carrying his sister, Emmanuel led the way. Subdued, Danielle trailed along behind them, with her bound hands attached to the back of the cart.

Tension permeated the air with the stench of sweat and drudgery and dread—a foul odour that stung Lydia's nose and made her stomach roil. Every eye sought signs of a French presence. But the more level terrain allowed them to make better time than they had before. No one spoke of stopping for breakfast.

They reached the sandy beach late in the morning, and caught sight of *Legacy* floating serenely in the little cove. Lord Danbury led the men in a hearty huzzah at the sight.

Lydia offered a whispered prayer of thanks. She had never seen anything more beautiful. The gigs were lowered with a splash. She watched as the oarsmen pulled with a will until they were near enough to hail, and then nearer still.

In a short time, the gigs were close enough that the oarsmen hopped out and pushed them the last couple of feet to ground them. Captain Campbell had chosen to come ashore. He sat majestically in the front of one of the boats until it ceased its forward motion.

"You can see we were able to make all the additional repairs." He gestured to *Legacy*, bobbing calmly in the sea behind him. The captain caught sight of the enormous crate containing the throne. "You've found it then?"

"You sound surprised."

"Of course not; just pleased."

"I'm afraid your reaction will be short-lived, Captain. I have some bad news for you." Quickly, Danbury revealed the situation.

Captain Campbell showed no visible reaction to the news. "We'd best get the throne loaded. Won't do to dally." With a few barked commands, he sent one of the boats back to the ship for reinforcements. They had not dared to drive the cart onto the sand. The wheels would immediately become bogged down, stranding the vehicle in a matter of moments.

CHAPTER 27

"What do you think we should do?" Danbury asked the captain as he approached.

"Well now." Campbell removed his hat, and swiped at the sweat on his broad brow with his forearm. "Looks a challenge, doesn't it?"

Harting called from where he stood near the ox cart. "Pull up one of the skiffs. We'd have to load it in one of the boats later, and this way we won't have to transfer the thing."

"Brilliant," Danbury grinned wolfishly. At his order, three sailors ran to the shore and returned, dragging the boat across the beach.

Behind her, Danielle snorted. Lydia gritted her teeth, but did not turn around.

Louis and Emmanuel drove the oxen beneath a nearby tree. The gig's slat seats were hacked out to allow the throne to rest more snugly against the bottom. More men arrived from the ship to help.

Superfluous to the process, Lydia tried merely to stay out of the way, finding shelter beneath a coconut palm.

Catching a flash of movement from the corner of her eye, Lydia spun around to see Danielle Long attempting to scuttle away. The Frenchwoman's hands remained bound but she had been freed from the cart. Dashing after her, Lydia snatched at Danielle, catching her by the hair.

"No you don't."

"Let me go, trollop!"

Lydia regarded her dispassionately. The desire to make her pay for her betrayal had abated. In its place lay only a small lump of pity. Danielle swore at her, kicking and bucking. Hauling on the ropes that bound her, Lydia dragged the girl to a nearby palm tree. Her breath came in short, hard gasps as she lashed the end of the rope to the nearest palm, making certain that Danielle wouldn't be going anywhere. At last the job was done. Then she pulled out her notebook and scrawled a message in pencil relaying the details of Mr Long's murder. She addressed it to Poiret and tacked the note high on the palm tree, where Danielle could not reach it. If there was any justice in the world, the woman would pay for her crimes.

Lydia dodged a final, furious kick and turned away. She glanced back at Danielle. Dishevelled and red-faced, the woman stood tugging against the ropes with all her might, her lips pulled back in a snarl. A shudder rippled through Lydia.

Danielle caught her gaze. "Do not pity me, you… you…" She spat on the ground, but a bit of spittle remained hanging from her chin as thin and delicate as a spider's web.

Lydia turned away. The woman hurled abuse after her. Silent under the insults, Lydia returned to the edge of activity.

The men had reversed the process used to get the throne on the cart. The throne swung pendulously, suspended across a sturdy tree branch for a long, breathless moment. A sailor hurried the cart away, and the skiff took its place. The teams of men holding the ropes began to lower the throne into the boat. Ominous creaking issued from the tree.

"Careful, lads; careful," said Lord Danbury as he lowered the rope hand over hand.

The others followed his example, keeping up the steady pace he dictated. The throne nestled safely in the boat. The tree seemed to moan and then with a loud popping sound the branch collapsed atop the throne with a rush. For one heart-stopping moment it seemed the throne would tip and fall beneath this onslaught, but the men rushed forward and braced the crate with their shoulders. Lydia took an involuntary step forward herself, hand outstretched, though she was too far away to add her force to the effort. The throne steadied, and she exhaled heavily.

The oxen's lead ropes were hooked through the iron ring at the nose of the boat and then woven through the oarlocks. With the oxen securely hitched to the skiff, men took positions on each side of the boat to keep it from tipping in either direction. A couple of others lent their backs to the process, pushing while the oxen pulled.

In a few minutes they had crossed the sandy beach and the sea lapped the nose of the rowboat. The other two boats were dragged up beside the one carrying the throne and lashed securely on either side. They acted as pontoons, balancing the central boat and providing much needed buoyancy.

Lydia approached Lord Danbury. "My Lord, I would beg a favour of you."

He swabbed at his brow, huffing and panting, but a satisfied grin lit his features. "Name it."

Lydia swallowed hard. "I fear for Sophie's recovery if we leave her in this isolated spot with Danielle Long. I know you sent for Poiret and he should be coming for her soon, but in the meantime she could greatly harm the poor girl. Also, her tales of escaped slaves could bode ill for Sophie."

"What would you have me do?"

"Would you consider allowing her to join us?"

Danbury's jaw worked in and out for a moment. "I suspected as much." He sighed. "Complications."

Lydia glanced back at the trees to where Sophie lay, a tiny crumpled figure.

Danbury followed her gaze. "Oh, very well. Have you any paper?" He jotted a note to Poiret and enclosed a handful of coins to cover Sophie's price.

Holding the small, folded package he gestured with it towards Danielle. "Would you be so kind…"

Lydia accepted the parcel and approached the Frenchwoman. Despite her thrashing, Lydia managed to get this packet secured to the tree also.

Behind her, one of the ship's great guns boomed a harsh warning.

CHAPTER 28

Whirling to look, Lydia peered at the horizon, but could not see the source of the alarm. Coming abreast of the others, she saw the same confusion on the faces of the gentlemen as they scanned the horizon. Captain Campbell, however, was squinting at his ship.

With pulse sounding unnaturally loud in her ears, Lydia clasped her hands together to still their trembling.

"They've spotted a sail." Campbell set his hat more squarely on his head.

"Go. Go!" Harting waved the men towards the boats.

Men piled into the makeshift flotilla. Emmanuel carried his sister's small form, placing her carefully in the bow. The oxen were driven into the sea, dragging the ungainly contraption until the final bit of solid ground was left behind. The oxen were released from the boats and waded back to shore. The oars were deployed and the sailors pulled swiftly towards *Legacy*.

Lydia glanced back to see the oxen emerging from the sea. Behind them she saw Pierre-Louis Poiret and Monsieur Laurent with a couple of armed men emerge from the jungle and approach Danielle. The tableau grew smaller as they pulled further away but she caught a glimpse of Pierre-Louis' hand raised in farewell and returned the gesture.

The lurch of the boat as it pulled aside *Legacy* brought Lydia's attention back to the events at hand. She had been so engrossed that she had not even given thought to her usual fear.

A complicated system of ropes and rigging had been readied. In a mad flurry of activity, the crew secured the throne and hauled it up from above. Thirty minutes after spotting sails on the horizon, Captain Campbell, bellowing commands, set foot once more on his deck.

The sails snapped to attention, bringing *Legacy* about smartly. To Lydia the scrambling crew looked as chaotic as a mound of ants.

Lydia had Sophie transported below decks and comfortably ensconced in a hammock before joining the gentlemen and Captain Campbell on the quarterdeck. From this vantage point the French ship loomed nearer.

"We have to make it out of the cove before we will be able to pick up any real speed. We have the weather gauge, but the breeze won't pick up proper until we get out to sea," Campbell said.

"The French will be able to open up with a full broadside. They have plenty of time to take up position. Look, they are already bringing her about." Danbury pointed at the other ship, lumbering into a turn that would put her at the best angle to open up with her guns when *Legacy* tried to pass.

"Yes, but we hold the trump card," said Harting. "They can't sink us or they risk losing the throne. They can't even do major harm below decks, as they risk damaging it beyond repair."

"You're right," said Captain Campbell. "But they can shoot our rigging to bits, until we can do naught but wallow like an upended tortoise."

Harting gestured with his spyglass towards the other ship. "While they are aiming at our rigging, we can aim at what really matters."

A new light came into Campbell's eye. He rubbed his jaw. "We'll have to stay out of range of their grapnels." In an instant, Captain Campbell reversed his previous orders to his crew.

The men scrambled like roaches in a sudden light, striking the sails and leaving only enough canvas aloft to provide rudimentary manoeuvrability. Sharpshooters climbed aloft and the gunnery crews took up positions. *Legacy* had only twenty-eight guns, while the French ship had at least fifty, but they would make the best use of them they could.

They drew close enough to see the name emblazoned on their adversary: *Angélique*. With a threatening clatter the French raised their gun hatches. Lydia caught her breath.

All noise aboard *Legacy* had been snuffed out as if sound were as easily extinguishable as a candle. Lydia could not tear her eyes from the warship. They had only one opportunity to get past the *Angélique*. If they could make open water, they could outrun the heavier vessel. Should the Frenchmen catch *Legacy* with their lines in the narrow mouth of the cove, they would swarm the ship. They would be overwhelmed in moments.

Enthralled as a mouse before a snake, Lydia could not move, could not breathe. A heavily accented voice boomed from the French ship. "*Legacy!*"

Lydia jumped and let loose a little squeak.

"Strike your colours and 'eave to, in ze name of France."

"Pompous Frogs," muttered Captain Campbell. He shouted back to the disembodied voice. "Never!"

"'Eave to or face bombardment."

"Bombard away." Campbell's flippancy brought grins to his men's faces and they nudged one another.

In a quieter voice Campbell ordered the passengers below. Lydia moved slowly. Fascination with the life-and-death dance being played out between the two vessels made her sluggish. Neither gentleman made any movement.

There was a moment of utter stillness, then the French response was heralded by a puff of white smoke and a roar from one of *Angélique*'s gun hatches. The shot landed on the far side of the ship, throwing up a great geyser of foamy spray.

"Buck up, lads. We'll get past these Frogs and laugh at them when we do," Campbell called to the men.

"Miss," one of the sailors called to Lydia. "Miss, get below! And pray for us."

CHAPTER 28

"Of course."

Lord Danbury whirled round at the sound of her voice. "Get below. It is too dangerous on deck."

Lydia had no time to respond. The world was consumed in thundering. Above their heads, the foremast yardarm splintered. With a groan of rending wood, it toppled to the deck.

One of the cables, flying free in a wild arc, struck Lydia. It knocked her to the deck, snatching the air from her lungs. Gasping, she shook her head to clear it. On hands and knees, she scrambled for cover. Blocks and tackle pummelled the deck like hail. Prayer pulsed through her, more a cry of the heart than any formal words.

Men feverishly pounded powder and shot into the muzzles of their muskets. All around, the thundering of the great guns reverberated, followed by the fearsome whine of the balls as they tore by. The deck was soon awash in water flung up by wild shots.

Bitter gun smoke hung in the air, scouring the back of her throat with the scent of battle and death.

The *Angélique* had an advantage of height. As they came within range, a volley of gunfire burst from her deck. A smattering of strangled cries punctuated the deeper roar of cannon and muskets as men were hit. The sharpshooters in *Legacy*'s rigging fired back, holding their positions valiantly. Still the two ships drew nearer.

Mr Cabot waved his pistol in the air. "It'll be canister and chain shot next round, lads!"

Lydia abandoned her prayerful position. God could probably hear her even when she was moving. Half crouched, she scuttled to the nearest wounded man. The hands were desperately defending *Legacy*. There were few who could tend to the wounded. Stooping, she looped her arms under his and locked her fingers across his chest. She dragged the injured man down the ladderway. It was a good thing he was unconscious as she heaved him along—the pain of their passage would have been terrible, but certainly he would be in less danger of being shot again, or crushed by falling timbers.

Lydia flattened herself on the deck as a shrill screech split the thunder of the guns. Grapeshot sped overhead, cutting a merciless swathe through the men.

Lydia repeated the process time after time, helping the wounded away from the worst of the battle. Every breath was a prayer.

She slipped in a spatter of blood, falling for what must surely have been the hundredth time. Lydia clenched her eyes shut and her hands into tight fists and then released them. She couldn't bear to stand by and do nothing.

The smoke cleared for an instant as Lydia came on deck. They were abreast of *Angélique*. She craned her neck up at the vessel.

"Oh, God, please help us," Lydia whispered.

Below her feet, the gunnery crews could finally bring their guns to bear and they let loose with a long rippling broadside. The horrific noise redoubled, and the whole ship shook with the volume. Her ears rang, and the world went silent as a grave. Clasping her hands over her ears, Lydia hurried to the side of another wounded man. On the foredeck, she could see Mr Harting, tall and elegant as always, taking careful aim as he let off a round from his pistol.

Of its own accord, her gaze sought Lord Danbury. *God grant that he's unharmed.*

The injured sailor at her feet had a streak of blood running down his forehead. The wound must be under the hairline somewhere. He lay insensible, a dead weight. *Get on with it.* Reaching under his arms she linked her fingers atop his chest, hefting him up awkwardly. Gasping and staggering with the effort, she dragged him backwards across the deck.

She nearly had him to safety when from the corner of her eye she saw a French grapnel skitter across the deck and then clamp tight to a nearby rail, its teeth biting deeply into the wood. Her breath hissed through her teeth.

Snatching a knife from the belt of the wounded man, she dashed for the railing and hacked at the thick grappling line. A movement caught her gaze and she glanced up to see French sailors gesturing at her wildly.

Lydia dropped to her knees behind the suddenly flimsy protection of the rail. She could not stop her frenzied sawing. More canister shot whistled over her head. More lines thunked onto the deck. *Legacy* had to break free quickly or they would be overrun.

Some ten feet further down the deck, another grappling hook clattered and then bit into the rail.

Beside her the railing fractured, peppering Lydia with shards of shattered wood. Intent on her task, it took a moment for her to realize she had nearly been shot. The prayer revolving in her mind had been reduced to a single desperate shriek.

She ducked lower still. She almost had it. If only... The cable parted at last. Lydia took no time to celebrate. The acrid stench of the slow match, and foul smoke had seared itself permanently to her lungs. She was panting now, wheezing. The sea and sky had ceased to exist. Only the moment remained. The smoke and flame—and blood.

Using the rail as a screen she crawled on all fours to the next line and attacked the rope. A strong hand gripped her shoulder.

"Allow me," shouted Danbury, his mouth close to her ear. He raised a boarding axe in one hand.

Lydia scrambled aside and he took her place at the rail. Two competent strokes of the axe, and the rope gave way. *Legacy* was free.

A couple of feet away, another grapnel landed on the deck. *Not again.* Before it could find purchase, Lydia snatched it up and hurled it into the sea.

CHAPTER 29

Gradually, *Legacy* pulled away. As they came abaft the *Angélique*'s beam they gained a position where the situation reversed: *Legacy* could fire on her, but for the moment the French could not return fire. The French ship kept up a withering barrage of gunfire from the upper decks, but her cannon fell silent, biding their time.

Legacy's great guns roared their outrage. Her gunners aimed for the *Angélique*'s waterline. At such close range they could scarcely miss. After the first volley, the order broke down. The gun crews fired and reloaded as quickly as they could. They needed to inflict as much damage as possible in a very few minutes.

A hoarse cheer heralded the appearance of a gaping wound at the *Angélique*'s waterline. Another round hulled her once more. In a few moments the *Angélique* began to list, her bow dragged down by the water pouring through the holes gouged by *Legacy*'s wicked fire.

Captain Campbell ordered canvas packed on. The seamen jumped to the task, unreefing the sails and letting loose with every ounce of canvas the injured masts could bear. The sails immediately caught the wind, billowing out with a satisfying flapping.

Legacy swung away from the *Angélique* towards open water. A few angry shots followed them, but they no longer posed any real threat.

"Ha!" Captain Campbell shouted from where he stood at the wheel. "We were a bit more of a challenge than they thought, eh?" Blood trickled from a gash on his cheek and seeped from a makeshift bandage that encircled his thigh, but he grinned widely.

A cheer went up from the crew. Danbury grabbed Lydia, whirling her around in an exuberant embrace. "We did it!"

"Miracles still happen." Lydia grinned as widely as any of the hands. She shouted too. No one could have heard anything less. They had all been deafened.

"I think you're a lucky charm, Miss," called one of the sailors. "We made it through a cyclone, and now a battle we ought never to've escaped from. Normally women's bad luck on a ship, but I say as how you're good luck. First the storm and now this."

"I'm no lucky charm, Jonas. God must've heard our prayers."

"Well, if your prayers is that good then I wish you'd pray for me."

"Don't be impertinent." Danbury stepped towards the scruffy seaman.

A hoot of laughter went up from the listening men at this sally, and Jonas grinned sheepishly. "I didn't mean no disrespect, Miss, and that's a fact." The sailor scratched his head.

A command from above sent the sailors scurrying back to their tasks.

"I'd best see if Dr Marshall could use my assistance with the wounded." Lydia turned to go below decks.

Danbury touched her arm as she turned, and then drew back his hand as if she had scalded him. "Miss Garrett, a word please."

"Yes?"

"I… It's just… you must not risk yourself as you have been doing. I don't think I, that is to say, the mission could do without you now."

Lydia read the regard in his gaze and lowered her eyes. No use wishing for what might have been had the situation been different. She could manage no more than a husky whisper. "Lucky then that I am unscathed."

"Unscathed? You're covered in cuts, you have that arm injury, and you look tired enough to drop."

Lydia's gaze fell to take in her own dishevelled person. "I might have been killed," she said. "I came within inches of it. I shall be rather sore in the morning, but for now I am well enough. There's not a soul aboard who isn't scratched and bruised, including you. And there are a great many who are far worse off."

"There are men enough to care for them."

"I shall allow Dr Marshall to make that decision. If I can do something to alleviate their suffering, then I intend to do it."

Danbury sighed. A sensible man, he recognized defeat when it was upon him. "If you need me, I will be conferring with Captain Campbell. He needs to know we will be setting sail for India, not for home. Let's hope he takes the news well, eh?"

Lydia smiled. "If anyone can soothe him, you're the man."

"Your confidence is touching, if misplaced. Perhaps I ought to find Harting to act as my second. If you see him will you send him to me?"

Lydia nodded agreement, but she had already made good her escape.

* * *

Anthony sighed as he watched her fleeing form. He wasn't quite sure how he had managed to botch the conversation so thoroughly. Lydia Garrett was a mass of contradictions. She looked as fragile as the most delicate porcelain, but she had a core of solid strength that bent for no one. Shaking his head at the conundrum she posed, Anthony hurried to speak with Captain Campbell.

* * *

Hearing Harting's voice above her, Lydia hurried up the stairs to find him seated on an upturned bucket and working to remove slivers of wood from the face of a swearing cabin boy.

"You must be still or it will hurt all the more," Harting said.

"They didn't hurt near as bad goin' in. Leave 'em where they are." The lad wriggled and kicked.

CHAPTER 29

"They're sure to cause infection if I leave them. I'm nearly through. Hold still." His hand made quick darting motions, until at last with a bark of satisfaction he released his grip on the back of the boy's head. "Go wash your face and bathe it with camphor," he ordered. The child jumped to his feet and took off.

"Are you angling for Dr Marshall's position? It looked like you had done that before," said Lydia.

"No, but perhaps I shall study to be a physician when we get back to England. I imagine it provides as much excitement as espionage."

"The hours are just as poor, though."

"You have a point." He smiled. "You've become quite the heroine."

Lydia groaned inwardly. She had no desire for another lecture about staying prudently out of danger's reach. "I've done no more than anyone would have, given the opportunity."

"I beg to differ. There are quite a lot of people who would have run screaming given half a chance. You, however, seem to have no instinct for self-preservation whatsoever."

Lydia rolled her eyes at him, and attempted a distraction. "Lord Danbury requires assistance breaking the news of our new destination to Captain Campbell."

"Right-o." Harting rose.

Lydia thought for an instant that her efforts had been successful. No such luck.

"I wasn't being critical, you know. I admire courage in anyone and you've got it by the bucketful. Danbury and I were both worried for you, though. Not because we don't think you are capable, but because we should be destitute without you."

Lydia shook her head at him. "You know very well that's not true," she said, even as she wished it were. "Off with you. Lord Danbury will need all your skills at persuasion."

Harting did as instructed, but with an infuriatingly secret smile Lydia could not interpret. Shaking her head in a futile effort to clear it of distractions, she hurried to the orlop.

Moans and the stench of blood, sweat, and worse met Lydia as she entered the surgery. For an instant she considered retreat. Even the thick miasma of gun smoke and charred wood permeating the deck was better than the closed-in reek of the orlop.

Dr Marshall caught sight of her. "Miss Garrett, I'm glad you are here. Your assistance will be much appreciated."

The injuries ranged from a serious chest wound, where a splinter nearly a foot long and wickedly sharp had pierced a man's torso, to a broken leg caused by a recoiling gun, and an injured foot, hurt when a sailor dropped a cannonball during the heat of battle.

Every berth was occupied. While Dr Marshall and his loblolly boy handled a tricky amputation, Lydia stepped in to set a broken leg. Her patient lay supine on the operating table. His arms and uninjured leg were lashed securely in place to keep him from thrashing about. The man's eyes rolled about wildly. Sweat beaded his forehead and he bit down on the bit of rope she placed between his jaws.

Bracing her own feet against the rolling deck, Lydia pulled on his foot, carefully repositioning the bone. It took every ounce of strength she possessed to accomplish the task. At the end, she quivered from the effort. Her entire person was drenched in perspiration and the cut on her arm had reopened. Blessedly, the sailor had passed out in the midst of the ordeal. While he remained unconscious, she immobilized the leg so he could not undo her efforts.

As the worst of the injuries were treated, Lydia's tasks became more mundane. She worked with Marshall through the afternoon, washing and bandaging wounds, fetching water, and wiping faces.

The gentlemen joined her late in the afternoon.

Lord Danbury looked appalled. "Miss Garrett, you are running yourself ragged. Some of these patients look better than you do."

"Perhaps you would like to help then." Having reached the limit of her endurance, she had no patience or energy for disruptions.

"Of course we want to help. That's why we are here." Harting smoothly inserted himself between them.

Instantly contrite, Lydia begged pardon. "I'm sorry. Your help would be greatly appreciated. They've had nothing to eat. If you could ask the galley to send something…?"

"I assume you also have had nothing to eat," Harting said.

"I don't think I could eat anything."

"I'll have something brought in case you change your mind."

Lydia shrugged, too weary to argue. From across the room a man croaked out a request for water, and she automatically turned to him.

"Let me get it." Lord Danbury took the cup from her hand.

Harting excused himself to procure food, leaving Lydia with Danbury. She set about changing a dressing. They worked in silence for several moments.

"We took a count and, except for some minor cuts and bruises, all of the wounded are in here. By some miracle we lost only nine men in the battle."

Lydia smiled. "I am glad to hear it. They certainly fought well."

"Most of them are attributing our successful escape to you."

"Me?"

"Yes, they took you literally when you said you prayed."

"I meant it literally. I did pray."

"I know you did. I mean they seem to think you are akin to a saint. On first-name terms with God and all."

Lydia snorted. "I'm scarcely a saint—ask Danielle Long."

"You have a point. I don't think she found you fitting for canonization just yet." Danbury met her gaze and smiled at her. A gentle smile that suggested his opinion was contrary to Danielle Long's.

"Lord Danbury, I—"

Harting arrived leading a parade of men bearing armfuls of hammocks, blankets and trays of piping hot porridge. He took the spoon from Lydia's hand as she bent to help a sailor eat his meal.

"Let me do this. Sit in that chair over there and eat something. Danbury even pulled up a table so you don't have to worry about disarranging your lovely dress."

Lydia looked down at the filthy, blood-spattered rag she wore and grimaced. "I suppose I do look frightful. Little did you know the bargain you were striking when you granted me a clothing allowance."

"Yes, your bits and baubles are liable to bankrupt the nation. Come now. Go eat." He pushed her gently towards the chair.

Danbury patted the back of the chair, like a boy trying to attract a recalcitrant puppy. Lydia offered no resistance. She couldn't marshal her thoughts into an argument. Perhaps if she sat for just a few moments...

CHAPTER 30

"Danbury."

Anthony looked up and Dr Marshall motioned to Miss Garrett. She slumped in her chair, sound asleep. Her dinner lay untouched on the plate, though her fingers still loosely grasped the fork.

"What do you think we should do?" asked Harting. "She's absolutely worn out but we can't leave her there."

Danbury studied the problem. "If we wake her she'll insist on going back to work."

"Do you think we could move her without waking her?" Harting asked.

"I'll carry her and you open the doors for me."

Harting moved the side table out of the way and took the fork from her limp fingers. Anthony scooped her up deftly. Her head lolled back and rested against his shoulder. She half mumbled a protest. His heart did an uncomfortable little flip. His breath quickened. It was from fear of waking her, he reassured himself. He waited a moment to make sure she still slept, then made his way carefully to her cabin.

Anthony laid her down gently in her hammock. She didn't stir. Harting covered her with a blanket. Anthony's eyes narrowed as the agent lingered to brush a stray strand of hair away from her mouth.

He rounded on Anthony with a grimace that bordered on a snarl. "If you do not fulfil your bargain…"

Anthony's jaw tightened and he held up a hand. "What do you take me for, man? Have you learned nothing of me in the past months? I will find a suitable position for her when we return to England."

Harting lowered his head as if abashed and withdrew the insult. "Sorry, Danbury. It is just seeing her thus." He waved a hand at her still form and Danbury could commiserate. Lying there she seemed impossibly fragile—even though he knew her to be made of sterner stuff than the old oak of *Legacy*'s hull.

"Is Miss hurt?"

Anthony started at the soft question. He had forgotten the slave girl. She watched them with wide, dark eyes. Pain and exhaustion etched her features as if her face were made of something harder than flesh.

"She needs to rest."

"We will have Dr Marshall come check on you both as soon as he is at liberty," Harting whispered.

They tiptoed from the cabin, shutting the door behind them.

A pair of sailors walked by, conversing in gale force tones. Anthony shushed them, explaining that Miss Garrett had fallen asleep. Abject in their apologies, the men quickly spread the word. All evening the crew tiptoed when they came near the greater cabin.

Anthony watched the reactions with amusement. As a lovely young woman, Miss Garrett had already become something of a pet among the crew. A few older hands had clung to the old chestnut that women were bad luck on a ship, but now the tales of her adventure on Mahe, her courage during battle, and her compassionate care for their wounded endeared her to them all the more. Every man-jack among them was determined she should have her rest and whatever else they might provide for her.

He rather felt the same way. How had a girl of dubious reputation and embarrassed circumstances managed to captivate the interest of the sons of two noble and ancient houses, as well as a captain and an entire crew? All without resorting to flirting and flattery.

He again pictured Harting smoothing the tendril of hair from her face. The tenderness in the gesture had been palpable. Anthony's brow furrowed. He had come to like Harting, but perhaps the man would bear watching. After all, Anthony had got Miss Garrett embroiled in all this. It was incumbent upon him to provide her some measure of protection from unwanted advances.

* * *

Lydia woke at dawn—a little dazed, but ravenous. Sitting up, she winced as overextended muscles made their protests felt. She must have fallen asleep while eating, and Dr Marshall must have found someone to move her out of the way.

A list of wounded men filed through her mind. They would need help with breakfast. *Mmm, breakfast.* Her stomach growled. She changed out of her filthy blood-spattered dress. Another gown ruined. She daydreamed of a real bath with hot water and soap, but made do with a wash from the tepid water in her basin. At least she could don a clean dress.

Lydia knelt by Sophie's inert figure and smoothed damp hair back from a clammy forehead. The girl was feverish and moaned feebly at the touch. Lydia wet a handkerchief and wiped the girl's face. She needed something to help bring the fever down. She would ask the doctor. Stiffly she straightened and hastened down to the orlop.

Dr Marshall looked exhausted. Dark circles ringed his eyes, standing in stark relief against the paleness of his skin. His hair stood on end, proclaiming that he had run his fingers through it many times. She explained how Sophie had come to be wounded and brought on board with them and he promised to prepare an embrocation for her, but waved away Lydia's attempts to help. "You need more rest. Their shipmates will assist them now that most of the cleaning and patching has been done."

On deck, Lydia inhaled the crisp, pre-dawn breeze, gratefully filling her lungs with the fresh air. The scents of the sickroom seemed stuck in her throat. She paused for a moment to enjoy the quiet stillness of the morning. In fact, it was unusually quiet; the crew must be subdued after the battle.

"Ah, Miss Garrett, you're up. I hope yer feelin' fine."

The boisterous greeting made her jump. She turned to the speaker, one of the sailors. "Yes, thank you. I am."

"I'm glad to hear it, Miss. We was all worried about you."

"Worried about me? Why ever for?"

"Why, on account of you workin' yerself to the bone, and faintin' from pure exhaustion."

Another sailor called to the first. "Angus, you daft mule, be quiet or you'll wake Miss." He came around the mast and stopped. "Oh, Miss, you're up. I hope this great gob didn't wake you. How are you feeling?"

Lydia had to laugh. "I feel fine, thank you. I'm not sure what you were told, but I only fell asleep."

"And you had every right to, Miss. We showed those Frenchies not to mess about with honest, God-fearing Englishmen. Gave 'em what for, we did. I reckon they saw you and thought we had an angel on board helping to fend 'em off."

"I reckon they was right if they did," said Angus. "You saved my mate Liam, getting him below decks smart-like. Then you patched him up. I never seen a neater job. He's already back in his own berth. He said as how he might have died if it hadn't been for you. You ever need anything from old Angus Robb, you just ask."

Lydia blushed, fumbling for a response. "You are very kind. I just tried to help where I could."

"Aye, well, there ain't many high-born ladies of quality what would risk their necks. That took pluck. Like I said, you ask if you ever need anything."

Lydia cast about for a way to extract herself. "Sophie needs something nourishing to eat. Could you please check with cook and see if breakfast has been prepared?"

"Right'o, Miss. We'll bring it up for you whenever it's done."

"Thank you," she said, making her escape.

Calls of "Good morning, Miss," and "How are you feelin'?" followed her progress through the ship. She smiled and greeted each man courteously. By the time she reached the great cabin, she was near to running like some poor hunted beast. She closed the door and leaned against it to shut out the hullabaloo caused by her passage.

Lord Danbury glanced up at her entrance; he must have come in while she was on deck.

"Miss Garrett, good morning. I trust you slept well."

"Yes, thank you." Lydia abandoned the door. "You are awake early."

He stood, vacating the seat and offering it to her before pulling up another for himself.

Lydia took the chair willingly. She would not betray her discomfort, but every muscle ached. Even the strenuous efforts of their sojourn on Mahe had failed to prepare her body for the exertions of a sea battle.

"You were right about the men. They seem to have given me credit for our escape."

"Yes, I heard them. They are all smitten."

Lydia shook her head. "Perhaps it is because I have been the only woman on board."

Lydia and Anthony jumped as the door burst open and Angus trundled in, carrying a tray loaded with a breakfast of boiled oats. Apparently, *Legacy*'s cook did not ascribe to the notion that invalids should be fed broth and light liquids.

"Here you are, Miss; just as I promised," said Angus grinning jovially.

"Thank you. If this doesn't stick to Sophie's ribs and get her on her feet again, nothing will." *If only from a desire to avoid eating any more of this tasteless stuff.* Lydia smiled and accepted the tray.

"Now, don't you worry none, Miss. A proper breakfast is coming for you and the gentlemen. My mate Liam, what you patched up, is bringing it up when it's done. You deserve better than this here and we'll make sure you get fed right."

Lydia had to admit relief. "You are very kind, but please don't annoy cook by asking for special dishes for me."

"You've nothing to worry 'bout on that score. Cook is happy to do what he can and he told me particular that you're to ask for anything you want and he'll get it for you if he can. If we don't have it aboard we'll get it special when we get to India. If you don't mind waiting, that is."

"I am perfectly satisfied with whatever he makes."

"Ain't it just like you?" Angus grinned. "Sweetness itself. Not wanting anybody to trouble over you. He's as good as got your message. I'll tell him it myself." Knuckling his forehead, he closed the door softly behind him.

Lydia shook her head at the closed door. This sort of behaviour could easily become trying.

"Give them a few days and the adulation will die down a bit," Danbury said. His eyes positively twinkled. Given half a chance, he would chuckle.

Lydia glared at him. "It's unnerving to be thrust up on such a high pedestal. I'll be lucky not to fall off and land on *someone*." Pleased with her parting shot, Lydia flounced away to feed Sophie breakfast.

* * *

"Were you able to plot a direct course for Calcutta, Captain?" Marcus asked.

"Aye, we have provisions enough to see us to India. We were lucky to have the chance to water and victual on Mahe."

"I'm relieved to hear it. Time may still be of the essence in this matter." Marcus adjusted his cravat. Why had he said that? He wasn't relieved. It felt as if the proverbial sword of Damocles was suspended directly above his head.

CHAPTER 30

"What do you plan to do when we arrive?" Danbury asked.

"I shall approach the Governor-General and lay the whole story before him. A great deal will depend on how he receives us."

"What do you know of him?"

"Lord Wellesley will undoubtedly act. He is a great political friend to William Pitt. He has been effective militarily in India, but he can be... mercurial. The rumour was that he grew petulant when his victory over Tippoo Sultan only netted him a marquessate. He'd had his cap set at the Order of the Garter."

"Will he be an ally?"

"I'm no fortune-teller," Marcus sighed. "We must show him that it is in his interests to ally with us."

Campbell rubbed his hands together. "I tell you, gentlemen, I'll be able to dine out for years on the tales of this particular voyage. Though whether anyone will believe me is another thing."

Marcus wished he could feel as optimistic. He had ever struggled with second-guessing the decisions he made in the heat of the moment. If only he had been able to capture the traitor—the man had actually been on the island with them and yet he was no closer to even knowing his identity. Disappointment tasted sour in his mouth.

"Sail away, sir." A young man knuckled his forehead as he made his report.

Campbell stood. "Excuse me a moment, gentlemen."

Marcus and Danbury set to rehashing the final days on Mahe. The euphoria of escape had been usurped by frustration that they had not captured the murderer and the mood on board ship had begun to grow fractious. Though he made no mention of it, Danbury seemed pinched, the force of his ebullient personality diminished. Lost opportunities—the world was aswim with them. Marcus shoved aside his regrets. Wallowing would avail naught.

Legacy picked up speed perceptibly. Danbury broke off in midsentence. He and Marcus exchanged a look. Standing in concert, they went out on deck. Miss Garrett joined them, worry writ plain on her face. She eyed the captain as if awaiting judgment.

Campbell said something further to his pilot then left the helm, making his way to where his passengers stood. He came directly to the point. "I've good reason to think that ship off our beam is a French corvette."

CHAPTER 31

Dread cinched Marcus's gut tighter than the Prince of Wales's corset. What if this mission failed?

"Do you think we're in danger?" As ever, Danbury cut to the heart of the concern.

"We've pulled away smartly and may be able to shake her, but I'm wary. We've sighted the same ship twice before. She never seems to draw nearer, but neither does she lose sight of us for long. Her captain is sly enough to keep out of sight for the most part, and a good enough sailor to pull it off. I'd lay odds she's stalking us. Any normal privateer would make a dash and swarm aboard like a plague of infernal locusts." Campbell pushed back his hat and scratched his head. "This is something different."

"What do you suggest?" Marcus asked.

"I say we pack on sail and try to outrun her. *Legacy* hasn't nearly reached the limit of what she can do. I thought you gentlemen might have reasons for wanting to draw the sloop on, though, so I wanted to consult you."

"Could she simply be another ship using this same route? This is a trade route, isn't it?" Marcus asked. He wouldn't be one of those agents who leapt to conclusions. They invariably blundered and cost lives.

"Aye, it is, but that ship is no merchantman, nor is she escorting one. She is alone, and like I said, a normal privateer would be on us like lice—if you'll pardon the expression, Miss."

"Is it possible that *Angélique* had a consort?" Danbury said.

The captain shrugged. "There could have been a dozen ships hidden away in some cove, or coming around from the other side of the island."

Closing his eyes, Marcus rubbed them lightly. After a moment he looked up. "Then the traitor may be on this ship rather than *Angélique*. This unknown sloop may even have stopped to pick him up from their disabled counterpart."

A spark lit Danbury's eyes for the first time in days. He took to pacing. "With our masts and rigging damaged, it was slow going for a while. They'd have had plenty of time to catch us up."

Miss Garrett took one small step forward. "It would seem, Captain, that the answer depends on their intentions. If they mean to take us, we should run; if they intend to follow us, then perhaps we ought to let them. We could allow them to think we remain unaware of them, and set a trap."

Lord Danbury turned and stared at her from under lowering brows.

"I apologize, my Lord. I spoke out of turn."

"No, please. You make a good point. The trick is to discern what they intend."

The captain shrugged. "It seems to me that if they meant to overtake us they would have already done so. They have had ample opportunity, with all the advantages of surprise and even the darkness of night to mask their approach, yet they have not."

"If their spy is aboard that ship, I should dearly like another opportunity to bring him to justice," Danbury said.

Marcus voiced his agreement with this sentiment. Raising his spyglass, Marcus peered at the tiny fleck of white on the far edge of the horizon. If the spy were truly on board, he might have one more chance at redemption. The traitor would not escape again.

* * *

"Doctor, have you prepared the physic for Sophie?"

Marshall's hands were busy changing a bandage and he gestured with his chin towards the medicine cabinet. "The one marked with a bit of tar on the stopper."

Lydia pulled out the small brown bottle and lifted the stopper. It smelled of all things foul, but if it would aid the girl, she would make sure Sophie took her dose faithfully.

Offering a nod of thanks as she passed, she hurried back to the sun and air.

She opened the door to her cabin cautiously for fear of waking her last remaining patient. It had been wasted worry. Sophie was already awake, though she remained in her hammock.

Lydia took the girl's hand in her own. It was hot and dry, as fragile as a meadowlark. "How are you, Sophie?"

"I'm better. Thank you."

"I brought you a concoction that Dr Marshall prepared. It will ease your pain, and put you to rights in no time."

The girl attempted to raise herself, but Lydia placed a hand on her shoulder. "Stay yourself. You still need rest." She poured a dollop into a small cup and handed it to the girl. Sophie wrinkled her nose at the stench, but dutifully swallowed the lot, though it left her gasping. Lydia quickly handed her a cup of water to wash away the taste.

"Has Dr Marshall come to see you at all?"

"No, Miss."

Lydia frowned, but then pushed aside her irritation. He had had his hands full with all his patients. "I shall remind him to look in."

"You are very good, Miss."

Lydia waved aside the comment. "What would you like to do in London? I mean if you could have your heart's desire."

"I—" Sophie's gaze grew dreamy and she shook her head.

Lydia cocked her head, inviting further comment.

"I would like to—" A flush darkened her cheeks. She sighed and spoke again. "You said the ladies of London would like my gowns. I would most love to work as a mantua maker."

Lydia blinked. "You do beautiful work. I'm sure it will not be long before you have a line of clients at the door."

Lydia lifted the water to the girl's mouth again and she gulped it.

"Careful, slow down." She smoothed the girl's hair back from her face. "How do you keep track of your ideas?"

"I draw them. I get papers and charcoals, and I get them out, 'fore I forget." Fumbling at the pocket of her dress, Sophie removed a ragged little sheaf of folded pages and offered it to Lydia.

Lydia took the stack and paused in her ministrations long enough to leaf through the pages. The paper had obviously come from several sources. Many of the pieces had four or five drawings crowded onto each side. The quick sketches described graceful lines and an elegant sense of proportion.

"You're an artist with your pen as well as your needle."

Sophie ducked her head shyly. Lydia carried on as if she had not noticed Sophie's discomfort. "You've embraced the new French style."

"Monsieur liked to keep in touch with what goes on in his homeland."

"I find that I like this new fashion very much."

"It suits you."

"I think your gowns will be in great demand. Lord Danbury will ensure you get a good start."

"Miss—"

"Yes?"

"I'm sorry, Miss. I made some—guesses? No. I don't know de right word, but I thought wicked things 'bout you when you come to the house. I beg pardon."

Lydia could not feign ignorance. Patting her hand, she smiled. "Do not give it another thought. I'm well aware people may misunderstand my—circumstances. I am not unprepared for it. I do appreciate that you have revised your opinion of me."

Sophie refused to meet her eyes.

Lydia changed the subject to ease the girl's embarrassment. "Would you like something to eat?"

"I could not eat."

"It will help you to regain your strength. Just a little?"

"I don't think so, Miss."

"Then I shall fetch Emmanuel; perhaps he can convince you to eat."

* * *

Lydia stared up at the dome of the sky. The stars shone large and vibrant against the deepest indigo of night, bigger and brighter than any she had glimpsed in London. Dr Marshall joined her at the rail.

"As you requested, I looked in on the slave girl. I fear her condition is grave."

Lydia's mouth dropped open. "I have been with her most of the day. She seemed to be improving."

"That is often the way with gunshot wounds." He turned from his perusal of the sea to offer her a half-smile. "I have attended my share of duelists."

Lydia turned her face away. How could she have misunderstood Sophie's condition so drastically?

Marshall placed a hand on her shoulder. "Do not fault yourself, child. Patients often seem to rally, and just when we begin to hope, they falter." He cleared his throat. "I made her as comfortable as I could, and bled her to bring down her fever. But… perhaps you ought to say farewell and call her brother. I don't think she will last the night."

Numbly, Lydia fled to her cabin. Tears pooled in her eyes as she fell to her knees beside Sophie's hammock. Dr Marshall was right behind her and she heard him rustling about the cabin.

"Oh, Sophie. I'm so sorry," she whispered. She wanted to say more, but couldn't force the words past her heartbreak.

Sweat beaded on Sophie's forehead and she moaned softly. Fingers shaking, Lydia bathed the girl's face with cool water.

"Miss Garrett." The sharpness of the tone made her head snap up as if she had been slapped.

"Did I not tell you the stopper marked with tar?"

Her brow furrowed in confusion. "I'd…"

He held up the vial, its dark glass unmarred by a daub of tar or any other kind.

Lydia balled her hands into fists. Her nails dug into her palms. This was her fault. Negligence and foolish pride had kept her from taking greater care in selecting the appropriate bottle. She had never even thought to check it again before administering it. Who was she to be playing physician and surgeon? The tears spilled over, scalding her cheeks.

"Please leave us, Miss Garrett. Her brother must be informed of her condition."

Dumbly she nodded and stumbled from the cabin.

CHAPTER 32

Dry-eyed at last, Lydia stared as Sophie's body was sewn into a canvas bag with a cannonball for company. The ceremony was mercifully brief. Lydia wanted to hide away in her cabin. She fingered the pitiful scraps of paper she had salvaged. They were all that remained of a gifted artist's dreams. Lydia swallowed, pushing back against the regret that threatened to throttle her.

Emmanuel stood, a towering figure though his head was bowed in sorrow.

My fault. My fault. The aching knowledge drummed through her.

She approached him tentatively. "I am so very sorry." The words she marshalled with such effort emerged as little more than a whisper.

His gaze met hers and though she found anguish there she read no condemnation.

"I meant only to care for her."

"I know." His deep voice held no reproach, but neither did it offer any warmth.

"I… please." Her voice fractured. She breathed deeply of the salt air that stung her reddened eyes. "I have no right to approach you, but I beg you to forgive me."

He really looked at her then for the first time, his gaze searing into her until he seemed to have read her soul.

"You're a kind lady. You show us regard, though you know we are just slaves. But, I—" He looked away, out to the sea that surrounded them, or perhaps to something both nearer and infinitely further. "I will ask God to help me forgive. It will take time. I am not so strong all at once."

She bowed her head in acknowledgment, a defendant in the dock accepting the verdict. There would be no absolution. "I will trouble you no longer. Only, these were Sophie's. I think she would want you to have them." She extended to him the scraps of paper that held his sister's heart.

He accepted them with trembling hands and began to page through them. Unabashed tears dripped and spattered off his chin.

Lydia turned to catch Lord Danbury eyeing her. As much as she wanted to, she could not find it in herself to summon a reassuring smile. She needed to get away from all the watchful eyes and helpful hands. She hated the adoration from the seamen. Couldn't they see she was not worthy of their regard?

* * *

"Well, gentlemen. We've kept a close watch on that sloop and we've proved your theory. Their sails appear on the horizon once or twice a day, but then fall back almost as quickly. They've made no effort to draw nearer."

Anthony grinned and looked at Harting. They had another chance to get their hands on the killer. His fingers tightened experimentally. Once he got hold of him...

From the satisfied look on Harting's face, he had obviously already reached the same conclusion. "It has become a sort of game among the crew, to see who can spot the sloop on any given day."

Captain Campbell harrumphed. He was clearly not amused by the cat-and-mouse game. "I suppose you want me to keep to our course and string these fellows along."

"Doggedly, sir. Doggedly," Harting said.

"All right then." Campbell shook his head. "If you'll excuse me, gentlemen." Anthony had the distinct impression that the captain would have liked to sigh. Not that he blamed the poor fellow. If Anthony were skipper he wouldn't like risking his vessel either.

A flash of pale green muslin caught his eye, and Anthony looked down to see Miss Garrett staring out at the horizon. She seemed oblivious to her surroundings and her posture lacked the graceful assurance he associated with her.

The slave girl's death had hit her unaccountably hard. Miss Garrett had a compassionate nature, but why should she grieve so deeply for someone she had known only a few days? And yet the sorrow was there. It darkened her eyes and flattened the animation of her features. It was as if she had died with the slave girl and the figure at the bow was a mere ghost haunting the ship.

She was so pale. Had she been eating properly? Anthony took a step towards her, but then reversed his course. Perhaps Dr Marshall could take a look at her. No doubt she would accept his solicitude better.

* * *

The mouth of the Hooghly River yawned before them, a serpent ready to swallow them whole. Only a little further. Lydia stepped away from the gentlemen and peered back past the stern of the ship.

Yesterday, the white sails that had dogged them for weeks had grown larger and larger until they were the size of her hand when she extended it to the horizon. But then they had sighted a convoy of Indiamen with their Royal Navy escorts, and the sloop had melted away.

Now *Legacy* was surrounded by everything from great trading ships to navy frigates, junks to one-man rowboats. As if the river were a funnel, the vessels came together in a sudden rush, each vying for position as they waited for a pilot who could guide them through the treacherous sandbars that littered the waterway.

Danbury's liberal funding had procured a pilot more quickly than they might have expected, and *Legacy* wove her way among lesser ships like the stately lady she was.

Transfixed, Lydia stood at the rail and watched as the land glided past. Danbury paced along the rail in the waist of the ship, his hands clasped behind his back, his attention fixed on the exotic scene. Harting had his glass to his eye, and his free hand plucked at his cravat.

A fantastical Hindu temple nearly groaned beneath the weight of a surfeit of decoration. Lydia could not spy an inch that was not carved, painted or moulded. Ancient decay had worn other shrines into little more than moulded mounds of stone. Dilapidated hovels stood cheek by jowl with ostentatious new buildings painted in lurid colours.

Mr Cabot appeared at her side. "I've been to India twice before. It is difficult to take in all at once."

Mutely she nodded.

Legacy slowed as they neared Calcutta and the river traffic grew even heavier.

A frescoed building with a long colonnade sat at the edge of the river. A series of stairs as wide as the building led all the way into the water. Among jumbles of crates and boxes, men, women and children thronged the stairs. Others stood in the muddy brown water.

"What is that?" she asked.

Mr Cabot smiled broadly. "It's a bathing ghat. The Indians try to bathe at least once a day in running water, and since the Hooghly is the main tributary of the Ganges, they consider this water holy."

Lydia looked over the side at the brackish water. "It smells foul."

"Yes, well, they also use it for a variety of other purposes, including the disposal of diseased corpses." A glimmer of nearly sly humour flickered in his eyes at her horrified gasp.

Stonily she turned back to the river and watched in silence. Mr Cabot seemed not to notice her pique and remained by her side.

A flood of irrational panic churned her stomach. What if they failed to convince the Governor-General to go along with their plan? Swallowing hard, she placed a hand flat against her abdomen. She took a deep breath and immediately wished she hadn't.

CHAPTER 32

They sailed past Fort William, its battery bristling with the snouts of long black cannon. At last, Captain Campbell anchored near a dozen or so other ships.

Calcutta gleamed in the afternoon sun. The entire city seemed to be made of white marble.

"It looks almost… European?" Lydia said.

Cabot nodded. "Calcutta was really built by the East India Company. The northern areas where the company officials live are airy—palatial even."

"Since we speak of palaces, what is that building there?" Lydia pointed to an immense building some distance away.

Cabot leaned forward and squinted. After a moment he leaned back. "It must be the new Government House. I left the company not long after the foundation was laid. Wellesley meant to build a palace better befitting his dignity from nearly the moment he stepped ashore."

"You do not care for him then?"

Cabot shrugged. "He's a competent leader, but with his gifts he could have been great. He'll never achieve that though—he's too fussy. Too set on formality and too intent on making sure everyone knows he's in charge. No. People respect him, but they don't like him much and he doesn't like them."

Lydia's gaze strayed back to the massive white building. Would such a man champion their cause, or prove another hindrance?

* * *

Once ashore, Anthony hired a carriage for their use. A native man perched in the driver's seat, his head wrapped in a snowy turban, but bare-chested. A piece of cloth that extended to his ankles was wound around his body like a skirt.

Dr Marshall paused next to the cart. With a tug at his earlobe he addressed Anthony. "I understand you're going to Government House?"

"Yes, sir. Are you going that way? You're welcome to join us."

"I am. Thank you." The doctor climbed up.

Miss Garrett slid closer to Anthony to make room. The nearness of her body made his throat tighten. He stared at the passing scenery, studiously trying to ignore the warmth spreading from her thigh to his.

People teemed through the streets. Some were shabby, but more were dressed in brilliant colours that vied for attention. Most of the native men wore long, narrow-chested jackets that reached to their knees, and a sort of loose pantaloon beneath, secured tightly at the ankle. Each head was crowned with a turban. Most of the women wore garments not much different from the men's, but a few wore tight, short blouses and separate skirts, leaving their abdomens scandalously bare. Matching headscarves rested lightly, covering their hair. Gold glinted from earlobes, necks, wrists, and fingers.

Anthony's mouth dropped open as an ornate barouche crossed their path. It was pulled by a matched pair of zebras and driven by an Indian man in European livery. If ever there were a city built on excess they had found it.

They passed under a white marble archway surmounted by lions. Brackets were in place which indicated it would be a gate one day, but for the moment it offered no impediment to visitors. Scaffolding still shrouded portions of the east wing. But the enormous building managed to retain an air of cool detachment.

A dome sat centred over a rotunda and columned wings spread out on either side: it was a palace befitting imperial goals.

British soldiers in brilliant red dress coats guarded the main entrance. They stood unmoving as the visitors—led by Harting—approached. He presented his request to see the Governor-General and within a few moments a clerk appeared. Harting once more offered his compliments and credentials. They were whisked through halls and corridors, down colonnades, and up stairs. Everything gleamed with newness, from the black-and-white, tiled marble floor to the wall hangings.

At last they were deposited in a small, comfortably furnished antechamber. "If you could oblige us by waiting, gentlemen, miss." He inclined his head towards Miss Garrett. "His Lordship will attend you shortly."

"You are very kind," Harting murmured.

In a matter of moments, the impeccably mannered staff produced refreshments and then discreetly withdrew. Miss Garrett poured them each a draught of iced lemon water.

Harting lounged in his seat. "It isn't as hot as I feared."

"Hot enough." Anthony pulled out a handkerchief and swabbed his face.

Miss Garrett sipped at her glass, looking as cool as if she were made of marble—like everything else in this shrine to commerce. Anthony strode to the windows. They stood open, but little in the way of a breeze stirred the drapery. "I may very well strangle the next man who tells me I must wait before I can see this business through."

Harting raised his glass and a single eyebrow in sardonic salute.

The door opened again and the clerk reappeared. "Lord Wellesley asked that you meet him in the gardens. If you'll follow me."

CHAPTER 33

They found Lord Wellesley holding an architectural plan up to the building and giving the overseer marching orders. Anthony scrutinized Wellesley while he had the chance: friend or foe?

He was as tall and thin as a whippet, his broad forehead so high he was nearly bald. White hair contrasted sharply with thick, dark eyebrows. His nose was long and thin, perfect for looking down upon lesser mortals. And his mouth was delicate, almost feminine.

The clerk approached close enough to be seen and then backed away again. Wellesley finished his conversation then turned to them.

"Miss Garrett, Lord Danbury, Mr Harting." With infinite courtesy, he greeted each in turn. "I am Lord Wellesley. I understand you have arrived in Calcutta this very day with some urgent matter to discuss."

"Yes, sir." Harting produced his letter of introduction from William Pitt.

A single eyebrow went up as the Governor-General read the letter. Folding it neatly, he returned it to Harting. "Perhaps you would care to join me in my office. It appears the nature of our conversation should remain confidential."

He offered Miss Garrett his arm and ushered them back inside, through another labyrinth of corridors and into what must be his private sanctum. A large desk guarded one end of the room with a couple of stiff-looking chairs standing sentry in front of it. Wellesley bypassed this area, leading them instead to a more informal seating area made up of several couches. "Would you care for something to drink?"

"Your clerk was kind enough to have refreshments brought to us earlier," said Danbury.

"Part of the trick to overcoming the heat here is to make sure you drink enough," said Lord Wellesley. He rang for more refreshments. "Now, precisely how may I be of service to you?"

Harting took the lead. "Actually, we are here to be of some service to you." He carefully outlined the story of their adventures in detail, pausing only when a servant came in with drinks. The Governor-General interrupted rarely and the few questions he asked proved his attentiveness.

The telling of the tale took the greater part of an hour. At its conclusion, Wellesley leaned back in his seat. "So you've brought the Peacock Throne to India. It seems most irregular. Why not take it to England, where it could be guarded from every Nawab who got it in his head to set up a new dynasty?"

Harting took a long draught from his glass. "We felt the best course of action would be to pull Bonaparte's fangs by returning the throne to India ourselves. If, as a British gesture of friendship, we repatriate the throne, it loses its power to rally troops to another's cause."

The Governor-General tapped his lower lip with one finger. "I fear you may overestimate the Oriental mind. They embrace any excuse to cause trouble. I shall have to consider this matter carefully. We must make no mistakes for the French to take advantage of." He sighed and sat silent for a moment, tap-tapping on his lip.

Anthony struggled to keep the sneer within him from rising to the surface.

Wellesley's gaze returned from the middle distance with an almost audible snap and focused square on Harting. "Perhaps I have been too hasty. This may be for the best." He nodded. "Yes, Pitt was wise to place his confidence in you. This could be just the signal we need. We're hosting a ceremony and ball here on the twenty-sixth to inaugurate Government House. I intended to display Tippoo Sultan's throne at that time. We will show off the Peacock Throne at the same time. It will be a clear symbol of British dominance to all the native princes."

Anthony ground his teeth. He had the same sinking sensation he'd had as a boy when he leaped from the roof of the stables and discovered he could not fly after all.

* * *

Surely Marcus had heard wrong. God grant that the man wasn't that thick-headed. He concealed his anxiety behind the mask he had cultivated so long. For a languid moment he examined his breeches and plucked a stray hair from his knee. Only then did he turn his gaze to the Governor-General's. "I'm afraid that won't work, my Lord. Rather than avert a crisis, you tempt uprising."

"Calcutta is well protected by the garrison at Fort William." Wellesley's cheeks and the tip of his aristocratic nose turned cerise. He patently loathed those who argued with him.

Too bad, thought Marcus grimly. *I'm not one of your lap dogs to be bullied or bribed into submission.* "Calcutta is not the only British outpost in the country."

Danbury interrupted with the force of an explosion. "You'll not lay a hand on the throne if your intention is to rub the faces of the Indians in defeat. Such an attitude would, would—"

Marcus cut in smoothly. "The spy could position his puppet as the salvation of India and begin what would amount to a revolution. A mob could be storming Government House in a matter of a few hours. We may be better armed but we are vastly outnumbered. If the rajas band together we haven't a hope of survival. The French would have accomplished all they set out to do."

Danbury's chin stuck out at a pugnacious angle. "My father was entrusted with the care of the throne and I intend to see it returned to those who have the right to claim it. I am not a thief."

Marcus could not recall his Lordship embracing such a sentiment before, but he swallowed any urge to smile.

"So what do you propose?" Wellesley sat back in his seat with the air of one who has washed his hands of an affair and does not much care what is decided.

And here was the rub. What *were* they to do with the great monstrosity? Marcus exhaled through his nose. They ought to have chucked it into the Indian Ocean when they had the chance. Silence reigned as they considered the complexities of the case.

Miss Garrett cleared her throat. "Gentlemen, I do not wish to speak out of turn, but I believe the most practical course of action would be generosity." She looked to Marcus as if seeking support, but he had no notion what she meant. He shrugged minutely and shook his head.

She continued. "What I mean is, why not adapt Lord Wellesley's idea of displaying it at the ball? We can announce that we are returning a great treasure to India. It could be presented as a gesture of friendship between England and the princely states, rather than as a wedge to divide them."

"Yes." Wellesley set to tapping his lip again. "I can see a number of advantages to the idea. Our intentions would be clear, so the rabble cannot be roused by fiery speeches and innuendo. They will be forced to steal the thing if they want to raise a pretender to the throne like Tippoo Sultan."

"It would also make it seem we are unaware of the threat still posed by the French agent," said Danbury.

Marcus smiled wickedly. "We can set a trap and lure the spy into trying to steal the throne. We will present him with an attractive time for an attempted theft. He will know where the throne is to be, and we can arrange to make it seem we are quite lax, and it is loosely guarded. We shall be able to set the stage rather than wait for our opponent to act. Well done, Miss Garrett."

Miss Garrett flushed, her eyes gleaming almost as brightly as they had before the slave girl had died. It was good to see the animation returning to her features. Like seeing Galatea come to life.

"Then it is settled. We have a week to prepare. I'll keep a company guarding the throne at all times, in case they decide to strike sooner. I think it unlikely though. We will have the spy in a nice neat net, and when we've trussed him, I shall have the fun of feeding him to the sharks." Wellesley stood. "Where is the throne now?"

"Aboard *Legacy*. We thought it best to consult you before trying to bring it ashore," Marcus said.

"Just so. Well, we will have to make quite sure of its safety. Let me round up a few good men and a stout cart. I think I shall go with them. Will you be returning to your ship?"

"Yes, sir," Danbury said.

"Good. Then I should like you to show me this remarkable throne. I want to know what all the fuss is about."

"We would be happy to show you, sir, but there is one other matter."

"Yes?" A note of impatience tinged his tone for the first time.

"We would like to be in on the planning and capture of the French agent," Harting said.

Wellesley considered. "I suppose it's fitting. You have strung them along this far. Taking away your victory would hardly be sporting."

As they waited for the cart to be brought round and the men to assemble, Lord Wellesley seemed to become a different man. He was urbane and charming, certainly, but a well-mannered façade obscured the greater force of his personality.

"Have you made arrangements for lodging?"

"No, sir. Do you have any suggestions? We can always stay aboard *Legacy* if decent lodging is difficult to come by," said Lord Danbury.

"I should be glad to have you stay at Government House. It is time we had a building that reflects England. It has been rather a project of mine. There are a few things yet to be completed, but for the most part construction is finished."

"We should be delighted to stay. We were quite impressed with the architecture."

"We shall be happy to have you. It is always a pleasure to catch up on the news from home. In fact, Miss…"

"Garrett," said Danbury.

"Yes, I apologize, Miss Garrett. There is surely no need for you to return to the ship. I know a young lady who would enjoy meeting you. Mrs Adkins is a widow, but she has been a great help to me, acting as my hostess in my wife's absence. She is always desirous of new and pleasant company."

Marcus bit the inside of his cheek to keep from speaking. The metallic tang of blood filled his mouth. How dare Wellesley send Miss Garrett to fraternize with his mistress?

All innocence and goodwill, Miss Garrett smiled prettily. "I should be delighted to meet her, I'm sure."

The blood trickled down the back of Marcus's throat. He could not protest. He had known when manipulating Miss Garrett to his purpose that her virtue would be suspect. Before it had not seemed to matter when placed beside Pitt's imperatives. But now…

* * *

Miss Garrett departed. A moment later the clerk announced the carriage and the gentlemen made good their departure. Wellesley did not speak again until they were seated in the carriage. "I don't intend to be impertinent, but may I know how Miss Garrett came to join your expedition, and her role?"

Fighting the impulse to bristle, Anthony related the story.

"Ah, I see. And do you think her quite trustworthy? Did you confirm the source of her sudden affluence?"

Harting sprang to Miss Garrett's defence. "Indeed, I helped her secure the small income which she now claims. In all things she has acted above reproach. I can vouch for her loyalty."

Anthony regarded Harting. The man's familiar tone bordered on the impudent. His attentions towards her had always been marked. Maybe if Anthony failed to produce employment for her, the man would press her into some sort of liaison. His nostrils flared at the notion. It could very well explain why Harting had been hounding him to know what provision he had made. Blood pulsed at his temples. The rogue was plotting his seductions.

"She is priceless and unique," said Anthony. He regaled Wellesley with tales of Miss Garrett's courage and compassion during their adventures.

"It sounds as if this young woman has uncommon good sense, which makes her rarer than I first thought. So which of you fine young bucks is bedding her?"

Anthony blinked. He could not speak, could not move. If he did he would surely throttle the Governor-General and be slapped behind bars. His glance found Harting's and to his surprise found no gloating smirk resting there. Instead, Harting was flushed and breathing through his nostrils. His hands kneaded the knobbed head of his cane.

Perhaps Anthony had misjudged the man.

Silence reigned in the carriage for a long, long moment. "Come now, surely it would be foolish to let such an extraordinary feminine specimen escape you." Lord Wellesley grinned mischievously. "Ah, well, here we are."

Captain Campbell welcomed the Governor-General aboard with all the pomp and ceremony he could muster on short notice. The fanfare was mercifully curtailed by Wellesley's eagerness to see the throne.

Deep in the hold, Anthony took a crowbar and removed several of the slats from the crate containing the throne. Wellesley himself removed some of the weeds that padded the crate and peered in. He motioned for the light to be brought closer. Gold and jewels glittered enticingly in the spare light of the oil lamp. Pulling his head from the opening, Wellesley cleared his throat.

"Hmm, yes, I see. Quite aside from its political value, this must be worth an astronomical sum." He leaned back into the opening. "It seems to call to one, doesn't it?"

CHAPTER 34

L ydia found Mrs Adkins plucking a melancholy air on a small mandolin.

A statuesque beauty, Mrs Adkins' golden hair gave the appearance of luxurious length, even bound and dressed up off her neck. Her dress set off a graceful figure to perfection. The blue of the fabric, a few shades lighter than her eyes, made them look all the more vivid.

She inspected Lydia as if sizing up a rival—one she was confident of crushing in short order.

They circled each other in polite small talk.

"What has brought you to India?" asked Mrs Adkins at last.

Lydia picked her words with care. "I lost my cousin to a murderer, the same man who killed Lord Danbury's father."

"Oh my." Mrs Adkins raised a dainty hand to her mouth. "How dreadful. I knew him in London. A very nice man I always thought. And you are his son's… associate?"

Lydia nodded mutely.

"I suppose you have a chaperone."

Lydia shook her head. "Character is best demonstrated when there is no watchful eye to force one to do right. I am no one's courtesan."

One of Mrs Adkins' eyebrows shot up. "You must have done a great many interesting things."

Lydia hesitated. Was this a veiled barb?

Mrs Adkins seemed to note Lydia's consternation, and her cheeks coloured as well. "If I intend an insult, you shall be in no doubt about it." A smile broke through at the absurdity of the threat. An instant later Lydia was laughing with her.

Lydia collected herself. "We seem to be sniping at one another for no good reason."

Mrs Adkins reached for the glass at her elbow and sipped. "I am so accustomed to fending off supercilious busybodies I have begun to leap to the conclusion that every woman who arrives in Calcutta will try to take her pound of flesh from my person."

Lydia swallowed. Dear heavens, she had been defending her own reputation when the entire time she was in the presence of Wellesley's mistress.

"May I offer a bit of advice? The harridans around here can be… unkind." Pain lurked deep in the lady's eyes, and Lydia knew she was speaking from the heart of her experience. "Construct a small fiction. Say that one of the gentlemen is your guardian or some such. Your life will be easier."

Lydia bit her lip. Perhaps such a tale would stave off the rumourmongers. But her conduct gave her no cause for embarrassment. Perhaps it was time to refuse to be embarrassed.

"Well, now that we are to be friends, perhaps you will tell me something of yourself."

Lydia shared her story willingly since it seemed to distract Mrs Adkins.

"The little lost heiress!" Mrs Adkins clapped her hands delightedly at the conclusion of the tale.

"Hardly an heiress," Lydia protested through her smile. "My parents were as poor as church mice and I never had a claim on my mother's family."

"Nonsense. I shall make up a lovely story for you. You have the beginnings of a very nice novel in your tale, but it must have a happy ending. I'll have it no other way."

Lydia could not help but laugh.

"Perhaps one of your gentlemen…"

The blood seemed to freeze in Lydia's veins. She shied away from the insidious notion. Harbouring any such ridiculous hopes would only invite heartache. "It's out of the question, I assure you."

Mrs Adkins shrugged, apparently unperturbed by Lydia's harshness. "And now you are in this very unique position—able to travel the world. If the proper misses of London society knew what they were missing—"

The tramp of booted feet sounded in the hall, and they paused in their conversation.

Lord Wellesley pushed through the door, followed closely by Danbury and Harting. "M'dear, you look in exceptionally good spirits. I thought Miss Garrett might be good company for you."

"You were very right, sir. She is a charming young woman and I thank you for sending her to me."

Wellesley patted her hand. "I have a few more guests for you. May I present the Earl of Danbury and the Honourable Marcus Harting."

Both gentlemen bowed.

"I am charmed to meet you both. Lord Danbury, you have my sincere condolences on your father's passing."

"You are very kind. He is sorely missed."

"I imagine so. He was one of the few who welcomed me in London, and I always appreciated his kind treatment. Please, won't you sit? I'm sure you're dreadfully thirsty after your exertions." She rang for refreshments.

Lord Wellesley excused himself, citing other pressing concerns. They spent the balance of the afternoon in Mrs Adkins' company until the time came to dress for dinner and they were shown to guest rooms.

Lydia's chamber was lovely. Decorated in a formal style, it was saved from pretension by the liberal use of beautiful Indian silks and native flowers, which gave the room an exotic flavour.

Lydia pulled off her sweltering garments and, after a quick wash, she exchanged wool stockings for the cooler luxury of silk ones, and allowed herself to be pushed into a chair in front of the vanity so a maid could dress her hair.

CHAPTER 34

Despite her best efforts, she found herself unprepared for the arch looks and knowing scorn that were sure to come. It rankled that any insolent fool might question her virtue and she had little recourse. When they'd left London, no one had anticipated this detour. Lydia had certainly never prepared for the possibility of having to defend her honour to a host of strangers.

The maid, Annette, cleared her throat pointedly and Lydia yanked her attention back to the looking glass. She regarded her reflection sceptically. She was in good looks. The maid had pulled the hair back from her face in a classic Grecian style, banding it with narrow white ribbons and securing the ends in a loose knot at the nape of her neck. Some of the curls escaped, framing Lydia's face and kissing her neck.

She met the girl's eye in the mirror. "You've done wonders."

Annette curtsied. "Thank you, Miss."

From down the hall a sonorous gong announced dinner. Lydia jumped from her seat. Her stomach churned as if setting up to make butter. Wistful thoughts of remaining in her room with the windows open to welcome in the evening breeze beguiled her imagination.

As the girl did up the last button, Lydia stepped into a pair of slippers. She turned around for an inspection. Annette smoothed a hair back into place and smiled. With that glowing recommendation, Lydia placed a penny in the maid's hand and hastened downstairs. She could not afford to be late and give Calcutta's denizens another reason to gossip.

* * *

Following dinner, the Governor-General's guests were treated to a concert by a violinist. Marcus watched Miss Garrett swaying minutely in her seat. Colour high, lips slightly parted, fingers unconsciously moving to the music, her gaze rapturously intent on the musician—she was a vision to behold.

He was not the only one taking note. Several of the men in the room openly studied her. Heat rose beneath his cravat, until—blasphemy—he wanted to rip it off. *Lecherous brutes*. He turned slightly in his seat to catch a better view of her audience. They looked like wolves sizing up a toothsome lamb.

The song ended and she returned his gaze, flashing a dazzling smile in response. Marcus revised his earlier opinion. He had done the other gentlemen in the room an injustice. They could hardly be blamed for admiring her. Luckily, she had the good sense to disregard their unwelcome attention. He always had believed her to be possessed of excellent sense.

In truth, Miss Garrett appeared to have no notion of the effect she was having on the gentlemen of Calcutta. As the violinist began his next selection, she once more turned towards the music with that whimsical half-smile and closed her eyes.

His eyes narrowed and he turned to find Danbury's face. There his Lordship was, with a pretty little thing to his right, but he paid her no mind. Like so many others, his eyes were fastened on Miss Garrett. Could it be that he had procured no employment for her by design? Perhaps the blackguard wanted to see her destitute, in a position of dependence. When her circumstances had been sufficiently reduced, she would be at his mercy.

Marcus could not release the tension in his jaw, but gave vent to his feelings by plucking a bloom from the nearest arrangement and shredding it. He was being ridiculous. His attention ought to be on the French spy, not Miss Garrett, no matter how fetching she looked.

He had to maintain his priorities.

He'd capture the man who meant to destroy England. Then he'd deal with Danbury.

* * *

The next morning Lydia found breakfast laid out in chafing dishes on the sideboard in the morning room. She was delighted to see that there was not a single ship's biscuit in sight. Inhaling the familiar scents of an English breakfast, she helped herself to eggs, toast and sausages before sitting down at the table.

With a cheery smile Lydia joined a newlywed couple she'd been introduced to the evening before, but the young woman's greeting was markedly cooler than their previous exchange. In a few pointed remarks, Lydia was given to understand that the new bride had heard tales.

Lydia tightened her grip on the teapot. Squaring her shoulders, she offered up a silent plea for grace. Head held high, she sipped at the steaming brew, but could not manage a bite of the food on her plate. Her throat had closed tight, perhaps from the effort of holding back tart comments.

Danbury entered and an impish impulse snatched hold of Lydia. She greeted him warmly. "Good morning, Anthony. I hope you slept well."

He blinked at her use of his given name. "Like a top, Miss Garrett. Quite a long day we had." He filled his plate and took a place across from Lydia.

"Tea?" she asked sweetly.

"Ah, yes. Thank you." He motioned towards her piled plate. "I see you've recovered some of your appetite. You've been getting too thin lately."

Amused at the scandalized expression on the young bride's face, and knowing what the woman believed, Lydia couldn't help but pique her a little more, despite Lord Danbury's quizzical expression. "Have you met Lieutenant Carrington and his lovely wife?" She waved an airy hand towards the couple.

The wife gave a tiny squeak of alarm at being singled out to a man she thought quite dissolute, but her husband rose, extending his hand cordially. He gave his bride an odd look. Either Lieutenant Carrington was unaware of Lord Danbury's supposed wickedness or he was not as shocked by it as he might have been.

Lydia watched Lord Danbury. The poor sweet man never turned a hair. Indeed, he seemed entirely unaware of any particular undercurrents. He greeted the lieutenant cordially and they spoke of the Marathas for a few moments until at last Mrs Carrington's continual plucking at his sleeve managed to gain her husband's attention.

The couple excused themselves from the table, Mrs Carrington whispering agitatedly in her husband's ear. Lydia shook her head at their departure and turned her attention back to her meal, finding that she was able to eat heartily after all.

* * *

Dinner was a smaller affair than it had been the previous evening. The company was made up entirely of Europeans. To Lydia's surprise, Dr Marshall was among the party.

Mrs Adkins made to introduce him. "We have not seen Dr Marshall this age. In fact, he tells me he returned to India just yesterday."

"Dr Marshall kindly acted as surgeon aboard *Legacy*. We are well acquainted." Lydia made her curtsy anyhow. With a pang, she realized how little she actually knew of him. "I did not know you had interests in India, however."

He offered a short bow in return. "My father's estate is a mere baronetcy in the Midlands, but my mother's family had extensive properties, not just here but in France, Italy and Switzerland as well."

"You must be exceptionally well travelled. Is that where you developed your interest in botany?"

"Indeed, there is an infinite variety of vegetation to be found in this world. All of it either useful or at least decorative."

The doors opened and Dr Marshall offered Lydia his arm. "May I?"

The table was laid with an extraordinary amount of silver, which glimmered in the candlelight. Servants stood behind each place and offered innumerable dishes with solicitous aplomb.

The colonel on Lydia's left nudged her arm familiarly. "I had not the least notion I was dining with an adventuress. I thought you must be someone's daughter, out for the first time."

"An adventuress?" Lydia asked coolly, one eyebrow arching of its own accord. Did she actually seem the type of woman who preyed on men for their money?

His red cheeks turned even redder. "I must watch my tongue. That did not come out right at all. I merely meant you must have had some remarkable adventures if you are embroiled in this affair."

Lydia frowned. Had news of the throne's arrival spread so quickly? She thought they'd meant to keep the matter quiet until just before the ball, in order to mitigate the risk of theft. "Mostly I did a lot of climbing and walking in beastly hot weather." Attempting to appear pleasant, she sipped at her soup and then set aside the spoon. "How did you come to hear about our adventures?"

He chuckled indulgently. "It's impossible to keep a secret in Calcutta. As grand as it is, we English are really just a village. Everyone knows what everyone else is up to. Especially if there is any hope of diversion in it. And you, my dear, are quite diverting." He raised his glass to her.

Lydia smiled. Perhaps there was a way they could turn the situation to their advantage? If a rumour was started that the throne was kept in a certain place, when it was in fact somewhere else all together, perhaps Le Faucon could be persuaded to attempt a theft even sooner.

Deep in thought, Lydia bent her head towards Dr Marshall as he told her a story about some plant or other he had discovered on some island or other. She tried to look attentive but only caught maybe one word in ten. She had more pressing things to think about.

* * *

Anthony grew so distracted watching Dr Marshall monopolize Miss Garrett's attention that he no longer made any pretence of attending to the young lady on his right. She had told him a number of boring and pointless stories about her brother, whom she thought he might know, despite his protestations that he had not had the pleasure. The dowager lady on his left snatched him back from his abstraction.

"I asked whether you will be at Government House for the ball," she said in response to his request that she repeat herself. Her deep, penetrating voice and her question—phrased, he thought, rather loudly in case he were hard of hearing—came at a moment of unintentional lull in the conversation around the dinner table.

Mrs Adkins answered for him, speaking from her place at the end of the table. "Of course Lord Danbury will be joining us for the ball. He and his colleagues are responsible for bringing the treasure back to India. It is all most thrilling, isn't it?"

"Treasure?" asked one of the diners, obviously not as up to date in his gossip as some in the room.

Lord Wellesley took the conversation in hand. "We are restoring a great historical treasure to India. A magnificent object. It will do much to show our good faith to the princes. These fine gentlefolk are responsible for preserving it from the French."

"But what is this treasure?"

Lord Wellesley's smile had something of the predator about it. "We are keeping it a secret—a whim of mine. I do love surprises, and this will be a thumping great one."

"How delightful," said the pretty but singularly dull young woman to Anthony's right. She gave him an adoring look and clasped her hands together in front of her bosom.

He shuddered and turned to speak further to the lady on his left.

"What have you discovered?" the older woman asked. "The Delhi diamond, a rajah's rubies, or is it Tippoo's Tiara?"

Anthony managed a game smile at this sally. "How did you know?"

CHAPTER 34

"Oh, la." The lady laughed too heartily and thumped him with her fan. "A lucky guess."

He took a swig from his glass and turned to the young miss at his other hand. She couldn't be all bad.

CHAPTER 35

"How far do you believe the rumours have spread by now?" Lydia asked. She and Mrs Adkins had just set to work. She stared at the neat piles of invitations on the desk. A great deal of work remained to be done.

Mrs Adkins sipped her coffee. "I am certain every English lady in the vicinity has heard the news and is anxious for details."

Lydia could not restrain an unladylike grin.

"This reminds me. I should give orders that I am not at home to visitors." Even as she spoke, a footman appeared.

Lady Groverton and the Misses Langley and Merrick all waited in the green drawing room.

"This is an uncivilized hour for callers. Though I believe I know what they want," said Mrs Adkins. "You will accompany me, won't you, Miss Garrett? I should value your support very much. Lady Groverton is something of a bulldog, and her daughters Marianne and Martha Langley are dreadful. Miss Merrick is inoffensive enough, but I'm not sure I am up to facing them all on my own."

"I shall certainly join you if you wish it."

Mrs Adkins' wry look clearly stated that Lydia was displaying the lack of caution characteristic only in a person who had not met the ladies in question. But she would not give her a chance to change her mind.

"Come. We'd better hurry down."

Down they went, entering the drawing room in time to hear one of the young ladies murmur something about a wicked adventuress being a guest in the house, and how mortified she would be to have to meet her.

The blood drained from Lydia's face in a rush, leaving her cold for the first time since arriving in India. Mrs Adkins reddened and her jaw tightened. She took Lydia's hand and gave it a reassuring squeeze before sailing in for a bout of verbal sparring.

"Good morning, Lady Groverton; ladies. How are you all this morning? I do hope nothing is amiss."

In a peculiarly deep, fruity voice, Lady Groverton reassured her there was nothing the least wrong. "We have been out this morning and realized we have not seen you this age. What have you been doing with yourself?"

"I am glad there is no trouble. It is such an unusual hour for calls I was quite taken off guard. May I present my very great friend, Miss Lydia Garrett."

Cool greetings were exchanged and Lydia endured the sharp appraisal of four sets of eyes. She returned the scrutiny.

Though a small woman, Lady Groverton's harsh features and coarse manner made her seem larger. Her daughters were plain, mirror images of one another, quite tall with large hands and feet. Their hair—the colour of mud bricks—was piled into elaborate coiffures that suited them poorly. Their lovely dresses did them no justice: the matching shades of rose-coloured linen clashed with their yellowish skin tones, making them look gawkier than they were.

Miss Merrick was a pretty creature, plump and rosy with soft brown hair curled and pulled back from her face with a great number of pins. Her manner was by far the most congenial of the group and she lacked the edge of hauteur demonstrated by the other women.

After lukewarm greetings there was a momentary lull.

"And where is your chaperone? I hope we will get to meet her soon." All of Miss Merrick's ruffles and bows seemed to be fluttering, though there was no breeze.

"No," said Lydia, not unkindly. She could not bring herself to be cutting to the blushing young woman. "I do not have a chaperone."

"But didn't you come out with a party of gentlemen?"

"I did indeed."

The fact that the adventuress had brazened her way into their very midst seemed to dawn on the ladies all at once. Lydia calmly sipped from the ubiquitous lemon water.

"I understand that there was some sort of expedition led by natives on some dreadful little island."

Lydia lowered her glass. "There was a battle at sea against a French ship-of-the-line as well."

Marianne Langley was shaking her head so hard her many braids were in danger of tumbling down around her ears. "Don't you find such activities taxing? It is… why, it is unfeminine. I'm sure I would never wish to—"

Lydia had no compunctions about cutting short the elder Miss Langley. "Not at all."

"Is Mr Harting still travelling in your party?" asked Miss Martha Langley. She was obviously not one to lose sight of the most important thing: an unattached and wealthy male.

"Yes, Mr Harting is a charming gentleman. The fourth son of the Viscount of Wiltshire. I should be delighted to introduce you to him if you desire."

"Lucy Carrington told me he is very handsome and quite well off," said Miss Merrick, rallying.

"He is both. He also has beautiful manners. I am sure he will make quite a stir among the young ladies of Calcutta."

"How did you find the treasure, and what is it?" Lady Groverton asked.

"I do apologize." Lydia smiled as sweetly as she could manage. "I cannot discuss the treasure. The Governor-General would be greatly put out with me, and I would not care to distress him. Once it is safely returned to the Indian people, the veil of secrecy will be lifted. Until then, I am afraid, I am bound to silence."

CHAPTER 35

The ladies' smiles grew even chillier—more like grimaces than expressions of good humour. But Lydia caught Mrs Adkins restraining a grin.

Despite cajoling and clumsy attempts at verbal entrapment, they could get no more information from Lydia. Nor could they get Mrs Adkins to invite them to the ball, though they did everything but demand an invitation.

Finally the ladies gave up, departing in a huff. As the door closed behind them Lydia distinctly heard the phrase "no shame". She turned to find Mrs Adkins wheezing and holding her sides.

"My dear, you were magnificent—so polite and immovable, and… and British. A beautiful thing to see." She sighed and shook her head. "I shall have to invite them. The old dragon's husband is an important man, but I did enjoy withholding the satisfaction of it for the moment.

"Did you see Martha's face when you said you had no chaperone? She looked as if she had eaten something sour. Women such as we have a bad reputation, but I never met one with such a scandal-loving nature as those pious young ladies we just entertained."

CHAPTER 36

The day of the ball dawned clear and bright—a day made for frivolous pursuits. Still, Lydia was unable to go back to sleep. The weight of unfinished tasks made her restless.

It was too early for most of the household, and she breakfasted alone. Now she was up, but could not accomplish any of the tasks that wakened her with their clamour. Mrs Adkins would not be ready for her assistance for at least an hour.

She fingered her small notebook. At least she could make lists. The garden beckoned and she stepped outside to enjoy the last hint of freshness before heat took hold of the new day.

Every flower and shrub in the quintessentially English garden catered to British sensibilities. Government House was not the place for the exotic flora of India, but rather the familiar larkspur and poppies of home. It was formally laid out, and even though Lydia's taste leaned to the modern fashion for natural, rambling gardens, it was a pleasant place, especially with the dew still fresh on the ground.

She strolled amongst the blossoms for a while. Finding a bench, she made all the lists she could think of. If she were honest, her restlessness stemmed less from the arrangements for the ball and more from anxiety about the throne. There had reportedly been no attempts on either the throne itself or the location where it was supposedly hidden. If the murderer meant to turn thief, then his opportunities to do so were fast slipping away. If an attempt was to be made it would be made soon. They had conceived a good plan—but it had drawbacks. If anything went wrong, there could be grave consequences.

She plucked a stray leaf from her skirt. The peace of the garden pulled at her. Absently, Lydia caressed the leather cover of her cousin's diary. It was the only thing she had of him, and she had taken to carrying it as a talisman, even though it had no further intelligence to offer that could be of practical assistance.

At last she stood and shook out her skirts. There was much to be done today. Hopefully, someone would now be up to help.

Ahead of her in the path, Dr Marshall stared at Government House. As if sensing her scrutiny he turned towards her.

"Good morning, Dr Marshall."

"Miss Garrett." He waited for her to catch him up. "It is a beautiful building, isn't it?" He did not wait for her response. "So unlike most of the architecture in India—a real symbol of British authority. It would be terrible if anything were to befall it."

"What do you mean?"

"You mustn't be frightened." He took her hand and patted it. "Many of the Indians aren't pleased with the British dominance of their commerce and government, but they are not likely to become violent, unless some outside force acts upon their passions."

Lydia withdrew her hand from his grasp. "I appreciate your reassurance."

The doctor continued. "My pleasure, Miss Garrett. As you know, I have had business in India for many years. I have come to know something of the region. If we placate the rajas, they will keep the people in line."

"You have a great grasp of politics then?"

"No great understanding is needed. These are simple people. We've already made many improvements, such as building Government House. We will continue to bring civilization to these people. If anything, they should be grateful for our intervention."

For some reason what he said, though it reflected the pompous self-satisfaction of many of the British she had met in India, did not ring true. Was the doctor making sport of her? She could not make him out, so changed the subject in the hope of distracting him.

"Tell me more of your family and home in England."

"I told you of my father last evening. My mother was a Frenchwoman. During the revolution, her family's French holdings were seized by the Committee of Public Safety. Of course, she had most of her jewellery, and her family had the foresight to ship over some of their prized possessions before hostilities broke out. Now that the revolutionaries are gone from France I have some hope that the rest of those properties will be restored."

They had returned to the house now, and Lydia stepped inside. "Pray, excuse me. I must run and assist Mrs Adkins. There is much yet to be done."

Government House was waking and the stirrings soon became a positive hum of activity. Mrs Adkins supervised the preparations for the ball as the flowers were put in place and other last-minute details seen to. She deputized Lydia, setting her to work overseeing the process in the entry hall and public rooms.

Luncheon was a hurried affair. Lydia took time only for a glass of the pervasive iced lemon water by way of refreshment before hurrying back to her tasks. They worked through the normal afternoon rest and when Mrs Adkins insisted it was time to dress for the ball, Lydia was soaked with perspiration and cross from trying to do too many things at once.

She trudged up the stairs to her room, intending to wash and change quickly.

"Miss Garrett."

Brow furrowed, Lydia turned. "Yes, Mr Harting?"

"May I have a moment please?"

Lydia mustered a grudging smile. "I fear—"

"It will not take long, I promise."

He ushered her inside a small sitting room which was probably in general use by lower-level functionaries who were entertaining other low-level functionaries. Even here there was a moderate showing of

CHAPTER 36

British grandeur with a number of knick-knacks on display and fine, brocaded furniture. Inside, a young Indian woman stood with head respectfully bowed and fingers linked primly in front of her.

"I thought you might require a ball gown for the evening." Harting extended a scrap of paper to her. Lydia recognized it immediately and accepted it with trembling fingers. It was one of Sophie's drawings.

"Where did you get this?"

"I requested it from Emmanuel. I thought this would be a means of honouring the girl Sophie. When I told him my plan he was quite willing." He seemed intent on assuring her that he had not come by the drawing through illicit means.

With a flourish, the Indian woman produced a gown from where it had been secreted. Lydia caught her breath. One hand flew to her mouth in wonder.

The delicate silk was pure white, shot through with silver thread making it shimmer as it caught the light. Drawing near, she realized the silver threads created a subtle paisley pattern very common in India, but usually executed in garish colours. The sleeves were fitted, ending at the elbow. Every edge was trimmed with intricate crystal beadwork. A short train completed the gown, trailing behind in a graceful arc.

"I asked Mrs Deepta to make it for you."

"It's lovely." Lydia extended tentative fingers to brush the airy fabric. She wanted to say something more, to somehow express how much the gesture meant, but she could not find the words.

"I'm afraid you'll have to hurry now."

Lydia raised her eyes from the gown and met Harting's. The tenderness she saw reflected there froze her in place.

As if in a dream she watched as Harting raised a hand. With infinite gentleness he brushed a thumb across her lips. Enthralled, she raised a trembling hand to cover his. A warm tingle started in her fingertips. It spread through her palm, her wrist, and up her arm, until it settled in her belly.

Her breathing grew shallow even as her pulse pounded loudly in her ears. Unbidden her lips parted slightly. Harting lowered his mouth towards her.

Crash!

The spell shattered. Lydia whirled round.

The little seamstress stood in the midst of smashed porcelain. Fear quivered in every line of her being. Lydia had not seen what happened, but the poor woman had likely just brushed against one of the endless array of pots and urns and jars that decorated the interminable galleries of Government House.

"So sorry. So sorry," the woman whispered. She stooped to pick up the pieces.

"It does not matter." Lydia bent and raised the woman to her feet. "Don't fret now. I'll call for a maid to clean up this mess."

The seamstress nodded and blinked back tears.

"Thank you for the dress. It is the loveliest gown I have ever seen." The woman bowed.

Harting placed a hand under her elbow, gently steering her away. "I'll handle this. You should be preparing to dazzle the citizens of Calcutta."

"Are you certain?"

"Yes, of course, go. Go and make yourself presentable." His small smile and the warmth in his eyes brought the heat back to her cheeks.

"I carry this for you, *Missee Sahib*." The seamstress retrieved the gown and carried it lovingly from the room.

In a daze, Lydia followed.

* * *

A lukewarm bath welcomed her to her room. Lydia slipped into the water and sighed. Even tepid, the water felt refreshing. She raised a hand to her face. Were her cheeks still red? She hugged her legs to her chest and rested her forehead against her knees.

CHAPTER 36

What had she been thinking? Such behaviour justified the assumption that she was an adventuress. Her cheeks flamed again as she remembered the feel of his thumb on her mouth. How could she ever face Harting again? She couldn't even say precisely how she felt about him. Until that afternoon she had striven not to view him in any sort of romantic light. And what of Lord Danbury? She groaned.

Lydia lingered longer than she had intended. The maid's noisy arrival in the outer room brought her back to reality with a start, and she jumped from the bath, sloshing a prodigious amount of water over the side with her. She flung her dressing gown over the mess to sop up the water and hurried to the other room.

The maid set to with brush, pins and comb, poking and pulling until Lydia's hair was arranged to her satisfaction. She carefully placed a pair of silver-beaded combs among the piled curls so they would show to best advantage. Having helped Lydia don the rest of the ensemble, she stepped back to admire her handiwork, darting forward to tuck a curl in here or pluck away a bit of fuzz there.

Finally, she allowed Lydia to look in the glass. The gown fitted her to perfection. The way it shimmered and caught the light made her think of melting ice. The impression of coolness made her seem a being apart, untouched by the wilting heat. She looked as elegant and refined as Sophie could have wished.

"Will I turn into a pumpkin if I'm not back in my room by midnight?"

Seeing the confused look on Annette's face, she realized she had spoken aloud. She offered her thanks and a generous tip for the girl's hard work.

Straightening her shoulders and taking a deep fortifying breath, Lydia stepped from her room.

Chapter 37

The ballroom buzzed with activity. Mrs Adkins stepped away from the people she was speaking to when she saw Lydia.

"My dear, you are exquisite. That dress is indescribable, and I thought you needed the help of my paltry seamstress. Whoever made it?" The older woman took her hands and held them away from her body.

"A Mrs Deepta. She made it from a sketch by a friend of mine."

"I adore it. I have seen some examples of the new fashions, but this is more gracious than anything I imagined." Mrs Adkins tapped Lydia with her fan, and offered a knowing smile. "You are going to be busy in the morning. Every unattached gentleman and officer will be calling on you. And all the ladies will be pursuing you for your seamstress."

Lydia blushed at the compliments and returned the sentiment. Mrs Adkins was in good looks. Excitement pinked her cheeks and her midnight blue gown had a dramatic flair that suited her.

The eight hundred guests were unusually prompt. Curiosity about the treasure, and the mysterious trio who had brought it to India, was too high for anyone to chance missing a thing. Instead of a trickle of arriving dignitaries, there was a flood—a gushing eddying mass of humanity intent on entertainment.

The noise in the ballroom grew exponentially as the guests poured in. This was going to be a long evening.

A flourish of music from the orchestra betokened the first dance. Lord Wellesley, with Lydia as his partner, opened the ball with the mincing, intricate steps of the minuet. The moment the minuet ended a new tune struck up, and a handsome young lieutenant from Essex promptly claimed her. After the fourth dance, she was thirsty and relieved that she had blocked off the dance on her card. An eager captain immediately offered to fetch a glass of negus. Gratefully, she accepted his offer and stepped out to the terrace to await his return.

The press of humanity had made the ballroom exceedingly close. In contrast, the terrace seemed nearly cool. Many of the guests were taking the air, and she conversed with the young officer in complete propriety.

Danbury appeared at her side. She had forgotten that he had claimed a slot on her card. "I believe the next dance is mine." He offered a gentlemanly bow.

"Lead on, Lord Danbury." Relief broadened her smile. While the attention she received might be flattering, the interrogations about the treasure were importunate, and she had grown weary of fending them off. It would be a pleasure to lower her guard.

* * *

Excitement hung in the air like a physical presence. But perhaps that was simply a cloud of clashing perfumes. Anthony had always disliked balls, fêtes, soirees and all the other formal interactions of society. They were guaranteed to make a man feel like a great oaf.

This once, though, he would make an exception to his antipathy. He would do anything to catch his father's murderer—even dance past midnight.

At least he had this respite. Miss Garrett could make even dancing pleasant. Her delicate fingers resting in his own broad grip made his pulse drum to battle-stations tempo.

As they came together she leaned close. "How do you think things are proceeding? Has anything happened?"

"Nothing as yet. Everything is in place. The throne has a couple of guards outside the door. It would look suspicious if it did not. The rest are hiding."

The Peacock Throne had been moved that afternoon into the marble hall—so named not just for the soft grey marble underfoot, but also for the greater-than-life-sized statues of Roman emperors that were inset in niches along the wall. Flanking these, in the style of a Roman atrium, tall columns were covered in *chunam*, a sort of plaster made of burnt shells that was carved and then burnished so that it glowed like old ivory. Wellesley had given them all a lecture on those columns. He was inordinately proud of them. In addition to its merit of size and location, this hall had two wide verandas which ran along the east and west sides of the room. The strategic placement of a large tapestry over a small side entry effectively hid the passage from view, making a sort of hidden room in which soldiers were mustered in readiness.

The dance separated Anthony from Lydia then brought them together again.

"When do you expect action?"

"Harting thinks something could happen at any minute. I expect them to wait until after the ball. It would be foolhardy to try to remove the throne with so many people about, but we must be prepared for all eventualities."

Lydia nodded acknowledgment, then changed the subject. "Evening dress suits you remarkably well. You look quite distinguished."

"Why, thank you. I believe I mentioned before how fetching you look." Anthony heard himself utter the lukewarm praise, but the words held no relation to his actual sentiments. Miss Garrett looked like a moonbeam, straight and luminous. No other woman in the room could hold a candle to her. The pure white column of her gown shone like a beacon in a sea of florid silks and satins.

Pleasant appreciation lit the face of every gentleman who caught sight of her. Even the ladies turned their heads to watch her progress, sending quick, darting glances her way.

"And you dance very well." Miss Garrett was trying valiantly to keep the conversational ball in play. Anthony shook himself.

"Were you afraid I might not?" he asked in mock indignation.

"Not at all. You seem to be able to turn your hand to anything you set out to do, but it is a pleasant change not to have my toes trod upon. My last partner was not nearly so proficient."

"All in the line of duty, Miss Garrett. We must all make sacrifices for the greater good."

"Then perhaps you will allow me to tread upon your poor toes for a quarter of an hour."

"If I must suffer, at least you have only those pretty slippers rather than a pair of great clumsy Hessians."

She swatted his arm. "I suppose I shall have to find some other way to make sure you are doing your fair share of sacrificing."

"Pray, ma'am, no threats if you please. You have sacrificed so nobly that there should be no call for the rest of us to suffer. Although…" He caught sight of Harting leading a resplendent Mrs Adkins, and jerked his chin in their direction. "It looks like he ought to be doing more sacrificing, I'm sure."

* * *

Harting certainly looked as if he were enjoying himself. Lydia bit her lip. A flash of annoyance sizzled through her, but then faded as quickly as if it had been one of the fireworks at Vauxhall. Despite what had almost transpired she had no claim upon him. Nor could she ever.

Their dance ended and Lydia took her leave of Lord Danbury, pleading the need to assist Mrs Adkins with her responsibilities. A survey of the flushed, excited faces surrounding her was all it took to convince her that the ball was a roaring success, even before the supper tables had been laid out.

Anticipation about the treasure had the guests in high spirits. They danced and chatted with gusto. Even those who could not— or would not—dance, having sought refuge in the card room, were in an unusually good humour.

Lord Wellesley's taste and refinement were praised on all sides, and when supper had been laid, the food proved a further source of delight. It was by far the most successful ball of the season and the guests were enjoying themselves immensely.

Lydia was thrilled for Mrs Adkins' sake with how well the ball fared. Every detail was perfect. While the guests were drawn to the supper table like a tidal wave, Lydia took the opportunity to slip back out to the terrace. She breathed deeply of the scented night air and sighed, deciding to stroll out into the garden.

Even after dancing, the restless need to move propelled her forward. She fidgeted with her fan, wandering into the garden with no particular destination in mind.

Could they have allowed for every contingency? Their enemy was cunning. He would not allow himself to be easily trussed. "Miss Garrett?" An inquiring voice at her elbow pulled her from her reverie.

"Lord Danbury. It's growing quite warm in there, isn't it?"

"Yes, quite." A pause stretched between them until at last he extended his arm. "May I walk with you?"

"Of course."

He offered the confiding smile that never failed to lighten her mood. "To be honest, I've had dashed all I can handle of prying questions and impertinent stares. I can now fully commiserate with trained monkeys."

Some of the tension in her shoulders eased. "Precisely. I'm rather pining for the anonymity of London at the moment."

Jasmine and roses scented the air. Strategically spaced torches offered dim and flickering illumination. On the other side of the hedgerow a woman giggled.

He covered her hand on his arm with his. "I haven't forgotten my promise, you know. I shall find you an appropriate post when we return."

Lydia ducked her head. "I know that, my Lord, and I thank you."

They had reached a sort of cul-de-sac and were forced to halt. He turned to face her and his hand caressed her cheek as if she were immeasurably fragile.

"Miss Garrett, I'm not as erudite as Harting, but—" He broke off and groaned. Then both hands were cupping her face, and his lips were on hers, warm and sweet and gentle.

For an instant she sank into the kiss. A delicious whirling, sliding fall. As natural and necessary as breathing. She wrapped her arms around his neck and he pulled her closer.

His lips moved to nuzzle her ear. "I've waited. I didn't know. I feared—"

She jerked away, panting a little. Her heart pounded wildly.

His eyes widened and it was as if she'd opened some compartment in his soul and poured in pain. And then suddenly his expression shuttered over—his face was the shade of a brick wall, and just as impassive. "I'm so sorry. I know that your position is dashed awkward. I shan't press you again, nor will I allow anyone to say—"

"No, my Lord." She held up a hand. "I cannot, but it is because I… I have used you mercilessly."

Stiff and formal he waited for her to continue.

Tears pooled in her eyes. She fumbled for a way to phrase her confession without seeming to cast stones. "At Mr Harting's request I have been passing along information about you. Information I gleaned from searching through your papers."

His eyes had grown cold—so cold that goose flesh prickled her arms.

"Your inheritance?"

She nodded, miserable. "It was from the government. Payment in advance." The chill had been replaced by a scorching, searing, suffocating heat.

Lord Danbury inclined his head with a little jerk. "I am sorry to have troubled you, ma'am. I trust you'll excuse me."

He strode away from her as if escaping a foul odour.

Deaf and blind to any others, Lydia wandered the garden. A bench presented itself. She groped for it and sat down heavily. She might never get up again.

Gravel crunched and a shadow loomed over her. "Miss Garrett."

Lydia could not quite force a smile as her merciful solitude took flight. "Good evening, Dr Marshall. I hope you're enjoying yourself."

"I am. The ball is an absolute triumph. I know you had a great deal to do with its success, so you should be congratulated." He proffered a glass. "I thought you might be thirsty." He held out a glass of negus.

"How kind." Her words were automatic, as was her acceptance of the glass he held. She drank deeply, scarcely tasting the punch.

"No trouble at all. I hoped you would honour me with the next dance."

"I regret that I have already promised it or I would happily oblige."

"No matter. I shall endeavour to enjoy your company now." With an abrupt change of subject, he continued, "Do you know what time they plan to unveil the throne?"

"Sometime towards the end of the evening," Lydia said. Something was wrong. Her tongue felt thick and slow. She blinked, trying to clear her head. The world spun sickeningly.

"Are you all right, Miss Garrett?" The doctor placed a solicitous hand at her elbow and helped her rise. "Perhaps a turn around the garden?"

Lydia followed. She craned her neck to look up at him, but the simple act of turning her head made her stomach lurch, and she battled to keep from disgracing herself. Closing her eyes, she allowed herself to be led further from the light and activity of the ball.

What was wrong with her? She blanched. *Please don't let there be anything amiss with the game from the buffet. It would be terrible if all the guests were to fall ill.*

Lydia's mind whirled, disordered and chaotic, unable to focus. Thoughts seemed to slip through her grasp as soon as they formed.

Dr Marshall nudged her gently to a bench and she collapsed gratefully on the cool stone. Her senses cleared for a moment and she heard the doctor whispering.

"*Elle est ici.*"

Her heart plunged to her feet. She turned to look at him, fighting to concentrate—to understand. Darkness consumed her, dragging her into a deep void.

CHAPTER 38

Lord Wellesley led the party into the receiving hall. A murmur of excitement built among the guests. At Wellesley's request, Harting and Anthony made their way to the front of the crowd. The audience quieted and an expectant hush filled the hall.

Anthony had to restrain a snort as Wellesley eulogized their courage and resourcefulness. *What rot.* All he wanted was to find the murderer and go home.

The crowd pressed closer as latecomers edged into the hall. The spy had to be amongst them; he could smell evil in the air. He eyed the assembled guests, looking for someone out of the ordinary, a visage twisted with cruelty and avarice. It was hopeless. Every face he looked in seemed to hold a measure of one or the other. But then, Miss Garrett had proven that looks could deceive. He strangled the thought and buried it beneath his determination to find the murderer.

Wellesley had moved on, and now waxed lyrical about bridges being built between Britain and India because of the heroic return of the treasure to Indian soil. Anthony glanced over to Harting. The man's eyes had glazed over. At least he didn't seem to be buying the tripe Wellesley was selling either.

He searched the faces of the crowd for Miss Garrett. How was she enduring the posturing? She was nowhere to be found. Smart girl. She had a positive genius for looking after her own interests. A taste as bitter as wormwood filled his mouth.

As the audience began to shift and whisper, the Governor-General stepped back. With a flourish he whipped the covering from the throne. The crowd inhaled as one body.

Jewels caught the light and refracted it into miniature starbursts. The grand Peacock Throne of the Mughals shone as if lit from within. Spontaneous applause burst from the crowd. Many of the guests approached the throne, touching it with soft hands—some reverently in respect of its beauty, others greedily as if touch might help them guess its value.

Wellesley's men would have to watch the crowd, or the throne would be picked clean of jewels by morning.

A group of men clustered around Lord Wellesley, congratulating him on a coup of diplomacy. Others pressed closely around Anthony and Harting, avid for the tale of their adventure. Anthony indulged them—partially.

It would never do to cause a panicked search for French spies. He found himself hailed as a hero, but he could not accept the praise heaped on him. His true goal had yet to be accomplished.

At last the crowd began to disperse and Harting collared him. "Have you seen Miss Garrett?"

"Not since the buffet was laid." He fumbled with his cravat, trying in vain to repair the damage inflicted by the crush.

"I wonder how she's holding up. The crowds might have trampled the poor girl if she were as inundated as we."

"I'm sure she will have managed." Anthony would rather not see Miss Garrett again. Ever.

Harting shook his head. "No, I'm sure she would have attended the unveiling. I think we ought to look for her."

Anthony sneered. "Are you sure she isn't off performing some errand for you?"

Harting stepped back. A light seemed to have been snuffed out somewhere within him, eliminating the friendly gleam in his eyes. "I haven't asked anything of her."

Anthony glared at him.

Harting sighed. "May we discuss it later? For the moment I have an unpleasant suspicion that all is not well."

Shaking his head at the tacit confirmation, Anthony breathed out heavily. The edge of betrayal sliced him open like a fillet knife. "I'll go this way." It was a harsh bullfrog's croak of a voice, but at least he hadn't issued the challenge that had sprung to his lips. He had to get away from Harting before he did something impulsive.

He circled the reception rooms and glanced out at the gardens. Miss Garrett was nowhere in sight. Hangers-on hampered his every movement, introducing themselves and peppering him with questions he did not wish to answer. At last he approached a servant and asked him to summon Miss Garrett.

The instant he stood still, avid officials desiring his confidence clustered around him as if he were some sort of magnet. Would this evening never end? Doing his best to at least appear gracious he slapped on a polite smile.

Some twenty minutes later Harting approached. "Excuse me, gentlemen. May I borrow Lord Danbury for a moment?" His lips were turned up in a semblance of a smile, but he bore such an air of reproach that the crowd fairly melted away.

He was to the point. "Did you find her?"

Anthony's hands clenched into fists. "I did not."

"Did you even bother to look?"

The urge to shout nearly choked him. "I looked. But frankly I am much more interested in finding a murderer. She likely took to her bed with a megrim. I'd do the same if I weren't set on finishing this business."

Harting shook his head. "I had a servant check her room. She isn't there." His gaze looked past and around Anthony, searching the guests for a slender column of white. For the first time a stirring of unease niggled at Anthony. Almost involuntarily he looked over his shoulder.

Lord Wellesley stood nearby speaking to a bewigged and gartered gentleman. Anthony touched Harting's arm. "Come, let's inquire with Wellesley. He may know something." They approached him and begged pardon for the interruption before presenting their concern.

"No, come to think of it I haven't. Of course, I haven't seen Mrs Adkins in a good while either. Perhaps some crisis over musicians or some such called them away. Ah, thank you," he said to a waiter who approached him with a note. "Excuse me a moment, gentlemen." Lord Wellesley unfolded the missive. He paled, his face tightening into hard lines and his eyes turning wintry.

"Lord Danbury, Mr Harting, please join me in my study. Lord Chester, I must beg you to excuse us."

Anthony and Harting exchanged glances. Something was terribly wrong. They hurried to follow Lord Wellesley's rigid form. Once the door shut behind them, he flung the letter on the desk.

"Their lives are threatened."

"Who?"

"Miss Garrett and Mrs Adkins." Wellesley's voice was vehement.

Harting leaned close over Anthony's shoulder to examine the letter. It was short and to the point.

Treasure is defined by man. What do you treasure, gentlemen? You will follow directions and deliver up the Peacock Throne, or Mrs Adkins and Miss Garrett will die. Further communication will follow.

Lord Wellesley stepped from the room and ordered a passing servant to find the ladies and ask them to join him in the study. The servant scurried away, the harshness of the command lending wings to his progress.

"We will have to post guards on the ladies. They must be cautioned to take the greatest care with their safety," said Harting.

Tension stemmed further conversation as they waited in agitated silence for the ladies to present themselves. Lord Wellesley rang for another servant and sent him to find the commander of the forces tasked with protecting Government House.

Captain Stevens arrived a scant few minutes later, breathless and still clutching a pair of playing cards. These he tucked quickly out of sight as he perused the note.

Still there was no sign of either lady.

The servant returned, but his downcast demeanour boded no good. "I am sorry, my Lord, but I have searched everywhere. I cannot find the ladies."

Anthony took to pacing while the poor man underwent a close interrogation. The servant answered readily enough and it appeared he had performed a thorough, if hurried, search. Captain Stevens excused himself to gather a few soldiers and make an in-depth search.

"Be discreet, Captain. I do not want to upset my guests," said Lord Wellesley. "It will cause chaos and make our task more difficult."

He turned to Anthony and Harting. "I hate to think it, gentlemen, but I fear they have been kidnapped. Whoever this villain is, he is not stupid. He has ensured he will have them in his power if he wants to do them harm."

"I thought the French possessed more scruples. To abduct and threaten ladies…" Harting looked ready to fling himself on a horse and join battle if only he knew where the enemy lay.

"I should not have allowed Miss Garrett to accompany us in the first place." Anthony dropped into a seat, head in his hands.

"No, my boy, this is not your doing. This is the fault of a wicked enemy. Self-recrimination will avail nothing. We must think. I refuse to allow the blackguard to get away with this." Lord Wellesley's features spoke of grim resolution.

Anthony raised his head, but could summon no enthusiasm. He had erred badly and now Miss Garrett was in danger. "You're right, of course."

"Sir, did you know the waiter who delivered the note?" Harting asked.

"I…" Lord Wellesley thought about it. "Why, no, I didn't recognize the man. The waiters for this evening are all soldiers. Not our usual servants. I thought it a wise precaution. Captain Stevens will have a list of their names."

"It might be expedient to discover who gave him the note."

Captain Stevens soon returned. The ladies were nowhere on the grounds of Government House. The search had been discreet but thorough, and he was confident in his report.

Anthony seemed to have trouble breathing, as if someone had struck the air from his lungs. At Lord Wellesley's request, Stevens immediately produced the list of sepoys employed at the ball. These were each brought in and interviewed briefly. No one had seen anything unusual. None could help pinpoint what time the ladies had been taken, although various soldiers had noticed them at different times throughout the evening. Anthony began a timeline to try to discover the approximate time the kidnappings occurred. In the end it contained so many holes as to be almost useless.

They interviewed twenty sepoys before recognizing the man who had delivered the note. Harting quizzed him at length, but he had little to add.

He had spotted the note propped prominently on one of the buffet tables as he passed. It was addressed to Lord Wellesley in a large bold hand and marked urgent, so, although he thought it odd, he made a point of seeking out the Governor-General and delivering the note with all haste. He had not seen who left the letter, nor had he noticed anyone loitering around the table. Nothing else struck him as out of place or unusual.

"I hope I didn't do wrong, sir. I thought you would want the letter right off. That's why I brought it straight along."

Lord Wellesley's shoulders slumped, but he waved away the man's concern. "Go on now, but do not speak of our interview to anyone."

Still looking slightly dyspeptic the soldier bowed and departed.

"Well, gentlemen, that was even less helpful than I had feared. What are we to do?"

Neither Harting nor Anthony could answer.

CHAPTER 39

Lydia woke slowly. She lay on the floor of a carriage—a carriage apparently travelling a wretchedly kept road because it bounced and lurched wildly. Abominably sick to her stomach, the sole thought she could muster was a longing for the vehicle to cease its violent motion. Her head ached fiercely, and her hands had been bound behind her. Wrenching pain lanced her back, arms and shoulders.

Hers was not the only body supine on the carriage floor. It took a few minutes to summon the strength of will to raise her head and see who shared her predicament. She could not see the person's face, but recognized Mrs Adkins' regally styled ball gown immediately.

"Ah, you've woken. I expected the drug to last longer."

Lydia turned her head, alarmed at the voice, but she could not say anything. It was all she could do to keep her teeth clenched against the bile rising in her throat.

"Perhaps it's just as well. I shan't have to have you carried in."

Lydia relaxed back onto the floor; it would be wise to conserve her strength. The figure in the corner continued to speak. He said something more about the effect of the drug, but she had stopped listening. Her entire being was intent on trying to determine some clue as to where they were. Her captor was apparently very confident. He had left the landau's curtains open, probably in order to facilitate a breeze in the stuffy compartment.

Through the gap she could see the stars high above. She wracked her sore brain, trying to remember what Captain Campbell had taught her on board *Legacy* about the stars, and how one could use them to gauge direction and speed. It took a good while, but at last she had her bearings. The coach was travelling roughly northeast.

She thought they were still in the city, but not in one of the heavily populated areas. The dark bulk of buildings was occasionally visible to her from her cramped position, but there were few other signs of life—no cooking fires, no people speaking, no dogs barking or donkeys braying. Even this late at night there would be some sign of habitation in a residential area.

Lydia sniffed delicately as a hint of salty sea air stung her nose. They were close to the ocean. Were they headed for the docks? If she could get away, maybe she could find *Legacy*.

The shadowy figure raised his voice. "Miss Garrett, you are not attending. I asked if you know who I am."

Lydia responded only because she did not want to anger him. "Yes, Dr Marshall, you are Le Faucon."

"Bravo, Miss Garrett. I knew you were a bright young lady. I did wonder if you would ever work out who I am."

The carriage pulled up sharply and Marshall leaned forward to open the door and climb out. He reached back in, pulled Lydia to a sitting position, and helped her slide out of the carriage.

"I do regret the damage to your beautiful dress—it was really magnificent," he said conversationally.

Was he mad?

"My associate up in the box will retrieve Mrs Adkins for us. Why don't you allow me to show you your lodgings? I wish the accommodations could be better, but I had to work with the resources to hand."

Lydia surveyed her surroundings carefully. She needed something, anything, to help her pinpoint their location. The darkness was so complete it swallowed all landmarks. Not that she would recognize the area even had it been midday. She had seen little of Calcutta and its environs.

Dr Marshall gripped her elbow firmly, and led her into a cavernous building looming directly in front of them. He escorted her through a large open room, the space almost entirely taken up with chests of exotic goods stacked nearly to the rafters – cotton, indigo and the critical saltpeter. Further along there were shelves lined with tea chests. Logs of ebony and mahogany made a kind of mountain at one end of the building. There was even a pile of tiger pelts and ivory tusks. At the far end of this warehouse they entered a narrow passage with several doors opening on to it. Marshall led her to the end of this long corridor, opening the last door.

It swung in onto a space that might once have been an office of some sort. The original furniture—a couple of desks and some broken chairs—had been shoved to one side and two pallets lay on the floor. Three narrow, boarded-over windows were placed high along what she thought must be the outer wall.

The carriage driver carried in Mrs Adkins, who remained insensible.

Marshall lit a smoking oil lamp that sat on the desk. Then he excused himself. "I shall return momentarily. You will write a short note to your companions verifying your continued existence. Please don't do anything rash while I am out of the room, Miss Garrett. Both my friend here and I are well armed, and, while I would regret the necessity, I will not hesitate to kill you if you attempt to escape."

"You would not regret it nearly so much as I would." Lydia jerked her arm free.

"I knew you were a wit." He smiled politely at her bravado. "I shall be back with pen and paper."

Lydia thought frantically. She must find a way to communicate what little she knew about their whereabouts. Too soon Marshall returned, bearing pen, paper, and ink. He loosed her bonds and pulled a chair to the desk for her to sit down.

"May I have a moment?" Lydia chafed her hands and arms. She needed a few more minutes to think. "My hands fell asleep while bound and until the blood returns they will not cooperate."

"Certainly, my dear. Do not try to be clever though. Mrs Adkins is far more valuable to me as a hostage than you. I will sacrifice you in a trice the moment you become more of a liability than an asset."

"I would not dream of trying to be clever. I can hardly think. My head still aches from whatever drug you used." Lydia snatched up the pen and began to write.

> *My dearest Gentlemen. By this time you must be a ware that Mrs Adkins and I are gone from Government House. There must be no recriminations; neither you nor the ast ute soldiers on guard could have prevented this. I have been instructed to write something to assure you of the authenticity of this communication. Lord Danbury, I beg you to remember that when we first met I wore a gown of indigo blue cotton, and put too much salt in your eggs so that Peter scolded me. Please take the greatest care and do not endanger yourselves.*
> *Lydia Garrett*

Marshall took the note from her and read it with narrowed eyes. Lydia tried to look unconcerned, and kept her breathing as even as she could.

"This will do." He bent at last to add a postscript to the bottom of the note. "I must be off, my dear. Someone is bound to have found my note at Government House, and I should not be found missing as well. It might arouse suspicion. I will see you in the morning. If you have need of anything, my man will be posted outside your door. Do not try his patience. He has instructions to silence you if need be." Leaving this threat hanging in the air, Marshall departed, closing the heavy door behind him.

Lydia heard a rustle from the pallet where Mrs Adkins had been laid and she rushed to her side.

"Are you awake?" she whispered.

"Yes." It was more a groan than proper speech. "Could you untie me, please? I feel very ill."

Lydia hastened to free the woman. "It will pass soon, except for the headache. I'm feeling much better already."

"Was that Dr Marshall?"

"Yes, I believe he kidnapped us in order to force Lord Wellesley to turn the Peacock Throne over to him. They must have some raja or sultan in the wings waiting to make a grab for power."

"He is a devil. I would never have thought it of him. He can be pompous but I would not have thought him a traitor."

"I understand his mother was French, so perhaps he does not feel England is his country."

"Nevertheless I would not have believed him capable of such deceit. Wellesley will never consent, you know. He will resent the demands. He may even grieve for me." She smiled ruefully as if she doubted the notion. "But he will never allow himself to be dictated to by such means. He cannot. If word got out, he would be ruined. None of us would be safe. Every time someone wanted something they would snatch a body from the street and then make their demand. It would be ridiculous. No, I'm afraid that we shall have to prepare for our fate, whatever it may be."

Lydia almost confided that she had sent a secret message in the note she had prepared, but decided at the last to keep her own counsel. It would be unkind to raise hopes which might come to nothing. She did not know what the future held and while she trusted Mrs Adkins they might be placed under duress. What she did not know she could not divulge.

* * *

At Government House time had turned into a torment. Marcus could not sleep, but neither could he do anything productive. He had not the least notion what to do. It was a torment to sit about wringing his hands. He should know what to do. He was the Honourable Marcus Harting; he always knew what to do.

He must break free from this hesitation and do something. He had not been at such a loss since Lyons. Nightmare images stormed the barriers he had erected in his mind and he was there once more.

The guillotine's blade glimmered red with blood in the sunset. The scent of death in the air, the fanatic gleam in the eyes of the populace. The press of the wooden barrel that had been his prison. His salvation. His uncle, standing tall and straight with his hands bound behind him, stoically awaiting his turn before Madame La Guillotine. The thunk at once solid and liquid. The roar of approval from the mob.

Hatred.

Others had consoled him, counselled him. He had been but a lad of sixteen. There was nothing he could have done to prevent the massacre. He had been right to obey his uncle's order to remain hidden. But Marcus had vowed never to be so powerless again and he had spent his lifetime thwarting Fouche, Napoleon's spymaster, the man who had engineered that day's bloodbath.

But here he was again. Unable even to begin to assist the person he had come to care for most in the world.

A servant appeared at his side. Lord Wellesley insisted they should eat. He dragged himself from his seat and plodded blindly to the breakfast room. Danbury sat at the table, his face white and drawn; the same look that a soldier sported after an unexpected defeat. Did Marcus look as rumpled and haggard himself?

The food might have been dust for all he could taste.

The other guests staying at Government House had not been informed of the abductions, but they seemed to sense something was wrong from the solemn countenances of their companions. The congratulations on the capital ball of the previous evening died on their lips, and the conversation trickled off into a puzzled silence.

Dr Marshall arrived at the table, hale, hearty and brimming with bonhomie. The downcast aspect of his audience seemed not to affect his own spirits in the least as he peppered them with humorous anecdotes.

Marcus ground his teeth. Why would the man not be still? His temples pulsed in aching rhythm. Dr Marshall prattled on as if he intended to do so all day. Thankfully a clerk interrupted him to present Lord Wellesley's compliments, and ask Lord Danbury and

Mr Harting to join him at their earliest possible convenience. They leapt from the table murmuring swift farewells and practically flew along to the Governor-General's study.

"Gentlemen," Lord Wellesley greeted them, waving a note. "One of the servants found this propped on a side table in the entry hall. I questioned the girl, of course, but she knows nothing. Somehow this villain has a means of gaining access to Government House whenever he wishes. I tell you, he must be caught!"

Marcus grabbed the note, read it silently, then passed it to Danbury, who looked ready to rip it from his grasp.

Danbury read aloud the short portion of the note the abductor had penned. "This is a sign of my good faith. The ladies have not been harmed, and will not be harmed unless you fail to obey my smallest instruction. Further communication will follow." He then read Lydia's brief message.

"Lord Danbury, is the note authentic?" asked Wellesley.

"Yes, sir, I believe it is. I would recognize Miss Garrett's hand anywhere. I have seen it often enough. Yet something is wrong. I must think—"

"What do you mean?" asked Marcus.

"To begin, I think she had wore a dress of brown linsey-woolsey. Very cheap stuff. I made no complaint about the amount of salt in the eggs. I didn't even have eggs. And her lout of a relative was called Fenn. What can she mean?"

Lord Wellesley stood and came around his desk. Both he and Marcus leaned in, reading the note again over Danbury's shoulder.

"Is anything else odd?" Wellesley asked.

"Just… I have never seen her penmanship quite so sloppy."

"She must be under a great deal of strain." To Marcus his words felt thick, lumpy, almost furred with anxiety.

"Yes, but there is something contrived about this note. I could be mistaken, but I think she is trying to send us a message."

Time stretched out, lengthening as it always did when Marcus least wanted it to.

Eventually, he and Lord Wellesley drifted away to discuss what steps they could take next. Men were already scouring the countryside searching for the ladies. Every servant had been discreetly questioned. No one had seen anything, either at the ball or anywhere else. The sole clue that had been unearthed had come some hours earlier, when one of the soldiers had found Miss Garrett's dance card in the garden. Even that proved nothing; she might have dropped it during her abduction, or she might have dropped it earlier in the evening. Who could say?

Marcus and Wellesley debated again and again whether they could turn over the throne in good conscience, and on the other hand how they could consider not turning it over when lives were at stake. Mindless discussion. Marcus hadn't the slightest intention of allowing Miss Garrett to remain in the hands of some fiend. He would find some way to reach her regardless of Wellesley's reluctance to trade the throne.

Danbury took no part in the conversation. Indeed he seemed scarcely to hear them. All his attention was directed on studying the note.

"There is no way to keep such a decision secret. If we give in to this fiend's demands it will soon be obvious to one and all that the throne has disappeared, and Britain shall be accused of losing it…"

"I have it!" Danbury sprang to his feet jubilantly.

Marcus whipped around and joined Danbury in examining the note.

"I shall kiss the clever minx when I see her again."

Marcus stiffened, but Danbury's excitement drew him, in spite of himself, as he waved the scrawled note.

"Look, gentlemen; look. You'll notice first the short structure of the lines. There is plenty of space for her to have made the lines longer but she wanted to draw our attention to specific words. Look at the last word of the first line."

"Aware?" read Marcus.

"Yes, but see she has left a slight gap between the 'a' and the rest of the word. Now look at the last word of the second line."

"House," supplied Lord Wellesley.

"Yes, don't you see? Warehouse. They must be in a warehouse. Now, see, she went on. Look at the spacing of these words." He pointed at the note emphatically. "They begin to run together, except for the last word, which has a curious little break in the middle."

"Nor the astute," the two men read the words aloud to themselves. Marcus said triumphantly, "Northeast! She meant they travelled northeast!"

"Precisely, and then there is the bit about the eggs and dress: all things that didn't happen, so we need to look at the individual words. Gentlemen, I think she is trying to tell us they are being held in a warehouse somewhere northeast of here. A warehouse that contains indigo, cotton, and saltpeter." Triumph blazed in every line of Danbury's features.

Marcus nodded, his heart bounding within him. It made sense. Yes. Yes, they had it at last. A starting point.

Lord Wellesley groaned. "Sir, we are in India. Every warehouse in Calcutta holds indigo, cotton and saltpeter. They are the primary exports."

Marcus's delight faded, but Danbury remained dogged.

"This information is valuable, sir. It narrows the field of search a great deal."

"But I fear it does not narrow it enough."

Marcus intervened between the two. "Lord Wellesley, there is an aspect of this situation which causes me great concern. But perhaps with this information we can turn it to our advantage."

"Yes?"

"I fear there is a traitor in our midst. Both Mrs Adkins and Miss Garrett are intelligent individuals. They could not have been lured away by someone they did not know and trust to some extent. The ladies must have gone at least part of the way willingly; no one could have abducted them by force from the middle of the dance floor. In addition, these infernal notes keep popping up in what one would assume were secure locations. It's too much to suppose this spy can break in and out of Government House at any hour of the night or day without leaving the slightest evidence behind him. The French are good, but not that good."

"I see your point." Lord Wellesley rubbed his chin thoughtfully. "I hate to think of such a thing, but it is a possibility."

"How do we use this to our advantage?" asked Danbury.

"If we know who has had access to Government House at the times these notes were left, and we can find out who has interests in a warehouse to the northeast, we can begin narrowing down our suspects."

"Who do we trust to help us with our investigation?" asked Wellesley.

"I suggest you use only those men in whom you place your utmost trust. If duty kept them from the ball last night, then so much the better."

"We must proceed with the utmost caution. Lyd… Miss Garrett no doubt risked her life to give us this information. The fewer people who know of it the better. If the spy gets any notion we are getting close he will move them and any advantage will be lost. He may even kill Miss Garrett," said Danbury.

Lord Wellesley pushed away from his desk. "This spy is a clever fellow. He won't give us time to plan. He is going to keep us off balance and move matters along quickly. Caution must be our first concern but haste our second."

CHAPTER 40

Lying on their skimpy pallets, Mrs Adkins and Lydia discussed their situation at length. After some hours they gave up on futile speculation. They needed to sleep. Whatever they faced they would handle it better rested. But while this was a good idea in theory, in practice it wasn't so easy.

Lydia tossed and turned. The pallets were better than sleeping directly on the hard packed earth, but not by much. In any event, her senses strained for the sound of movement in the corridor. The waiting for something worse to happen made it difficult to truly contemplate sleep. Eventually, however, exhaustion overwhelmed her.

The sound of the key turning in the lock instantly roused Lydia from the fitful sleep she had attained. Feeling at a disadvantage sitting on the floor, she stood to face their kidnapper, stooping to help Mrs Adkins do the same as he entered.

"Good morning, ladies. I trust you slept well?" Dr Marshall came in with the air of a physician attending his patients.

"I cannot imagine why you would think so," Mrs Adkins said in a tone meant to freeze him in place.

"Tut, tut, there is no call for incivility. I brought you breakfast." The doctor extended a package and a small ewer of water.

Lydia would have liked nothing better than to fling the parcel at his traitorous face, but they would need the food. It was wiser not to cultivate his displeasure. She stepped forward and accepted the meal, murmuring thanks she did not feel.

"Now see, Mrs Adkins. Miss Garrett knows how to behave." He turned to Lydia. "But of course she is the kind of woman who knows which side her bread is buttered on. Adept at pleasing a man, isn't she?"

Lydia's cheeks flamed as if he had slapped her.

"Do not regard him." Mrs Adkins put an arm around her shoulder.

Lydia could not be mollified. "At least I have not betrayed all those who have a natural claim to my loyalty and affection."

"Affection." Dr Marshall turned a mottled shade of red. "Do not speak to me of affection. The English are the coldest, most undeserving race on the earth."

"How can you say that? I have seen no Englishman treat you with anything but courtesy and kindness."

"You know nothing. The English system is constructed not on kindness, but on predatory self-interest. My father, the respected baronet, is nothing but an abusive wastrel." Bitterness dripped from his words like rancid honey. "But merely because of his status as an Englishman, the brute had the right to wrest me from my mother, whom he treated as a harlot. He made my childhood a misery until I prayed to God to die." A vein pulsed at his temple, and his eyes were watery.

Lydia stared at him steadily. She could almost glimpse the frightened little boy he once had been. Her heart softened for a moment as she imagined his boyhood. It must have been an agony; but did that justify his subsequent behaviour? "I'm sorry for your distress, but you are a doctor. You should value human life more dearly than anyone, and yet you have murdered to advance your cause."

Marshall shook his head, disdain radiating from him. "Miss Garrett, you are utterly naïve. The one thing being a physician has taught me is that human life is cheap. None of the tinctures and potions we apply cure anyone. They merely alleviate the symptoms, *if* the sufferer is lucky. Children die all the time when, contrary to all rights, their loutish parents survive."

Marshall paced the small confines of the room. The vehemence of his feelings spilled over into his tone. "Ask any poor young girl who has got herself into trouble, and you would know that the price to end a human life is much less than the cost of an additional mouth to feed if the child were allowed to live. And if all this is not enough to prove the point, then go into any rookery in the city and you will discover precisely how little a life is worth. Men will slit your throat for a farthing."

Lydia opened her mouth to argue but the doctor continued. "No. I shall thank you not to sermonize. The only way to get on in this world is to take what you want. Your platitudes cannot deter me."

"And what is it that you want?" Lydia asked mildly.

Marshall stopped in mid-stride. He looked at her with such contempt that what remained of her compassion for him shrivelled. "I shall restore the glory of my mother's family, and I will see that England receives the recompense she deserves for her tender care of her children."

"And you believe this is the best means by which to accomplish that goal?"

"Of course it is. General Bonaparte has given me his personal assurance that my service will result in the restoration of our family lands."

"But surely possessions alone will not suffice to make you happy?"

"Enough! This is no debate in the House of Commons. Eat, and if you so desire, pray that your friends obey my commands, and that you see another day." Having delivered what he apparently believed to be an effective parting line, he whirled and stalked away.

"Let's see what he has brought us to eat. It is a good sign. At least he does not mean to kill us immediately. Otherwise, why bother to feed us?" Mrs Adkins took the bundle from Lydia, who still gripped it in numb fingers. "Naan." Mrs Adkins held up a flat, round disc. "It is the local kind of bread. It can be quite good if it's fresh."

"The proverbial bread and water," said Lydia in weak jest.

Mrs Adkins smiled obligingly.

Lydia could not shake the unsettling effect of Dr Marshall's passionate discourse. What an unhappy wretch. Had he ever known love? Bitterness had eaten away his soul like lye, until nothing remained but his rage and pain.

They sat on the floor as if at a picnic, though without the same sense of frivolity. Now that the sun was up they could see that the windows were not as tightly boarded as Dr Marshall might have wished. Thin slits of sunlight filtered through, allowing them to examine their cell more closely. Fed and somewhat rested, they considered their situation anew.

"It seemed hopeless last night, but perhaps we can engineer an escape. Those boards look old and dry," said Lydia with an appraising look at the windows.

The door behind them flew open and banged against the wall. Lydia started, biting her tongue. Their guard, the driver from the night before, stood in the doorway with a basin of water and an incongruously fine linen towel.

"Monsieur says you will want to wash." He stalked into the room and set the items down, carelessly sloshing water. "I will bring drinking water later." With this surly pronouncement he left.

Mrs Adkins clutched her heart. "I thought for a moment he had heard us and come to put a violent end to our plotting."

"So did I," said Lydia, a little chuckle escaping—less mirth than the cusp of hysteria, quickly brought under strict control once more.

"If we are going to attempt an escape, we must be very careful. I do not think my heart could take another such scare. What are our options?"

"If you will listen at the door for the guard, I will go through the furniture to see if there is anything we could use as a tool or a weapon."

Lydia searched the desks and other furniture thoroughly, but found nothing useful. A broken pen nib, a stray button and a quantity of knotted string were the extent of her discoveries. Disappointed but undaunted she dragged a chair beneath the window and stood on it to examine the situation.

"There's no glass. It has all been broken out. If I had a knife or something like it, I think I could pry out some of these nails and remove the boards."

She climbed from the chair and replaced it in front of the desk. Mrs Adkins joined her and they sat on their pallets in silent contemplation of the predicament.

"In the novels I have read, the hero pretends to be ill. When the guard comes in, he is overpowered and the hero escapes," Mrs Adkins said.

"I don't think I could overpower the guard. Could you?"

"Not overpower him, but perhaps we could light the lamp. When he comes in, we could throw it at him and then run out."

"That might work." The scrape of a shoe in the hall caught Lydia's ear. "Wait. I think I hear him coming."

They watched the door expectantly. The lock turned and the door swung open. The guard brought in the pitcher of promised water. "Monsieur will be back with lunch," he muttered, before slouching back into the hall and closing the door behind him.

"Mrs Adkins, do you think you could charm him into leaving us a butter knife with our next meal?"

"Please call me Rosalie. If we are to die together, I'd like you to know my name." She straightened. "Wait. I've had another idea. Help me take off my stays. The busk and boning might work to remove the nails. It would be better if we could escape without a confrontation."

With Lydia's aid, Rosalie removed her stays and pulled out the long thin strips of whalebone that gave then their structure. When she had redressed, Lydia replaced the chair beneath the window and climbed back up while Rosalie took up position by the door. Lydia set to work diligently, wedging the edge of the whalebone under a rusty nail, and beginning to pry the nail loose.

The day grew progressively hotter, until it felt as if they were in a fiery kiln. No breeze or breath of air penetrated their cell, and they grew miserably overheated. Lydia took a break to drink from the provided pitcher. She had made progress, removing three nails from the bottom board, but it was agonizingly slow. Rosalie insisted on taking a turn wielding the whalebone and they switched positions.

By mid-afternoon, drenched with perspiration and exhausted, they had removed all the nails from the bottom board save two at the top, which they had purposely left in place. It would not do for the guard or Marshall to come in and find the board missing. Under the cover of night, they would pry out the last couple of nails in each board and make their escape.

"I do wish that whoever put these up had not been quite so thorough in his task," said Lydia as she began on the second board. Far from the perfect tool for the job, the thin whalebone kept slipping. Her hands were scraped and bleeding in several places. Rust discoloured her fingers and she carefully kept from getting it on her dress. Quite apart from the natural instinct not to ruin a gown, she did not want rust stains on her skirts giving away their plans.

The bone snapped once more and Lydia's knuckles were again grazed, drawing blood against the rough boards. She gritted her teeth, but refrained from crying out. *God grant that we do not run out of whalebone before we run out of nails.*

"Someone is coming," whispered Rosalie.

Lydia jumped from the chair and shoved it back into place. The key rattled in the lock. She dropped the whalebone behind the desk and plunged her hands into the water basin. The door swung open, and a smiling Dr Marshall appeared.

"Did you miss me, ladies?"

Lydia did not respond, but continued to wash her hands and then her face slowly, as if unconcerned.

From the pallet, where she lounged as if she had lain there all day, Rosalie complained loudly about everything from the heat, to the food, to the lack of facilities.

Lydia took up the towel, patting her hands and face dry. She breathed a prayer of thanks that Rosalie had distracted the doctor and she had the chance to fold the towel neatly and hide any stray streaks of rust or blood.

"I fear I am not as proficient at hosting these little events as I might be," Marshall said dryly. "Perhaps I will improve with practice. My friend Philippe tells me you have been very quiet today. What have you been up to, my dears?"

Finished with her ablutions, Lydia sat on her pallet. "We have been catching up on our needlepoint. What else?"

Marshall turned to her and smiled humourlessly. "Keep a civil tongue in your head or you might find it missing altogether." He turned back to Rosalie. "Mrs Adkins, I do not believe you were awake when I informed Miss Garrett of the precariousness of her position. Her life is of little value to me—and only in so far as it keeps those who do value her in line. Pray remember this if you are tempted to try something I might not like."

Lydia stared at the back of his head. His manner was markedly different from what it had been that morning. He seemed determined not to be drawn back into any sort of conversation.

Marshall left the room, calling to Philippe. "Bring in the food and allow the ladies to use the facilities, one at a time. I shall return later."

CHAPTER 41

A maid found another note just after tea. Anthony and Harting were poring over a mountain of paperwork in Lord Wellesley's study when it was brought in.

> *Gentlemen, I have assured you of my good faith by presenting proof the ladies are still alive. Now you will obey each of my instructions to the letter or your ladies will no longer remain in that happy state. Lord Wellesley, you will bring the Peacock Throne to the ruins of Kali's temple, near the village of Shiankam, at midnight. Only Lord Danbury may accompany you, and you must both be unarmed. We will conduct an exchange. Your treasures for mine. If troops are even suspected, the ladies will die.*

It was time for a council of war. They had learned a great deal throughout the exceedingly trying day, but little of it was of any use. They had list upon list of people and properties, but narrowing it down was proving even more difficult than they had feared.

Captain Stevens entered, leading a native woman with wide fearful eyes.

"Sir," said Stevens, bowing to Lord Wellesley. "This young woman may have seen who left the note."

Anthony leapt to his feet, and the woman started nervously.

"What did you see?" asked Lord Wellesley urgently.

In halting English, the woman delivered her story. "I scrub floor in the hall. Most days we do this more early, but the ball makes extra work. I work behind the plants. The man come in. He turn head like he does not want someone to see. So I am wonder, and I watch. He puts paper on table and goes away."

"Did you recognize the man? Do you know who he is?"

"Yes, sir. It is the…" She screwed up her face searching for the right word. "The doctor. I do not know his name. So many guests."

Anthony frowned. A doctor? And then all of a sudden it was as if someone had finally turned a tapestry over to reveal the picture rather than the knotted underbelly. Of course it was Marshall—with his French mother and burning desire to see her properties restored. Who better to help him in his quest than Bonaparte? He had mentioned his high-flown patients. No doubt they were the source of his intelligence as well as his wealth.

Beside him, Harting shook his head. They both ought to resign all claim of sense for not having seen it sooner.

"You are certain of what you say?" asked Wellesley.

"Yes, sir."

"Good girl. Here is a guinea. Run along now." The girl fled Lord Wellesley's presence, smiling and clutching her unheard of wealth.

Harting was on his feet. "It can only be Adam Marshall. By Jove, I never would have guessed it."

Wellesley shook his head mournfully. "Stevens…" He turned towards the captain.

"My men are already looking for him," said Stevens, anticipating the order.

"Does he own any warehouses?" asked Marcus.

Anthony pawed through the stacks of paper they had accumulated since the kidnappings, all the information they had been able to compile regarding the British and their holdings in and around Calcutta, until he came up with the list he wanted. "Here it is," he said. "He owns three warehouses, but only one is northeast of Government House. I am going."

Harting stood and pulled at his cuffs. "We will all go, but we must be careful. We'll approach it on foot. Don't want to put the ladies in any greater danger."

Anthony felt for the sword at his side. He would put Marshall in danger, or die in the attempt. And then deliberately he released the blade. No more impulsiveness. He must think. His reckless cruelty had placed Miss Garrett in danger from the first. If he had been kinder they would have danced together again and she would have been safe. He would not make the same mistake again.

They made their plans quickly. Dr Marshall had been spotted leaving after luncheon and Lord Wellesley left orders to detain him upon his return. They didn't trouble with a carriage but mounted horseback to ensure speed. In less than half an hour they were away, flying towards the warehouse at a gallop.

* * *

Lydia and Rosalie had eaten their lunch quickly. With renewed vigour, Lydia attacked the boards of their prison windows. Marshall appeared from time to time. With each visit he became more openly hostile, as if his anger fed off anxiety.

His shift in temper worried Lydia. His behaviour might be all affectation in order to frighten them, but Lydia sensed an instability beneath his façade. Urgency welled within her, lending energy to her efforts. The longer they remained within his power, the more likely it was that he would carry out his threats.

Night came early in India, and they lit the lamp in order to see what they were doing. All the nails save the final two on each of the three boards had been removed. Desperation sped Lydia's movements. With frantic haste she worked the remaining bit of bone.

The whalebone bit into her palm, scoring it once more. Tears scalded her cheeks, but she could not stop now. Necessity prodded her. They must escape soon or not at all.

The grating of the key shocked her. On the other side of the door, Marshall berated Philippe for falling asleep. There had been no warning.

Rosalie gasped, looking at her wide-eyed.

Lydia started to scramble from the chair, but the whalebone remained wedged tightly under the head of the nail. She gave it a mighty wrench and it pulled free, but she lost a precious second. Flinging the piece of whalebone into the shadowed corner, Lydia leapt down. There was no time to replace the chair, so she stood in front of it trying to regulate her breathing.

Marshall seemed to sense their apprehension the instant he opened the door. He eyed Lydia and the chair. In a single bounding step he leapt towards her and grabbed her hand, holding it up to reveal the scratches and rust stains. His eyes went automatically to the window, and he shoved Lydia aside. She stumbled and fell against the wall.

He examined the boards grimly and hauled Lydia up by her hair. "I warned you not to try to be clever." He slapped her, making her eyes stream, but Lydia had had enough.

She fought back, hitting, kicking and biting. From one corner of her eye, as if from a great distance, she saw Rosalie shove against Philippe, who held her back from the fray.

Lydia's strength was no match against Marshall's, but fury drove her, and it took him several minutes to subdue her. Breathing heavily, with his knee in her back, he pinned her hands to the ground above her head. He ripped off his cravat and used it to pinion her arms behind her. Hauling Lydia to her feet, he delivered another resounding slap that would have toppled her had he not still been holding her up with his other hand.

Lydia gasped for air. His weight had pushed what breath she had from her lungs. His slap had disorientated her. Her head ached, and her other wounds smarted, but she was pleased to note she had left an ugly scratch across his cheek, and had even managed to bloody his nose. With any luck she had caused more damage than she could see.

Marshall touched his face and blood came away from where she had scratched him.

"You have more of your father in you than you credit," Lydia rasped.

Rage suffused his features, making his eyes even darker. His fingers bit into her shoulders as he shook her savagely. Rosalie shouted for him to stop, and even Philippe released his grip on Rosalie to put a hand on his arm.

"Monsieur, she may still be useful," he said. "The exchange is only a few hours away. It would be a pity to waste any advantage."

Marshall seemed to come to himself and he released Lydia, who slumped to the floor. Rosalie knelt by her side, smoothing the hair back from her face.

"I am well," murmured Lydia. The words sounded less reassuring than she would have liked.

"Philippe, bind their hands, and put them both in the carriage."

"Yes, Monsieur." Philippe ducked his head, knuckling his forehead respectfully.

Rosalie did not struggle with Philippe as he bound her wrists tightly behind her back. He hurried her out to the carriage and returned for Lydia, who still lay dazed on the floor. Philippe picked her up and put her over his shoulder as he would a large sack of flour. Marshall had taken up a position on the box. His assistant had barely climbed up beside him when Marshall flicked the reins.

CHAPTER 42

Captain Stevens led the way into an area of docks and warehouses. Anthony, Harting, and Lord Wellesley followed closely on his heels. They took care to dismount and leave their horses at a distance from Marshall's warehouse. The place appeared to be deserted, but they approached cautiously, using the shadows as cover.

The main entry was closed, but not locked. They entered quickly and quietly, making as little disturbance as possible in the dusty, motionless atmosphere. The group broke apart to search independently.

Spying a long corridor at the far end of the building, Anthony immediately headed for the darkened passage. Marshall would have wanted to confine the ladies if possible. Methodically, he opened each door and moved to the next.

A chair sat outside the last door, and Anthony was not surprised when this final office turned out to be the prison.

Too late. He closed his eyes as guilt bombarded him anew. "They have already been taken away." He called to the rest of the men, his voice jarring in the smothering silence. "They're gone."

Anthony stepped into the chamber. He lit the lamp and held it up to see whether he could discern anything. Perhaps Miss Garrett had had time to leave another clue. Furniture was jumbled against one wall. A chair sat beneath one of the windows. A basin and pitcher sat on one of the discarded desks. Two pallets lay at the other end of the room.

The other men piled into the room behind him, glaring at the austere space as if they could force it to tell what had occurred within its dreary confines.

"The chair under the window," Anthony said. "Why is the chair under the window? It's not as if they could look out." He walked over to the window and regarded it closely. "They are a dashed plucky pair." He held the light high. "Look at this."

Gouge marks scored the boards where something had bit into the wood and prised out nails.

Captain Stevens returned from one of the other offices with another lamp to better illuminate the scene. They clustered around Anthony.

Harting frowned. "Whatever did they use? I can't imagine he would have left them tools."

Casting about for an explanation the men held up the lamps and examined the small space. Light glinted off dull ivory. Harting retrieved a shard of bone resting in the corner and held it up for inspection.

"It looks to be whalebone," said Captain Stevens.

"From what?" Anthony took the pale sliver and held it flat on his palm.

They all regarded it a moment longer.

"Why, I think it must be a piece of whalebone from a lady's stays," Wellesley said after a space.

"I tell you, gentlemen, I should not have wanted to be the one to have kidnapped those two—they are formidable." Captain Stevens shook his head.

"They would have made it clean away soon. These boards are almost free." Anthony tapped one with the back of his knuckle and sent it to the floor in a cloud of dust.

"They must have been interrupted and taken away before they could finish," Harting said. He rubbed his forehead as if trying to wrap his mind around the fact that they had indeed failed.

"Gentlemen, look at this." Captain Stevens pointed gravely at a spot on the floor. "This looks like blood."

CHAPTER 42

Again the lamps were brought to bear while they examined the spattered discolouration.

Harting knelt and touched the spot. "It's still damp. They cannot have been gone long."

"What sort of monster is he?" demanded Captain Stevens.

Enraged, Anthony did not attempt any comment. He would reserve his thoughts on the matter until he caught Adam Marshall, at which point he intended to demonstrate his feelings fully.

"Gentlemen, we have a decision to make. I cannot turn over the throne. So what will we do?" Lord Wellesley asked.

Anthony bristled. "We will turn over the throne. I brought it here. And as I've intimated before, it is not a present to the crown. By all rights it is mine and I will turn it over without a qualm if they will trade Miss Garrett for it."

Harting nodded sharply in agreement. In his fashionable jacket and elaborate cravat he looked markedly out of place in the dusty warehouse. But the savage expression on his face would have made him at home among a band of brigands. "We can minimize the political damage by simply announcing that the throne was stolen. We already made a gesture of goodwill towards the people of India. We will make certain they know the French have stolen it from them again."

Murmurs of agreement rippled through the circle of men. Lord Wellesley straightened his shoulders. "We are agreed then. We will recover the ladies."

"God help the murderous coward once he no longer has them in his power. I will hunt him to the end of the earth." Anthony clenched the hilt of his sword spasmodically.

They raced back to Government House. There was little time to spare if they were going to make it to the temple ruins at the appointed time. Anthony was strongly tempted to retain his sword, but Lord Wellesley insisted they follow the instructions explicitly, so he left it with Harting.

The throne had been crated and loaded into a stout cart for

just such an eventuality. They climbed up onto the box and Lord Wellesley took the reins.

"We shall be back as soon as we can. I want a regiment prepared to go after the fiend the instant we return."

"Yes, sir." Captain Stevens saluted smartly.

The cart ground away, gaining speed slowly as it turned out of the courtyard.

* * *

"You realize I must go after them," Marcus said.

Captain Stevens nodded. "Of course. Men and horses are waiting around the other side of the stables. We will need to delay a little. It would not do to get too close and allow ourselves to be spotted."

"There's no cause for you to disobey an order. Reinforcements will be here any moment. As you say, though, we will need horses."

Stevens raised an eyebrow, but nodded and headed to the stables.

Marcus paced the courtyard restlessly. Bats wheeled overhead, silent but for the rush of air as they swooped and dived too near. A single oil lamp hung near the door, but its paltry light did little to illuminate the area.

The scuff of a shoe on flagstone brought his head up as if the change in position could sharpen his hearing.

"Is that you, Mr Harting?"

"Captain Campbell, I'm glad you could come."

"Of course I came. When your man told me what had happened, I could scarce credit it." Campbell approached. Behind him loomed the hulking forms of more than twenty seamen.

As the men entered the feeble circle of light Marcus could see they were armed and scowling. Every man-jack looked as if he was itching for a fight.

CHAPTER 43

Again Lydia woke, groggy and sore, on the floor of a carriage. She appeared to be making a regular habit of it, she thought ruefully. Pain spiked through her as the carriage jolted through a particularly deep rut. A foul tasting gag made her mouth impossibly dry. *Please God, do not let it be Philippe's loathsome neckerchief.*

The carriage pulled up smartly and ceased its jostling, for which Lydia was profoundly grateful. In the sudden hush, she could hear Dr Marshall talking quietly to Philippe.

"It is all very well to foment rebellion in India. But if we can remove Lord Wellesley as well, the English will be in desperate straits. It will take months to get a new Governor-General in place. English strength in India will be broken and while they pour men into the breach, General Bonaparte will strike at their heart with an invasion force."

"You are brilliant, Monsieur. You have ordered everything perfectly."

"Well, I had not originally intended an assassination," said Dr Marshall modestly, "but matters have arranged themselves so nicely it would be a shame to waste such a prime opportunity. When I think of the things that have gone wrong…" He sighed. "In spite of everything things may come out better than I dared hope."

Energy surged through Lydia. She looked around wildly for Rosalie and found her slumped on the carriage bench behind her. Relief followed on the heels of her fear; the woman had been bound but not gagged. She must have behaved well.

Lydia's wild gyrations wakened her.

"Dear, you are awake. Are you all right? He didn't hurt you too badly, did he?" She leaned towards Lydia, but with her hands tied behind her back the impulse to comfort was checked.

Lydia shook her head violently and rubbed her face against the carriage floor in an attempt to dislodge the gag.

"What's wrong?" asked Rosalie. "You frighten me. What is wrong?"

Outside, a masculine voice hailed Marshall in French. This must be some of the crew from the French sloop. Lydia listened intently and realized from their conversation that they had heaved to in a sheltered cove just north of a village—which village, she could not make out. They were ready to load the throne and escape as soon as the exchange had taken place. Marshall began to discuss his plans with the men, but he must have been moving away. The sounds grew fainter until they were inaudible.

Lydia prayed fervently for help and continued to struggle with her bonds. There was no give at all in the ropes. She must warn someone of the trap.

Marshall returned and opened the carriage door. "They should be here any moment. Shall we set the stage?" He lifted Rosalie from the carriage and then turned back. "Do not try my patience, Miss Garrett. You have irritated me and I will kill you if you give me the slightest bit of trouble. Do you understand?"

Lydia nodded mutely, trying to look docile—which was not difficult given that she was bound and gagged. He pulled her from the carriage and stood her beside Mrs Adkins.

"Come along now, ladies. We must make sure you are displayed to best advantage."

Lydia's gaze swept the scene wildly. Thankfully, the night was clear, with a bright moon illuminating the landscape. They were in the ruins of some sort of building. Fantastical carvings covered every remaining surface. It must be some sort of temple.

Dr Marshall led them into a wide courtyard in the centre of the structure. He positioned Mrs Adkins with Philippe in the shadows at one side and dragged Lydia, stumbling along behind him, to the other.

Lydia could hear the rattle and slide of rocks as men took up their positions around the courtyard. A long, tense silence ensued. Lydia frantically worried the knots that bound her hands behind her back. She thought they gave way a little, but she was by no means certain: her fingers had grown numb and she feared testing the notion. It was imperative not to give away what she was doing. Without doubt Marshall would keep his promise if she provoked him.

A hail from one of the lookouts caused everyone to jump. "They're coming."

* * *

Anthony surveyed the temple as they approached. "This is a godforsaken spot if ever I saw one."

"Kali is a Hindu goddess associated with death and change. Her followers once performed horrible human sacrifices here," said Lord Wellesley.

"Then I am even more correct than I supposed."

They lapsed into silence as they drew nearer. No one approached and they saw no one as they pulled in front of the temple.

"Perhaps we ought to drive through those arches. It looks as if there might be an inner courtyard," said Anthony.

Lord Wellesley nodded and flicked the reins. They rumbled slowly through the arches, which formed a short tunnel, until they came to the central courtyard.

A man stepped from the shadows, pushing Mrs Adkins forward with him. "I see you followed my instructions," he said in a French accent. "Please step away from the throne. I must warn you, gentlemen, not to try anything dangerous—you are surrounded by my men."

Lord Wellesley and Anthony climbed from their seats, taking care to appear non-threatening. Anthony's every sense was attuned to the slight rustlings as the men surrounding them shifted their weight and fidgeted.

"Have they hurt you, my dear?" called Lord Wellesley.

"No, darling, but I think Miss Garrett may be rather badly injured," she answered before her captor jerked her arm and she subsided.

Anthony's hand reached for a sword that was not there. "Where is Marshall? We know he is behind this. Is he even more of a coward than we imagined?"

"Bravo." Marshall stepped from the shadows behind them. "I had hoped to keep my identity secure, but it is no matter. The *coup d'état* has been accomplished."

Anthony spun round to face Marshall. His heart gave a wrench when he saw Lydia with the man. One eye looked swollen and puffy, and her mouth had been tied so tightly shut, he could see where the bonds bit into her flesh. Still, she could stand on her own. He took comfort in the hope that no permanent injury had been done.

"You have been pitifully sloppy, Marshall. The little corporal will not be pleased. You didn't accomplish any of the things you desired. You may have the throne, but it will do you no good."

"Wrong as usual, Danbury. I have accomplished even more than I first hoped. It will be interesting to see what happens to India when there is no English leader in place." Marshall raised the pistol he had been holding casually at his side and pointed it directly at Lord Wellesley.

CHAPTER 44

Lydia had been unable to free herself from her bonds, but she could wait no longer. In a single desperate movement she whipped around, barrelling into Marshall with every ounce of strength she could muster. He staggered backwards while she went sprawling and tumbling sideways down a short flight of stairs. The shot he fired went high and wide, but the sound reverberated through the courtyard. A stunned pause froze everyone in place for a fraction of an instant as people tried to comprehend what just had happened. Then chaos surged into the void.

Lydia craned her neck to see what had become of Lord Wellesley. She was just in time to catch a glimpse as Danbury pushed him beneath the cart, trying to shield him with his own body.

Rosalie wrenched free of Philippe and ran towards the Governor-General. Marshall's men charged the cart with an outraged howl. From behind them, Lydia heard another mighty shout. Harting appeared in the arched entryway of the temple, leading a band of men who poured in behind him. The warning from the lookouts had come too late.

The clash of swords and curses pealed through the courtyard like an awful chorus of bells. Marshall swore viciously and darted down the stairs to grab Lydia, who struggled to gain her feet without the use of her hands. He snatched her upper arm, his fingers digging deep into the soft flesh.

Lydia refused to be a convenient hostage. She writhed and struggled in his grasp, hoping at least to delay his escape. The train of her dress wrapped about her legs, tripping her, and her weight carried Marshall down too. He was up again in an instant, trying to cuff her into submission while at the same time dragging her away with him.

* * *

Anthony succeeded in getting Lord Wellesley and his paramour safely tucked beneath the cart. Fortunately the horses were cavalry beasts, used to warfare, and they remained complacent as the fighting raged around them. Eager to join the battle, Anthony sought wildly for a weapon.

Harting tore past, practically chasing a great hulk of a man who—despite his size—had no apparent idea of how to handle a sword.

"Danbury." He tossed Anthony his sword, still in its scabbard.

Instantly forgiving him for every deception, Anthony caught it and bounded to the top of the cart to survey the scene. He wanted to join battle with only one man.

"Lordship, she's over there," old Angus Robb hollered with a jerk of his thumb.

Anthony finally caught sight of Marshall as he dragged Lydia through the portico at the far end of the courtyard. Rage slithered through Anthony. He leapt from the cart and darted after them. He shoved and slashed his way through the battling figures in his path. Once free of the struggling men he ran flat out.

Marshall turned and spied Anthony. He pushed Lydia to the ground. An instant later he thought better of his plan and jerked her upright again, putting his sword to her throat.

Anthony stopped some fifteen paces from the couple. He couldn't reach them in time to prevent Marshall slitting her throat.

"Surely you are more of a man than to murder a helpless woman? Let her go and fight me," Anthony said.

"Helpless? She is the least helpless woman I've met in my life.

CHAPTER 44

This entire debacle is her fault. I do have plans for her, however." Marshall pushed the point of his blade even further into her flesh until blood oozed in a thin line down her throat. "I made her a promise."

Anthony took a step forward, but stopped as Marshall's lips pulled back in a snarl. He held up his free hand in a staying gesture. "The others will be coming soon. You should fight me now or you will never get away." He advanced again, cautiously.

"I will kill her if you do not stop." Marshall retreated a step.

Anthony continued to close the gap between them.

He made a dismissive wave of his sword. "There are plenty more where she came from, but I will not allow my father's murderer to get away again." His muscles were so tense he could scarce continue his deliberate advance.

Marshall seemed to realize the only way he was going to get away quickly would be to fight and win. With a savage cry he shoved Lydia at Anthony and attacked.

Thrown off balance as she hurtled into him, Anthony scarcely managed to raise his sword to fend off the blow.

* * *

Hands tied behind her, Lydia could not crawl out of the way; instead, she rolled awkwardly away from Danbury. She kicked out at Marshall and the blow went home enough to cause him to falter for an instant. It was all the time Danbury needed to recover himself, and he rallied with a vengeance.

She scrabbled out of the way. She ached to help Danbury in some way, but feared tripping him up rather than Marshall. Once she managed to get clear of the men, she struggled into a sitting position. She could hardly breathe. Horror constricted her lungs like a snake.

Back and forth the figures danced. Lunging, feinting, parrying. Attacking and then retreating. Marshall drew first blood with his initial rush. But Danbury gradually gained the upper hand. After several passes it became apparent that Danbury was the stronger, more skilled, of the two. Still Marshall battled on with the sober determination of a bulldog, making up with sheer audacity what he lacked in finesse.

Danbury lunged, forcing the doctor to retreat. Marshall's swings were becoming erratic, less powerful. He half stumbled, but righted himself almost instantly.

"Yield," demanded Danbury.

Marshall did not respond, doggedly fighting on. He was breathing hard now, his face red and streaming with sweat. Danbury pressed his advantage. He drew blood again. A slick, red stain spread across the doctor's thigh.

"Do you yield?"

"I yield," Marshall said, his voice pitched high by strain. He bent over panting and braced his free hand on his knee.

Danbury reached for Marshall's sword. Uttering a primeval yell that made Lydia shiver despite the heat, Marshall lunged in a desperate attack. Danbury twisted away. Marshall's sword pierced jacket, waistcoat, and shirt, coming out on the other side. Danbury's sword found more solid fodder.

Dr Adam Marshall gazed down in astonishment at the blade protruding from his gut. He dropped his weapon and stumbled to his knees. He appeared shocked at being confronted by his own mortality. His hands found the wound, attempting feebly to staunch the blood.

Danbury knelt and pulled the sword from Marshall's body. He took out a handkerchief and, removing Marshall's hands, pressed the cloth against the wound. Marshall groaned pitifully and his eyes glazed over with pain. Lydia heard an English huzzah and realized the Frenchmen in the temple had been routed.

In an awkward writhing motion, she gained her knees and crawled to where the duelists sat on the ground. Nodding frantically, she succeeded in signalling Danbury to remove her gag.

She spat out the flannel wadding and said, "You are not injured?"

He put a hand to the blood that seeped along his abdomen; he was breathing heavily. "Only a scrape."

Lydia nodded towards the doctor. "Then help him lie flat."

Danbury did as directed.

"Keep firm, direct pressure on the wound. Your cravat would make a handsome bandage to help slow the bleeding." Danbury scowled, but removed his neck cloth with one hand. Already his handkerchief could absorb no more of Marshall's lifeblood.

Following Lydia's instruction, Danbury attended the dying man.

Footsteps pounded towards them and Danbury called for someone to take his place. A sailor did so, and Danbury turned to Lydia.

Utterly drained, Lydia sat statue still. Danbury crouched by her side and held her close.

"Are you all right?" The gentle embrace was too much, and she began to cry.

Danbury pulled back. "I'm sorry, I've hurt you. I ought to have released you from these bonds. I'm sorry." He cut her hands apart. Cupping her face in his hands, he brushed the curls from her eyes. "Now are you all right?"

"You should not have come alone; it was too dangerous." Lydia hiccoughed but summoned a smile.

"My dear girl… I'm so sorry for the things I said. I was angry, but from the beginning I have been using you just as much to help solve all this. I had no place to—"

Danbury pulled her close. Her head rested securely against his broad chest. His fingers tangled in her hair.

"Oh, but you did. I've felt so dreadfully guilty. I cannot tell you how sorry I am that I ever suspected you, or agreed to the plan." Lydia couldn't restrain a final sniffle. "Could I have a handkerchief, please?"

Harting appeared now and offered a fine square of linen to Lydia. She wiped her eyes and blew her nose gratefully. She knew she must look awful, but she was too tired to do much more than push her tangled hair back from her face. Danbury helped her to her feet as Lord Wellesley approached.

"He's dead then?" asked Lord Wellesley.

"Not yet." Danbury gestured to where a couple of men still laboured over the fallen man. "He will be soon."

"I shall see if he will give us any information about the French intelligence services. Excuse me." Wellesley walked stiffly away.

Rosalie stayed with Lydia and the two embraced. "I am indebted to you forever."

"Not at all," rasped Lydia. She longed for a cool drink. The flannel stuffed in her mouth had left her feeling as parched as a desert.

"Come along, let's get you back to Government House and have a physician look at you." Harting shepherded her away from Danbury and the crowd with infinite tenderness.

In a matter of moments, Lydia and Rosalie were ensconced in Marshall's carriage and on their way back to Government House. It was a fairly comfortable conveyance if one were not trussed and dumped in a heap on the floor, thought Lydia.

Neither Lydia nor Rosalie attempted conversation. In the grip of deep exhaustion they both fell asleep long before the carriage rattled up in front of the mansion.

Their arrival at Government House prompted a flurry of activity. Harting rang for a pitcher of lemon water. Accepting the offering gratefully, Lydia drank long and deep. The relief of the first swallow was unlike anything she had ever experienced.

She had no notion what would happen next, but with her hands unbound she felt as if she could face anything. Right after a nap.

CHAPTER 45

Lydia did not wake until well after the lunch hour. She groaned when she sat up, and held her head in her hands. Every movement caused some new ache. A glance in the glass by the bed revealed that both her eyes had been blackened and her lip split. Her face was pale and puffy. She winced at her vanity that these facts should bother her so much.

Annette had a meal and hot water brought up so she could bathe Lydia's wounds.

"I'm glad you're safe, Miss." The girl bobbed her head shyly.

Lydia thanked the girl for her kind wishes. When the meal arrived, she ate with a good appetite. Despite her pains, she felt better. The emotional storm of the night before had passed. Lydia pushed the covers aside and edged her legs over the side of the bed. She needed to discover what was happening.

Annette looked horrified. "Miss, the doctor says that you are to rest. Lord Danbury came around this morning to see you. He said he will be back. If you want him now, I will send for him."

"No," said Lydia. "There is no hurry. I thought he might need my help with something."

"I think he would be displeased if you ignored the doctor's advice."

Lydia had had enough of doctors feeling they could imprison her, but she held up her hands in mock surrender and climbed back into bed. She dozed a while. When she woke again it was eventime, and someone was knocking softly at the door. Rosalie stayed for a short time, and then Lydia read for a while. Another knock sounded. Lydia looked up hopefully.

The maid opened the door a crack and spoke to the person on the other side. Then she turned to Lydia. "It is Mr Harting. Do you wish to see him?"

"Yes," said Lydia without hesitation.

Annette helped her into a loose morning gown and pulled her hair back in a simple knot at the nape of her neck. She stood and made her way carefully from her room to the sitting room next door. Lying in bed all day had kept her from realizing the extent of her injuries. Now she was recalled to them with a vengeance.

She found Harting staring out of the open window at the garden. It was the nearest to repose she had ever seen his features.

"My dear." Harting turned and took her hands, gently leading her to a couch. "We were all so worried. Will you be all right?" He gestured to the angry bruises on her face and arms.

"Yes, I shall be quite all right. There's no cause to fret. Bruises heal quickly. Now tell me all that has happened."

Harting congratulated her on the note she had written and then described the search they had conducted. He detailed the final demand from the kidnapper, how Danbury and Lord Wellesley had ridden off alone.

"Have you captured all the conspirators?"

"Wellesley managed quite a nice haul. In addition to the men we took last night, he dispatched two English frigates after the French sloop. She and her entire crew were captured."

"They didn't put up a fight?"

"They made a short-lived attempt to run, but didn't get far. The English intercepted them, and after a short battle, *Égalité* struck her colours. The officers and crew are being questioned about Marshall and their knowledge of his plans."

"I am sorry to have missed all the excitement."

"Indeed, they also found the spurious Shah Akbar and Jahan Pasha. They wished to be on hand to set their coup in motion."

CHAPTER 45

"From the Earl's letter?" Lydia shook her head. "I had come to believe them mere figments of imagination."

"They're real enough. From what I gather, Akbar was the one who took the tale of the throne to France. He and Fouche worked out this plan. Akbar acted without French sanction when he sent that letter to the Earl, however. He thought it would frighten the old gentleman into speaking. When Marshall learned of the letters he was furious and brought forward his plan. To give him what little credit he is due, murder had not been his intent. It seems Akbar once more took matters into his own hands and was also the one to exercise his flair for the melodramatic by leaving the carved knives. He's lucky Marshall didn't murder him for his poor judgment."

Lydia found that she had been leaning closer and closer to him as the tale unwound. She straightened and at once regretted it.

Harting touched her arm.

She waved away his concern. "I'm well."

"The story of your kidnapping has begun to spread, and the French are thoroughly discredited." He grinned and sipped at his lemon water. "A swarm of well-wishers, and others who find it expedient to demonstrate their loyalty to the British, have been thronging Government House."

"Did Dr Marshall have any intelligence to offer in his final moments?" asked Lydia.

"Not as such. He was unrepentant to the end, though he took a great while to die. Belly wounds are nasty things." Harting hesitated.

"What is it?"

"He did give me a message for you. I believe you may have made quite an impression on the fellow."

Harting did love to draw out a story. Lydia bit the inside of her lip.

"He said it was his doing that Sophie died. He poisoned her because she would have recognized him as the French agent. Told you the wrong bottle, and then changed them later."

Lydia's mouth dropped open. She shook her head as tears welled in her eyes. Could it be true? Harting handed her a handkerchief and she buried her face in it. It defied belief. A small measure of pity welled within her for Dr Marshall. A wretched man whose soul had been disfigured by hatred.

"What do we do now?" Lydia asked.

"Matters have been wrapped up so satisfactorily there is little left to be done. I must write a dispatch to Mr Pitt, giving him the good news. Otherwise, I imagine our most pressing concern will be to outfit *Legacy* for a triumphant return to England."

Lydia swallowed her misgivings. "Mr Harting, I must beg to speak with you about what passed between us." It seemed an age ago.

"Miss Garrett, I must render my heartfelt apologies. I had no right, no excuse—"

She held up a hand. "No, please."

Harting reached for her hand.

A throat cleared. Danbury stood on the threshold. "Apologies for intruding. I can return at a more convenient time."

Lydia straightened, wincing at the sudden movement. "My Lord, I pray you, do not go. I'm most anxious to speak with you."

Danbury entered slowly, pulling a posey of flowers from behind his back. He presented them to Lydia with a flourish.

"I thought these might brighten your day."

Lydia accepted the gift with a bright smile. "Thank you, my Lord. It was kind of you to think of me. I've been hoping to speak to you all day. We never completed our conversation of the other evening."

Harting stood and excused himself, kissing her hand in farewell. When he had gone Danbury took his seat.

"How are you feeling?"

"I am much better, thank you. Though the physician insists I play the invalid."

"You've been through quite an ordeal."

"A few bumps and bruises, no more."

Danbury murmured something polite and an uncomfortable silence ensued.

The words rushed into her throat, but as each clamoured for preference she was rendered mute. It took nearly two minutes for her to choke out a weak sentiment. "My Lord, I can only express my great regret for my actions." She hurried on in a rush. "I understand that they must engender disgust. I release you from your promise to help me find a position. And I cannot thank you enough for risking your life to come after me."

Danbury took her hand. "Miss Garrett... Lydia, I could never have done otherwise. My dear girl, when you were taken and I thought of the things that might happen... And then we received your brilliant note. I was never so proud of anything in my life. Anyone would have thought I wrote the thing. But then I saw Marshall there with you, and I feared..." He trailed off. "This episode took at least five years off my life."

"Perhaps you could value each of those years for me, and I could make payment in instalments?"

He chuckled, but as soon as the laugh light in his eyes died he was glancing about the room restlessly. "I must beg you to accept my apologies. I know you did not act without good reason."

"Not good enough." Her throat was tight and achy. "Though I do want you to know, I never thought you guilty. I was determined to prove your innocence."

Another awkward silence filled the space between them. In a tangle of words they both spoke at once. Lydia insisted that Danbury continue.

His features remained clouded. "I must apologize for my forwardness at the ball and again last night. I meant no disrespect."

Swallowing hard to dislodge the lump in her throat, Lydia rushed to assure him.

"Oh no, sir. I never dreamt you did. Truly." Lydia broke off. Her hands kneaded the fine shawl Annette had draped her with mercilessly as she continued. "Rosalie Adkins has asked me to stay here as her companion. She felt we worked well together."

Anguished eyes sought hers. "I beg you to reconsider, Miss Garrett. I know there may be some awkwardness attached to your presence in our party, but surely there are more important things to consider than the opinions of others. I cannot believe you wish to remain in India."

Lydia could not bear to look into his eyes any more, and turned her gaze to her hands crushing the shawl into submission. "There is little reason for me to return to London. No family and no friends to miss me."

Danbury covered one of her hands with his. He turned the palm up and examined the cuts and scratches there for a moment. Gently, he raised the hand and brushed his lips across the tender skin.

Fierce heat spiralled through her and she began to tremble. His gaze held hers, and she felt herself falling, sliding into the deep blue pools.

"You must know how…"

A rustle in the doorway brought his hoarse words to a halt. Lydia snatched her hand free. Harting entered looking flushed. He clutched a sheaf of papers in his hands.

"Mr Harting?"

"I apologize for interrupting you again, Miss Garrett. May I enter?" He closed the door behind him.

"Of course." Lydia recognized the gleam of excitement in his eye, and her heart quickened.

A disgruntled Danbury stood.

Harting glanced at him. "Pray, do not go. The news I have brought may affect you as well."

With one eyebrow cocked, Danbury resumed his chair. Harting dragged another seat close to Lydia's.

He drew close and leaned in, speaking in a conspiratorial tone. "My contact in the Home Office has sent a coded message. It just arrived by way of Mahe. I must return to England as soon as possible. He has an assignment of the utmost importance."

Danbury nodded. "*Legacy* should be able to set sail in less than a day. She has already been victualled."

"Excellent. I have been requested to recruit an agent to help me in this endeavour. Miss Garrett, I hoped you would allow me to prevail upon you to fill this office. I do not believe there will be much danger; it is a simple courier role."

"Absolutely not. Miss Garrett has done more than her share for England. I refuse to allow her to face such hazards again."

"She could be a valuable resource. Her wit was a great help in this affair, as it will be in the next."

"I forbid it."

Harting's eyebrow arched in patent challenge. "You are in no position to forbid anything."

Lydia touched Danbury's hand. "My Lord." She kept her voice low. "We both know Mr Harting well enough to realize he would not ask such a thing without having considered all his options."

Harting nodded his head in acknowledgment of her argument.

"I cannot in good conscience refuse his request. Indeed I have no wish to do so." She looked from one man to the other. "This adventure has had its share of trials, but I have never felt so… alive."

Danbury looked away for a moment. The silence in the room stretched taut. Lydia had no desire to hurt him. Her heart ached at the thought that he might believe she had rejected him in some way. How could she explain?

After a long moment he turned back to them. "Harting, it looks as if you've acquired two agents for the price of one. I will not let her be pulled into this alone. I am going to stick nearby and keep an eye on her."

Harting grinned and clapped him on the back. "I'm glad to hear it, brother. Let's get to work."

"Shall I notify Lord Wellesley?" asked Lydia.

"No." The reply came in chorus.

She'd had no place making the offer so the answer was not

unexpected. She smiled to herself even as the gentlemen stood to prevent her from any such exertion.

"You must rest and get better." Danbury looked severe.

Heads together the gentlemen left the drawing room laying out hasty plans for departure.

Lydia threw a cushion at the closing door. How like men! They should know by now that she was no hothouse flower. A laugh bubbled up from her belly. They would learn.

HISTORICAL NOTE

One of my chief pleasures in writing historical novels is immersing myself in a world that is as foreign to our modern sensibilities as any high fantasy setting. I've done my best to get the details right, but there is also a good deal of invention on my part. And sadly, some of the really good stuff I was unable to use in the story because, frankly, no one would have believed me.

It may interest readers to know that the Peacock Throne was real. Crafted at the order of the great Mughal ruler Shah Jahan, it was supposedly captured in 1737 by Nadir Shah of Persia. I say supposedly because one of the seed ideas for this story was born when I realized that the Peacock Throne carried away from India looked nothing like the Peacock Throne that had been painted and described in Delhi. The first thing that popped into my head was: "What happened to the real throne?" With a moniker like the Peacock Throne, I was quite certain that it must have been something fantastic—and I promptly set about imagining what that might have been.

I tried to stay true to French strategies when it came to the development of the overarching plot to distract and divide British forces. I alluded to it in the story, but Napoleon had already attempted to reach Tippoo Sultan by invading Egypt and marching overland. Those plans never came to fruition, and when Napoleon realized that there was fresh political turmoil at home to be taken advantage of, and little chance of further victory where he was, he abandoned his men in Egypt and hastened back to France.

Sprinkled throughout the story are real people such as William Pitt and Lord Wellesley. I tried to distil what I learned about these gentlemen into characters that were fairly true—at least to who they were perceived to be by historians and biographers. Although if I'm honest, I can only hope that a contemporary would have recognized them.

Finally I would draw your attention to one of the most fascinating twists of history that didn't make it into the story. On the island of Mahe in the Seychelles, *Le Jardin du Roi* spice plantation remains to this day. The lovely woman who runs it traces her lineage back to French nobles who fled the French revolution. This great great ancestor of hers claimed to be the lost dauphin. Late in life he confessed—or claimed, as your point of view may dictate—to be the surviving son and rightful heir of Louis the XVI and Marie Antoinette. There is a surviving legend that the lost dauphin was smuggled out of prison by English aristocrats and ultimately made his way to Mahe with a few loyal retainers. My character Pierre-Louis Poiret is based on this man. I hinted at his heritage but couldn't bring myself to announce it out loud in the story. I feared that readers would refuse to suspend disbelief for such a stretch, even if it was one of the better-supported parts of the story!

Any and all errors in accuracy are my own. Some were made for the sake of the story, but others will have snuck in because I didn't think to question my own assumptions on a given topic. Please forgive these oversights. If you've spotted something glaring, I'd love to hear from you! I can be contacted through my website: www.lisakaronrichardson.com.